The Brass Ring

By Mavis Applewater

CHAPTER ONE

March 1989

Jamie Jameson sat along the side of the road seated in her roommate's green Volvo. Jamie was mentally debating what was worse at the moment, being seen in a green Volvo or having just been pulled over for speeding, again. Jamie couldn't help herself. This was Massachusetts; everyone drove like a Freakin idiot. Jamie fumbled for her driver's license knowing that she probably wouldn't receive any form of a citation. Yes it was good to be blonde. Jamie checked her hair and make up in the rear view mirror as the tall uniformed figure approached. Her green eyes glinted merrily as she noticed that the officer was a woman. Jamie suddenly felt her day had just gotten better.

There was a tap on her window and Jamie turned to find the statuesque beauty staring down at her. *'Oh my!'* Jamie thought as she drank in the tall beauty standing outside of the car. She hurriedly rolled down her window as her heart began beating out of control. "License and registration." Came the cold demand. Jamie grimaced slightly at the officer's icy demeanor.

Jamie felt her mouth go dry and decided to play up her hair color for all it was worth. *'This could be fun.'* Jamie thought wryly. After all, she often flirted with male cops just to beat a ticket, even though she that was not what she was looking for. Now this woman was definitely someone she would enjoy flirting with. As Jamie handed over the requested items to the tall dark officer, she briefly brushed the officer's strong hands.

Jamie smirked as she felt the officer tremble slightly from her touch. "Do you know why I pulled you over?" Jamie's heart dropped slightly as the icy facade remained firmly in place. *'Why do they always ask that? Of course I know why you pulled me over, I was driving like a bat out hell.'*

"No?" Jamie lied as she flashed her most innocent smile and batted her eyes at the dark beauty.

"You were speeding," came the curt response. *'Well no kidding Sherlock.'* Jamie mentally groaned as she smiled brightly up at the woman whose legs seemed to go on forever.

"I was?" Jamie gasped slightly adding a hint of an accent to her tone. *'Yup, time to lay on that blonde charm. Please let her be gay . . .. Please let her be gay . . .. Please let her be gay and single.'* Jamie silently chanted to herself as she once again smiled up at the officer. "I had no idea." Jamie lied once again. "Was I going very fast Officer . . . Calloway?" Jamie added noting the name on her nametag. In truth she wouldn't have noticed the nametag at all if she hadn't been looking at the woman's chest.

"Yes. You were doing sixty in a forty mile an hour zone," came the frigid reply. Jamie saw herself grimacing in the mirrored sunglasses the officer was wearing. "This is a Maryland license. Are you from out of state, Miss. Jameson?" *'Gee you think?'* Jamie mentally groaned realizing that she was quickly loosing ground.

"Yes, I'm a student at BC." Jamie sighed conceding defeat.

"I see," the officer noted. "And this registration says that the vehicle belongs to Claudia Turner."

"My roommate." Jamie sighed again knowing that she was indeed going to get a ticket, and Claudia was going to be her usual pissy self about it.

"I'll be right back," Officer Calloway snapped in her ever-present icy demeanor.

Jamie slumped down in her seat resigned to her fate. She found herself glancing in the rear view mirror, catching a glimpse of the cop's well-defined backside as she strolled back to her patrol car. Jamie waited for what seemed an eternity as she watch the tall dark cop chatting away with her partner in the patrol car. *'Great! Just my luck, maybe she's straight, or just not interested in me. Maybe she thinks I'm a dork. Maybe she looks totally gross out of uniform. Yeah right and maybe pigs will fly!'*

Jamie had been so lost in her own little world she failed to notice Officer Calloway's return. "Sign here," came the firm command as the officer shoved a clipboard with the violation attached into Jamie's face. Jamie angrily penned her signature to paper and handed it back to the officer. "In the future drive more carefully." The cop sternly warned as she gave Jamie the citation along with her driver's license and the registration for the ugly Volvo.

"Thanks." Jamie snorted as she tossed the items onto the passenger seat.

"Have a nice day." Officer Calloway added in a mocking tone.

"Do they make you say that?" Jamie groused.

"Yes." The cop responded flatly as she turned away.

Later that day Jamie found herself storming into her dorm room. She tossed her backpack onto the bed and the spare set of keys to Claudia's Volvo onto her roommate's bureau. "Of all the rotten . . .." she growled, recalling her afternoon's exploits. "The first woman I've been attracted to in months, and she doesn't even notice me. And she gives me a . . ." Jamie's heart stopped momentarily as she suddenly realized that she had left the speeding ticket in the car. "Oh shit," she growled knowing that Claudia would check on the car as soon as she could.

Jamie raced down the staircase not wanting to waste time on the ancient elevator. She was on a mission, knowing her anal roomie would check every inch of her precious Volvo to insure Jamie had not marred the ugly vehicle. It always amazed Jamie that Claudia allowed her to use it all. As Jamie bolted out of the main doorway and raced towards the parking lot, she suddenly remembered that she had forgotten the spare set of car keys that Claudia insisted that she use. *'Don't know what she's afraid of... that I'll drive down to East Bum Fuck and ransack Mommy and Daddy's house?'* Jamie thought in disgust; not that she wanted to carry around Claudia's *Jesus Saves* key chain. However, the spare set was on a key chain that held only the keys to the car and read, *'The wages of sin are death'*.

Realizing that she had forgotten the hideous key chain, Jamie came to a complete halt, almost tumbling to the ground as she spun around and raced back into the dormitory. Once again she opted for the staircase as she ran back up the four flights towards her room. Bursting into the room, she was greeted by the sight of her roommate glaring at her. "You were speeding!" Claudia bellowed as she held up the slip of paper as proof.

"Jesus, Claudia." Jamie rolled her eyes as she snatched the citation out of Claudia's hands. Claudia inhaled sharply at Jamie's expletive.

'Way to go Jamie! First you get busted with the ticket, and now you take the Lord's name in vain. Claudia is bound to have an aneurysm for sure. How did I get stuck with her for the last two years? Oh yeah no one wanted to room with either of us. So the dyke and the Jesus Freak were forced into it.' Jamie's mind was racing as she tried to calm herself. "Look I'm sorry," she said trying to placate her now fuming roommate.

After a solid hour of lecturing from Claudia, Jamie found herself retreating out of the room muttering. "Bad day?" A familiar voice called out to her.

"You could say that Becky," Jamie groaned as she greeted her friend.

"Let me guess, Claudia?" The brunette chuckled.

"How did I get stuck with her?" Jamie whined. "Never mind I know. I should have never told Tammy, but somehow I thought we were friends. How did I know when I came out to her she would blab to the entire dorm."?

"Hey you know that Toni and I never cared," Becky pointed out. "If we weren't already rooming together either one of us would have roomed with you after Tammy asked for a new assignment."

"I know," Jamie sighed.

"And you know that people really like you but they are just too chicken shit to room with a lesbian because someone might think that they are gay also." Becky draped a comforting arm around her friend.

"Yeah, or they might catch it." Jamie chuckled feeling slightly better.

"Right." Becky laughed. "Never mind you are the only dyke in the building who has the guts to admit it. How many times has one these little Miss prim and proper gals gotten wasted so they would have an excuse to make a pass at you."

"Don't remind me." Jamie sighed. "Just a few more months before I am off to Med School."

"So, what got Claudia's knickers in a twist?"

"I got a speeding ticket while I was driving her precious little car," Jamie explained as they walked towards the elevator.

"That bucket of bolts can actually speed?" Becky asked surprised.

"Who knew?" Jamie laughed, as she looked at the ticket in question. "Damn it! Seventy Five bucks!"

"How fast were you going?" Becky inquired.

"About twenty five over the posted limit," Jamie confessed. "Seventy Five bucks and a lecture from Claudia. This day totally bites."

"What was the lecture about?" Becky asked.

"Oh, being responsible when borrowing other people's possessions, blah, blah, blah." Jamie responded with a roll of her eyes. "Oh, and of course her usual reminder that I'm going to hell. You know that one really frosts my cookies. Because only one of us is a virgin, and it isn't the bible thumper."

Jamie felt better after chatting with Becky and decided she deserved a night out; it was after all the weekend. Claudia walked into the room and gave her a disgusted snarl. "Where are you going?" Claudia asked with her arms folded.

"To a lesbian bar," Jamie said flatly knowing it would bother her roommate.

"Ugh." Claudia blanched. "You can't . . ."

"Use your car," Jamie finished for her with a smirk. "No kidding."

"You shouldn't go to places like that; it's disgusting," Claudia added in a distasteful tone.

"How would you know?" Jamie shot back deciding it was time to torture Claudia. "Have you ever been to one? Come on

Claudia, fess up; have you ever felt up another woman? Stuck your tongue in a woman's mouth while gently caressing her breast? Feel her nipple harden from your touch? Gotten all hot and sweaty while your bodies pressed together in the heat of passion? Feeling yourself getting so wet that you thought that you would explode from her touch?" Jamie hadn't done most of those things either, but that wasn't the point.

Jamie watched in amusement, as Claudia turned pale and bolted out of the room. "Now that was fun," Jamie smiled as she finished getting dressed. Jamie stepped out into the hallway and carefully locked the door behind her. She turned, hearing footsteps rapidly approaching. "Where's the fire?" Jamie called out as she spotted Becky barreling towards her.

"Don't ask," Becky sighed heavily as she threw her overnight bag over her shoulder. "I just finished my paper for Stedman's class. I was supposed to meet up with Steve over an hour ago. I swear I don't understand why we have to take some of these classes. My, don't you clean up nice." Becky winked at her friend.

"Thank you," Jamie smiled in response. "I wouldn't say that too loudly; you don't want Claudia to get the wrong idea."

"I've woken up in stranger places," Becky scoffed. "Where is Broom Hilda anyway?"

"Bathroom losing her lunch," Jamie explained with delight.

"What did you do?" Becky asked in an accusing tone.

"Me?" Jamie gasped in mock indignation as she flipped her long blonde hair out of her face.

"Uh huh," Becky snorted. "So where are you off to?"

"Somewhere Else," Jamie answered with the name of the popular woman's bar she was going to that evening.

"Good for you," Becky answered as the headed towards the elevator. "Maybe you'll meet someone nice."

"I'll settle for someone half way decent looking who can dance," Jamie answered as she pushed the call button for the elevator, which was now creaking in response.

"You never know," Becky encouraged her.

6

"What's the sense of it; after graduation, I'm out of here," Jamie pointed out as the ancient contraption finally squeaked open. Reluctantly the two students entered. "Why do we trust this thing?" Jamie wondered aloud.

"Our youthful sense of adventure," Becky laughed. "Don't tell me Claudia is actually letting you use her car?"

"Are you serious?" Jamie chuckled. "One, I doubt she'll ever let me near it again, and two, she has made it perfectly clear that she doesn't want her car seen within a five block radius of *one of those places!* "

"Yeah, someone might get the false impression she actually has a pulse," Becky teased. "I'm heading into the city. Do want a lift?"

"Thanks, but you are already running late," Jamie responded with relief as the elevator doors opened. Over the past four years Jamie had learned not to use the elevator if she really needed to get where she was going. Like most of her dorm mates, she'd found herself trapped in the mechanical prison once too often. "I'll just take the *'T'*."

"Don't be silly it's on the way," Becky offered with a warm smile.

Jamie accepted her generous offer, not looking forward to riding on the crowded subway on a busy weekend night. That and the MBTA was about as reliable as the dorm's elevator. Jamie arrived at the club early enough not to have to pay any cover charge and treated herself to a Disaronno on the rocks. She took a sip of the nutty amber colored liquor and sighed deeply. Leaving a tip for the bartender, she made her way to one of the back tables where she could see everything and everyone as they entered. Knowing that the upstairs would not be open to dancing for at least an hour, she sat back and people watched.

Jamie was content in watching the growing crowd. She had always been a friendly, outgoing person, except when it came to meeting women. She was fine once the conversation started, but she was strangely shy when it came to chatting with women in a club. She, of course, understood why. At twenty-two, she was a virgin. She wasn't ashamed of this; she had never wanted to sleep with the boys she met in high school. When she finally admitted to herself why, it had taken all of her courage to just tell another person. That had gone badly to say the least. Her sophomore year at BC had become a living hell after her roommate Tammy had told anyone and everyone who would listen, effectively turning Jamie into an outcast in the all girls' dormitories.

It was strange really, Jamie was waiting for true love before giving herself to someone, but of course everyone assumed that since she was gay, she would sleep with any woman she could get her hands on. *'If they only knew!'* Jamie laughed to herself. Half of the gay women she met stayed away from her because of her lack of experience, and the other half found her innocence just a little too interesting. It was the second half that frightened her most. So here she sat sipping her amaretto in the most popular women's bar in Boston, almost two and a half years since she had come out, wondering if she would ever meet Miss. Right.

The crowd was beginning to pick up when Jamie spotted a tall, raven-haired beauty entering the club. *'No, it couldn't be!'* she thought to herself as she drank in the woman's beauty. The woman in question was dressed in faded blue jeans that were ripped slightly on one knee, a white tank top, and a faded denim jacket. As the woman turned towards the bartender to place her order, Jamie knew whom she was. She would know that butt anywhere. The woman turned back around unaware of Jamie's ogling.

Jamie found herself inhaling deeply as she watched the woman remove her jacket and lounge carelessly on the barstool. It was the eyes. They were the most amazing shade of blue Jamie had ever seen. *'Oh my, Officer Calloway, why would you hide those under such tacky sunglasses?'* Jamie was not surprised as she watched a group of women gather around the cop. She was after all drop dead gorgeous.

Jamie went to take a sip of her drink and realized that while she was lusting after the policewoman, she had drained her glass. Knowing that she now had an excuse to return to the bar, she quickly inspected her own attire. The black silk vest that showed just a hint of cleavage and her black jeans were a good choice. She grabbed her glass and made her way over to the bar. She had considered heading over to where the policewoman was perched, but at the last moment her courage failed her. She took a spot where she could watch the woman, and hopefully she could be seen as well.

Jamie ordered another Amaretto and waited for the tall beauty to notice her. Jamie nursed her drink already feeling slightly buzzed from the first one. After finishing her second drink and failing to be noticed by the object of her affections, Jamie was feeling a little bold and slightly drunk. Jamie hatched a plan. She would just go over and give the woman a hard time for writing her up this afternoon. Not a good plan, but it was all she had. Jamie placed her glass on the bar and blazed a determine path over to the brunette.

Jamie never knew how or why it happened but just as she stepped up to the brunette who was engaged in a conversation, she tripped and landed right in the policewoman's lap. Jamie's ears were ringing from the laughter that suddenly rang out. Through the chuckling Jamie heard a deep sensual voice asking if she was all right. Strong hands lifted her up from her embarrassing position, and she suddenly found herself staring into pools of crystal blue. "Speeding again?" the same sensual voice asked her as Jamie felt her entire body turn beet red when the question evoked another round of laughter.

"My mistake," Jamie responded in a hurt tone as she brushed away the policewoman's hands. Then she gathered what little dignity she had left and walked away.

"No wait." The policewoman reached out for her as Jamie started to stumble once again. Strong arms held her carefully, preventing her from falling and embarrassing herself further. "Ugh!" the petite blonde snarled as she steadied herself.

"CC I've always known you had a way with women," a tall dark skinned woman to Jamie's right snickered, "but now you have them throwing themselves at you!" More laughter ensued as Jamie took a sudden interest in her footwear. "Damn, girl, what's your secret?" Jamie was plotting her escape as more and more comments were being made at her expense.

"Look I'm sorry for intruding," Jamie muttered as she turned to CC.

"You're not," CC responded unable to meet Jamie's eyes.

"CC, her eyes are a little higher than that," the dark woman teased her friend.

At that moment Jamie realized that CC had been addressing her cleavage. The tall brunette turned an unnatural shade of red and buried her face in her hands. Feeling slightly relieved that the shoe was finally on the other foot, Jamie relaxed slightly. "Maybe if I had been wearing this earlier today, you wouldn't have given me that speeding ticket?" Jamie quipped.

"She didn't?" One of the policewoman's cronies laughed. "Shame on you CC."

"Tell us Sweetie, was the big bad CC mean to you?" The first woman placed a gentle arm around Jamie. "Come on what did she do? She didn't frisk you now did she?"

Both CC and Jamie blushed furiously at the comment. "Enough!" CC barked out. "You'll have to excuse them; they don't get out very often." CC apologized.

"Oh come on CC, lighten up." Her friend teased. "Isn't she beautiful when she's angry?" The woman addressed Jamie. "I'm Kendra by the way."

"Jamie," the blonde answered as she relaxed slightly.

"Nice to meet you Jamie." Kendra smiled keeping her arm around the smaller woman's shoulders. "Now tell us all about how mean Robocop over there was to you. She didn't do a strip search did she?" Jamie's mouth hung open, uncertain how to take the woman's teasing.

A growl escaped from CC. "They have opened the upstairs and I'm going to dance," CC snapped coldly and stormed off.

Jamie swallowed hard as she watched the taller woman's retreating form.

"I blew it," Jamie muttered as the crowd surrounding her dispersed.

"No, no sweetie." Kendra, who had remained reassured her.

"I should go and apologize," Jamie said with a hint of sadness.

"No," Kendra replied firmly as she gave her a slight hug. "I did this. Sometimes I just don't know when to quit. Look, I'll go and soothe her ruffled feathers. Then you could . . ."

"Never mind," Jamie cut her off in a dejected tone. "I think I'll just cut my losses now so I can leave here with some dignity."

"Come on sweetie," Kendra encouraged her. "Trust me, her bark is much worse than her bite."

"Thank you, but I've made a big enough ass out myself for one evening." Jamie responded.

"No you didn't," Kendra answered gently.

"I fell into the woman's lap," Jamie snorted.

"Well it was certainly an ice breaker," Kendra teased her.

"Oh yeah it was real smooth," Jamie sighed. "Look, thanks again, but I'm just going to dance and then head out of here."

Jamie walked away with her shoulders slightly slumped and made her way upstairs. She was careful to stay clear of CC. A woman approached her who was about her height with thick glasses and asked her to dance. "Why not," Jamie found herself saying as she walked off to the dance floor. The woman wasn't a bad dancer, but she just wasn't a terribly good one either. Jamie endured two more dances with her, all the while scoping the crowd for CC. She spotted her at one point leaning against a wall talking with Kendra.

After leaving the dance floor, Jamie made her excuses to the woman she had been dancing with and decided it was time to leave. She descended the staircase feeling a sense of loss at the way her entire day had gone. Just as she reached the bottom of the stairwell she felt a hand on her shoulder. She turned and found herself captured in a fiery blue haze. She could feel her emerald eyes twinkle in response.

"Wait," the tall beauty said in a voice that almost sounded as if it was pleading with her.

"Yes?" Jamie responded in a slightly nervous tone.

She watched the tall woman shift nervously from one foot to the other. Uncertain at what she should do, Jamie just stood there and felt her mouth go dry. "Was I going too fast again?" Jamie finally offered hoping to prod the policewoman into speaking. "Huh?" the woman responded with a blank stare. They remained that way for a lingering moment as Jamie felt her eyes drift down to the taller woman's chest. Jamie was losing herself in a delightful fantasy when CC decided to speak once again. "I Uhm . . ." CC stammered as Jamie returned her gaze to a more appropriate position.

"Yes?" Jamie repeated in a curious tone.

"Dance . . . you . . ." CC stammered like an idiot.

"Excuse me?" Jamie questioned as she tried to understand what the woman was trying to say. Jamie watched the policewoman fight some internal battle as she chewed on her bottom lip. Jamie glanced at her watch quickly while she waited for CC to compose herself. It was getting late, and if she wanted to catch the train, she would need to leave very soon. "I have to go," Jamie finally said regrettably.

"No." CC managed to blurt out as Jamie looked at her in bewilderment. Jamie found herself amused by the policewoman's nervousness. It was hard for her to fathom that this was the same woman who had treated her so coldly earlier in the day. "I . . . Uhm . . ." CC began to stammer once again. "Wow." She finally said as she blew out an exhausted breath. "I'm sorry. I'm not usually this much of an idiot," CC finally managed to say. "I wanted to know if you would like to dance with me," she blurted out finally.

"Here?" Jamie responded with a slight chuckle, trying to ignore the way her heart had begun race. She was relieved as she watched the slight smile emerge on CC's face.

"No I meant upstairs." CC answered with a slight blush. "You know, where the music is."

"I'm sorry," Jamie answered with a slight frown.

"Oh. Well okay." CC sighed heavily. "Sorry," she offered to the smaller woman as she turned to walk away.

"Wait," Jamie called out as she panicked slightly. Reaching out, she touched CC's arm gently, feeling a sudden surge of warmth. "It's just that I need to catch the train. My roommate won't let me use her car anymore since I got that ticket this afternoon," Jamie explained hurriedly. "Not that I like to take her car to clubs anyways. She's a bit of a phobe." *'That's putting it mildly.'*

"Sorry about writing you up today." CC curled up her lips in embarrassment. "I was going to let you off with just a warning. But my partner is a bit of a hard ass, and I'm a rookie. Plus I'm not out on the job. You know how it is."

"Yeah, I do." Jamie sighed deeply and glanced at her watch once again. "I need to go."

The last thing Jamie wanted to do at that moment was leave. But the thought of adding cab fare to her already over extended budget at that moment was unthinkable. "What if I gave you a lift home? That way you could stay for one more dance," CC offered hopefully.

"Really?" Jamie asked brightly.

"Yeah" CC responded with a shrug. "I mean, it's the least I can do."

"Okay," Jamie agreed, barely containing her excitement.

The couple returned to the second floor and made their way through the sea of bodies. They danced shyly to 10,000 Maniacs *'She drives Me Crazy'*. Jamie felt that the song was more than appropriate. Without speaking about it, the couple remained on the dance floor for several more songs, their bodies drawing closer and closer together. As a slow song began that neither was familiar with, CC looked down at her with a questioning gaze. In response Jamie wrapped her arms around the taller woman and drew her close.

13

The sensation of their bodies touching for the first time sent an electrifying jolt through Jamie. She heard herself moan as the sensation settled in a southern location. She snuggled closer as she felt CC wrap her arms around her back. The swaying of their bodies and the feeling of CC's hands roaming across her back caused Jamie's breathing to grow heavy as she felt her thighs begin to quiver.

Jamie looked up at her dance partner and once again found herself captured by the woman's beauty. She tilted her head up just as CC was bending down. Their lips brushed together slightly. They smiled at one another shyly before pressing their lips together once again. Jamie felt her body taking over as she pressed herself against CC's firm body. She found herself moaning deeply as she felt CC's tongue beginning to tease her bottom lip.

Jamie parted her lips slightly. CC accepted the invitation and began a gentle exploration of Jamie's mouth. Jamie was lost in the thrilling sensation. She found herself exploring CC's body. Her hands began to caress the taller woman's breasts. She felt slightly light-headed as two nipples hardened beneath her palms. She heard the taller woman moan deeply. The sudden thrill that shot through her body caused Jamie to tear her lips from CC as her hands remained firmly in place. Jamie cast an alluring gaze up to her dance partner. "Take me home," Jamie requested in a husky tone just loud enough to be heard over the music. Her companion simply nodded mutely. Jamie lowered her hands and wrapped her arms around the taller woman.

On the drive to the dorm the only conversation consisted of Jamie providing directions. The air was filled with an electrifying sexual tension. Once CC pulled her aging Mazda up in front of Bowdich Hall, she shifted the car into neutral and pulled on the emergency brake. The two women found themselves sitting there in a heated silence, unable to look at one another.

14

"So?" CC finally offered. "Can I call you?"

"Yes!" Jamie blurted far too quickly. She blushed at her overly eager response. *'Smooth,'* she chastised herself mentally. Clearing her throat quickly, she made an effort to regain her composure. "I mean that would be nice." She turned to find two bright blue eyes twinkling back at her. "Do you have anything I could write my number on?"

CC looked around quickly and reached over to the glove compartment. In her movements she accidentally brushed against Jamie's chest. Jamie moaned involuntarily from the contact. Their eyes met in a misty gaze causing a surge of heat to pass between the two women. Jamie felt the shy kiss brush gently across her lips. Her heart began to race from the tender contact. Without thinking she laced her fingers through the taller woman's long silky tresses and pulled her closer to her. As their kiss quickly heated to a passionate level, their hands began to fumble to release their seat belts.

Once free from their restraints their hands began a sweet exploration of the other's body. The windows of the aging Mazda quickly fogged up as the two woman tried to press together, each craving a deeper connection with the other's body. More than once CC's knee or the side of her body rammed into the car's stick shift. "Nuts!" she exclaimed suddenly as she pulled away. "We're rolling." Quickly CC reengaged the emergency brake.

Both women blushed as they once again captured each other's gaze. Then suddenly they were both overcome with a fit of giggles. "Uh hum," Jamie cleared her throat managing to quiet her laughter. "I think we were looking for something." CC cast an alluring glance at her companion. "Pen and paper," Jamie suggested brightly.

"Right," CC responded in a deep tone. Leaning across the tiny vehicle once again she managed to open the glove compartment. Once opened an array of items spilled out onto Jamie's lap. "Oh God!" CC exclaimed in embarrassment as she quickly retrieved a variety of items, mostly ketchup packets off Jamie's lap.

Finally managing to find a pen that worked and a napkin, CC handed them over to Jamie. The blonde quickly wrote down her telephone number, chuckling slightly when she had finished.

"What?" CC questioned her.

"I guess it's true what they say about cops," Jamie laughed as she held up the white and pink napkin from *'Dunkin' Donuts'*.

"Hey," CC responded with a mock snarl as she snatched the napkin away from Jamie. "I travel down to Rhode Island a lot on my days off, to visit my kid sister."

"That's sweet," Jamie answered with a smile.

"Yeah well," CC muttered trying to brush off the compliment, "I don't get along with my Mother or Stepfather but Stevie means the world to me."

"You're just a big softie, aren't you?" Jamie teased.

"Am not," CC protested in vain.

"Uh huh." Jamie chuckled slightly. "I should go," Jamie added in a quiet tone.

"Right," CC sighed.

"I don't want to," Jamie confessed. "But if I don't, I think the temptation would be too much, and as attractive as I find you, I don't think compromising my virtue in the front seat of your car is a good way to start off. "

"Compromising your virtue, eh?" CC teased in return.

"Yeah well," Jamie swallowed hard not wanting to go into details in fear of scaring the woman off. "When you call just ask for me. I'm in room 403."

"Okay," CC answered with a bright grin. "And you are right." Jamie stared at the woman in confusion. "I don't want things to go to far too fast either. I like you, and I would like to get to know you better," CC reassured her with a gentle caress on her arm.

"Thank you," Jamie answered with a sigh of relief.

CC walked Jamie to the main door of the dormitory, and after another heated lip lock, she made her way inside. As she climbed the staircase, she wondered if CC would call? And if she did, how long would it take for her to do so? Jamie climbed into bed and dreamt of the tall policewoman. Jamie would not need to wait long before CC called. The following morning the call came. They talked for over an hour before some of her dorm mates began to complain about her tying up the only telephone on the floor. CC was seeing her sister that weekend but suggested that they go out the following weekend.

The following week passed far too slowly for Jamie's tastes. She had spoken to CC at length every day and agreed to a picnic on Saturday. CC arrived early, and they made their way to Cold Springs Park, which was located in a neighboring town. They relaxed and played all day, and much to Jamie's delight, they even took several rides on the antique carousel. They each vied to catch one of the brass rings but neither was successful. It was the perfect first date. They talked about everything, and much too Jamie's relief, CC was neither put off nor overly eager by her lack of experience. The only disagreement the two had was over the carousel, which CC insisted upon calling a Merry-Go-Round. Despite the differences in linguistics, the two shared a perfect afternoon, and it looked to Jamie that more would follow. The only thing CC requested was that Jamie keep their relationship quiet for now, fearing fallout within the department.

May 1989

Jamie and CC stumbled into the dorm room in a fit of giggles. "I had fun today," Jamie said as she closed the door behind them. "Your kid sister is quite a handful. I didn't think we would ever get her off of that carousel. You would think someone who just turned sixteen wouldn't enjoy that kind of thing," Jamie added as she pulled her tall girlfriend in for a hug.

"Her? What about you?" CC teased as she found herself lost in Jamie's deep green eyes. "And around here it's called a Merry-Go-Round."

"Hey at least I got the brass ring," Jamie laughed as she held up a solid brass ring in triumph, "and it's a carousel you Yankee."

"I can't believe my baby sister is sixteen," CC sighed as she wrapped the small blonde into her arms tightly. "I worry about her so much. Living with our parents, well our Mother and her Father isn't a healthy situation."

"She has you," Jamie pointed out, "and she seems to have her head on straight."

"True." CC sighed heavily. "It's just that some days I don't know if Stevie is going to grow up to be a stand up comic or a master criminal."

"For your sake I hope it's the smell of grease paint she follows," Jamie said as she relaxed into the warmth of CC's embrace. "It wouldn't do having one Boylston's finest arresting her own sister."

"Boylston's finest." CC chuckled. "I've only just finished my probation period. Have you thought about taking some self-defense classes? I worry about you walking around campus late at night."

"Hmm." Jamie sighed contently as she took in the scent of her girlfriend's leather jacket. Tilting her head up she found herself captured by the deep blue eyes that made her heart skip a beat. It was hard to believe that they had only known one another for a little over two months. *'Who could have imagined that getting a speeding ticket could be so rewarding?'*

"What are you thinking about?" CC asked her as she stroked Jamie's long blonde tresses.

"Us," Jamie nuzzled closer to CC. "About the day we met."

"I gave you a speeding ticket," CC snorted. "I could barely keep my hands from shaking as I wrote out the traffic citation. I wanted to let you off with just a warning, but I wouldn't have heard the end it of from Max."

"I know," Jamie said with a smile as she brushed her lips gently across CC's. "I was very disappointed. It was the first time in my life being a cute blonde didn't pay off."

"Oh it did," CC purred at the memory. "But you know how it is. God, I hate being in the closet."

"I know sweetheart," Jamie comforted her. "It sucks. I hope when I get to med school things will be different than they are here."

"Speaking of which, where is your gruesome roomie any way?" CC scanned the room carefully for the offensive party.

"Claudia is spending the weekend with her boyfriend," Jamie offered softly as she claimed CC's lips once again.

"Really?" CC moaned against Jamie's mouth.

"Uh huh," Jamie confirmed as she stole another kiss. "You know I never thought I would see you again after the way you totally ignored my flirting with you while you wrote up that ticket. Imagine my surprise when I saw you sitting at the bar that very night. I thought you were pretty hot in your uniform but seeing you there in those tight blue jeans . . . well, it was almost too much for me."

"Oh is that why you told me off?" CC teased her as her lips began an assault on her neck.

"Hey I had to do something to get your attention." Jamie moaned as she felt her knees begin to quiver. "And I didn't really tell you off. I was just embarrassed after falling into your lap."

"That certainly got my attention all right," CC whispered hotly in her ear.

Jamie pulled away from CC slightly and looked deeply into her eyes. "I love you," She said in a nervous tone. Her entire body trembled. It was the first time she told her; in fact it was the first time she had told anyone. She stood there in breathless anticipation waiting for CC's response. She needed to hear it before they went any further. CC had been more than patient, in fact, it was Jamie who had caused them both to retreat into a cold shower on more than one occasion. But CC had been right about waiting until they were both sure.

"I love you too." CC smiled brightly. "More than you can possibly know James." Jamie released the breath she had been holding. Those were the words she needed to hear.

"I like the way you say that," Jamie purred.

"What?" CC smiled slightly. "When I tell you that I love you? Because I do you know. Or is it when I call you James?"

"Both," Jamie confirmed as she ran her hands along CC's stomach. "I think it's cute when you call me James."

"I am never cute," CC countered with a mock scowl. "Besides, your name is Jamie Jameson, certainly someone has called you James before."

"Well that's true Caitlin," Jamie teased her.

"Ugh," CC rolled her eyes in disgust at her real name.

"I know only Stevie can get away with calling you that." Jamie chuckled slightly. "But I like the way you say my name. In fact I like the way you say everything."

"Do you now?" CC kissed her on the top of her head.

"Yes, I do," Jamie said softly as she took CC by the hand and started to lead her over to her bed. "Do you know what I want to hear you say now?"

"No," CC squeaked as she realized where Jamie was leading them. Her heart was beating rapidly, and her palms began to sweat.

"I want to hear you say that you are going to make love to me," Jamie offered directly in a husky tone. Jamie reached up and pulled CC to her and captured her lips. Their kiss quickly

21

deepened as their tongues battled for control. CC could feel her jacket being removed as Jamie pulled her down onto her bed. "Wait," CC gasped suddenly. "Jamie, are you . . ."

"Don't ask me if I'm sure please," Jamie laughed slightly. "I'm the one attacking you."

"But it's just that your first time should be special," CC tried to explain.

"This is special," Jamie stated gazing at CC intently. "I love you, and you love me. I'm here, and you are here, and Claudia is off with her Neanderthal boyfriend. To me this is special. Do you want this?" Jamie added shyly as her hands began to roam across the front of CC's tank top.

"Yes," CC admitted shyly with a slight blush. "Yes, I want to make love to you." CC's hands began to feel their way under Jamie's tie-dye T-Shirt. CC's mind was racing as she felt the warmth of her young lover's skin responding to her touch. Now would be the perfect time to tell Jamie everything. Her thoughts were cut off by the sudden awareness of Jamie's fingers caressing her breast.

CC's moaned with pleasure as she pulled Jamie closer to her. Jamie felt as if she was going to explode as she felt CC's nipples respond to her touch. Jamie felt herself being lowered onto the bed as CC began to pull her T-Shirt up. Jamie allowed CC to remove her top as her own hands continued their exploration of CC's body. Jamie moaned deeply as CC began kissing her neck. The sensations sent a jolt through her body. Never before was she so happy that she had waited for the right person. Caitlin Calloway was indeed the right person. She was beautiful beyond words, and she held the key to Jamie's heart.

CC continued to kiss her way down Jamie's neck enjoying the sensation of tasting the young blonde's skin. Her hands roamed down Jamie's back, feeling their way to the clasp on her bra. CC felt very proud of herself as she unhooked the garment easily. Slowly she removed Jamie's bra and took in the sight of the beauty that was now lying beneath her. "You are so beautiful," CC whispered. Time seemed to stand still as she allowed her fingers to explore every inch of Jamie's exposed skin.

Jamie blushed as she watched her lover touch her body. This felt far too good to be true. She halted CC's movements as she began to pull the tank top off of her body. She needed to see her . . . needed to feel her body next her own. Jamie sat up slightly as CC raised her arms allowing Jamie to remove her top and then her sports bra. They both began a slow exploration. Fingers gently touching as their hearts beat in unison. Without realizing what she was doing, Jamie bent her head slightly and captured CC's breast in her mouth.

CC moaned as her body arched in response to Jamie's ministrations. "I love you!" CC gasped as Jamie took more of her into her mouth. The emotions were swirling out of control as Jamie began to lavish the other breast with the same attention.
"I love you," Jamie murmured softly against CC's skin. CC held her closer as she kissed the top of the blonde's head. Jamie groaned softly as she broke away from the taste of CC's body.

They looked into one another's eyes, each captured by the passion they found there. Silently they lowered themselves onto the bed and lay side by side, just looking at each other. CC reached over, not wanting to break the spell and slowly began to unbutton the shorts Jamie was wearing. Jamie's breathing began to catch as she felt the cotton material being stripped away from her body. Jamie almost exploded when she felt CC's fingers lightly teasing the elastic band on her panties. Reaching up she gave CC a reassuring kiss.

CC accepted her invitation and slowly removed the remainder of Jamie's clothing. Barely having time to catch her breath as she finally viewed the woman she loved in all of her natural beauty, CC felt soft gentle hands lowering her back down. Jamie undressed CC, kissing her way across the newly exposed flesh. They found themselves lying side by side once again simply drinking in the wonder of the other's body.

They both shifted slightly, closing the distance between their bodies, hands exploring as they kissed passionately. Pressing closer together they opened themselves to the other. Jamie was lost in the perfection of the moment as they each touched the other's passion, gently exploring the wetness that greeted their hands. They entered each other at the same moment, each taking all that the other had to offer. The jolt of pain had been unexpected as CC's fingers tore the barrier of her innocence. The pain vanished quickly as CC's thumb began teasing her clit.

Jamie shuddered as CC's fingers stroked her. She could feel her lover's body tremble as her own fingers followed in the same passionate rhythm. As their hips ground together in a wild tempo, each of them seemed to want to possess the other. Feeling the sensations wash over her, Jamie mirrored CC's movement and was greeted by a deep moan from her lover. They cried out together as the waves rushed through their bodies.

They clung to each other as their bodies continued to tremble. Covered in sweat, they exchanged gentle kisses as their breathing began to slow. "That was . . ." Jamie's voice squeaked slightly.
"Are you okay?" CC inquired in an equally exhausted tone.
"Oh yeah," Jamie gasped. "Is it wrong to . . ."
"What?" CC encouraged her in a slightly nervous tone.
"I want to . . ." Jamie's words were cut off as CC kissed her deeply. "Yeah that's what I want," Jamie panted as the kiss ended.

Jamie's fears were put aside as she realized that her lover wanted the same as she did. They both wanted more. Their kissing quickly grew out of control. Each of them allowed their hands to explore the other's body. Jamie found herself on her back pulling her lover's wetness to her mouth. She trembled as she felt CC tasting her for the first time. Jamie inhaled the scent of her lover's passion as she pulled her down to her eager mouth. She wanted to drink all that CC had to offer; her heart was pounding from excitement and fear. Her nervousness quickly vanished as she felt CC tremble when her tongue tasted her for the first time.

Jamie found herself lost as her tongue began to tease her lover's clit. They drank in one another's passion, shifting occasionally as they tried to please their lover. Jamie almost lost it, finding it hard to focus on pleasing CC while her own body was reacting to the sensation of CC's tongue entering her. At times each fumbled as they struggled to maintain their own control, but somehow their bodies knew what to do. They fit together perfectly, and once again the two lovers found themselves climaxing in unison.

Later Jamie found herself wrapped in CC's arms with her head lying on her lover's chest. She listened to the gentle beating of CC's heart and her steady breathing. She lost count of just how many times they drove one another over the edge. Jamie was amazed at just how many different ways there were to make love. She was confused at times but found her lover's gentle touch reassuring. Jamie had come out of the closet almost three years ago and was never happier that she had waited for just the right person to be with. The entire evening had been sheer poetry in motion. Her parents were going to freak when she switched to a med school up here. But she had so many offers, and no one could doubt Harvard's credibility. One of the best programs around and she could stay close to CC. The money was going to be a problem, but she could make it work. Jamie yawned slightly as she noticed the sun coming up.

CC shifted beneath her. "Why are you still awake?" CC said quietly as she kissed the top of her lover's head.
"I'm too happy to sleep," Jamie purred as she snuggled closer to CC. "I could stay like this forever."
"Me too," CC sighed. "But I have to leave."
"No," Jamie whined.
"Sorry, James," CC groaned. "Duty calls. Time to go protect and serve."
"You could protect and serve right here," Jamie suggested as she reached up and kissed her lover.

CC considered the idea for a moment, as she tasted herself on her lover's lips. Reluctantly she removed herself from the warmth of Jamie's embrace. After several kisses and a little pleading CC managed to get dressed. "I'll call you tonight, and we can go out." CC offered as she kissed Jamie. She smiled as her lover pouted in response. "Hey I have to go home," CC repeated. "I can't very well show up at the station without a shower first. People will talk."

"I suppose," Jamie grumbled. "But I think that hickey on your neck will give you away."

"Brat," CC teased in response. "I love you, James."

CC kissed her lover once more before walking out of Jamie's dorm room for what would turn out to be the last time. The days passed, turning into weeks. Jamie never received as much as a phone call from CC. Jamie called and left message after message on CC's answering machine. She eventually called the station only to be given the run around by CC's fellow officers. It didn't take an oracle to figure out that it was over. Jamie never bothered with Harvard and decided to attend George Washington instead. Jamie could never forgive CC for tarnishing the memory of a sweet night of passion into the disgusting image that she had been used.

The Present

Dr. Jameson stripped off her rubber gloves and tossed them into the trash. Nurses looked at her expectantly. "Time of death twelve twenty six am." That was it a life ended and there was nothing she could do to save the man. Her head was throbbing; it had been a long day. For a brief moment she wished she had followed her parents advice and gone into private practice. She loved emergency medicine, her only regret was returning to Boylston, but the offer from the hospital had been too good to refuse. In the six weeks since her return to the town where she spent her undergraduate years she had been on edge.

"The cops want to talk to you," One of the nurses explained.

That was the reason Jamie had been on edge. She hated the police. Well not all of them, just one in particular. The one who she had so willingly offered her virginity to only to have the woman walk out of her life without so much as a goodbye. It had been more than a dozen years since CC left her, and it still hurt. Perhaps that is why she never allowed anyone to get that close again. She certainly allowed them into her bed, but never into her heart. Jamie's return to the city had made her nervous. Luckily her schedule kept her busy, and since this was a big city, she had yet to cross paths with CC. Perhaps she never would. "Peachy," Jamie muttered in response as she finished filling out the chart. "Tell them I'll be just a minute." Jamie closed the chart and ran her fingers through her short blonde hair.

Stepping out into the corridor Jamie knew who it was instantly. Blue eyes widened as she spotted Jamie and the brief smile quickly vanished from the tall brunette when she saw the look of hatred cross Jamie's features. Jamie steadied herself and approached the two detectives. "I'm Dr. Jameson; how can I help you?" She said coldly crossing her arms defiantly across her chest.

There was a deafening silence as she glared at the tall woman. "I'm Detective Sampson and this is Detective

Calloway," The man offered finally. "We have a few questions to ask you about the man you just treated." Jamie noticed that Detective Sampson seemed a little uneasy. She cast a final glare at CC before turning to his direction. "How can I help?" Jamie answered in monotone voice.

"How is he?" Detective. Sampson asked.

"He's dead," Jamie responded firmly. "We did all that we could."

"Trust me he wasn't worth it," Detective. Sampson added. "But did he say anything?"

"No," Jamie answered bluntly.

"Nothing at all?" Detective. Sampson pushed.

"No," Jamie repeated in the same cool fashion. "He was unconscious when he was brought in and he never regained consciousness. Now if that is all I'm very busy." Jamie turned on her heels and marched off. She could feel CC's unwavering stare as she stormed into the doctor's lounge.

"Jesus CC, what's up?" Her partner asked. "You never let me do the questioning."

"Shut up!" CC snapped and started down the hallway. Detective Sampson simply complied, not wanting to face his partner's temper.

CC forged a determined path down the hallway and her heart skipped a beat as Jamie reemerged from the doctor's lounge. "Was there something else Officer?" Jamie snarled as she stared into CC's eyes.

"You . . ." CC stammered.

"Yes?" Jamie's voice never betraying the fear she was fighting at facing the one person in her life that had truly hurt her.

"James," CC began softly.

"Don't," Jamie cautioned her coldly.

"So you're just going to pretend that we don't know each other?" CC asked in disbelief.

"Works for me," Jamie snapped back. "Now if you'll excuse me it's very busy here tonight."

Jamie tried to step away from her. CC reached out, but Jamie pulled away harshly. "Don't," Jamie repeated coldly. "Anything you had to say to me, you should have said a very long time ago." Jamie stomped off leaving CC just standing there in a dejected manner.

"Another one of your conquests?" Her partner snickered from behind her.

"Shut up, Max," CC growled.

CC entered the townhouse quietly, hoping not to disturb anyone. She needed to be alone with her thoughts and idle chatter with her kid sister was not on the menu. Jamie was back, and CC hadn't a clue as to what she should do. CC closed the door and turned to find Stevie standing in the living room wiping the sleep from her eyes. "What are doing up?" CC asked trying to sound causal. "Is Emma all right?" She asked suddenly concerned that something might be wrong with her eleven-month-old niece.

"She's fine," Stevie yawned. "What's wrong?"

"Nothing," CC lied. It unnerved her the way her kid sister could always see right through her.

"Uh huh," Stevie replied in disbelief.

"Nothing is wrong," CC lied again. "Just a tuff day at work." She could tell by the expression on Stevie's face that she wasn't going to buy it. "I just ran into someone that I hadn't seen in a long time."

"With you that could be anyone," Stevie snorted.

"James," CC stated bluntly.

"James?" Stevie yawned not quite comprehending. Her eyes widen suddenly. "James? As in Jamie, the love of your life?"

"She's not . . ." CC began to argue.

"Oh please Caitlin," Stevie scoffed. "Who are you trying to convince here, me or you? Did you tell her?"

"Tell her what?" CC whined not happy with the path this little chat was taking.

"You know what," Stevie responded defiantly. "The truth. Did you tell her what happened?"

"No," CC grumbled simply wishing to rewind the clock and make all of this disappear. The real question was just how far back she wanted to go. Back to tonight where she astoundingly ran into Jamie, or back to twelve years ago when everything changed. "The woman hates me, and she no longer wants to hear why I walked out on her."

"But you didn't walk out on her," Stevie argued. "You think she might want to know that?"

"Well she doesn't so just drop it," CC growled.

"No." Stevie fumed. "I watched you lying in that hospital bed calling out her name day after day. I watched you shut out everything and everyone, except for Emma and me. Never getting close to another woman all because of what happened. Tell me the truth here Sis, don't you think she has the right to know?"

"Stevie drop it," CC pleaded. "Please. Jamie hates me, and maybe it's for the best."

"Is it?" Stevie pushed.

"Please let it go," CC sighed heavily. "I did."

"Did you?" Stevie asked quietly as she placed a comforting arm around her older sister's shoulder.

"Stevie please," CC pleaded one last time. "I'm tired, I'm cranky and I simply want to see the peanut and go to bed."

Stevie simply raised her hands in defeat and returned upstairs to her own bedroom. CC breathed a sigh of relief as she removed her coat and went about her nightly ritual of putting her gun in the lock box in her closet. She showered and changed into a beat up old T-shirt and a pair of flannel boxer shorts. She wrapped a towel around her wet hair and put the kettle on. Then she made her way up to Stevie's room where her sister was sleeping soundly. Then she quietly snuck back downstairs to the room next to her own. Peeking over the crib she found her little peanut. Emma, her niece, was sleeping just as soundly as her mother. The sight of her niece never failed to melt her heart.

Knowing that she shouldn't, she lift the infant out of her crib. She could never resist spending time with the precious little angel. Sometimes CC found it unbelievable that her brat kid sister was someone's mother. Bright blue eyes stared back at CC. *"Oh yeah, that's my girl."* Emma gurgled softly as her aunt cradled her into her arms and carried her out into the kitchen. Stevie had long since given up on trying to stop CC from kidnapping her daughter in the middle of the night.

CC prepared hot chocolate while cradling her niece carefully in her arms. The sun was just beginning to rise, gently kissing the morning sky. CC inhaled the scent of her niece. "Why is it you smell so good? Huh?" She asked the little bundle in her arms. This was their time together. CC sighed deeply as she settled down on the couch in the living room. "You know your Momma gave me a hard time this morning," CC explained as Emma kicked her legs. "Don't tell her this, but this time I think she might be right."

CC sipped her hot chocolate, careful to keep it out of Emma's inquiring grasp. "Life is funny, Emma. A long time ago I met the most beautiful woman in the world. Everything was perfect until . . ." CC grimaced slightly as Emma tugged on her hair and then gently removed her raven tresses from Emma's small fist. "I take it you want to hear the story?" She cooed towards little Emma. *'Man, the guys on the force would drop dead if they could see me now.'* But she told little Emma everything during their morning ritual. Emma after all was a very good listener.

She shifted and sank into the sofa, resting her niece on her chest as she began to tell her story. She had left Jamie's dorm room and gone home happier than she had ever been in her life. The only thoughts she had were of the night before and the night to come. She would see Jamie that night and tell her again just how deeply in love with her she was. Later that day everything changed. It was a simple traffic stop. At least it should have been. Her partner called in the plates of the aging Honda. It was nothing more than a busted taillight. She should have been more careful. CC never saw the gun. She knew the dangers when she joined the force, but somehow she never thought it would happen to her.

CC never expected to end up lying in the middle of Dunster Street bleeding just because of a busted taillight. The first shot rang out and ripped into her stomach. She had been stunned as the burning blazed through her abdomen. Somehow, whether from reflex, training or out and out fear, she managed to draw her own weapon and fire. She hit her target but not before a second bullet ripped into her body. For weeks she drifted in and out of consciousness unaware of her surroundings. Her only cognizant thoughts were of Jamie.

By the time her mind could fully focus on where she was, more weeks had passed. She awoke to find her kid sister sleeping in a chair. The awkward teenager had run away to be by her sister's side. It had taken the department weeks to track down her mother. Not surprisingly to CC, her mother made no effort to see her. When Stevie found out she hitch hiked her way up from Providence to Boylston. The two had always been there for one another.

CC had been shocked by the amount of time she had lost. Her first thoughts turned to Jamie. Stevie told her that she had called out for her. But everyone with the exception of Stevie assumed that James was her boyfriend. "I have to call her," CC insisted.

"She's gone," Stevie reluctantly admitted to her sister. "I tried to call her but by the time I got here she was already gone. The dorms are empty now. Do you know how to get in touch with her parents? I assume she went home for the summer," Stevie offered hopefully only to be greeted by CC shaking her head in the negative as the tears began to fall.

CC could feel her heart breaking at the news. "Why?" was all she could say. It didn't take her long to fit the missing pieces together. The punk that had shot her was an FBI informant. CC was never given the full details of what this guy was working on or why he panicked when she pulled him over. She had her suspicious, but was never told anything. The entire incident as the FBI put it was unfortunate and swept under the rug. There had been no mention of it in the press. It had been almost two months since she found herself lying in the middle of Dunster Street. Jamie had no idea what had happened. All she knew was CC had left her room after a night of passion with the words, *"I'll call you."* This was bad. She had to find Jamie and explain what happened.

It was later in the fall of that year when CC finally returned to duty. It hadn't been hard for her to convince a judge that her kid sister would be better off in her care. Life with their mother and Stevie's father was a living hell. Stevie's father was a sick bastard and there was no way she could continue to let her stay there. CC hadn't been welcomed in her Mother's home since she came out of the closet. Not that she had ever received a warm reception prior to that. Thanks mostly to her stepfather; Albert Beaumont had never succeeded in his twisted attempts to get his hands on his stepdaughter or daughter. CC watched over her teenaged sister and regained her strength both physically and mentally.

Her sister started school and even though she felt betrayed by the department, CC returned to work. Now it was time to find Jamie and tell her what happened. It wasn't very hard to track down the med student. Feeling the need to do this face to face, CC flew down to DC and rented a car. She felt nervous as she parked across the street from the dormitory. But she never doubted that once Jamie knew the truth they could start over again. Nothing could have prepared her for what happened next.

She had just stepped out of the car and was preparing to cross the street when another car pulled up. Jamie stepped out. CC's heart skipped a beat at the sight of her lover as the early morning sun caressed her golden locks. Of course if CC had been thinking clearly she would have wondered why Jamie was just coming home at this hour. Or perhaps she would have noticed the driver of the car, a tall redhead stepping out and walking over to Jamie.

CC felt as if she had been shot once again, and she watched in horror as the two women embraced one another. She was certain that her heart died that day as she watched her lover sticking her tongue into another woman's mouth. The tears welled up in her eyes, and she felt sick. She threw open the car door and climbed inside, hiding from the sight of betrayal. She was crying so hard that she never noticed the other woman's departure. For a brief moment she looked up and caught a curious look from Jamie. Never certain if Jamie had seen her, she drove off and never looked back.

"Well that's the whole story, Peanut," CC whispered to her niece. Emma simply blew bubbles in response. "You are such a good listener. I guess I never told Jamie the truth because she had replaced me so easily. Never fall in love, Emma; it's just not worth it. Of course you may never get the chance to date. Between your parents and me, I don't think any gentleman caller would stand a chance. Of course I think your Dad has your prom gown already designed. I don't know why I'm worrying about all of this. It's not like Jamie and I would still be together. I mean look at your Mom. She and Katrina were the perfect lesbian couple and look what happened."

"Katrina decided to have an early midlife crisis," Stevie's voice interrupted her. "What are you telling my daughter?"

"Nothing," CC feigned innocence.

"Uh huh," Stevie chuckled as she reached out for Emma.

"No," CC whined.

"She needs to be fed," Stevie pointed out. "So unless you can do that . . ."

"Oh," CC blushed as she reluctantly handed Emma over to her Mother.

"Some big stuff cop you are," Stevie chuckled as she returned to her bedroom. CC followed the duo upstairs in hopes that she could take Emma back downstairs. By the look on Stevie's face as she sat down in the rocking chair CC knew that Emma would be sleeping in the crib in her mother's room. Stevie opened her blouse she began to feed her daughter.

"Does that hurt?" CC inquired, truly curious about the ritual.

"Hmm," Stevie winced slightly. "Sometimes. Now what is this about a prom dress?"

"I was just telling the little peanut that her Daddy probably has already designed one for her." CC chuckled.

"Probably," Stevie said with a smile. "But what's the point of having a father who's a big drag queen if he won't design clothes for you? Nobody does Liza better than your Daddy. Do they sweetie?" Stevie smiled down at her daughter. "Do you know what you are going to do yet?"

"About?" CC asked suspiciously.

"James," Stevie answered directly.

"Not a clue," CC sighed in defeat.

Jamie shifted slightly, trying not to disturb her companion. She eased her way out of bed, hoping not to awaken her new friend. Jamie blinked slowly as she focused on the loud decor of the strange apartment. *'What is it they say? I would never choose this wallpaper,'* she thought as she searched for her missing clothing.

"Where are you going?" a voice murmured from the bed.

"Time to go," Jamie answered bluntly as she pulled her jeans on.

"But . . . I thought that maybe," the brunette began in a desperate tone.

"Sorry . . ." Jamie paused as she tried to recall the woman's name, unable to decide if it was Trudy or Tracy. Perhaps it was Stacy. No, it definitely began with a "T". Jamie shook her head, deciding to move on. "I don't do overnight. I told you that." Jamie's tone was gentle and yet unwavering. "It's late. I need to get going," Jamie offered as she pulled on her T-shirt and then covered it with her charcoal sweater. She pulled on her leather car coat and leaned over to kiss the woman goodbye.

"Can I call you?" the brunette inquired hopefully.

"No." Jamie turned away, tucking her underwear into her coat pocket.

"Oh, that's right. You said that too." The brunette sighed heavily. "An honest cad."

"Something like that," Jamie confessed as she fished her car keys out of her pocket. *'Never get attached and never tell them you'll call when you know you won't. You taught me that, CC.'*

Jamie found herself sitting in her car outside the brunette's apartment building. Another one night stand. Granted, it wasn't something she did very often. Well, not anymore. Seeing CC at the hospital had not only shaken her, it had reopened a very old wound. After work she made it to the bar by last call and found herself escorting the tall brunette out of the bar before the lights were turned up.

She had hoped that a night of sexual exploration would extinguish her demons. But once again it left her wanting more. Those first few months in med school, Jamie had found herself wandering from one woman to the next until she received a very unorthodox wakeup call.

It was one night when she found herself in a stranger's apartment. They were naked and fooling around on the woman's bed. Much to her surprise, the woman's girlfriend entered the bedroom. Jamie panicked. Surprisingly the woman wasn't angry over Jamie's presence. In fact she was thrilled and decided to join them. Jamie found herself being made love to by two women as they explained to one another just what they should do to Jamie. The experience was wonderful, but at the same time it had unnerved her. She realized that these two women had planned the evening. This wasn't who she was.

From that night on Jamie decided not to be such an easy target. She dated more and started insisting on safe sex. After time had passed, she gave up on meeting the right woman and concentrated on her studies. Although she still went out and occasionally satisfied her carnal desires, for the most part Jamie simply focused on herself and her career. Now here she sat wondering where in the hell she was. *'Getting too old for this, Jamie. You're in a strange town with your underwear in your pocket,'* she mentally chastised herself. Finally she started the car and headed off towards what she hoped was a main road that would lead her back to the highway.

Two hours later she found herself completely lost and her gas tank nearing empty. She pulled over across the street from a park and tried to get her bearings. She looked across the street; her eyes widened as she noticed the wooden sign - 'Cold Springs Park'. "How in the hell did I end up here?" she mumbled absently.

Without remembering how or why, Jamie found herself walking through the park until she stood in front of the carousel. The antique was still beautiful. The brass plaque was still there, explaining the age of the carousel and the restoration dates. It had been the first and last place CC had taken her. It was the last good time they'd shared, the last date with CC right before she left a shattered naive girl behind. "Fool," Jamie groaned as the tears began to fall.

A noise off in the distance snapped her back to reality. As she turned, she half expected to see CC standing there. Jamie shivered at the thought and then quickly realized that hanging out in the park in the middle of the night was far from safe. Despite having taken CC's advice about taking a course in self-defense, she had no desire to utilize her martial arts training in an empty park in the middle of the night. She twisted her keys through her fingers as she hurried back to her car. She knew her way back to Boylston from here and hopefully she'd have just enough gas to get home.

CC stood in the shadows and watched as her former lover retreated. She didn't understand why she'd driven out here. But once she spotted Jamie, a silly part of her said it was fate. Not that she was hoping for reconciliation. But Stevie was right. Jamie deserved to hear the truth. Now she only had one problem - how was she going to get the stubborn blonde to listen to her? Just what are the right words for totally abandoning someone? Of course, that wasn't what had actually happened. CC rubbed her throbbing temple and decided to leave. She didn't need to tell Jamie tonight. In fact, what she needed to do was go home and get some sleep.

Later that evening as she was lying in bed trying to sleep, her mind kept spinning. Thoughts of the younger innocent Jamie filled her; she wondered how and when she was going to tell Jamie the truth. Life had been so simple back then. They were young and in love. They gave each other their innocence. Why had she never told Jamie that it had been her first time as well? After seeing Jamie kissing a stranger, CC had never really opened her heart to anyone again.

Many women tried to get through to her, but the stoic policewoman only offered her body and never her true self. Her tossing and turning continued. CC showed up for work the following night completely exhausted.

"Hey, CC," her partner called out. "You look like shit."

"Thank you," she snapped.

"Ooops." The older man cringed. "At first I thought maybe you got lucky. But from your nasty attitude, I'll assume that you struck out."

"What are you talking about?" CC snarled as she flopped down in her chair. The rickety metal chair squeaked under her weight.

"That Doc last night," he continued, oblivious to the fact that he was treading on shaky ground. "You couldn't take your eyes off her. I can't blame you. She's a real looker."

"Shut up," CC growled. "We have work to do." CC watched with some degree of amusement as her partner's eyes widened in fear.

CC's night was long and boring. It was quiet. In fact, things had been a little too quiet. Just as she relaxed enough to enjoy the reprieve, all hell broke lose. There had been another shooting. CC grabbed her coat and her partner. As they drove to the scene, she said a silent prayer that she wouldn't end up at the hospital again looking into those angry green eyes.

After they finished taking statements from the witness, who of course hadn't seen or heard a thing, they went to Boylston General. CC braced herself as she stepped through the electronic doors of the emergency room. She flashed her badge at the receptionist and made her way to the nurse's station.

"I'm Detective Calloway," she explained.

"Yes, I know." The heavyset woman smiled at her. "Dr. Jameson will be with you just as soon as she can."

CC groaned as she fought back the desire to bang her head on the counter until she lost consciousness. *"What the hell."* She reasoned as her head fell against the counter.

Jamie rubbed her eyes tiredly as she allowed the orderlies to escort her newest patient from the room. A nurse had already informed her that the police were waiting. Nothing new since it was a gunshot wound. Jamie braced herself as she said a silent prayer that CC wouldn't be one of the officers waiting to question her. She had already lost enough sleep because of her ex-lover. She stepped out of the curtained area and gritted her teeth as she watched her former lover banging her head on the counter. It would have been comical if it weren't CC.

"Who am I kidding?" She found herself smiling. "It's damn funny. I'm glad to know I'm not the only one who's freaking out over our paths crossing again," she said quietly as she approached the detectives. "What the hell. I could use a little fun." She shrugged as she stepped up to the nurse's station.

"If you get blood on the counter, you'll have to clean it up yourself," Jamie stated dryly. She smirked as the taller woman suddenly halted her movements. She winked at CC's partner who was just standing there looking bewildered. CC raised her head and glared at the doctor. Jamie felt her heart drop. CC looked so tired and defeated. She was about to reach out to her. Stopping herself, she withdrew her hand. "I take it you're here because of the guy I just sent up to surgery?" she asked in a professional manner.

"Yes," CC responded in the same cold professional tone.

"He'll make it," Jamie answered, not even blinking as she stared down CC's icy gaze. "And before you ask, he didn't say anything. If that's all, I have work to do."

"Fine," CC snapped as she turned away, her movement causing a basket of files to topple over. Jamie suppressed her laughter as the tall brooding detective growled. Jamie just stood there as the flustered woman bent over to pick up the mess. The laughter that was threatening to emerge suddenly died as she found herself leering at CC's backside.

Thankfully, CC and her partner were too busy cleaning up the mess to notice her overt ogling. As they returned the items to the desk, Jamie found herself blushing. CC turned to her, seemingly understanding what she had just done. The taller woman flashed her a cocky grin.

Jamie clenched her jaw and folded her arms across her chest, glaring at CC who seemed far too happy with the turn of events. "I have work to do," Jamie spat out as she turned away. CC's laughter was burning her ears. She didn't turn around until she was certain that they'd left. Turning slightly, she caught sight of CC walking down the hallway. She glimpsed once more at the woman's rear end. She gasped slightly as CC turned and winked at her.

Jamie's head fell onto her chest as she fought back the anger that was building up inside of her. She sighed in defeat, knowing that anger wasn't the only emotion she was feeling. As she felt her nipples straining against her T-shirt, she hated her body for still finding CC attractive.

A few days later, Jamie was back at work. She was beyond exhausted at that point. Since her last run in with CC, she hadn't been able to sleep for more than a few hours. She wished that it were anger that was keeping sleep from claiming her tired body. It wasn't. Her mind and body were betraying her. She found herself lost in the thought of touching CC. The ache had been building steadily, and she was fighting a losing battle to get past it. "Tonight," she tried to reassure herself as the ambulance doors swung open. "I'll get some sleep tonight."

"Talk to me," she commanded the EMT as she looked down at the frail teenage girl on the stretcher.

"Seventeen year old female," the EMT said hurriedly. He began to run off her vitals. Jamie could see the concern in the man's face as he spoke. "Drug overdose. We found these at the scene," the man explained as he handed her a vial of sleeping pills.

"Intentional?" Jamie continued as they wheeled the girl into one of the bays. "Okay people, on my count," she instructed the staff as they lifted the small girl onto the table.

"Yes," the EMT confirmed her earlier question. "She was on the phone with a crisis center. The counselor called it in."

"Can they do that?" Simon Fisher one of the interns questioned.

"Yes," Jamie snapped. "Okay people, let's pump her stomach."

"Parents are on the way," the EMT added as he gathered up his things. "So is the councilor. Off duty cop," he added before leaving.

Jamie was taken aback by the sadness in the older man's eyes. It was never easy when it was someone so young. She focused her energy on saving the girl. The monitors screamed out. "She's crashing!" Jamie yelled out as they ripped open her clothing. "Tube her," she instructed her resident.

Jamie continued to work on the teenager long after life had slipped away from her. "Fuck," she growled finally, stripping off her latex gloves and tossing them on the floor. She pinched the bridge of her nose, fighting back the tears. Jamie knew that the girl had died only moments after she came in contact with her. Something inside of her just wouldn't let her go. Now she had to. Weakly she announced the time of death.

Jamie carefully pulled a sheet up to cover the tiny body. "I'll get her cleaned up," Evaline, one of the nurses, offered as she touched Jamie's arm lightly. Jamie nodded mutely, taking one last look at the girl she failed to save. She stripped off her gown and brushed back her errant blonde bangs, knowing that now she had to face the girl's parents, and in a clinical manner inform them that she had failed to save their child's life.

She stepped out of the room, grabbing the chart as she went. She signed off on the paperwork, taking a quick glance to note the girl's name and her parent's names. She handed the paperwork over to the desk clerk and noted that it was after three a.m. "I'm done for tonight," she muttered grimly. The clerk simply nodded in understanding. "Where are . . . " She stopped her inquiry, noting the resemblance to the girl, Susan. " . . . never mind. I see them."

As she approached them, she spotted a lone figure hiding in the corner. CC looked like she had been through hell and back. "Oh baby, why are you still doing this?" she murmured quietly.
Jamie spoke carefully to Mr. and Mrs. Johnson. They were shattered. She tried to be comforting as Susan's mother screamed, "Why?" Jamie watched CC out of the corner of her

eye while she tried to comfort the grieving parents. She watched as the brunette was sucked into her own private hell.

CC had been five when her brother committed suicide. Jamie had heard the story of how the young girl had found him hanging in his bedroom. She knew that CC had been a volunteer for a teen crisis hotline back when they were dating. She'd always been proud of her for turning her own tragedy into something positive. Watching and knowing that it was CC who had been the one on the telephone with Susan was tearing Jamie apart.

Jamie was miffed that the Johnson's rebuffed her offer to provide them with phone numbers of councilors. They seemed to be blaming the crisis hotline for their daughter's suicide. Jamie tried to shake it off. They were in shock. She finished talking to them as she watched azure eyes filling with tears. CC wrapped her arms around herself, as she stood there alone. Jamie called for a nurse to take the Johnson's to see their daughter.

After they left, she stood and ran after CC who had stormed out of the waiting room. It didn't take her long to find the woman outside, clinging to the brick wall as she wept. Jamie choked as she watched CC slump down on the ground. Jamie raced over. She knelt down and wrapped the distraught woman in her arms. CC curled up in her embrace and wept.

Jamie's head was pounding as she tried to open her eyes. The effort alone caused a searing pain to stab at her already muddled brain. Finally she managed to prop open one eyelid. The sight that emerged before her was startling and very pleasant. She blinked open her other eye. Then she blinked once again. Seeing that it wasn't a mirage, she stared intently at what she had been using as a pillow. *'Yep, that's a breast. A really nice breast,'* she said to herself as she snuggled closer.

She closed her eyes, enjoying the comfortable warmth emanating from the naked body beneath her.

Just as she was just about to drift back to sleep reality came crashing down around her. Her eyes flew open as she bolted up into a sitting position. "Oh God," she groaned as her head pounded violently. Feeling the chill of the morning air, she looked down to find herself completely naked. "Oh God," she repeated as she wrapped the sheet around her.

As she pulled the sheet around herself, she managed to reveal the naked body she'd been resting on. "Oh God," she said again, only this time her voice was filled with desire. CC groaned from beneath her. "Please stop saying that," the brunette pleaded as she placed a pillow over her head. "What the hell am I doing in bed with you?" Jamie shouted, which only increased the pounding from her hangover. She winced in pain, swaying for a moment, and feeling slightly nauseous. Something caught her eye. "When did this happen?" she inquired as her fingers began to trace a soothing pattern over the scars on CC's abdomen. CC reached out to clasp her hand while still hiding her face under the pillow.

Jamie pulled her fingers back as if she had been burned. "Never mind," she berated herself. "Let's get back to the first question. Why are we in bed together?"

CC threw the pillow off her face and stared up at Jamie who was straddling her. Jamie realized her position and bolted from the bed. Her emerald eyes widened at the sight of CC's magnificent body. Before she could surrender to the primal urges coursing through her, she tossed the sheet onto CC, successfully covering the temptation but not diminishing her desire.

"I can't believe you," Jamie snarled as her head spun.

"What?" CC gasped as she pushed up to her elbows.

Jamie looked around frantically for her clothing. "You got me drunk and took advantage of me," Jamie accused her, sensing that it wasn't the truth.

"I what?" CC stammered.

"Didn't you?" Jamie asked weakly as some of the events of the past evening began to rear their ugly head.

"No," CC protested. "In fact I tried to slow things down."

"It doesn't matter," Jamie reasoned. "Where are my clothes? And where the hell am I?"

"I think you threw your clothes over there," CC informed her. "And you're at my place."

Jamie stumbled to the far end of the bedroom to find hers and CC's clothing strewn all over the place. As she bent over to retrieve her pants, she noticed several well-placed hickeys on her body. "What are you, part vampire?" Jamie grumbled as she tugged on her pants.

"You started it," CC purred playfully. "Do you want to see mine?"

Jamie was furious at the way CC was taunting her. "No," she growled in response. "I just want to get out of here," she fumed as she tugged on her shirt and jacket. She was far too flustered to search for her underwear.

"Stay?" CC implored her.

"Not a chance," Jamie flared, as she hopped up and down in an effort to put her shoes on.

"We need to talk," CC offered gently.

"No, we don't," Jamie argued before something occurred to her. "You said that last night," she mumbled.

"Yes, I did." CC sighed deeply. "Right before you tore my clothes off."

"It was a mistake," Jamie blurted out as she stumbled to the door. She threw it open and then slammed it behind her. The sound of a baby crying pierced through her head. She turned to see a brunette woman standing in the living room holding a screaming infant. "She has a wife and kids," she muttered.

"Who does?" The woman looked at her in confusion as she tried to comfort her child. "Rough night, James?" The woman smirked.

Jamie's jaw dropped in realization. "Stevie?" Jamie stammered. "Little Stevie?" she babbled. As she looked past the woman out the picture window, another realization struck her. The nausea returned and threatened to choke her as she stared out the window.

"Something wrong?" Stevie inquired.

"I live here," she stammered as she stared out at her parking lot. "I live next door." She felt sick.

"Jamie?" CC's voice beckoned from behind her.

Jamie turned to find CC clad in an old pair of sweatpants and a rumpled T-shirt. "I need to go," she muttered absently before she turned away and walked out the front door.

CC rubbed her throbbing temples as she stared at the door Jamie had just slammed. "Want to talk about it?" Stevie offered in a sweet tempered tone. CC turned and cast a weary bloodshot gaze at her younger sister, who was holding her fussing daughter in her arms.

"No," she answered, the heartbreak evident in her voice. Her bottom lip began to tremble. "Yes," She whimpered as she walked over and removed her fussing niece from Stevie's arms. "First I need to hold the Peanut."

CC held her niece tightly, taking in the sweet scent of the infant's hair. It was the only thing that would bring her peace at the moment. "Don't ever grow up on me, Peanut," she cooed to squirming infant who was clinging tightly to her seeming to understand her pain. "Is she okay?" CC asked as Emma clung more tightly to her. "She feels a little warm."

"I've called her doctor." Stevie explained. "She's running a little fever and she has been fussy all night. I'm sure that it's nothing." Stevie's tone was neither comforting nor convincing.

"What did the doctor say?" CC asked hurriedly.

46

"I haven't talked to him yet." Stevie continued. "I've left a message with his service. I'm just waiting for him to call back."

CC looked over at her sister who seemed more than a little concerned. CC sensed that Stevie would feel better is she was the one holding her daughter. Reluctantly she handed the infant back over to her mother. "So?" Stevie began slowly as she seem to relax slightly now that Emma was nestled in her arms. "While we are waiting for Dr. DeMarco to call, why don't you fill me in on what happened last night?"

"Last night I was working at the hotline." CC swallowed back the bile that was creeping up on her. "It was near the end of my shift when I got a call from a teenaged girl, named Susan. She sounded odd when she began to talk to me. I suspected something right away. Her tone was so flat and unfeeling."
"Oh God!" Stevie choked out.

"Susan was having problems dealing with her feelings towards other girls." CC continued as the tears began to well up in her eyes. "I talked to her. I did everything by the book, you know. But I just knew that she'd done something. It felt like an eternity before she admitted that she just wanted to stop the pain. Then she told me about the pills. I stayed calm while I was talking to her. It wasn't easy. I just kept her talking and got her to tell me where she was. I just kept her talking while I waited for the ambulance to reach her. I really wasn't on the phone with her for that long but it felt like forever. After the EMTs reached her, I rushed straight to the hospital." CC paused for a moment to look over at her sister who was holding her breath. "She didn't make it, Stevie," CC choked out.

"I'm so sorry Caitlin," Stevie offered in a soothing tone. "Do you want to talk about it? It must have brought back memories of Donny." Stevie added in reference to the brother she had never known. "You need to talk to someone," she encouraged CC.

CC brushed away her tears and smiled shyly at her sister. "I did," she mumbled as she felt a blush creeping up on her. "Jamie was Susan's doctor. I ran outside of the emergency room and collapsed when I realized that Susan had died. Jamie came to me. We ended up going to the bar across the street from the hospital. It was hard for her as well to lose a patient that was so young. We talked and talked about it. We didn't talk about the past or us, just about the senselessness of it all and the waste of such a young life. Unfortunately, while we were talking we also drank, margaritas," CC added with a grimace as the pain of her hangover shot through her.

"Oops." Stevie snorted. CC knew by the smug expression her sister was sporting that she was holding back her laughter.

"No kidding," CC agreed in a wry tone as she rolled her eyes. "At closing time we stepped outside, agreeing that neither of us should drive. I hailed a cab and I turned to her to ask if she wanted to share the cab. The next thing I knew we were making out."

"Uh huh." Stevie snickered.

"I tried to put a stop to things," CC frantically tried to explain, "but we just kept kissing and touching each other. Somehow, while we were groping one another, we ended up in the taxi. I gave the driver our address. Well, you can figure out what happened after that." CC folded her arms tightly across her body feeling the tequila induced aches and pains coursing through her.

"Well it isn't the worse thing that could happen," Stevie theorized. "After all that is how we got little Emma." Stevie laughed as she tried to quiet her still fussing daughter. "Let me guess; Jamie wasn't happy when she woke up next to you?"

"Happy?" CC groaned. "She was bordering on violent. Face it. I'm not the woman of her dreams; I'm more like the woman of her nightmares."

"Go talk to her," Stevie instructed her sternly.

"Have you lost what's left of your mind?" CC asked in a horrified tone. "She hates me."

"No, she doesn't," Stevie, argued. "She's next door. Go talk to her."

"Next door?" CC said as she shook her head in confusion.

"Our new neighbor," Stevie explained. "The one we haven't met yet. Go to her. It's time for the two of you to bury the hatchet."

"I'm just afraid she'll want to bury it in my skull," CC responded sincerely.

"Stop being a coward," Stevie flared at her harshly. "Go and talk to her. If she stays angry with you, then you haven't lost anything. If she understands, then maybe the two of you can save your friendship. Go!" Stevie shouted, sending a sharp jolt through CC's throbbing head. Emma stirred slightly.

"What about Emma?" CC protested.

"I'll come get you when the doctor calls," Stevie growled.

CC knew she was fighting a losing battle yet she wasn't ready to concede just yet. Stevie's eyes burned into her. She felt her resolve crumbling. Without bothering to put on a coat or shoes, she stepped outside. She shivered from the cold. She was just about to retreat back inside her own home when she heard the lock being bolted behind her.

Jamie allowed the water to rush over her body. The hot water and steam from the shower were helping her painful physical state. She leaned against the tile wall. The events of last night were finally creeping back to her. They had talked like old friends, only they weren't. Tequila had been a poor choice. But she knew she needed it, and she needed to be there for CC. Unless someone saw the horrible things that they saw on a daily basis, they wouldn't understand the pain or the need to reach out to someone in an effort feel alive again. Then the bar closed and it was time to leave. Jamie knew she was in no condition to drive and neither was her companion.

She was relieved and disappointed when CC raised her arm to hail a taxi. She had been fighting the tingling sensation pulsating through her body all evening. She reasoned that it was the alcohol making her notice the intoxicating scent of her former lover. Reason decided to abandon her when their eyes met just as a taxi pulled up in front of them. They moved together as if drawn by some unseen force. Their lips met instantly. The kiss lacked any shyness or hesitation. They simply exploded into a fiery passion. Standing in the shower, Jamie's hand absently felt her still swollen lips as she recalled the raw aching need that had coursed through her the night before.

Jamie's stomach clenched as the memories flooded her senses. The kiss had deepened, and she found herself sucking on CC's tongue. All she wanted at that moment was to take this woman to bed to fulfill all of her carnal desires. She cupped CC's backside, pulling her closer to her. The cab driver squawked. Jamie pulled away from the warmth of the taller woman's body, yanked the door open, and started to push CC inside the taxi. "We should talk," CC protested as Jamie followed her inside.

"No," Jamie argued, the effects of the tequila clouding her thoughts. She closed the door and pressed her smaller body into CC's. "Jamie . . . we need to talk." CC gasped as Jamie kissed her neck, sucked on her pulse point, and slid her hands across CC's chest. She pushed the taller woman back and straddled her. As she teased CC's nipples through the material of her shirt, she reclaimed her lips.

She plunged her tongue into the warmth of CC's mouth as her hands fumbled, slightly uncoordinated from the alcohol. CC moaned into her mouth as her body arched. "Still want to talk?" Jamie recalled herself whispering hotly just before dipping her tongue into CC's ear.

"No," CC panted unsteadily as Jamie continued to press her body into CC's.

As her mouth and tongue continued their assault on CC's ear and neck, she could hear CC give the driver her address. "Why didn't I get it then?" she berated herself. "Because I was loaded," she groaned in realization. Jamie didn't make a habit of drinking like she had the previous evening. She recalled how the two of them wrestled passionately in the back of the taxi and how she had drifted in and out of the present. Images of their first and last time together flooded her mind.

The memories, the taste of CC's body, and the tequila all mixed together to fuel her passion. Somehow she had managed to unbutton and unzip the leggy brunette's blue jeans. She only halted her movements when CC suggested that they slow down. She managed to climb off of CC and they both sat up. She nestled herself in CC's arms. Even in her drunken state, she knew how right it felt to have this woman hold her.

CC kissed the top of her head. Soon they found themselves kissing again. This time they took the time to explore. They shared slow gentle kisses as their tongues danced together. There was a wonderful tenderness to their kisses as they snuggled. Jamie must have drifted off during the cab ride. She could only recall the warmth of CC's body as she nestled against her.

Then she found herself in a strange apartment being led to the bedroom. "We should sleep," CC suggested as they both staggered slightly. Jamie was about to agree when one look into those crystal blue orbs re-ignited her passion. She recalled pulling CC's jacket off and casting it aside. This time it was CC who reclaimed her lips as Jamie found herself pulling at the taller woman's still unfastened pants.

Jamie felt a returning flush of desire as she recalled how her lower anatomy had pulsated while they hurriedly undressed one another. Before she knew what was happening, they were both frantically tearing the blankets back and pulling one another down onto the bed, rolling around as their bodies melted together.

Jamie could still taste the tender flesh of CC's body and the taste of her passion as she feasted upon her wetness. The moans

51

and groans that escaped from both of them! It was as if she was a moth and CC was the flame. She couldn't recall how many times she screamed out her lover's name. Or how many times she reciprocated the gift.

A sudden blast of cold water jolted Jamie back to reality. "Son of a . . .," she screeched as she quickly retreated to the back of the shower. Tentatively she reached out, trying to avoid the icy spray of water. Finally she managed to shut the water off. Climbing out of the shower, she wrapped herself in a towel. Her head was still pounding as she threw on a pair of sweats.

Slowly she walked downstairs, her body aching from her overindulgence. She smiled slightly as she padded her way into the kitchen, thinking that alcohol wasn't the only thing she had overindulged in. "My God, I don't think I've ever behaved like that." She chuckled as she started to fill the teapot with water. Despite how and who she had been with, she had to confess that her carnal desires had been sated.

A knocking at the front door sent a searing pain through her temples. She flinched as she put the teapot on the counter and shut off the water. "Please stop," she begged as she made her way towards the insufferable noise. "Stop," she repeated in an irate tone as she opened the door. She found CC standing on her stoop, shivering from the cold. A sudden flash from the previous evening washed over her. *CC was bent over in front of her as Jamie rode her backside, pressing her wetness hard into the policewoman as she begged for release.* A blush covered her body as she tried to make the image disappear.

"Can we talk?" CC inquired sheepishly.

"No," Jamie replied in a weary voice.

CC shifted nervously from one foot to the other as she wrapped her arms around herself to fight off the cold. Hearing

Jamie's response was almost a relief. Now she could simply go back to her condo and crawl into bed. She could picture pulling the covers over her head and hiding out until next spring. She looked over to see her sister glaring at her from the front window. CC shrugged at her younger sibling in an effort to convey that Jamie wasn't interested in talking. Stevie's glare grew fiery as she pointed towards Jamie's doorway.

CC rolled her head in defeat, turning back towards Jamie who was just leaning against the doorway looking very pale. "I'm sorry," CC began. "But we need to talk. Now may not be the best time, but Stevie has locked me out and isn't letting me back in until we talk," she explained in an exhausted breath.

"I always liked that Stevie," Jamie chuckled. "I'm just not up for this," she added in a tired voice.

"Please," CC pleaded. "If you shut the door on me too, I'll be stuck out here in my bare feet. I could freeze to death."

"It's not that cold," Jamie reasoned.

"Oh, come on," CC grumbled, her patience worn out. She was hung over, cold, and pleading with her ex-lover to let her talk to her. None of these events were sitting too well with the brooding brunette. "What's the worse that could happen? You'd end up hating me? You already do."

"Yes, I do," Jamie responded as her jaw clenched. "Come in."

CC blew out a sigh of relief as Jamie stepped aside and let her in. Her body brushed slightly against the smaller woman's. She heard the moan escape from Jamie. CC bit down on her bottom lip as she tried to ignore the sudden tingling sensation her body was experiencing. Knowing that Jamie's audible response had been involuntary, she chose to ignore it. Now if she could just get her lower anatomy to do the same, she might just get through the morning with some sense of dignity.

She felt her body warming as the door clicked shut behind her. "I meant what I said," Jamie grumbled as CC turned to her. She couldn't help noticing how absolutely adorable the small blonde looked. Her hair was all rumpled and damp, and her sweats hung on her. "I don't want to talk. But it is chilly out. You can hang around here until your sister decides to let you come home. I'm going to bed." Having had her say, Jamie brushed past her and headed up the staircase.

CC stood there with her mouth hanging open. "Could I feel more like a total dufus at the moment?" she muttered as she stood in Jamie's living room. "I could just watch some television," she reasoned. Then her shoulders drooped as she realized that Stevie was right. "Ah, what the hell," she conceded. "Might as well face the music. Even if I'm twelve years too late." Drawing on her last ounce of courage, she climbed the staircase.

Tentatively she stepped into Jamie's bedroom. She found her ex-lover lying face down on the queen-size bed on top of the covers. "Jamie," she began shyly, feeling her courage abandon her.

"I'm in hell," Jamie groaned without lifting her head off the pillow.

"Look, if you don't want to talk, that's fine," CC stated firmly, feeling her courage returning. "But you can listen."

"If I listen to what you have to say, will you let me sleep?" Jamie moaned in disgust. "It's my day off and some guy keeps pounding on my head with a jackhammer."

"Yes," CC reassured her. After all, the same guy was beating on her head.

"Speak," Jamie commanded her.

"That morning I didn't walk out on you," CC began to explain, suddenly feeling better. It felt good to finally tell the one person that had been hurt the most by the unforeseen events that had occurred that day. "I was on patrol. We pulled over a car with a broken taillight." CC's body tensed as she recalled the terror she had lived through that day. "I never saw the gun," she continued as Jamie lifted her head and stared at her. CC couldn't read the expression in her eyes so she continued. "I was shot twice. It was bad. For weeks I drifted in and out of consciousness. My only clear thoughts were of you. No one knew about you since I was in the closet back then, so no one made an effort to find you. Except for Stevie. She ran away from home when she found out. The story never made the press. The guy was an informant who was about to expose an FBI conspiracy. He ended up dead not long after that. The whole thing was covered up."

CC stood there, waiting for what seemed like an eternity for Jamie to respond. She watched as Jamie's face scrunched up. "Was that before or after Scully and Mulder escaped from the space craft?" Jamie asked her bitterly.

"It's the truth," CC asserted. "By the time I was able to understand what had happened, you were gone."

"Are you under the disillusion that I would buy that load of horse manure?" Jamie spat at her as she climbed off the bed.

CC found herself standing toe to toe with a very angry little blonde. The veins in the younger woman's neck were bulging as her face turned purple. "Who do you think you are talking to?" Jamie snarled as she poked the taller woman in the chest. "I'm not some bimbo you picked up in a bar," Jamie flared as she poked CC once again.

"It's the truth," CC repeated firmly as her body winced from Jamie's assault.

"The truth?" Jamie spat back. "You wouldn't know the truth if it bit you in the ass." She poked CC once again, even harder than her first two attacks. CC could feel the anger welling up inside her.

"Fine. Don't believe me," CC shouted bitterly. "I know what happened. I wasn't the one who ran off and bedded someone else."

"Where do you get off?" Jamie yelled in return.

"You were my first," CC said as she gritted her teeth. "I loved you."

"What?" Jamie uttered in disbelief as her eyes narrowed.

"You weren't the only virgin that night," CC answered in a flat even tone of voice.

Jamie's eyes widened. "That's it," Jamie said in a low harsh tone. "Get out." She pointed to the doorway.

"Jamie," CC drew a breath to steady herself. "I'm not lying."

"Out!" Jamie commanded her firmly as she nudged the taller woman towards the door.

As she continued to guide CC back downstairs and out the doorway, Jamie released a string of obscenities that embarrassed the policewoman. The front door slammed behind her. Once again CC found herself standing outside in the cold morning air. "That went well." She sighed as she approached her doorway. She knocked on her own front door. "Stevie, can I come home now?" she pleaded desperately.

Jamie collapsed against the door and began to sob hysterically. "Why would she say those things?" she cried out to no one. "What if it's true?" The tears fell harder; nothing made sense. She couldn't think. She was tired from lack of sleep over the past week. Her body ached from her hangover, and she couldn't recall the last time she had anything to eat. All she knew for certain was that last night, for a few short hours, she'd found herself in CC's arms.

Her mind argued that it was the last place she should find herself, but her heart disagreed. It felt right. It felt more than right. It felt like it had twelve years ago. It seemed like a lifetime ago, but the pain was still as fresh as the first night she sat up waiting for the phone call that never came. "Could what CC told me be the truth?" she cried out in the emptiness.

The angry pounding on the door rattled through her tired body. "It's her," she said quickly as she pulled herself to her feet. She wiped her nose on her shirt before opening the door. CC wasn't standing on the other side. Instead she found a very angry Stevie holding a crying infant.

"Crying?" Stevie asked bitterly. "Good, because so is my sister."

Jamie backed away fearfully from the doorway. The baby cried harder. "You have no idea how hard it was for her to come over here and face you," Stevie continued as she kicked the door close. For the first time in years, Jamie suddenly feared for her life. The infant continued to cry. Jamie looked at the baby. At first she had assumed that it was her mother's yelling that caused her discomfort. Now her trained eye led her to believe that there was something wrong.

"My sister worshiped the ground that you walked on," Stevie continued. "You broke her heart."

"What's wrong with the baby?" Jamie asked her quickly.

Stevie just shook her head and stared at her blankly. "What's wrong with the baby?" Jamie repeated, her professionalism kicking in. Stevie seemed uncertain what to do. "Look," Jamie offered in a calm tone, "you can keep telling me off. I'm a bitch, okay? Now we all agree. What's wrong with the baby?"

"I don't know," Stevie stammered. "I've been waiting all morning for her pediatrician to call, but he hasn't yet."

"Can I take a look at her?" Jamie held out her arms. Seeing the indecision on Stevie's face, she said, "You can still tell me what a complete jackass I am."

"Deal," Stevie agreed as she handed her daughter over to Jamie.

Jamie pulled a comforter down off the back of the sofa before laying the crying child down. "Hey there, peanut," Jamie cooed to the child. "Not feeling good?"

"CC calls her that," Stevie commented absently.

"My bag is in the kitchen. Would you grab it for me?" Jamie asked.

Stevie returned quickly with the black bag in hand. "How long has she been like this?" Jamie inquired as she began a careful exam.

"She woke up early and was a little fussy," Stevie explained as Jamie continued her exam.

"What's her name?" Jamie asked as she took the baby's temperature. "I know. No one likes that part of the exam," she reassured the infant.

"Emma," Stevie informed her. "And you're still a jerk."

"Hey Emma." Jamie tickled the child. "She has a slight fever. Is CC telling me the truth?"

Jamie peeked into Emma's ear and her suspicions were confirmed. "How long have you been waiting for her doctor to call?" Jamie inquired.

"All morning," Stevie offered. "And yes, CC told you the truth. A guy who was about to rat out a bunch of cops, FBI agents who were helping a certain Southern mob boss shot her. You know the one - elderly gentleman, likes to where a Red Sox's baseball cap, and no one knows where the hell he is."

Jamie continued a careful exam of Emma's tired little body. She checked her bag to see if she had her prescription pad and then wrote out a prescription before redressing Emma and handing her back to her mother. "Emma has an ear infection. It's very common at her age."

"Really?" Stevie relaxed as she cradled her daughter.

"Here this should help." Jamie handed the prescription to Stevie. "I think you should see a pediatrician, I know someone. I could call her if you'd like?"

"Thank you," Stevie said sincerely.

Jamie felt the tears building as she dialed her friend's number. "She was all alone?" Jamie asked. "At the hospital?" Jamie choked at the thought of CC lying helpless with no one there for her.

"Yes," Stevie responded coldly.

"Sandy, Jamie Jameson . . ." she spoke into the telephone. She explained about Emma and Sandy agreed to see the infant immediately. Jamie then relayed the information to Stevie.

"Thank you for Emma," Stevie said.

"But I'm still a total jackass." Jamie sniffed as her heart shattered. "I didn't know. Why didn't someone tell me?"

"No one knew about you," Stevie explained softly. "I was the only one who knew who she was calling out for in her sleep. But when I arrived you were already gone. By the time she found you, it was too late. The day she did find you, you were sucking face with some girl."

"The things I said to her," Jamie whimpered as she brushed the tears out of her eyes. "Do you have a car?"

"Yes, and I know where to go," Stevie confirmed. "What are you going to do?"

"I need to talk to CC," Jamie confessed as she grabbed up her sneakers.

"No kidding," Stevie laughed.

"One question, Stevie," Jamie started carefully. "Who's little Emma's Daddy?"

"Long story." Stevie smirked as they started out the front door. "If the two of you haven't killed one another by the time I get back, I'll tell you."

"Fair enough." Jamie agreed.

CHAPTER TWO

CC was lying on her bed staring up at the ceiling. The last twenty-four hours had been hell on earth. A young girl had died, something that despite her sense of reasoning she felt responsible for. Then she slept with Jamie. Not a bad thing. In fact it was very nice - too nice. She was kicking herself for that as well. She should have been stronger and not let it happen. But there was something about the way Jamie kissed her. One touch of her lips and CC was lost, thinking with the wrong part of her anatomy.

The harshness of Jamie's words hurt her deeply. She knew that the whole thing sounded unbelievable; still she had hoped that the feelings they had once shared would have made a difference. Apparently she was mistaken. CC was just lying there, fighting with the knowledge that Jamie had never cared for her the way she had cared for Jamie. "A part of me still does," CC admitted to the empty room.

A shy knock on the door disrupted her agony. "Come in, Stevie," she called out softly, hoping that the doctor had finally called. The door creaked as it opened slowly. CC sat up to watch it. "What the hell?" she muttered, wondering what her little sister was up to. She felt her body temperature rise slightly. Her crystal blue eyes widened as she watched the petite blonde step shyly into the room.

"It isn't Stevie," Jamie announced carefully.

"I can see that," CC concurred, a slight bitterness creeping into her voice.

"Stevie took Emma to the doctor," Jamie continued in an uneasy tone as she stared at the floor.

CC started to lift herself off the bed, her head pounding violently from the quickness of her action. "Ouch," she moaned as two hands placed themselves on her shoulders. "I need to go with her," CC protested as Jamie pushed her back down onto the bed.

"She's already left," Jamie explained as she sat on the edge of the queen-size bed. "I took a look at Emma and it looks like she has an ear infection. I sent Stevie to a pediatrician I know and trust."

"Is that serious?" CC asked impatiently. "Ear infections?"

"No," Jamie reassured her. "It's quite common."

CC lay back down, crossing her arms over her chest. She was trying to understand why was Jamie there. They sat there in a deafening silence. CC stared up at the ceiling as Jamie sat on the edge of the bed with her back to her. "I need to get my car at some point," CC muttered absently in an effort to break the silence.

"Me too," Jamie stammered.

"Why are you here?" CC finally asked as she braced herself for another outburst.

"Stevie took me out to the woodshed." Jamie chuckled slightly, still keeping her back to CC.

"Huh?" CC said as she shook her head. Her movements sent another jolt of pain through her head. "Ouch," she exclaimed as she began to rub her temples. "Never again," she moaned in agony. "Jose Cuervo and I are not friends."

"Stevie told me what happened," Jamie continued, the sadness evident in her voice.

"So did I," CC noted with a hint of bitterness.

"I know," Jamie conceded.

"Now you know." CC sighed. "Why didn't you believe me?" CC's voice grew harsh. "I was in love with you."

"I didn't know that," Jamie explained as she finally turned to her. CC's heart dropped as she took in Jamie's drawn features and puffy eyes. "I thought you had used me."

"I didn't," CC replied softly as she took Jamie's hand.

"Why didn't you tell me sooner?" Jamie whimpered. "God, CC! You were all alone."

CC couldn't stand to see Jamie hurting. She reached up and pulled her former lover down. Jamie instinctively curled up next to her and CC wrapped her arms around the smaller woman. "By the time I found you, it was too late," CC explained. "You had moved on, and I doubted that you'd believe me."

"Losing you hurt so much." Jamie sniffed. "I never really trusted anyone after that," Jamie said as she snuggled closer.

"Neither did I," CC confessed as she allowed her body to relax and enjoy the warmth of Jamie's body. "It's over," CC offered tenderly as she rubbed Jamie's back. Her stomach clenched as Jamie's hand slipped under her T-shirt. "Maybe now we can save our friendship," CC said hopefully. Her skin tingled as Jamie rubbed her abdomen.

"I would like to try," Jamie responded honestly.

CC wondered why she had suggested friendship? The smell of Jamie's shampoo was invading her senses. The feel of Jamie's hand was causing her stomach to flutter. Not to mention they were lying so close together that CC could feel Jamie's breath on her skin. At that moment, friendship was the last thing on her mind.

Her body tensed as she fought against the sudden awakening of her libido. Jamie lifted her head and looked at her questioningly. CC watched as the blonde opened her mouth to speak. Their eyes locked. Before she could think or stop herself, she kissed Jamie.

Their lips and bodies instantly melted together. CC could feel the years of anger and mistrust fading as their tongues met. The kiss deepened slowly as their bodies pressed together. There was nothing hurried in their movements. They explored the warmth of each other's mouth as their hands slowly and softly caressed each other's body.

Shyly they ended the kiss. Jamie traced CC's jaw line with her fingers. CC leaned into the touch. Suddenly old fears and demons emerged. "We can't do this," she said softly as her heart disagreed.

"I know." Jamie sighed deeply. "That was the past. Too many years and too much pain for both of us," Jamie said as she smiled sweetly. "I should go."

"No," CC responded tenderly as she pulled Jamie into her arms. "If your body feels as rotten as mine does, the walk back to your place will kill you." Jamie groaned in response. "Let's get some rest, and then we can figure out just how we're going to get our cars back."

"Okay," Jamie agreed as she snuggled against CC's body. "I'm glad that you're back in my life. I would like to try becoming friends."

"Me too," CC concurred as she felt Jamie's breathing deepen. She did want Jamie back as a friend. Now if she could just stop her lower anatomy from pulsating, everything would be all right. She felt Jamie clutch her T-shirt. Looking down, she realized that the doctor had drifted off to sleep. CC brushed her hair back. Holding the blonde a little tighter, she quickly fell asleep.

CC ushered the irate man towards the holding cell. He wasn't really a man. He was nothing more than a boy. His misfortune was that he was just old enough to be tried as an adult. He may have looked young and innocent, but the youth had blood on his hands. He had been aiming for a member of a rival gang when he shot down a little girl on her way home from Sunday school. It saddened the policewoman that two young lives were now ruined because of something so senseless. The only thing that eased the pain for her was that the case was finally wrapped up and the little girl's family could rest easy knowing that the idiot responsible was going to jail.

When she and Max cornered him, the little bugger was so frightened that he wet himself. She was a little miffed at the way Max was taunting him about it as they escorted him down to Central Lockup. "Give it a rest, Max," she growled as she looked towards the guard. The guard was about to open a cell. "No way," CC protested as she pointed down the narrow hallway. "He needs to be isolated."

"What did this little pip squeak do?" the older man asked as he towered over the boy.

"Never mind," CC snapped, her blue eyes flashing with anger.

"He killed a kid," Max announced loudly as CC cringed.

There were certain things that didn't sit well with other inmates. You might be a lowlife drug dealer or a thief but even this group had their standards. And anyone who hurt a child was a marked man. Most people didn't seem to understand that most of them had children themselves.

"The gang shooting?" the guard grumbled as he stared down at the youngster. CC nodded in confirmation. "Follow me. I have a dark corner for the little weasel."

As they followed the guard, the jeers from the other inmates started. CC could feel her prisoner tense up through her grip. CC tightened her grasp as they approached the cell and the taunting increased. She could see Max loosen his hold as he snapped his head back. "Shut up!" he screamed at the rowdy inmates.

"Shit," she muttered as her prisoner began to squirm. Max had loosened his hold just enough for the youngster to free himself. CC was slammed against the wall. The scuffle was short lived. She was a lot bigger than the boy and he was handcuffed. They locked him in his cell, but not before CC had been slammed into the iron bars when they undid his restraints.

She watched as the youngster scrambled around his cell like a caged animal. CC felt slightly woozy from her head making

65

contact with the cement wall. "Nice going," she growled at her partner.

"I'm sorry," Max apologized quickly.

"No you're not," CC spat out as she walked back down the corridor. "Keep an eye on him," she instructed the guard. Despite the fact that they had already taken his shoes and anything else that he might use to harm himself, she knew that he was about to face an endless night of taunting.

Finally they stepped outside to find that the sun had set. CC swayed slightly and fought back the bile that was rising in her throat. "Calloway?" Max asked, his voice trembling slightly. "Are you all right?"

CC nodded her head only to reach out so she could hold onto the wall of the building. "No," she managed to choke out. Max steadied her as he led her to their vehicle.

"I'm taking you to the hospital," he stated firmly as he lowered her into the car.

"Fine," she conceded. "But you can do the paperwork, jackass."

A short while later CC found herself sitting in the emergency room waiting area with an ice pack on her head and one hell of a headache. She let Max call it in to the precinct and handle everything. She thought it was only fitting since he had been the cause of her pain. It gave her a small sense of pleasure that he would be getting home very late after dealing with the paperwork and their lieutenant.

Finally a nurse escorted her into a curtained exam area. Max tried to follow but retreated when she glared at him and said, "Sit!" The nurse instructed her to put on the ugly paper Johnny and have a seat on the exam table.

CC held up the flimsy sheet of paper in disgust. "It's my head," she protested. The gray-haired woman just stared at her and then scowled as she crossed her arms, daring CC to argue. "That didn't work for my mother," CC said in defiance.

"Are you going to be trouble?" a familiar voice questioned her as Jamie stepped into the room.

"Officer, you wouldn't be giving my nurse a hard time now, would you?" Jamie mocked her.

"Howdy, neighbor," CC jested as her stomach clenched. After the night they had slept together and disastrous morning that followed, the two women had been getting along. It was all very friendly although CC couldn't stop feeling something more for the blonde doctor. She was becoming very good at convincing herself that it was just old emotions. That is until she would see Jamie. It was always that first glance that would make her heart skip a beat. So far she had successfully managed to hide her feelings from everyone except herself.

"What?" she asked, realizing that Jamie had been speaking to her.

"I said, are you going to be a good girl?" Jamie repeated. Despite her teasing tone, CC didn't miss the look of concern on the smaller woman's face.

"I'm always good," CC jested in response as she winked playfully, hoping to lighten the mood.

"Humph," Jamie scoffed as she blushed slightly. "Behave," she cautioned CC as she ran her fingers through her short blonde hair.

"Okay, you win." CC sighed as she rolled her eyes. "I'll put on the paper napkin." She watched as the two women stood their ground. "I don't need an audience." She shooed them away.

"Oh, she's shy," Jamie joked to the nurse before they departed the room.

Later CC was tugging on the paper Johnny, trying to cover her body as Jamie flashed a pen light in her eyes. "Stay still and follow the light," Jamie scolded her.

"I can't help it," CC groaned as she tried to close the gap in the back of the gown. "I feel so exposed."

Jamie sighed as she lowered the light. "CC, I'm a professional," she explained gently. Then she glanced over her shoulder at her nurse who was carefully recording CC's vitals onto a chart. Jamie leaned in. "Besides, I've seen it before," she whispered in CC's ear. CC blushed as the inside of her thighs quivered slightly. "You're adorable when you blush," Jamie whispered teasingly.

"Stop it," CC cautioned her as she gritted her teeth.

"Behave and I will," Jamie instructed her as she pulled away. "Now let's try this again. Follow the light with just your eyes."

CC decided to cooperate just so she could get out of there. Jamie seemed to be placated as she continued her exam. "You're not going to ask me who the President is again?" CC teased as Jamie examined her shoulder.

"No, although Howdy Doody was an interesting answer," Jamie said flatly. "Quite a nasty bruise you're sporting back here."

"What about those?" the nurse inquired.

CC bit back a laugh, knowing that the nurse had spotted the fading hickeys that Jamie had left there. "Those seem to be old," Jamie squeaked out.

"Oh, those?" CC began, knowing that Jamie was blushing behind her. She jumped slightly as a cold metal stethoscope was placed on her back. "Good Lord! Don't you warm those things?"

"Take a deep breath," Jamie instructed her in a flat tone.

The exam continued as Jamie poked and prodded every inch of her body and then shipped her off for x-rays.

Later CC was sitting on the exam table swinging her legs, bored out her mind. Her head had stopped hurting and she just wanted to go home. Finally, after what seemed like an eternity, Jamie reappeared. "So did you find anything interesting?" CC questioned her.

"No," Jamie responded as she sipped her coffee. "Just as I suspected, your head is completely empty."

"Cute," CC scoffed as she looked around to ensure that they were alone.

"You can get dressed now," Jamie offered with a smile.

"Thank you." CC sighed with relief.

"As I was saying, you're fine but just a little beat up," Jamie continued. "What happened?"

"Difference of opinion," CC lied as she began to get dressed. "Uh, Jamie . . . there's something I would like to talk to you about," she began hesitantly. CC knew she had to ask, and it had been bothering her since they'd woke up together that morning. "That night." She paused for a moment as her mind searched for the correct words. "We weren't careful," she finally spat out, unable to look at Jamie.

"I understand," Jamie said gently, CC could feel the small blonde approaching her. "CC, look at me," Jamie requested softly. CC swallowed hard before turning to face her. Jamie gave her a reassuring smile. "I had the same concerns myself. It wasn't a very smart thing to do. In fact, I had myself tested a couple of days later. I'm fine. If you want I can set up a blood test for you."

"Thanks." CC sighed with relief as she finished putting on her clothes. "I would like a test. I'll see my own doctor though. Thanks for not being offended."

"Why would I be offended?" Jamie responded. "We had unsafe sex, not knowing one another's sexual history. So how are you getting home? Even though you checked out, I would feel better if you didn't drive."

"I'll have Max take me home. It'll be his penance." She chuckled as Jamie gave her a curious look.

Later that night, CC indulged in her favorite activity. She sat on the sofa cradling her niece in her arms. "So Emma, what am I going to do?" she asked the cooing infant. "Don't tell anyone, but I think I'm falling for her all over again."

A soft knock on the front door interrupted her thoughts. "Now what?" She sighed as she stood, carrying Emma to the door. The scowl she was sporting quickly vanished when she opened the door and found Jamie standing on the other side.

Jamie stared up at CC who was cradling Emma in her arms. A rush of emotions assaulted the blonde as she drank in the sight. *'I don't think I've ever seen anything more beautiful,'* she thought blissfully as her heart began to pound in her chest. Her emotions had been on overload ever since CC had unceremoniously reentered her life. She blinked in confusion as she suddenly became aware that CC was talking to her.

"Sorry," she apologized as she shook her head in an effort to clear her thoughts. "It's been a long day," she added, hoping that the tall policewoman would accept the feeble excuse. "I just stopped by to see how you're doing."

"Come in," CC offered in a friendly manner as she stepped aside.

Jamie accepted the offer and stepped into the condo. She tried to calm her racing heart as CC closed the door behind her. Jamie's mouth went suddenly dry as CC moved towards her. "Have a seat," CC said as she sat down onto the sofa.

Jamie shrugged out of her jacket and took her place next to CC. "So," she began slowly, trying to sound as normal as possible. "How are you feeling?"

"Much better," CC replied. "Although the doctor who tended to me did seem to enjoy giving me a hard time."

"Nasty wench," Jamie teased as she reached out and allowed Emma to capture one of her fingers in her chubby little hand. "And how are you feeling, little one?"

"She's doing great." CC beamed as she tickled her niece. "I want to thank you for taking care of her that day. "

"You don't have to thank me," Jamie said, brushing aside the compliment.

"Well, I think that I should," CC continued in gentle tone. "Given everything that was going on that day, it was very thoughtful of you to put everything aside and look after my little peanut."

"I'm just glad that she's feeling better," Jamie said as she finally forced herself to look into CC's eyes.

Time came to a halt as she fell into the electric blue gaze. *'Will I ever stop wanting you?'* she asked herself in desperation. Even when she had convinced herself that she hated this woman, her heart and body still ached for her touch. Emma gurgled, breaking the trance the two women found themselves locked in. Jamie watched as CC turned her attention back to her niece. She couldn't help noticing that CC's breathing was erratic. Of course she was only aware of this since her gaze had drifted down to CC's breasts.

"I should put her down," CC commented quickly as she stood, cradling the tired infant in her arms. Jamie simply nodded in response, thankful for the reprieve. She used the time alone to collect herself. Lusting after CC was understandable and very dangerous. *'Well, dangerous might be a little extreme. It's simply unwise. Although when she looks at me, I'm not certain why that is. What would be so wrong about rekindling what we once had?'* Jamie's mind rationalized as CC reentered the room.

"Can I get you something to drink?" CC offered.

"No, thank you," Jamie answered as she tried to bury her lustful thoughts.

CC smiled as she sat down next to Jamie. Emma's absence seemed to create an electrifying energy between them. CC reclined slightly and winced as her shoulder pressed into the sofa. "Still hurts?" Jamie inquired, thinking how lame the question sounded. *'Of course it still hurts, you moron. She has a bruise the size of Nebraska on that shoulder,'* she mentally kicked herself.

"A little," CC lied as Jamie rolled her eyes in response.

"So, what happened today?" Jamie inquired, desperately seeking a topic of conversation that would lead her mind away from CC's body. Internally, Jamie was fighting back the urge to reexamine the injury and kiss it to make it better.

"We were escorting a prisoner and he didn't want to go to jail," CC explained flatly as she shifted her position. The movement caused their thighs to brush against one another slightly.

Jamie's body trembled from the contact. "So why were you so upset with Max?" she asked as she pretended that she was unaffected by the touch.

"He was baiting the guy," CC explained, once again adopting a flat dry tone. "He turned his attention away briefly." Unaware of what she was doing, Jamie gripped CC's thigh as her eyes widened in anger. "The thing is, I think he was pushing this kid's buttons on purpose," CC concluded.

"Why would he put you in jeopardy like that?" Jamie growled as her grip tightened.

"I don't think he wanted to put me in danger," CC explained quickly. "I think he was trying to push the guy into doing something stupid so he'd have an excuse to beat the crap out of him."

"What an asshole," Jamie blurted out.

"Not really," CC reassured her as she laid her hand on top of Jamie's hand. It wasn't until CC's hand touched hers that Jamie realized she was holding on to her. Not only had she gripped the taller woman's firm thigh tightly, she seemed to be hovering over the slightly reclined woman.

Jamie's heart beat wildly as her breathing became erratic. She was so close to CC that she could feel her former lover's breath on her skin. Jamie swallowed hard as CC reached up and cupped her face in her hand. Jamie fought back a moan as she leaned into the touch. CC's legs parted slightly as Jamie unconsciously leaned her body closer. CC's lips looked so inviting and they were so close. All she had to do was lean in a little closer.

From behind them came the sound of someone clearing her throat. The couple bolted up quickly. Stevie stood there looking very embarrassed. Jamie stood up quickly, weaving slightly.

"Sorry," Stevie apologized shyly. "I didn't mean to interrupt."

"Oh no, you didn't," Jamie lied as she blushed furiously. "I was just checking out . . . I mean, checking on your sister."

"I see." Stevie chuckled in amusement. "And how is my sister fairing this evening?" Stevie teased as CC glared at her.

"I'm fine," CC growled at her younger sibling.

"Well, it's late and I should be going," Jamie stammered, feeling very disoriented by the entire situation. "Glad to see you're feeling better," she offered to the smirking policewoman. Jamie snatched up her jacket and tripped as she made her way to the doorway.

"I'll see you out," CC said from behind her.

Jamie's stomach clenched as she realized that her escape had just been postponed. CC opened the front door for her and the two women stepped out into the cool night air. "You are far too amused by all this," Jamie chastised her as they lingered in the doorway.

"I'm sorry," CC replied softly. "You were so flustered. I shouldn't have teased you."

"It was just so . . . " Jamie's voice trailed off as she tried to organize her thoughts. Her mind was screaming for her to invite this woman back to her place. They stood there in an awkward silence as Jamie fought back the image of CC lying in her bed only a short distance away.

"It just old emotions," CC rationalized as Jamie tried to quiet her throbbing lower anatomy. "It would be a mistake," she stammered.

"Yes," Jamie confirmed, not truly believing what she was saying. "We're just becoming friends again. Given our history, the whole thing would be so wrong."

"Right," CC agreed and Jamie felt her heart break just a little.

They found themselves staring at one another once again, cloaked in another cloud of silence. "Well . . . Uhm . . ." Jamie finally said, hoping to relieve the tension. "Goodnight."

"Goodnight," CC replied. Neither of them moved.

Jamie just stood there, losing herself in a sea of blue. Jamie's mind and body were locked in an intense battle over what her next move should be. Before she could reach her decision, CC's gaze dropped to the ground. Jamie suddenly felt a little foolish. "Goodnight," she repeated and quickly made her departure.

Once she was safely inside her own home, Jamie locked the door. Dropping her coat on the floor, she quickly unzipped her pants. Bracing her back against the living room wall, she slipped her hand into her pants. "Oh my God," she moaned as her hand was flooded by the river of passion that had pooled between her thighs. Her eyes fluttered shut as she began to touch herself.

Her mind filled quickly with images of CC kneeling before her. As her fingers plunged in and out of her center, she imagined that it was her former lover touching her. The young doctor's body responded as her hips swayed in rhythm. She was so close to climaxing, but for some reason she couldn't cross over the edge. Frustrated, she removed her hand from her body. "Damn it," she moaned as she banged her head against the wall lightly. "I need to get past this," she whimpered. "Don't I?" she choked out as she slid down onto the floor. The confusion and doubt finally took their toll. The guilt returned in full force. "I left her all alone!" She began to weep.

Once she had cried herself out, Jamie dragged her tired body upstairs. After taking an extended shower, she climbed weakly into bed. Thoughts of CC quickly invaded her senses. She tried once again to pleasure herself and once again she failed. She tossed and turned for several hours as sleep evaded her grasp as well.

CC yawned exhaustedly as she signed the last report on her desk. It had been a long day. Happily it consisted of nothing but paperwork. The good people of her fair community had managed not to kill one another for the past few days. It was nice to have calm looming over the city.

CC decided that life was going pretty well. Emma was feeling good. Stevie had landed a couple of new clients and was very busy. CC was proud of her little sister. She'd started her own web design company early on. She was doing well and could work out of the house. The little stinker had turned out all right. She ran her own business and still managed to be a full time mom.

Now if CC could just stop lusting after the pretty blonde doctor who lived next door, life would be perfect. It had been a couple of weeks since CC had been injured and the two almost kissed. During the days that followed, CC tried to convince her that it hadn't happen. That Jamie wasn't going to kiss her. That it was just wishful thinking.

But CC knew the truth. What else could have been happening? Jamie was lying on top of her, their faces so close that she could feel the blonde's breathe on her skin. CC smiled at the memory of how it felt to have Jamie's body pressed against her own. *'Oh, don't be going down that road, Caitlin,'* she cautioned herself.

Thankfully Jamie never brought it up. They didn't talk about it or the one drunken night they'd spent together. It seemed to be working. They had fallen into an easy sort of friendship. It was all very neighborly. They would say hello as they passed, or she would invite Jamie over for coffee in the morning.

Since they both worked the late shift they could spend time together. Not a lot of time, just simple friendly gestures. CC would be lying if she said things were completely comfortable between them. Jamie was still her ex-girlfriend and there would probably always be a slight awkwardness between them.

CC wrapped up her work and said goodnight to Max. On the drive home she thought it was odd that Jamie was, for all intents and purposes, the great love of her life yet the two had only been intimate twice. And the second time was more than a little hazy for both of them. Every once in awhile, CC would be chatting with Jamie and something would spark a memory from that night.

At that point, CC would suddenly grow uncomfortable. It wasn't easy sitting next to someone while you were thinking about the hot sex the two of you had once shared. CC would usually come up with an excuse to end their conversation. Tiredness usually worked. They worked odd hours, and neither seemed able to get enough sleep. There were times when Jamie would do the same. CC secretly wondered if the blonde was experiencing the same sense of déjà vu.

As CC pulled into the parking lot, she looked around for Jamie's car. She was disappointed when she didn't see it. It was fast becoming her routine to look for the little Honda. If she found it, she would look over at Jamie's condo to see if any lights were on. Usually there were. CC would then knock and invite Jamie over.

She'd been nervous the first time she knocked on Jamie's door, but the friendly response instantly relaxed her. A few times it had been Jamie who extended the invitation if she arrived back later than the policewoman.

CC hoped that would happen this evening. She enjoyed the time she spent with Jamie and Emma at the end of the day. Yet she still cautioned herself not to hope for anything more. CC stepped into the home she shared with her sister and instantly flinched. The sight she saw in the kitchen gave her the creeps. "Ugh," she squeaked.

"Tsk," Stevie chided her as she continued using the breast pump. "Some big tough cop you are. You stand over dead bodies all day long, and then you freak watching someone express breast milk. You are such a big sissy."

"Am not," CC scoffed as she started to walk away, feeling a little queasy from the sight.

"Right," Stevie said as she rolled her eyes. "Remind me not to allow you to help my daughter with her homework."

"Whatever," CC blew her off as she retreated into her bedroom.

After she showered CC found Stevie working on her computer. "Don't wake her," Stevie cautioned her as CC loomed over the crib set up in Stevie's office, which was located next to CC's bedroom.

"But . . . ," CC started protest.

"Brad is picking her up in a few hours," Stevie explained patiently. "She'll be very cranky if you wake her."

"Right, I forgot." CC sighed in disappointment. "So that's why you were doing that thing."

"That thing?" Stevie chuckled. "Yes, Caitlin. That's why I was expressing breast milk."

"Does he have to take her overnight?" CC pouted.

"He's her father," Stevie explained in exasperation. "He would like to spend time with her."

"I know," CC grumbled.

Stevie looked up from her work and studied her sister for a moment. "No James tonight?" she inquired, slightly surprised.

"No," CC clipped.

"Sorry," Stevie apologized quickly. "I just thought that you two were . . . never mind."

"You thought what?" CC questioned her as she looked over Stevie's shoulder. For the life of her, she couldn't understand what she was looking at on the computer screen.

"Nothing," Stevie hedged.

"Uh huh." CC sighed in disbelief. "Stevie, I'm not getting back together with Jamie. So just drop it."

"Okay."

"I mean it," CC asserted.

"Okay," Stevie agreed.

"I'm serious," CC stated with conviction. "We're just friends. Not even close friends, just neighbors."

"Oh, is that why you two were making out the other night?" Stevie questioned her absently as she continued to work.

"We weren't making out," CC corrected her as she watch Stevie shut down her computer. Stevie stood and cast a look of disbelief at her before exiting her office.

Frustrated, CC followed Stevie into the living room. "We weren't," she growled.

"Fine. You weren't making out," Stevie conceded. "You were just wrapped up together like two snakes in heat. My mistake."

CC massaged her throbbing temple. "Stevie, let me try to explain things to you," she began slowly.

"I hope you do better than the time you tried to explain the facts of life to me." Stevie giggled.

"I didn't know you knew already." CC grimaced as she recalled the long ago conversation. "I certainly didn't know you were gay." CC looked quickly out the front window, trying to see if Jamie had returned. She frowned, realizing that she hadn't.

"Look, Stevie." CC returned her thoughts to her sister who was eyeing her suspiciously. "Jamie is a part of my past. It's nice that we no longer hate one another. But too much has happened between us and it's been a long time. We've both changed."

"Then why did you sleep together again?" Stevie pried.

"We were drunk and emotionally vulnerable," CC said, trying to defend her actions. "I don't know if you can understand that."

"Caitlin." Stevie chuckled. "I'm an adult. In fact, I have a child of my own. That's how I became a mother. Honestly, Sis, I think the two of you are using it as an excuse. I think you slept together because you wanted to. I also think that you still have some very deep feelings for the good doctor."

"Don't be ridiculous," CC gasped.

"Am I?" Stevie asked her seriously. "If you don't care then why do you keep looking out that window to see if she's home yet?"

CC wanted to crawl under a rock. She couldn't argue with her sister. She didn't understand what was happening. Stevie said goodnight gathered up Emma and went upstairs to her bedroom. CC stood alone, trying to convince herself that Stevie was wrong.

CC finally gave up and retreated to her own bedroom. Tossing and turning, she managed to get a couple of hours of sleep. When she woke up again, the smell of coffee was coming from the outer room. Dragging herself out of bed, she found Stevie changing Emma's diaper in the living room.

"Hey, my stinky little peanut," CC cooed at the child. Stevie laughed at her silliness. CC cast a pleading look at Stevie.

"Go on." Stevie laughed as she handed her daughter over to CC.

Stevie cleaned up the mess and washed her hands as CC held her niece, teasing her. Emma gurgled up at her aunt. "Do you want some coffee?" Stevie inquired.

"It's not that decaf crap you drink, is it?" CC inquired hesitantly.

"No." Stevie smirked. "I made the real stuff for Brad. He's running a little late. He had to work some after hours party last night."

"Well, if he's too tired . . . ," CC began as Stevie handed her a fresh cup of coffee.

"He's still coming to take Emma," Stevie chided her. "Give it up."

CC shrugged innocently. She allowed her eyes to wander to the window once again, smiling slightly when she saw Jamie's car in the lot. Feeling much better, she decided to enjoy the few moments she had with Emma. She carried the infant and her coffee out on the deck.

It was a delicate balancing act. She had to keep the coffee safely away from Emma. Stevie opened the sliding door for her and left the two of them alone. CC placed her coffee down on the table and lifted her giggling niece over her head. She began making a series of silly noises much to the delight of her niece and, by the chuckling she heard, someone else was amused as well.

She lowered Emma safely in her arms and cradled the child before looking over at the adjoining balcony. Jamie was leaning against the wall, still wearing a jacket. Her hand covered her mouth. She appeared to be fighting off a fit of laughter.

"You tell anyone and you die," CC cautioned the doctor as she allowed her well-trained eye take in Jamie's appearance. Green eyes flashed in amusement. "I have a gun," CC reminded her playfully.

"Your secret is safe with me," Jamie responded warmly.

They stared at each other for a moment. CC felt her heart breaking. Being a detective sucked at times. It only took her one quick scan to know that Jamie had just returned home. And by the smudge of lipstick on the blonde's collar, CC could safely assume that she wasn't working late. CC continued to smile despite the sudden rush of sadness. All the while she reminded herself that it was none of her business.

Jamie had been standing out on her deck for a few moments feeling lost. Last night had been a turning point for her at least she hoped it was a turning point. Her shift at the hospital had been uneventful, the usual mix of heart attacks and extracting objects from person's orifices that really had no business being there. She was looking forward to heading home and spending sometime with CC.

That is when the familiar panic she had been experiencing lately crept in. She was growing far to fond of spending time with the attractive policewoman. Not to mention her hormones were reaching the point of exploding every time she was near the tall dark haired beauty. She couldn't deny the sexual desire that seemed to be coursing thru her veins. But sleeping with CC wasn't really something that she considering doing at this moment in time. She was fearful that if she rushed into CC's arms she would do so because of the memory of what they had once shared. Or out of sheer lust. Neither would be the basis for a good relationship. And if she were to reunite with her former lover, she wasn't going to settle for anything less. Then of course there was the question of what did CC want?

The thoughts had been troubling her since the two had slept together a few weeks ago. When the some of her co-workers suggested going out that evening Jamie felt it might just be the thing she needed. The thought of spending time away from CC and not dwelling on something she might never have was something she felt that she should be doing.

There was also the chance that perhaps she could find some release for her pent up frustration. Her hormones certainly didn't rule Jamie, but she was after all human. And finding herself constantly turned on by someone she couldn't have was beginning to wear on her. Add to that, she couldn't seem to alleviate the situation herself. This aspect was really working her nerves.

She went to the bar with her co-workers who were either gay or gay friendly and ran into Liz. The brunette had pursued the young blonde doctor before. But Jamie never gave her a second glance. Last night Jamie had a sudden change of heart. In hopes of releasing herself from the pain she was feeling she decided to give Liz a chance. They ended up in Liz's car. During the heavy petting session, Jamie became upsettingly aware that no matter how hard the brunette tried, Jamie wasn't going to be able to climax. Liz was persistent. Jamie tried to clear her mind to focus on something that would help her along the way. It turned out to be a poor choice. She ended up doing the one thing you should never do. They were kissing and it wasn't Liz's name that crossed her lips.

"Why did I think of CC? Why was it her face that entered my thoughts at that moment?" She thought as she recalled the hurt look on Liz's face. She apologized profusely. They straightened their clothing. Liz just walked away from her in a stony silence. Jamie went to rejoin her friends to find they had departed.

Jamie drove around for hours trying to figure out the mess her life was becoming. Once again she found herself standing in front of the carousel at Cold Springs Park. Now she was home and feeling exhausted. She watched as CC stepped out on the deck with Emma wrapped up in her arms. She watched in amusement as the policewoman cooed and giggled with the infant.

'I should have come home last night. It is where I wanted to be. So why did I go out and try to get laid?' She questioned herself as she fought back the laughter. CC was beyond adorable at that moment. She found herself blushing as she and her former lover exchanged a friendly banter.

"Why is Emma so dressed up this morning?" Jamie inquired knowing that she was grinning like an idiot.

"Her Daddy is coming over." CC answered brightly as she adjusted Emma's little outfit.

"Oh." Jamie answered more than a little curious about Emma's father.

"Would you like to come over for coffee?" CC asked in a friendly tone.

"Yes." Jamie answered quickly before she had a chance to think about it. Then she frowned. "Would you mind if I hopped into the shower first?"

"Go ahead, when you're ready just climb on over." CC readily agreed. "If we are not here then we will be inside."

"Thanks." Jamie replied in gratitude.

She rushed inside her home and dashed up the staircase. She wanted to join CC for coffee. But she had no desire doing it when she looked like hell and had the scent of another woman on her body. Jamie showered quickly and tossed on a pair of sweats and a t-shirt. Jamie knew what had been bothering her. For most of her life she had avoided relationships and simply sought pleasure on occasion, whenever she needed it. Dating wasn't something she did very well.

She had chosen to live her life like this because of a misplaced sense of mistrust. Now that she knew that CC had never meant to hurt her, she couldn't foresee continuing as she had in the past. Last night had proven that those days were indeed behind her. As she stepped over the railing onto CC's balcony her only question was, *'But what am I suppose to do about it now?'*

Jamie found everyone in the living room. She smiled as CC refused to hand Emma over to her Mother. "Is she holding your daughter hostage?" Jamie inquired as Stevie glared at her sister.

"It would appear so." Stevie teased. CC yawned as she held her niece tightly. "Did you get any sleep last night?" Stevie asked with concern.

"Couple hours." CC replied yawned once again.

Jamie felt a pang of concern that CC hadn't been sleeping. "Would you like some coffee James?" Stevie asked.

"Yes, thank you," Jamie replied eagerly since she had no sleep at all.

"Caitlin, go get Jamie some coffee," Stevie instructed her sibling firmly.

Jamie watched in amusement as CC curled up her lips and snarled. "Fine. Don't think I miss the attempt in tricking me into giving up the peanut," she grumbled as she stood and handed Emma back over to her Mother.

"That was too easy." Stevie said with suspicion. She sniffed for a moment before taking a quick peek into her daughter's diaper. "I should have guessed," Stevie said in disgust as she rolled her brown eyes. "You only love her until she leaks. Come on Emma, Mommy needs to change you before Daddy gets here."

CC chuckled as she led Jamie into the kitchen. Jamie couldn't help but notice the definition of her muscles as she reached up to the top cabinet. Jamie couldn't suppress the sigh that escaped from her. CC turned to her and gave her a curious look. Jamie blinked guiltily knowing that it was clear as to what she had been thinking. The sigh wasn't a, *gee I'm tired or even a hurry up and get the damn coffee.* No it was clearly the kind of sigh that screams, *wow you have a hot body*!

Jamie stood there chewing on her bottom lip trying to think of something to say. Anything that would get her out of the embarrassing situation that she had placed herself in. It was hopeless and she knew it. "Sorry," she muttered finally as CC handed her the coffee. CC smirked at her and shook her head in amusement. As she turned back to replenish her own cup of coffee, Jamie took a quick glance up and down the woman's long legs. She said a silent prayer of thanks that CC was clad in boxer shorts.

"Enjoying the view?" CC taunted her as she turned back around. Jamie had already been busted and decided to just go with it.

"Yes." She smirked confidently. CC's blush showed that the leggy brunette was thrown slightly by Jamie's bravado. "I see that you are still working out," Jamie continued amused by the flustered _expression on the normally stoic policewoman's face.

'What the hell am I doing?' Jamie suddenly panicked, realizing that she was flirting with her ex-girlfriend. But it felt so right. She couldn't deny it, just being around CC made her crazy. She placed her coffee cup on the kitchen counter and tried to steady herself.

"Are you all right?" CC inquired carefully. Jamie shook her head in confusion.

CC placed her own coffee mug down and wrapped her arms around Jamie. The doctor felt herself melting into CC's touch. Instinctively Jamie wrapped her arms around CC's waist as the brunette rubbed her back gently. "Sometimes when I'm around you . . ." Jamie began softly as she laid her head against CC's chest. Nothing in the world felt as good as being held in CC's arms.

Jamie lifted her head and found herself locked in an electric blue gaze. She felt her pulse racing as she watched CC tilt her head slightly. The only thought racing thru Jamie's mind was that she wanted to kiss CC. No, she needed to kiss this woman. Their faces were only a breath apart when the sound of a ringing doorbell interrupted them.

They stepped away from one another shyly. Each seemingly lost in their thoughts. Jamie turned away as CC backed away from her. Jamie sipped her coffee slowly as she wondered whether or not the interruption had been a good thing or a bad thing?

"That must be Brad," CC commented as she picked up her coffee cup. Jamie simply stared off into space, her body still reacting to the kiss they had almost shared.

"Brad?" Jamie responded absently as sounds from the outer room invaded her senses.

"Emma's father," CC supplied with a shrug.

"Really?" Jamie perked up. She had been a little more than curious about, little Emma's origins. Not that it really mattered. Emma was an adorable little girl. Jamie was just an overly inquisitive person.

"Come on." CC offered as she led Jamie back into the living room. Jamie grabbed her mug of coffee and followed the taller woman. Jamie looked at the tall dark haired man who was fussing over Emma. Something about him was familiar. "Hey Brad." CC called out happily.

"Girlfriend," Brad responded, and Jamie smiled realizing that Brad was a big queen.

"Brad this is . . ." CC paused with her introduction. " . . . Our neighbor Jamie." The blonde doctor smiled thinking that the situation was a little unusual.

"Nice to meet you neighbor Jamie," Brad said as he smiled over at her.

"She's the doctor who took care of Emma," Stevie added as Jamie tried to figure out where she had seen Brad before.

"Oh my God!" He squealed. "I can't thank you enough."

"It was no problem." Jamie brushed it off. "You look very familiar." She finally said.

"I well . . ." Brad stammered uncomfortably.

"Brad performs at a lot of the clubs in town." Stevie supplied.

"That's it," Jamie responded brightly. "It's Cher." She slapped her forehead.

"Excuse me?" CC nudged her.

"I saw you perform last night at Vapor." Jamie explained brightly. Then her heart dropped. Liz was a friend of his. That's why he looked so uncomfortable. He must have heard the whole story about what had happened. "You were very good," Jamie muttered quickly noticing the curious looks they were getting from both CC and Stevie.

"Thank you," Brad responded sincerely while still unable to look at her directly. Jamie knew that she had nothing to be embarrassed about. Still she didn't want CC to know she had been making out with another woman.

"You have everything?" Stevie asked as she checked the bundles of baggage she had loaded Brad down with. He nodded as she led him to the door. Everyone exchanged goodbyes quickly. Stevie stepped outside with Brad.

Jamie and CC just sipped their coffee trying to ignore the uncomfortable tension that was surrounding them. After what seemed like an eternity Stevie reentered the condo.

Jamie was relieved that Brad had left without a chance to reveal her activities the night before. "So that is Emma's father?" Jamie asked Stevie.

"Yeah." Stevie smiled brightly. "Brad is one of my best friends. He absolutely adores Emma."

"So how did . . .?" Jamie began uncertain if she had pry into Stevie's life.

"Brad and I go way back," Stevie cut her off. "We even shared an apartment in college. We both got dumped after being in long-term relationships. So we went out one night to cry on one another's shoulders."

"And drink," CC added.

"We woke up the next morning, saying we didn't, did we?" Stevie laughed. "When I found out I was pregnant, it was pretty clear that we did. We were both surprised to say the least. "

"You were surprised?" CC grunted.

"Enough out of you tuff stuff," Stevie chastised her. "Okay now, both of you out."

"What?" CC yelped. Jamie just stared at her blankly.

"The contractor is coming over." Stevie sighed. "You are not going to be here. Emma's room has taken forever because of you." Stevie accused her sister. "Jamie do me a favor and take her out of here." Stevie pleaded.

"But I'm exhausted," CC whined.

"You are not staying here," Stevie growled. "You keep interfering. Jamie please take her with you, so I can move my daughter out of what is suppose to be my office."

"Okay," Jamie agreed before she could think about it.

"Good," Stevie said with satisfaction.

"But . . ." CC began to argue.

"No buts," Stevie flared. "If you had your way Emma's room would stay down here next to yours until she's ready for college. No, go play with Jamie."

Jamie's jaw dropped at what Stevie had just said. "Fine," CC grunted as she stormed off towards her bedroom.

"Jamie, thanks for doing this," Stevie said gently. "Oh and Brad is a big gossip queen. I heard about last night." Stevie said flatly as she held her hand up to stop Jamie from saying something. "It's none of my business. But I want you to understand something. I know the first two times you hurt my sister it wasn't your fault. Do it again, and I'll make you sorry you were born."

"I have no intention of hurting her." Jamie said with anger.

"I know that," Stevie said quietly. "I'm just telling you how I feel." Jamie stood there, understanding that Stevie was simply looking after her sister. She tried to brush away the uncertain feelings she was experiencing. As CC reemerged from the bedroom dressed in jeans and a sweater, Jamie realized that she had just agreed to spend the entire day with the woman.

CC shifted nervously as she stood in Jamie's living room. "So," she said as she sucked on her teeth, trying to appear calm, "what would you like to do?"

"I feel like we've been sent off on a play date." Jamie chuckled as she tugged nervously on her T-shirt.

"I know," CC admitted as she finally lifted her gaze to meet Jamie's. "So, you want to make out?" CC teased, hoping to break the tension.

Thankfully Jamie laughed in response. "Would you totally freak out if I said yes?" the blonde questioned her as she continued to laugh.

"Yes," CC answered honestly as she released a breath of relief. "How did we end up here?" Jamie stared at her with a curious _expression. "I mean, we had a good thing and then everything was over. Now I just don't know how to act around you. Somehow it was easier when you hated me."

"Not for me," Jamie said with sincerity. "I had all this anger. I had a fear of commitment. Now, I realize that I've wasted a lot of time. I shut people out. All of it was based on a misunderstanding. I don't know what I should be thinking or feeling. The only thing I know for certain is that I'm still attracted to you." CC felt her heart skip a beat at Jamie's admission. There was a but or a however coming though - she could feel it. "But I'm not certain if what I'm feeling is because of the you in the here and now or because of what we had and lost."

"I feel the same," CC admitted. "I still find you very attractive. Why wouldn't I? You're a beautiful woman." Jamie blushed shyly and the sight tugged at CC's heartstrings. "But I don't know if it's you or the past that's calling to me."

"Well, why don't we just start over?" Jamie suggested with a shy smile. "Forget about the pressure of the past and just let things happen. I could live without the speeding ticket this time though," Jamie added playfully.

"I don't know about that," CC hedged. "So neighbor, now that I've been banished from my home, what should we do today? Since we haven't really hung out together since we were dating."

"I have an idea," Jamie said with a mischievous grin. "I just need to get changed."

"Should I be nervous?" CC called after her as she yawned.

She settled down on the sofa and fought back the need for sleep. She glanced around Jamie's home. It was simple. CC could see that the doctor had yet to fully unpack. It lacked something. If she hadn't known that Jamie lived there she would never have guessed that this was the outgoing blonde's home. She thought about what Jamie had said about mistrusting people and fearing commitment. CC felt a chill run through her, knowing that she had inadvertently been the cause of that. She also realized that she'd been doing the same with her life.

"Ready?" Jamie said from behind her. "You'll need a jacket," Jamie added as CC grimaced. When she returned to her home to retrieve her jacket, she promised Stevie that she wasn't staying. She wondered as she climbed into Jamie's car if she was really ready for this. And just what did this confusing mess mean? Jamie started the car and pulled out of the parking lot. CC was still lost in her thoughts. *'Jamie said she wanted to become friends again. Is that all? Should that be all? Was it possible that they were meant to be more? Or was it just her hormones that were driving her insane?'*

"What are you thinking about?" Jamie inquired as she maneuvered her car.

"I'm just wondering where in the hell you are taking me," CC lied.

"Patience," Jamie chided her.

"Right." CC snorted as she allowed her eyes to flutter shut.

CC's eyes fluttered open as a wave of confusion washed over her. Slowly she began to recall where she was. She sat up and looked over at Jamie. She felt a slight wave of disappointment that the blonde doctor was wearing sunglasses. She really loved Jamie's eyes. "Sorry," she apologized as she looked out the window with curiosity. "Was I asleep long?" she asked as she stretched out her arms. She grimaced in annoyance when her hands hit the roof of the car.

"Not long," Jamie informed her. "Are you working tonight?"

"No." CC yawned.

"Me either," Jamie informed her. "Good thing since I think we both need to catch up on our sleep."

"Hmm," CC sighed in agreement. "Why are we on Route One?" she inquired, taking in the tacky stretch of highway littered with every type of restaurant imaginable.

"You'll see," Jamie taunted her as she pulled into the right hand lane.

CC could see the large orange dinosaur coming closer. "Oh no," she groaned as she began to realize just what Jamie had in mind. "You have got to be joking." Much to her distress Jamie pulled into the parking lot next to the soft-serve ice cream stand.

"You promised me," Jamie said with a pout.

"Isn't there a statute of limitations on something like that?" CC whimpered.

"No," Jamie refuted as she removed her seatbelt.

"Can't we just go back to your place and watch cable?" CC suggested hopefully.

"No," Jamie said flatly as she stepped out of the car.

"It's too cold," CC protested as she got out of the car.

"Come on, you big baby," Jamie chastised her. "Look at it this way - the course will be empty."

"The course?" CC groaned. "It's not real golf," she added as they approached the booth. "You're serious?" CC continued to groan as Jamie paid the teenager and received two putters and two golf balls.

"I've always wanted to come here," Jamie said brightly as she walked over to the miniature golf course. "And you promised," Jamie added sternly as she waited for the brooding policewoman to catch up with her.

CC had promised her, but that was over a dozen years ago. She had managed to avoid this little activity back then. Now she was doing penance. She was at the Route One Golf and Baseball Park. Better known as the putt putt place with the big ugly orange dinosaur. She had always thought of the big monstrosity as a sure fire way not to miss the exit for Route 99.

"What is it?" Jamie pried. CC thought the blonde seemed far too amused by the situation.

"The truth is that I completely suck at this," CC confessed reluctantly. "I mean I'm not just bad at it; I suck wind."

"Cool, more fun for me." Jamie chuckled as she handed CC a putter. As the brunette felt the walls closing in on her, Jamie swatted her on the backside and nudged her towards the first hole.

"Okay," Jamie said triumphantly as she perused the scorecard. "There's a six stroke limit for any hole. You can move the ball a club head from the boards. No more than four players to a group. Balls leaving the carpet should be placed at the point of departure. There's no penalty."

"I think that one's going to come in handy." CC sighed as she watched Jamie place her ball down in the proper place.

As Jamie stooped over, CC was given a very nice view of the blonde's firm backside. "Then again, this could be fun," she noted in amusement. It took Jamie three strokes to sink her ball. CC marked it down on the scorecard. She crinkled her forehead as she tried to write with the stubby little pencil. She handed Jamie the card and said a silent prayer as she positioned her ball. After six tries Jamie took pity on her and they moved to the next hole.

The next hole was the Ocean Wave. CC felt slightly better when it took each of them four strokes to sink their balls. But the next hole was the Chinese Pagoda. Jamie managed to sink her ball in two strokes and almost caught CC staring at her ass. Once again, CC exhausted all of her shots and they moved on.

The Bowling Alley was very easy, just a straight shot across the oversized pins. It took both of them only two strokes. "You're getting better," Jamie said in an encouraging tone.

"Bite me," CC snarled as she set up her next shot at the Lighthouse. She could feel Jamie's body standing very close to her own as she putted. She did fare better as Jamie took three shots and she took four. It was far less embarrassing than having to pick up her ball without sinking it.

At the Dinosaur's Cave she was having trouble once again. She noticed Jamie putting down her own putter. "Let me help you," Jamie offered as she wrapped her arms around CC's waist. CC's mouth went dry as Jamie's hands covered her own. The feel of Jamie pressed against her body was making her head spin. "Like this," Jamie explained as she guided CC.

"I've got it," CC choked out, needing to distance herself from Jamie's body.

Her body temperature dropped once Jamie stepped away from her. CC's vision was bleary and her palms were sweating. She swung wildly. Her blue eyes focused on the red ball that flew off the course, over the fence, and into the traffic on the highway below. They both cringed as angry motorists honked their horns. CC braced herself for the sounds of cars crashing into one another. Thankfully, the sound never came.

"Way to go, Tiger Woods." Jamie chuckled.

CC spun around and glared at her. Jamie covered her mouth with her hand. CC knew she was fighting back the laughter. CC growled as Jamie's eyes widened fearfully. "I'll get you another ball," Jamie offered quickly before dashing off to seek refuge.

"We couldn't have gone to the batting cages or played skeet ball?" CC moaned in embarrassment.

Jamie returned, still trying to hide her smile. "Not a word," CC cautioned her sternly. They continued on and CC thankfully fared better. She even managed to score a hole in one at the Rocket Ship. Jamie seemed more than a little miffed by that. After completing the eighteen holes they returned their equipment. CC glared at the teenage boy in the booth who was chuckling at her.

"How about some ice cream?" Jamie suggested.

"It's freezing out and you want ice cream?" CC asked her in bewilderment.

"Yes," Jamie responded brightly. "Loser pays," she added as she dashed down the hill to the ice cream stand.

"Brat!" CC called after the blonde as she chased after her. CC caught Jamie around her waist just before she reached the building. "Gotcha!" she cried triumphantly as she pressed Jamie up against the wall of the ice cream shack.

"You cheated," Jamie protested as she panted heavily.

"Liar," CC grunted as she pressed Jamie's back against the wall. "Admit it," CC demanded as Jamie struggled playfully against her.

"Never." Jamie laughed as she struggled.

CC decided that she was being challenged and pinned Jamie's arms to her side. "Bully," Jamie choked out as she continued to try to free herself. CC could feel the breath escape her as she realized how closely she was pressed against Jamie's body. Jamie's face was flushed from the cold, and her green eyes twinkled merrily up at CC. The tall woman could feel Jamie's breath whispering gently across her cheek. Jamie seemed to loosen her grip.

Their eyes locked and CC felt her mouth suddenly go dry. For the second time in the past few hours, CC felt herself being drawn in. She released her hold on Jamie's arms and felt them wrapping around her body. CC blinked for a moment before stepping away. *'It would have been so easy to just kiss her.'*

She felt Jamie's hand resting on her stomach. Jamie turned into her body and rested her head on CC's shoulder. The taller woman relaxed into the touch, knowing that her ex-lover was fighting the same battle. CC held her for a moment. Jamie sighed deeply before taking a step away. "Come on, tough stuff. Buy me an ice cream." Jamie jerked her head indicating that they should move.

"Why exactly am I buying the ice cream?" CC groused as they walked around the building.

"Because I said so," Jamie snorted defiantly. "It's closed," Jamie pouted as CC yawned.

"I can't imagine they get much business on a day like this," CC noted with another yawn.

"Still exhausted?" Jamie asked sympathetically as she stroked CC's arm. The taller woman simply nodded in response. "Me too," Jamie concurred. "We should head back. Maybe the contractor's done for the day and you can get some sleep," she added hopefully. "Why have you really been banished?" Jamie inquired as they headed back up to her car.

"I have no idea," CC explained quickly. Jamie just cast a doubtful look in her direction. "Well, they say that I keep interfering," CC explained. "I don't," she concluded firmly.

Jamie laughed as she unlocked the car. "I don't," CC repeated as they got into the car.

"Oh poor baby," Jamie mocked her. "Wrongfully accused. How do you endure such a burden?"

"Laugh it up, Blondie," CC growled as her mind wandered back to the playfulness they had shared a few moments ago.

Jamie drove them home. CC's hopes of being able to go home and crawl into bed were dashed the moment they pulled into the parking lot. "The contractor is still here," CC noted grimly.

"Still in exile," Jamie said softly. "Why don't you come in and watch some television with me?" Jamie suggested.

"You don't mind?" CC asked, fearful that she was intruding. "I mean if you had plans for your day off, I understand. Stevie can be a little stubborn, but I'm almost certain she wouldn't let me freeze to death."

"Caitlin, the only thing you're keeping me from doing is my laundry," Jamie explained as they stepped out of the car.

CC cringed slightly at the use of her first name. "Okay," CC agreed, not really wanting to end her time with Jamie. After they entered Jamie's townhouse, they kicked off their shoes and jackets. They relaxed on the sofa and instantly began to fight over the remote control. Eventually they settled on watching a Law and Order rerun on A&E. CC noticed that they had each chosen to sit in a manner that put a little distance between them. As they watched the program, CC fought to keep her weary eyes open. It wasn't long before she lost the battle and drifted off to sleep.

Jamie stirred slightly, feeling very comfortable. She blinked her eyes open to find herself resting in CC's arms. Somehow the pair had fallen asleep and wrapped themselves up in one another. She was feeling the same sense of warmth and belonging that she'd had that morning when she went over to CC's and apologized. The two women had fallen asleep together that morning as well. Of course she had to admit it always felt good when CC held her. There was something so comforting about the being in her arms.

She inhaled lightly, taking in the soft delicate scent that was CC. Her lips curled in a smile of recognition. It was the same. After all these years she still smelled the same. It had always amazed Jamie that CC seemed so strong, casting a look of stoic indifference on everyone she encountered. But she smelled soft and delicate. It was her true self, the one she kept hidden.

Jamie shifted slightly, hoping that she wouldn't awaken the slumbering policewoman. CC continued exhaling slowly in a steady rhythm. Jamie just wanted a few uninterrupted moments to enjoy the feel of CC's body lying beneath her own. She lifted her hand slowly and placed two fingers against CC's full lips.

Jamie's pulse beat in a calming rhythm as CC's breath caressed her fingertips. She guiltily indulged in the simple pleasure for a few more moments, knowing that it was probably the last time in her life she would have the opportunity to experience the sweet sensation. Fearful that CC would awaken and find her fingers pressed against her mouth, Jamie regretfully removed them. She began to lift her smaller body off of CC's larger inviting frame. Her green eyes were still gazing dreamily at CC's lips.

Before she could stop and think she did the one thing she had desired all day; she lightly brushed her lips against CC's. She had only intended on placing a sweet gentle kiss on those lips that had been beckoning her all day long. She hadn't expected the sleeping woman to respond. Jamie was certain that CC was awake when she felt lips kissing her back.

The feel of CC tugging on her bottom lip overrode her senses. Jamie instinctively parted her lips. CC drew her tongue into her mouth and suckled it slowly. Jamie heard a deep moan and was uncertain who had released it. CC's hands clasped her body and drew her in, pulling her body closer. Jamie parted CC's legs with her thigh as her hips began to dance sensually against CC's body. A desperate need to breathe forced Jamie to break free of the passionate kiss.

As her body rocked against CC's, she peered down through half-opened eyes to see that CC was in fact still asleep. Anxiety flooded Jamie's senses as she pulled away from CC's touch carefully. "This is so bad," she groaned quietly, and she felt her knees start to buckle as she stood. She braced herself as she moved over to the edge of the sofa.

"I'm cursed," she reasoned as she looked down on the sleeping woman who seemed unfazed by their intimate encounter. "Jamie," CC murmured as she turned onto her side and then curled up in an adorable manner. Jamie whimpered at the sight. *She is so cute,'* Jamie thought as she fought to control her breathing. Jamie found herself reaching out towards CC's slumbering form. Quickly she snatched her hand back. *'Bad blonde,'* she chastised herself as she headed up the staircase.

She stared at her rumpled appearance in the mirror above her dresser. She took in her flushed features and snorted in amusement. Jamie blinked as she looked down at the top of the dresser. Sitting there was a small wooden box. She ran her fingers over the intricate carvings. Small simple ankhs covered the top. She tried to remember what CC had said when she gave it to her. It had been so long ago; she couldn't really recall the exact words. It was something about eternity. She lifted the lid of the medium-sized box. The scent of cedar greeted her. The only item inside was the now tarnished brass ring she had grabbed from the carousel that last day she had spent with CC.

Jamie rarely opened the box; yet she often questioned why she had kept it along with the silly brass ring. Whenever she wondered why she still held onto both items, she would toss them into a drawer so she wouldn't be forced to look at them and be reminded of the painful memory. Eventually the box would always reappear. For the first time, she didn't feel anger when she looked at them. This time she only felt regret.

She ran her fingers through her short blonde hair in a tense manner. She snapped the box closed and began to look for the blanket she had come upstairs to retrieve. She gathered the old blanket and a couple of pillows and headed back downstairs. Jamie glanced out the picture window, noting that the contractor's truck was still there. She smiled slightly, feeling happy that CC would have to remain in her company for a little while longer.

Jamie placed the blanket over the sleeping woman and then carefully tucked the pillows under her head. She fought against the overwhelming desire to kiss CC once again. She stood slowly and looked down at CC who was sleeping so peacefully.

Jamie rubbed her tired eyes before heading back up the staircase. Once in her bedroom she shed her clothing and climbed under the covers. It wasn't until her head hit the pillow that she realized that it had been over twenty-four hours since she had gotten any sleep. She didn't count the warm catnap she'd shared with CC. Looking over at the open door, she debated for a moment on whether or not she should get up from the warm cocoon and close it.

"Screw it." She sighed wearily. "If she does come up here, she won't see anything she hasn't seen before," she reasoned, closing her eyes as her weariness washed over her body.

It was difficult being around CC and yet it was wonderful at the same time. She knew without a doubt that the sexual tension flowed both ways. Still they needed to be careful. What if that was all there was? Also there was a part of her that was still angry at CC. Twelve years! In all that time CC had never made an attempt to explain what had happened. If Stevie hadn't pushed her, CC probably never would have told her the truth.

Jamie understood what had happened. But what about later when some time had passed? CC could have tracked her down and sent her a letter. Granted, Jamie probably wouldn't have read it, but that would have been her choice. That's what made her angry; CC never gave her an option to discover the truth. "Big jerk," Jamie muttered bitterly as she yawned. "Big gorgeous jerk." Jamie sighed as her mind conjured up images of the woman sleeping on her sofa.

Jamie started drifting off to sleep. She was torn between needing to talk to CC about the things that were bothering her and wanting to go downstairs to continue what she had started earlier. Jamie turned in the darkness to find a pair of crystal blue eyes staring down at her. She didn't hesitate as she drew CC down to her. She kissed her deeply, their tongues dancing together sensually. "Please, I need you," Jamie gasped as the kiss ended. Pulling back the blankets, she drew her lover to her. "Take me," Jamie pleaded as she kissed CC's neck. She could feel the weight of her lover's body pressing against her as she opened herself to her. CC entered her as they kissed. She could feel her lover plunging in and out of her as her thumb stroked her clit. "Don't . . . stop!" Jamie cried out.

The intensity of their passion sent a jolt through Jamie. Her eyes snapped open as she looked around her darkened bedroom. She groaned, realizing that she'd been dreaming. "Weenie," she scolded herself. If she was going to have a dream that good, the least she could do was sleep long enough to finish. The sound of feet running up the staircase startled her. "Oh no." She grimaced as she realized what was happening.

CC appeared in her doorway, panting and looking around in a frantic manner. *"Great! She can sleep through us making out but my dream wakes her up!"* Jamie blushed, wishing she could just disappear at that moment. "Are you all right?" CC gasped as she scanned the room.

"I'm fine," Jamie snapped as CC stared at her in surprise.

The taller woman approached her bed. "I heard you screaming," CC explained as she neared Jamie. The blonde just wanted her to go away so she could finish playing out the fantasy that had emerged in her dreams.

"I was having a bad dream," Jamie lied.

"But you were calling out 'Don't stop'," CC said as she knelt beside the bed. Jamie watched as CC's eyes widened in sudden understanding. Jamie blushed to her roots as she pulled the blankets over her head. She could feel CC tugging on them. She knew that it was impossible to die of embarrassment but at that moment she wanted to. "Jamie?" CC pleaded with her as she continued to tug on the blankets.

"Go away," Jamie whined as she continued to hold the blankets in place.

"Come on. You're being silly," CC coaxed her as she started to laugh.

"I don't care." Jamie fumed at the sound of CC's laughter.

CC continued to tug on the blankets as her laughter increased heartily. Furious that the tall woman was enjoying her discomfort, Jamie released her hold on the blankets while CC was still pulling. Jamie's sudden release caused the tall policewoman to crash down on the floor. Jamie looked over the side of the bed to find a pile of blankets shaking with laughter. "This is not funny," Jamie scolded the pile.

"Yes it is," CC laughed as she emerged from the blankets.

Jamie couldn't help but smile at CC's unruly appearance. Her hair was mussed up, and tears were running down her chiseled features. CC's laughter suddenly ceased as her eyes grew wide and her mouth hung open. Jamie watched as CC's breathing became ragged. The blonde stared at the woman sitting on the floor curiously. The coolness of the night air suddenly alerted her to what CC was staring at. She was sitting before the taller woman completely naked.

Jamie reached out for the blankets, stopping suddenly as she realized that all of the bedding was on the floor wrapped around CC. The tall raven-haired beauty slowly rose to her feet. Jamie's mouth was suddenly parched. CC placed the blankets back on the bed, covering Jamie slightly. Leaning over to tuck the blonde in, her breath whispered across Jamie's exposed skin.

CC's long hair brushed against her skin as the taller woman adjusted the sheets on the bed. "What were you dreaming about?" CC inquired in a husky tone that sent a delightful shiver down Jamie's spine. CC tilted her head slightly. Jamie found herself lost in a smoky blue haze. "What were you dreaming about?" CC repeated in the same rich tone.

Jamie couldn't respond despite the reaction her body was having to CC's voice. She could feel her nipples harden as her stomach clenched. Her mind and her body became engaged in a heated debate. She craved this woman's touch. She needed to feel their bodies melting together more than she needed air to fill her lungs. *'You know that you still love her. How can this be wrong?'* her heart screamed out from deep inside of her soul.

She watched as CC leaned closer to her. "Why are we fighting this?" CC asked as her voice dropped even lower in tone. Instinctively Jamie's thighs parted in anticipation. She felt helpless to stop CC from approaching her. Helpless to stop her as she lowered the sheet that was covering her body. Once again she was revealing herself to her ex-lover. "You are so beautiful," CC murmured sincerely as she sat down beside Jamie. They sat there simply staring deeply into one another's eyes, still not touching as a wave of electricity flowed between their bodies that remained only a few inches away from one another.

A flicker of hesitation clouded Jamie's cherubic features. "Don't," CC said so softly that Jamie had to lean in to hear her. CC cupped her cheek gently. Jamie leaned into her tender caress. "Would it be so wrong to be together one more time?" CC continued to speak softly as Jamie laced her fingers through CC's long silky hair. "No thoughts of the past or the future."

Jamie placed two fingers against CC's quivering lips, knowing the brunette was searching for some justification for them to spend the night together. Her action silenced the nervous woman seated next to her. "I don't want to tell you what I was dreaming about," Jamie stated in a low confident tone. CC's brilliant blue gaze lowered slightly. Jamie's fingers lingered on CC's lips. She could feel the exasperated breath caressing them.

Lowering her fingers from CC's lips, she placed them tenderly under her firm chin. She lifted CC's face so that she could see her eyes shining back at her. "I don't want to tell you," Jamie repeated softly. "I want to show you," Jamie offered before placing an urgent kiss on CC's full lips.

CC responded eagerly as the kiss deepened. There was nothing to stop them - no ringing bells and no unwanted intrusions. It was just the two of them. Jamie brushed aside the nagging doubts and fears. She began to suckle on CC's bottom lip. She could feel the taller woman leaning into her body. The feel of CC's clothing brushing against her exposed skin was driving Jamie insane.

She parted CC's lips with her tongue and entered the sweet inviting warmth of her mouth. As she enjoyed the gentle exploration, she lowered her own body onto the bed and pulled CC down on top of her. Their tongues engaged in a duel for control as the kiss deepened. CC parted Jamie's firm thighs with her leg.

Jamie could feel her excitement pooling between her legs. Her body arched against CC's denim clad thigh. Her body tingled as CC's body moved against her in perfect rhythm. "I want you," Jamie gasped as she broke away from the kiss. Her fingers dug tightly into CC's shoulders. "I need you, Caitlin," Jamie continued in a ragged tone as she felt CC's lips on her sensitive neck.

CC broke away from Jamie's neck as her body arched. Jamie looked up at her lover who was supporting herself above her. Jamie shifted her legs so she could wrap them around CC's well-toned body. "God," CC panted as she continued to thrust against Jamie's body. "You're still so beautiful." Jamie could only whimper in response as she thrust her wetness against CC's faded blue jeans. The friction against her throbbing clit was making her entire body pulsate with desire.

Jamie pulled CC down to her, needing to feel their bodies connecting. She gasped once again as the material of CC's shirt brushed against her sensitive nipples. CC began to nibble on her earlobe as Jamie clawed at the material of CC's shirt. Jamie's entire body trembled as CC dipped her tongue in her ear.

She pushed CC away slightly so she could capture her lips in a fiery kiss. Their hips continued to dance together in a sensual rhythm. She felt CC pulling her closer as large hands roamed down her naked back. Jamie's senses were nearing the edge. She fought against the urge to just allow the orgasm to overwhelm her. There was something more she needed. She needed to feel her lover filling her completely.

Reaching over, she captured one of CC's hands and pushed it down with a gentle insistence between their bodies. She could feel her lover shifting. CC pulled away from the passionate kiss as Jamie continued to guide her hand down to her damp curls.

Their eyes locked as CC freed her hand and ran her fingers slowly along Jamie's wetness. The blonde fought to control her breathing as long knowing fingers continued to explore her. A single digit pressed against her opening, teasing as it entered her slightly before pulling away. Jamie moaned in frustration as CC began to slowly stroke her clit. "You're driving me crazy," Jamie whimpered.

"Good," CC teased as she wiggled her eyebrows.

CC continued to tease her in a slow delightful manner. "Is this what you were dreaming about?" CC inquired in a deep rich tone as she pressed two fingers against her entrance.

"Yes," Jamie gasped, praying that her lover would continue. Jamie opened herself up further, offering all of herself to the dark woman.

Jamie's body rose off the bed as CC entered her slowly. She felt CC's fingers reaching her very core. CC wiggled her fingers inside of her before retreating slightly. Jamie found herself lost in a sea of crystal blue as CC plunged in and out her. She clutched the bedding as her hips glided in unison with CC's knowing touch. She saw something in CC's eyes that captured her as she felt the pad of CC's thumb tease her clit.

CC's rhythm grew more insistent as Jamie's body trembled. Jamie's mind filled with thoughts of touching every inch of CC's body. She needed to make this woman feel as wonderful and as loved as she did at that moment.

Jamie could feel herself nearing the edge as CC's rhythm reached a wild pace. Jamie's head fell back as the explosion rumbled through her body. Her eyes snapped shut as CC continued to pleasure her. She could feel warm kisses covering her skin as they worked their way down her body. She was still trying to recover from her climax as she felt her lover's breath on her thighs. Her body continued to spasm uncontrollably as CC began to suckle her.

Jamie's head was spinning as CC's fingers and her mouth pleasured her completely. "Dear God!" Jamie screamed out as

102

CC feasted upon her, drinking in all that she had to offer. The strange ringing in her ears mixed with a faint crimson flash in her mind as CC continued. Dimly aware that she had blacked out for a moment, Jamie felt her body explode once again.

Her senses went into overload as she pushed away from CC. "Need to breath," she panted as CC finally lifted her head. CC's crystal blue eyes danced merrily as she looked up at Jamie. She moaned slightly as she felt CC's touch departing from her body. She pulled the taller woman up to her and captured her in a sweet kiss. Her mind reeled, as she tasted herself on her lover's lips.

"Did you get your blood test back?" Jamie asked softly as she began to pull CC's shirt out of her jeans. CC nodded with a reassuring smile. "Good," Jamie purred before pulling CC's shirt up and off her body. She ran her fingers slowly across CC's shoulders, enjoying the feeling of warmth emanating from her lover's skin.

The sound of the telephone ringing disrupted their actions. They both turned and glared at the offending instrument. Jamie turned her attention back to CC, choosing to ignore the ringing phone. "The machine can pick it up," she said softly as she cupped CC's face. A distant chirping was added to the disturbing sound. Both women grimaced as Jamie's answering machine clicked on. "This isn't happening," CC moaned as she stood. "That's my cell phone. I left it downstairs."

"Don't," Jamie reached out to halt CC's movement. "It's our day off," she reasoned as she heard an unfamiliar voice on her answering machine. "Dr. Jameson, this is . . . " the frantic voice began as Jamie's pager began to vibrate on the nightstand next to the telephone. "It's the hospital," Jamie said with regret as her shoulders slumped.

"It can't be good if we're both being called," CC muttered bitterly as she headed out of the bedroom.

Jamie snatched up the telephone receiver quickly. "This is Dr. Jameson," she growled into the receiver. She listened as the woman explained the situation. CC had reentered the bedroom. She tossed her cell phone onto the bed, grabbed her T-shirt and put it on. Jamie ended the telephone call and climbed off the bed.

She fumbled slightly as she wrapped herself up in a blanket. "There's a fire downtown," she explained to CC.

"I know," CC said sadly.

"Why did they call you?" Jamie inquired fearfully.

"There've been some casualties," CC said carefully. "It looks suspicious. There isn't much I can do until the fire department finishes and the investigation team goes through everything. But I need to start talking to some of the survivors."

Jamie shifted uncomfortably for a moment. Suddenly, it was that awkward moment when they would be forced to deal with what just happened. Jamie didn't regret a single moment of their day together. The only regret she had was that their blissful day had been interrupted. "I need to get to the hospital," Jamie explained quickly.

CC simply nodded in response, a grim expression clearly written across her face. "I really want to finish this," Jamie said boldly. "Today was great. Every moment of today was simply wonderful. I would really like to see more of you."

"Yeah?" CC asked with a brilliant smile.

"Yeah," Jamie confirmed with a smile of her own.

"Okay." CC smirked confidently. "We both need to get going. We can talk later."

CC leaned in and kissed Jamie gently before she departed from the bedroom. Jamie ran her fingers across her lips and smiled at the tingling sensation she still felt. Jamie felt ten feet tall at that moment. She shook her head before heading towards the shower. She needed to focus on what was happening at the hospital. She decided that was a good thing. The emergency wouldn't allow her the time to second-guess what was happening between her and CC.

CHAPTER THREE

Jamie rubbed her throbbing temple as she hid in the break room. The ER was a mess that night. When she entered it looked as if all hell had broken loose. Burn treatment wasn't her specialty and thankfully the more severe cases had been directed to Mass General since they were affiliated with the Shriners Hospital. Still some victims slipped through. The last patient's injuries had been devastating. Jamie knew that there was nothing she or anyone else could do for the man. She did the best she could. Leaning over the unrecognizable man, she could smell his burnt flesh. "I'm going to make you more comfortable," she told him in a soothing tone. She needed help and she knew it. Jamie was a talented doctor but she was in over her head with this patient. "I'm going to get some help," she told him as she reached out to touch him. She pulled her hand away, knowing the slightest touch would only serve to inflict more pain. That's when she heard it. "Don't," he managed to choke out.

Jamie's green eyes blinked in disbelief as she fought back the tears. It wasn't often when she was faced with the knowledge that it would be more humane to simply allow a patient to go. Jamie struggled with her emotions, knowing that he was in unbearable pain and his chances of survival were very slim. His body had been burned so badly that Jamie was surprised that he was still alive. Simon, the resident assigned to her, just looked at her, thinking that she had the answers. Stella, the nurse assisting them, gave her a sad knowing glance.

Jamie paused before giving Simon instructions. "Where are you going?" Simon asked in a panicked tone.

"Simon, there's something you need to learn. Never be afraid of asking for help," Jamie said firmly. "I'm not qualified to treat this man. He shouldn't have been sent here."

Jamie sought out help, finally snagging Dr. Lustrum. The elderly surgeon agreed that there was nothing that could be done. Jamie did everything by procedure from that point on. Thankfully the patient passed away quickly. They did what they could to save his life even though they knew it was impossible.

Jamie sat in the break room nursing a cup of coffee when Simon entered in a somber mood. He sat down at the table across from her. "You knew, didn't you?" Simon asked her in an absent tone.

"Yes," she replied in a weary voice. "Simon, there was nothing that could be done. We're not God."

"He wanted to die, didn't he?" Simon continued.

Jamie bit her bottom lip, knowing it was the first time the young man had seen something so horrible close up. "Yes," Jamie confirmed. "We still need to do everything we can."

"I was relieved when he died," Simon choked out. "I shouldn't have been."

"Simon," Jamie began carefully as she reached out and squeezed his hand, "Mr. Barstow was in a lot of pain. There was nothing left to his body. Every breath he took was an agonizing hell for him. Don't be ashamed for feeling better that he finally found peace." As Jamie spoke the words, she wished that she could convince herself not to feel the same sense of guilt.

"Things are quieting down," Simon said softly as he began to caress her hand. "They should be letting us go soon. Did you want to get a drink or something?"

Jamie smiled slightly as she slowly pulled her hand away. *'Oh, this boy needs to pay more attention to the gossip around this place,'* she thought with a slight degree of amusement. "No thanks. I have someone waiting for me," she explained, hoping that he would get the message. It wasn't the first time the young man had shown an interest in her. Jamie had been trying to convey to him that she wasn't interested for some time now.

Thankfully Stella entered the break room. "Mrs. Barstow is here," the older nurse informed her in a dejected tone.

"Thanks," Jamie said in a heavy tone as she stood.

"Do you want me to go with you?" Simon volunteered.

"No, why don't you relax for a few?" Jamie said as she stepped out of the room with Stella following her closely.

"You know that boy has a crush on you, don't you?" Stella informed her.

"I know." Jamie grimaced. "I just keep hoping he'll get over it. Jesus, didn't anyone tell him I'm a big dyke?

"I know I did." Stella snorted in amusement. "He didn't believe me. "

Jamie rolled her eyes in disgust as she made her way to the waiting room to face Mrs. Barstow. She braced herself for the worst part of her job.

After she did everything she could to comfort Mrs. Barstow, she was informed that she could finally leave. She didn't argue; she headed off to collect her belongings. She just wanted to go home and see CC. She smiled as she thought about the dark-haired woman. As she tossed her lab coat into the laundry, Simon entered.

"I guess we're free," he said shyly.

Jamie simply nodded as she pulled on her black leather car coat, not bothering to change out of her scrubs. She wanted to go home and take a long hot shower and forget this night had ever happened. She wasn't in the mood for Simon's schoolboy crush.

"Dr. Jameson, are you sure you don't want to get a bite to eat or something?" he persisted, his big brown eyes staring at her hopefully.

"Yes," Jamie said firmly.

"Well, how about some other time?" he suggested.

Jamie bit back the groan as she calmed herself quickly. "Simon, you know that as your supervisor I can't really socialize with you," the blonde doctor stated firmly.

"I know it's discouraged but it isn't really against the rules," the young man persisted.

"Simon," Jamie spat out in a harsher tone than she had intended. "I'm seeing someone," she added in a gentler tone, hoping to finally discourage him. She wasn't up for the whole long pointless talk about her sexual orientation. Thankfully Simon simply nodded and began to change.

Jamie blew out a sigh of relief as she stepped into the corridor. She paused for a moment thinking about what she had said to Simon. For the first time in years she was seeing someone . . . or was she? Jamie felt the persistent throbbing start to build up in her already aching head. *'Oh great! Now I have to deal with the whole what-did-last- night-mean thing?'* As Jamie stepped outside, the sunlight caught her off guard. It was midmorning. Jamie simply wanted to wash away the smell of her patients and wrap herself up in CC's arms.

As she fished her car keys out of her pocket, she wondered if CC would take her into her arms. Just as she clasped her keys tightly, she saw the familiar and very welcome sight of CC approaching her.

"Hi," CC greeted her brightly.

"Hi yourself," Jamie said with a smile, fighting the urge to wrap her arms around CC's body. "Still on duty?" Jamie asked, taking notice of CC's badge hanging around her neck.

"Yeah," CC groaned. "You all done?"

"Yes," Jamie said with a nod. "I'm just heading home." Jamie could feel her stomach flutter and her palms start to sweat as she debated what she should say or do.

The two women stood in the parking lot in an awkward silence. Each seemingly wanted to say something yet neither spoke. "I need to get back to it," CC finally mumbled as she scrunched up her face.

"Right," Jamie managed to mutter in response as she kicked the gravel on the ground. "I'll see you later."

"Yeah, see you," CC responded absently before walking off towards the hospital entrance.

Jamie was kicking herself as she shuffled off to her car. "See you later," she muttered as she climbed into her car. "Could I be any lamer? Why didn't I just ask her what time she was going to be off duty?" Jamie rested her head on her steering wheel, wishing the throbbing in her head would cease. "Invite her over for breakfast?" She groaned, completely disgusted with her inability to simply talk to CC. Jamie eased her head up. "Okay," she calmed herself. "I know I want to start dating her again. Now all I have to do is find out what she wants. So I'll just sit her down and talk to her. Then I'll jump her bones."

It was mid-afternoon by the time CC returned home. She was beyond exhausted. She had spent all night and the entire morning collecting statements. An hour ago the report came back from the fire marshal. It wasn't arson. The fire was started due to faulty wiring. All of those hours had been a complete waste of time. She could have been snuggled up with Jamie. They could have finished what they had started the night before. Now she was emotionally and physically spent and she had to be back at work in a few hours.

CC yawned as she stretched her tired limbs. The townhouse was quiet. Emma was still with Brad and Stevie went out with friends. Her younger sibling was going to crash in town. She was happy that Stevie finally had some time to herself. CC thoughts quickly turned to Jamie. The blonde doctor was probably catching up on some sleep.

CC dragged herself off to take a long hot shower. Exhausted she climbed into bed after setting the alarm to wake her in four hours. "Sleep, I need sleep," the policewoman whimpered as her mind kept drifting back to the night before. Making love to Jamie had been incredible. That was the problem. CC had made love to her. Unlike their last encounter, this wasn't about sex. CC rolled over, annoyed once again as her inner voice reminded her that their drunken encounter hadn't been about sex either. Not for her.

"Now what do I do?" She growled in frustration as she punched her pillow. "I could barely speak to her when I saw her earlier. What if it was just a fling for her? She isn't the sweet naïve girl I left behind all those years ago. 'I'll see you later,' she said. What the hell does that mean?" CC sat up and stared at the telephone lying next to her bedside. "I can't call her; I don't have her phone number," she reasoned. "I could just go over there," she suggested. "No, if she wanted to see me she would have said something. She's probably sleeping anyway."

CC collapsed onto her bed in frustration. "Just take things slow, CC," she chastised herself. "Of course, yesterday wasn't exactly taking things slow, was it? I wish I hadn't seen that lipstick on her collar. I'd feel a hell of a lot better about things."

CC sighed heavily as she curled back up in an effort to get some sleep. She vowed that she would just take things with Jamie slowly. She needed to find out how Jamie truly felt about things. After all, Jamie lived next door. It wasn't as if they wouldn't see one another. CC listened to the empty sounds of silence. There was another matter she needed to direct her attention to, and she didn't want any interruptions. Smiling she slid her hand down her firm abdomen and began to touch herself. She'd been left feeling a little needy after her passionate encounter with Jamie had been interrupted.

A few hours later CC woke, still feeling irritable. Her mood had softened when she stepped into the living room and found Emma with Stevie. "Hey, peanut," she called out.

"You look like hell," Stevie commented with concern. "What did you and the nice neighbor lady do yesterday?"

"Nothing much," CC lied as she retrieved her giggling niece from her sister. "I got called in on that fire. Turned out it wasn't arson. But we had to work witness statements all night. I just got back a couple of hours ago."

"I'm sorry, Sis. You must be wiped," Stevie said with sincerity. "So what are you not telling me?"

"I don't know what you mean," CC scoffed. Something happened after Stevie became a mother. She seemed to possess this eerie sense of knowing when someone was lying to her.

"Right," Stevie scoffed as she glared at her older sibling.

"I need to get ready for work," CC responded coldly as she handed Emma back to Stevie. CC rushed off in an effort to escape.

"Caitlin," Stevie said firmly.

There was something in her younger sibling's tone that made her halt her movements. It frightened her. "It's nothing," CC lied once again as she shyly turned to face her sister. "I had a very nice day with Jamie."

"And?" Stevie pried.

"We kind of slept together again," CC mumbled.

"Have you lost your freaking' mind?" Stevie scolded her. CC's jaw dropped in surprise. "What does this mean? Are you two getting back together?"

"I don't know," CC answered her honestly. "What's the problem?"

"The problem is that you're still in love with her," Stevie responded gently.

"Don't be ridiculous," CC flared as she stomped off.

CC's anger continued as she showered and then dressed for work. She just wasn't quite sure what she was so angry about.

She grunted a terse goodbye to her sister and went out to her car. She noticed that Jamie's was gone. She knew that Jamie had already left for the hospital. She made a mental note to stop in and see her when she got home. CC turned the key in the ignition and was greeted by an irritating click. "Come on. Not tonight," she growled as she tried once again to start her car.

CC slammed the steering wheel, hurting her hand in the process. She muttered obscenities as she stomped back into her home. "Stevie, my car is dead again. Can I take yours?" she shouted.

"Go ahead," Stevie called out from Emma's room.

CC tossed her key ring onto the counter and snatched up her sister's. "Today is going to suck. I just know it," the irate policewoman grunted as she headed back out to the parking lot.

Jamie had caught up on some well-needed rest and then went to work. Her shift thankfully hadn't been as stressful as the previous evening. She often found herself thinking about CC. She pondered what the night before had meant? Jamie was displeased with Simon. It appeared that their little talk had not lessened the young man's crush. She decided that she could no longer handle him in a gentle manner. She had thought that their last conversation would have made things clear. She wasn't available and not interested in breaking hospital policy.

"Dr. Fisher," she said coldly as they stepped away from their patient. She had decided to start calling him by his last name, hoping the sudden change would make things clear to him. She handed him a box of latex gloves and a tube of KY gel. "You know what you have to do," she instructed him firmly.

Jamie fought back the laughter, knowing that the task she had given him was every young doctor's nightmare. Simon turned pale as he stared at the items she had handed him. He looked back at the overweight elderly man who was lying on his stomach groaning. "The patient is impacted," Jamie said firmly. "You need to clear his . . ."

"But?" Simon squeaked out, his brown eyes pleading for help.

"Dr. Fisher," Jamie repeated sternly. "This patient needs your help. Get to it and be gentle." She patted his chest before turning him towards the suffering man.

"There has to be another way," Simon pleaded. "I can't just reach into his . . ."

"Rectum," Jamie finished. "And clear it."

Jamie gave Simon a cocky smirk before leaving him to tend to the patient. It was a cruel task, but one that everyone had to endure at least once in their medical career.

"I can't believe you're doing that to him," Stella chastised her as she stepped out into the corridor.

"Everyone has to do an extraction at least once," Jamie said with a feigned innocence.

"Uh huh." Stella chuckled. "And the fact that he probably won't feel very romantic after having his hand up that guy's ass has nothing to do with it?" Stella accused her.

"Heavens to Betsy," Jamie gasped as she sauntered over to the nurse's station. "The thought never occurred to me."

"What's going on?" Evaline inquired with interest.

"Dr. Jameson is having Fisher do an extraction." Stella scowled.

"Ugh," Evaline groaned in disgust. "Nothing like pulling crap out of someone to start your night off. I swear, you doctors love torturing the youngsters. You do know that boy has a thing for you?"

"Yes," Jamie groaned. "I tried being nice. I tried explaining things to him. I even told him firmly that I wasn't interested. He just keeps looking at me with sad puppy dog eyes."

"Did you tell him that you're gay?" Evaline pried.

"Not yet." Jamie groaned in frustration. "I thought that maybe he'd get the hint. Heck, even if I was straight he's not someone I'd be interested in. Why is it that some guys just don't get it?"

"Speaking of your love life," Evaline continued merrily.

"Were we?" Jamie scoffed as she rolled her eyes.

"I just couldn't help noticing that you've been a little too chirper lately," Evaline explained, her curiosity clearly evident.

112

"Maybe I'm just happy to see you," Jamie teased.

"Right," Evaline scoffed. "Out with it."

"Out with what?" Jamie responded nervously.

"I saw you with that cop you were treating," Evaline taunted her. "There's something going on with the two of you, isn't there?"

"Actually, she's my ex," Jamie explained quickly, hoping to put an end to the conversation.

"And?" Stella pushed.

"And nothing," Jamie responded with a blush. "I need to check on Fisher," she blurted out quickly.

The rest of Jamie's shift was uneventful. Simon seemed less amorous after performing an extraction. Jamie gathered her gear together and headed out to her car. She yawned as she started her car. "I wonder if CC's home yet?" she pondered hopefully.

When Jamie pulled into the parking lot at home, she smiled when she spotted CC's car. Oddly Stevie's minivan seemed to be missing. Jamie parked her car quickly and bounced out into the parking lot. Her joy quickly vanished when she noticed that all of the lights at CC's townhouse were out. Jamie frowned, knowing that her plans to spend some quality time with CC had just gone up in smoke. "Rats," she groaned as she headed into her own home.

After tossing and turning all night long, Jamie finally managed to sleep for a couple of hours. The blonde doctor's mind was spinning. She tried to sort out what had happened between her and CC. Her mind hummed constantly, wondering if the sexual encounter meant anything, or if it was simply a case of their hormones getting the better of them.

Jamie shuffled down the staircase, sneaking a quick peek out her front window. She smiled when she spotted CC's car still there. Stevie's minivan was once again noticeably absent. "Good, maybe I can have a chat with CC without Stevie being there." She grimaced slightly when she saw the contractor's truck parked in the lot.

Jamie returned upstairs and took a quick shower. She dressed casually in a pair of jeans and a white T-shirt covered with her favorite charcoal gray sweater. She quickly blew her short blonde hair dry. She inspected her appearance in the mirror one last time before heading downstairs. She was barefoot. She smiled as she went out onto her deck. She had purposely chosen not to wear a bra or underwear. She felt slightly silly at the secret desire that things might progress between her and CC.

Jamie climbed over the railing and noticed that the sliding door was open, allowing the breeze to flow into CC's living room through the screen door. Shyly she lifted her hand to knock on the metal frame of the screen door. Her movement halted suddenly when she heard an unfamiliar voice moaning from with inside. "Yes . . . oh baby that feels so good." Jamie's heart sank as she listened to the sounds of pleasure emanating from the strange woman. Jamie felt sick as the bile rose in her throat. Quickly she went back over the railing that separated their decks. Jamie dashed inside and ran into the downstairs bathroom. Her body rocked violently as she released the contents of her stomach.

Jamie was curled up in front of the toilet, her head resting against the wall. "Why did I trust her again?" she choked out as her head throbbed violently. All she could think of was CC making love to another woman just on the other side of the wall she was leaning against. She blinked back the tears that were welling up in her eyes. "It was too soon," she chastised herself. "I went from hating her to falling for her all over again in less than a day. I'm a fool," she finally concluded.

CC rubbed her aching temple as she returned to the kitchen. She needed more caffeine if she was going to deal with her sister's attitude. Stevie was following close behind her. CC loved her baby sister dearly but at that moment she wanted to ring her neck. "Stevie," CC growled as she turned and gave the smaller woman a cold stare.

"Fine. I'll drop it." Stevie held up her hands and retreated into the living room. CC poured herself another cup of coffee and sighed heavily. The past few days had really sucked.

Her car still wasn't running and Jamie hadn't been around much. When she did encounter the blonde doctor, it was only briefly. Jamie seemed distant since the other night. She wasn't hostile, just distant. CC really wanted to talk things over with Jamie, but Jamie always seemed to be busy. Stevie's attitude towards Jamie just added to the mix. "I slept with her too soon," CC muttered absently.

"That's all I was saying," Stevie piped in from the outer room.

CC rolled her blue eyes in disgust. Gripping her mug tightly, she walked back into the living room. "Look, Stevie. Just drop it," CC stated firmly. "I know it was a mistake. I should have waited until we got to know each other again." CC found herself smiling as she watched her niece in her playpen try to put her foot into her mouth.

"I just don't understand why you slept with her," Stevie said in bewilderment. CC groaned at Stevie's persistence. "The two of you went from 'gee you're aren't the jackass I thought you were' to hopping back into bed together. I can understand the night you both got loaded, but this last time . . ." Stevie just shook her head.

"It felt right," CC explained. She was tired of having this argument with Stevie. For the life of her, she could not understand why her sister was so angry with Jamie. "We spent the day together, at your insistence I might add. It was like it was before. All the old feelings were still there."

"That's the problem," Stevie groaned bitterly. "You are not getting to know her."

"I know her," CC scoffed. "This is James we're talking about."

"No, this is Jamie Jameson," Stevie snapped back. "She's not the sweet naïve little college girl you remember."

"I know that," CC argued. "She's changed and so have I."

"Look, I like Jamie," Stevie defended herself. "But you're rushing into this. You're acting like nothing has changed. Come on, Caitlin. You slept with her and now she's blowing you off."

"She isn't blowing me off," CC protested. "She's busy. She had a life long before we ran into one another again."

"Open your eyes," Stevie warned her.

"What is this really about?" CC finally demanded.

"I just don't want you to get hurt again," Stevie said sincerely. "But Jamie isn't the little virgin you left behind."

"I'm quite aware of that." CC snickered.

"I'm serious," Stevie responded flatly. "I wasn't going to tell you this, but the night before the two of you hooked up together Brad saw her at the club. She ended up in the parking lot with some girl."

"Don't do this," CC warned her sister in a cold threatening voice. "I knew she was with someone that night."

"You did?" Stevie said in surprise.

"I'm a cop. I notice things," CC explained in a flat tone. "Let's just say the lipstick on her collar wasn't her color. What I didn't need was to hear the gory details."

"I'm sorry," Stevie said as she blinked in surprise. "I just don't understand why you would be with her so quickly knowing that she's promiscuous. Come on; it's a little sluttish."

"Don't," CC hissed out through clenched teeth. "I wouldn't worry about Jamie's morals if I were you."

"Excuse me?" Stevie gasped.

"Do you think Emma's room will ever get completed if you keep banging the contractor every time she comes over?" CC questioned her triumphantly.

"How did you . . .?" Stevie stammered as she blushed furiously.

"I notice things," CC taunted her. "I also know that you're not in love with her. You just need someone right now. She's a buddy," CC added with a shrug. She didn't want to argue with Stevie. They had always been close. She understood that Stevie was just looking out for her. But until she talked to Jamie she wasn't about to allow Stevie to trash her.

"What if that's all Jamie's looking for?" Stevie questioned her carefully.

"I don't know," CC answered honestly. "If that's all she wants then I guess that's it."

"What do you want?" Stevie inquired softly.

"I don't know." CC sighed as she sat down next to her sister, stretching out her legs. "Maybe we just needed one last time together to put everything behind us. Maybe it means something more. I don't have a clue. All I know was, at that moment, none of it mattered. There wasn't the past. No thoughts of the future. It just felt right. It felt right to hold her and kiss her."

"Okay," Stevie blurted out as she patted CC's knee. "Speaking of gory details, I don't need to hear everything." Stevie held up her hand as she grimaced. CC laughed as she swatted her sister playfully. "I just worry about you," Stevie added thoughtfully. "I can see that look in your eyes and it hasn't been there is such a very long time. Just try taking it slow. Maybe have a date or go out for coffee before the two of you get naked again."

"I promise," CC agreed, smiling as she stood. "With our schedules I just I hope I get the chance before the next ice age."

CC's smile vanished as she saw Jamie out in the parking lot hugging a small brunette. *'Who the hell is that?'* the policewoman's mind screamed. She felt her sister standing next to her.

"Oh boy," Stevie muttered as she grabbed onto CC's coffee cup before it could spill.

"Not a word," CC said sadly as she marched back into the kitchen.

Jamie hugged the small brunette tightly. The woman was one of the few people she knew that she could hug without reaching up. Meagan had chestnut hair and gray green eyes and was one of the truest souls that Jamie had ever met. She couldn't have asked for a better sister. Of course they had only officially become siblings a few years ago. But during all of those summer vacations and family trips they'd endured together, they had become sisters long before Jamie's father married Meagan's mother.

Jamie had endured a long hard week of sheer hell. It seemed to her that every person she encountered was just plain rude lately. She tried to write it off to her own emotional troubles. Granted, she was upset about CC, but she was trying to keep things in perspective and not fly off the handle. She needed some distance from the tall policewoman before she overreacted. She'd done that once twelve years ago and it cost her the woman she loved. So if it wasn't the possibility that CC was seeing someone, what was going on with the world? She'd also double-checked her calendar just to ensure that there wasn't another cause to the hostility that was surrounding her.

"Did you have any trouble finding the place?" Jamie asked her stepsister as she led her towards her home. Despite Jamie's over-analytical mind, she was notorious for giving horrible directions. She was infamous for saying things like 'you know, the place with the thing, turn right there'.

"No," Meagan responded brightly as they entered Jamie's townhouse. Jamie smiled, thinking that she'd done a good job in getting her sister up there from Maryland. "I just ignored what you told me and looked it up online."

"You doubted me?" Jamie gasped in mock horror.

"Yes," Meagan asserted firmly.

"I'm wounded," Jamie chuckled as they removed their coats.

"Did you just get off duty?" Meagan inquired thoughtfully as she settled down on the sofa.

"Yes," Jamie responded with a yawn. "I'll just put on some coffee for us," Jamie suggested warmly.

"If you need a nap or something, it's okay," Meagan interjected.

"No way." Jamie waved her off as she shuffled off to the kitchen. "I don't get to see you that often anymore."

"Okay," Meagan called out as she scanned Jamie's sparse living conditions. "Jesus, Jamie! When are you going to unpack?"

"It's getting there," Jamie called back as she carefully measured the coffee. "I've been busy," Jamie explained once she returned from the tiny kitchen.

"You look wiped, kiddo," Meagan noted thoughtfully. Jamie rolled her eyes at the term. Meagan was two years younger than Jamie. She'd been a bit of a wild child while they were growing up while Jamie had been a role model. Jamie always said that she'd saved everything up for when she came out.

Despite their differences the two had always gotten along. It didn't hurt that Meagan had finally outgrown her days of partying. Now the once feisty teen was a financial officer with a devoted husband.

"Are you certain you don't need to get some rest?" Meagan suggested.

"No, I'm fine, and I'm off for the next couple of days so we can spend some time together," Jamie explained. "I just had a really long week."

"You want to talk about it?" Meagan offered in a comforting tone.

Jamie shrugged as she sat down next to her sister. Perhaps it would do her some good to vent a little. "I don't know," Jamie mumbled as she collected her thoughts. Meagan quirked her eyebrows to encourage Jamie to continue speaking. "It just seems that lately I've been crossing paths with the rudest people on the planet. For example, the other day I was going to the post office. You passed it on the way here. It sits on a curve of the rotary."

"Not very safe," Meagan noted.

"That's why they put some lights there," Jamie explained quickly. "I pulled around the rotary and got stuck behind a car that's double parked. I can't go around because cars are coming up behind me. The driver can't see this because she's looking for something on the floor. So I beep my horn. I swear that's all I did," Jamie added in her own defense, knowing that Megan would assume that she offered the woman a single digit salute. "There were parking spots just a few feet ahead of her. She pulls up a centimeter and I'm forced to pull out into traffic and go around. Then I park in one of the spots and she pulls in behind me. We both walk up to the mailbox at the same time. She tells me 'you go ahead' in the snottiest tone I have ever heard. I never wanted to bitch slap someone so much in my life."

"You didn't?" Meagan laughed.

"No." Jamie blew out an exhausted breath. "I just rolled my eyes and mailed my letter. I really didn't want to get into it with her. "

"How rude." Meagan shook her head in disgust. "I did notice that the drivers around here are a little tense. What's with all the detours?"

"The Big Dig," Jamie groaned. "It's getting better. I know that Massachusetts' drivers have their own way of doing things. It's part of the charm of living up here."

"Something more than a rude driver is getting to you," Meagan pointed out.

"It's just that everyone I've run into this week has been like that," Jamie blurted out in exasperation. "I expect it at work. The folks I see there are sick or injured. It's hard to stay upbeat when you just broke your arm. But the other day I went to get pizza for everyone. I'm dressed in my scrubs, heading back to the hospital loaded down with several pizza boxes, and this guy shouts out, 'Hey, where you going with all that food? I'm hungry.' "

"Ugh," Meagan grunted in sympathy.

"I know what he said was innocent enough but it was the tone," Jamie bemoaned. "You know that flirty 'I'm a cool dude' tone. Did this guy actually think he was going to get my phone number or get lucky with me? Tell me truthfully. Does that random shouting out in the streets work with you straight girls?"

"No." Meagan laughed.

"It must work on someone since so many men do it," Jamie noted as she went into the kitchen to get their coffee.

She came back with the coffee mugs in hand. "Even in North Hampton or P-Town I've never heard a woman yell out 'Hey beautiful' or 'I love you'," Jamie explained thoughtfully.

"Maybe you just don't have sex appeal?" Meagan teased.

Jamie flicked her stepsister and then offered her a single digit salute. "And our parents always thought you were the nice one." Meagan sighed. "So are you going to tell me what's really stressing you out?"

"Well, there's this resident following me around at work," Jamie continued as Meagan rolled her eyes. "I keep explaining to him that I'm not interested plus I'm his supervisor."

"Have you told him that you're gay?" Meagan questioned her.

"No," Jamie admitted as Meagan gave her a curious glance. "I will but I just hate having to say that all the time. Why is it that you just can't say 'I'm not interested' without having to add an explanation?"

"I think I know what you are saying," Meagan responded. "Before I was dating Anthony and even after we were engaged, guys just wouldn't except that I didn't want to go out with them. You always have to explain why. Do women do that?"

"Oh yeah," Jamie groaned. "I had this friend back in my days at George Washington who started giving out the phone number to the local FBI office. She said it was easier then having to endure this long drawn out drama about why you don't want to give someone your phone number."

"I wish I had known about that little trick when I was single," Meagan laughed. "Okay, Jamie. You've stalled long enough. When are you going to tell what is going on with your ex-girlfriend?"

"I'm really trying to keep things with CC in perspective," Jamie explained carefully. "I told you what really happened twelve years ago and how it was just a huge misunderstanding?"

"Yeah, and I still say she had twelve years to tell you about the shooting," Meagan responded firmly.

"I do want to talk to her about that," Jamie muttered. "Well, I think she's seeing someone. Which makes things a little awkward since she's my ex-girlfriend."

"Well, face it. Once you get naked with someone, you never react the same way to them again. Even if you want to see them happy, or out of your life, or whatever, you still went to bed with this person," Meagan surmised.

"Yeah, and since CC and I ended up sleeping together recently it makes things even more difficult," Jamie said quietly in hopes that Meagan would miss what she said.

"Excuse me?" Megan choked, almost spitting her coffee out.

"It kind of just happened," Jamie squeaked out in embarrassment. "I was secretly hoping that maybe we could start dating or something."

"What do you mean it just happened?" Meagan berated her. "How does something like that just happen?"

"We spent the day together and it was great," Jamie started to explain.

121

"And you thought you'd celebrate by tearing one another's clothes off?" Meagan jested.

"Sort of." Jamie winced at the implication. "It just felt right."

"Are you sure it wasn't just old feelings?" Meagan suggested.

"Maybe," Jamie reluctantly admitted. "I just wish I had the opportunity to find out. Now I think it's too late."

"I don't know, Jamie," Meagan cautioned her. "If she's seeing someone so soon then she's not the person for you. I have to admit it is a little surprising to hear you talk about wanting to date someone. You've always been adamant about keeping your solitude."

"I've been doing a lot of thinking since CC reentered my life," Jamie confessed. "Maybe being alone isn't the paradise I've been telling myself it is."

"My, isn't this surprising," Meagan chuckled lightly.

"Oh, give it a rest," Jamie chastised her with another sharp flick. "Anyhoo, I want you to meet CC and her sister while you're here. Even if I've missed my chance of making things work with her, she's a really nice person. I feel bad that I've been avoiding her. I just needed some space on this one. I'd really like to keep her friendship."

"I'm a little curious as to why you haven't asked her if she is seeing someone," Meagan prodded.

"I'm scared," Jamie admitted with a heavy sigh.

"Blunt force trauma to the cranial cavity," the medical examiner noted dryly. CC tried to listen carefully as she stare at the lifeless body.

"Someone hit her on the head?" CC questioned Marissa with a yawn.

"Yes. Am I boring you, Calloway?" Marissa curled her lips in amusement.

"Not at all," CC waved off the remark. "I'm not sleeping well these days. What was she hit with?" CC blinked her blue eyes rapidly, trying to remain focused on Marissa's report.

"My best guess is a tire iron," Marissa explained. "You'd think they'd come up with something new. So what's keeping you up at nights?" Marissa pried.

CC rolled her eyes, knowing that Marissa would prod until she got a response. "Oh, you know - the job, my car has finally died, the usual stuff," CC lied.

"Uh huh," Marissa scoffed at the explanation. "Haven't seen you around town lately. I thought maybe some sweet young thing finally caught you," the dark-skinned beauty taunted the policewoman.

"Uhm, can we just focus on the case?" CC admonished her.

"So it's true," Marissa beamed.

CC was growing steadily more uncomfortable with the direction the conversation was taking. She had no idea where she and Jamie stood. She had been avoiding Jamie since her houseguest had arrived. It was childish and CC knew it. On top of that, CC had dated Marissa briefly some time ago and she never missed an opportunity to let CC know that she was still very interested. "Dr. Vergas, can we deal with the victim for just a moment?" CC snarled. "Was she sexually assaulted?"

"No penetration." Marissa went into detail. "I did a rape kit anyway. No signs of semen. But there is bruising between her thighs. I think our boy wanted to, but he was either interrupted or had equipment failure."

"What about the other thing I asked you about?" CC continued, making notes in the little pad she kept with her constantly.

"You were right," Marissa continued methodically. "The body was moved. She didn't die in the park."

"Great. So the park was a dumping ground." CC sighed as her temple throbbed. "No crime scene, and we have no idea who she is. You sent the dental impression over to Clooney?"

"Yes," Marissa answered her drolly. "Here's the full report."

CC accepted the file with a slight nod and started to leave the sterile environment. She hated going down to the morgue;

there was nothing rewarding about the experience what so ever. "Hey, Calloway!" Marissa called out.

"Yeah." CC sighed, thinking she had missed her opportunity to get out of the room. She tried to play the role of the big tough cop, but the sights and smells that surrounded her at that moment were making her sick.

"How about dinner on Saturday?" Marissa inquired with sly smirk.

"I don't think so," CC responded quickly.

"Come on. Its just dinner," Marissa pushed as CC's stomach became increasingly queasy.

CC was about to tell her in no uncertain terms that she wasn't interested but for some reason the brooding brunette found herself hesitating. "Fine." She accepted the invitation, thinking that perhaps going out with a friend was just the distraction she needed. "But it is *just* dinner," she emphasized, not wanting to lead Marissa on.

Later she was sitting at her desk looking over the medical examiner's report and her own notes and photos. CC drummed her fingers on her desk as she tried to piece together the evidence lying before her. "I hate it when you do that," Max grunted indignantly.

"Sorry," she grunted in response as she rubbed her face in her hands wearily.

"Okay, I'll get us some coffee." Max sighed as he stood, his chair creaking in relief once he had vacated it.

They had worked together for so long and, like most partnerships, they had each developed little habits that they knew drove their partner up the wall. CC would tap her fingers or fiddle with a pen or some other object. Max wouldn't have his chair fixed. Every time he stood, sat, or shifted, it would let out a high-pitched squeak that sent shivers down CC's spine. Max returned with two mugs of coffee; he handed one to CC before returning to his chair directly across their adjoining desks. CC glared at him as it squeaked.

"Let's go over it." Max sighed, ignoring her glare.

"White female, twenty-five to thirty years old. Blunt force trauma to the head, probably a tire iron. Marissa made a notation that it was probably a smaller one, like the kind that comes with a foreign compact car. The victim was found off the soccer field in Jackson Park, completely nude. Blonde, not natural," CC read off their findings.

"They never are." Max snorted.

"No rape but based on the bruising on the inside of her thighs, there was an attempt," CC explained dryly. "Probably why he killed her." Max nodded in agreement. "None of the victim's clothing or belongings were present at the scene which makes identification impossible for the time being. The body was dumped so the murder happened somewhere else. That's it for Jane Doe number . . . Good Lord, how is possible that that many women could just disappear?" She blinked her eyes in shock when she read the tag number. "Okay, died from a blow to the head; other than the bruising between her thighs, there's no sign of a struggle. The blood work came back clean so we can assume that she knew her attacker who couldn't step up to the plate. Her remains were dumped. Her identity and the site of the murder are unknown."

"Don't you love these easy cases?" Max joked half-heartedly. "You remember your first call after getting your gold shield?"

"What a nice guy." CC smiled. "He called us and then sat and waited while sipping his twelve-year-old scotch. He put the gun safely off to the side so we would know he wasn't a threat. He refused a lawyer and confessed."

"On the drive over I'd been lecturing you on the do's and don'ts and not to expect the suspect to just confess. Then this guy blurts out the whole story while offering to make us tea." Max laughed. "He was quite a gentlemen about the whole thing. I almost didn't want to put the handcuffs on the guy."

"You had to love it," CC agreed. "What happened to Mr. Henderson? I got home early from work and found my wife and best friend in bed together. I shot them both. Would you nice officers like a cup of tea?"

"I don't think I'd be that calm if I caught Shirley with my best friend." Max snorted. "Frank is an ugly guy," Max teased. CC couldn't resist laughing.

"Okay, I've got a couple of possibilities from Missing Persons," Max explained, getting back to business. "I don't think any of them are our girl. It might be too soon for someone to have reported her."

"Let's go," CC said grimly as she grabbed the Polaroid's of their victim and her jacket. She hated this part of the job. She was about to visit people who didn't know where their loved one was and she was carrying pictures of a corpse.

CC sat at her desk exhausted; she was no closer to finding out the identity of her victim. It had been hell visiting those hopeful families. They seemed so eager when they first arrived and then, when they realized what CC and Max were there for, they fell apart. There was a strange sense of relief when CC viewed their photos and informed them that the girl they had found wasn't their child. She left them no closer to finding the answers as to what happened to the young person they were seeking.

Max was shifting in his chair causing the squeaks to increase loudly. They were both frustrated. She was contemplating throwing her pencil at him when her telephone rang. The desk sergeant informed her that she had a visitor. She made her way across the squad room and out to the desk sergeant who simply pointed through the bulletproof glass to the lobby. CC's eyes lit up when she saw Jamie leaning against the wall. Her joy was short lived when she noticed the brunette sitting close by.

The sight of both women waiting for her startled CC slightly, and she braced herself for the awkward situation that awaited her. The tall policewoman brushed her bangs out of her face and quickly checked her appearance before opening the door and stepping out into the lobby. She approached the women as they chatted. "This shouldn't take to long," Jamie was explaining. "Why don't we check out that Mexican place for dinner tonight?"

"Hello," CC said, effectively interrupting the brunette's response.

Jamie jumped slightly, apparently startled by CC's arrival. She smiled as she looked up at the raven-haired beauty. "Hi," she responded in a voice just above a whisper. CC felt like she hadn't seen Jamie in ages. Mentally she was kicking herself for staying away.

"What brings you down here?" CC inquired shyly, suddenly feeling like a kid. Out of the corner of her eye, she caught a glimpse of the small brunette looking at her. CC knew when she was being sized up. She cast an icy blue stare down at the stranger. Much to CC's surprise, the small woman gave as well as she got. Neither seemed to be willing to give up.

"Uhm Caitlin …" Jamie said, interrupting their staring contest.

"Hey," CC groaned as she returned her attention to Jamie, "don't call me that."

"Sorry," Jamie chuckled lightly. "CC," she corrected herself. "I would like for you to meet Meagan."

"Hi," CC responded in a bored tone, not even glancing in Meagan's direction.

Jamie's jaw dropped; she was surprised by CC's rudeness. CC just folded her arms against her chest defiantly. Jamie tugged on CC's arm and pulled her off to a corner of the room. "Now I know you like to preserve your big tough cop image," Jamie sputtered. "But that's no excuse to be rude to my sister."

"Your sister?" CC gaped in embarrassment. Suddenly her face turned grim. "You don't have a sister," CC snapped in a quiet accusing tone. "You have three brothers."

"Meagan is my stepsister," Jamie corrected her.

CC tried to process the information as Jamie's face brightened slightly. The blonde seemed to suddenly understand everything. "CC, my Dad married Meagan's mother almost two years ago. Our families have always been close. Meagan's Dad passed away about eight years ago, and we lost Mom almost five years ago. Dad was really lost, and they just seemed to lean on one another. We were thrilled when their relationship turned romantic," Jamie explained in a very slow and careful voice.

"Your Mom died?" CC said sadly as she laid a comforting hand on Jamie's arm. "I'm sorry. I didn't know."

"How could you?" Jamie addressed her softly as she placed her hand on top of CC's. The blonde's thumb casually brushed the back of CC's hand. "We weren't even speaking to one another back then."

"I need to apologize to your sister," CC grimaced.

"Yes you do." Jamie gloated as she patted the back of CC's hand.

CC groaned before turning her attention back to Meagan. The brunette seemed overly amused by the situation. "I'm sorry," CC stammered as she offered Meagan her hand. Meagan shook her hand warmly. "I thought you were . . ."

"Jamie's latest hottie," Meagan teased. "Sorry, wrong team."

"Your husband would like that," Jamie snorted in delight.

"Yeah, laugh it up, Blondie," CC chastised her. "So is this why you stopped down here? Showing Sis all of Boylston's hot spots?"

"No. Actually I have a favor to ask," Jamie said grimly. "One of my interns is missing. She's only missed one shift, but Stella called me even though I'm taking some time off. It's just really out of character for her not to show up. The hospital called her apartment and I stopped over there before I came here."

"I'll look into it for you," CC volunteered immediately.

"Thanks," Jamie sighed with relief. "I don't want to alarm her parents just yet. These kids are under a lot of pressure, and sometimes they just freak out. Still, I wouldn't have pegged Sandra for losing control."

"Tell me about her," CC encouraged her.

"Her name is Sandra Bernstein. She lives in a two-family near Longwood," Jamie explained as she reached into the back pocket of her jeans and retrieved a slip of paper. "That's her address and phone number. She worked the night shift two nights ago and hasn't been seen by anyone on the staff since."

"What does she look like?" CC continued, thinking that the resident was probably spending time with her boyfriend.

"A little taller than me. She has blonde hair and green eyes. She's a little older than the rest of her classmates, maybe twenty-six," Jamie explained as CC's heart began to beat just a little faster.

"Is she a natural blonde?" CC inquired carefully.

"I don't know her that well," Jamie shot back quickly.

"Sorry," CC offered. "Did she have any tattoos or distinguishing characteristics?"

"Where is this going?" Jamie asked fearfully.

"Hopefully nowhere," CC said absently. "Can you wait here for a moment?"

Jamie nodded hesitantly as CC had the desk sergeant buzz her back into the squad room. She grabbed the Polaroid's off her desk and motioned for Max to follow her. She returned to Jamie who had turned white as a sheet. CC said a silent prayer that the nagging hunch she was experiencing was wrong. "James, could you look at some pictures for me?" she inquired carefully as Max looked on with interest.

"Oh God," was the only response Jamie offered as she accepted the photos. "It's her," she said after viewing the first one. Jamie thrust the photos back into CC's hand.

"Are you . . ." CC began hesitantly.

"Yes," Jamie said, cutting her off. "How?"

"We're still investigating," CC offered softly as she fought back the desire to wrap Jamie up in her arms. She could see the pain in the young doctor's eyes, and she just wanted to make it stop. "I'll need to see her employee file so I can contact her family."

"If it's all right, I'd like to call them before you do," Jamie requested softly. "I'll let the hospital know that you're coming over. I suppose you'll still need her file and need to check out her locker?"

"Thank you," CC responded as she began to absently rub Jamie's forearm.

Jamie gave her a halfhearted smile as she captured her hand and gave it a gentle squeeze. "Sorry, Meagan," Jamie apologized to her sister who was now standing beside her. "Looks like we're going to miss the museum."

"Tell you what." CC began to formulate a plan of action. "Why don't you come with me to the hospital? That way Meagan can take your car and do whatever she wants. I'll take you home;

it'll give me a chance to see Emma. Max, here's Sandra's address. Why don't you go chat up the landlord and see if you can get a look inside?" She handed him the slip of paper. He simply nodded in response.

"Mrs. Grayson," Jamie provided. "Her landlady is Mrs. Grayson; she lives on the first floor. She'll chat your ear off. But she's sweet."

CC watched as Meagan and Jamie conferred. "You have my cell number?" Jamie questioned her sister as she handed over her car keys.

"I just need a few moments." CC explained quickly.

CC gathered up her notes and jacket and went to rejoin Jamie. Max halted her movements by gently touching her on the arm. "That's James?" he inquired with a hint of sadness.

"Yeah," CC responded in confusion. "You've met Dr. Jameson before."

"And so have you," he noted dryly. "Twelve years ago?" he prodded. "I could never understand who James was. I had always suspected that you were gay."

"Let it go, Max," CC cautioned him.

"Right. We aren't suppose to talk about it," Max growled. "It never happened. I didn't get my gold shield after watching the rookie I was supposed to be taking care of almost bleed to death."

"Max, it was a long time ago," CC said softly, fighting against the familiar panic. "And you got your gold shield because you're a damn good cop."

"Right," he sneered, the bitterness clearly evident in his tone.

"Please, Max, let it go," CC cautioned him once again. She knew that both of them were still haunted by the demons that day had brought forth.

"At least the bastard got what he deserved," Max added dryly.

"Don't," she cautioned him sternly as she grabbed his arm tightly. "I don't want to think about that either." It was a nagging question that had haunted her for years. Was the man who had shot her that day later killed by the mob or by someone who didn't like the fact that he had gotten away with shooting a cop?

It was a question she prayed she would never know the answer to.

"Fine." Max shrugged it off. CC wasn't buying his sudden change in demeanor. "So is the good doctor the person you were seeing back then?"

"Yes." CC sighed in exasperation. "God, you're worse than an old lady. Can we get some work done now?"

As Jamie and CC drove to the hospital, the policewoman couldn't help noticing that Jamie was lost in thought. She assumed that it was the death of her young colleague. "Uhm CC . . ." Jamie began hesitantly, "why do you have your sister's car?"

CC looked at the blonde strangely; it certainly wasn't the question she was expecting. "Mine broke down a few nights ago," CC explained dryly, still feeling uncertain as to where this conversation was heading.

"So you've been using Stevie's?" Jamie said with a slight smile.

"Yeah," CC responded curiously. "Like I said, mine died. I really need to get a new one, but Stevie hasn't had the time to take me."

"I could take you," Jamie volunteered. "Are you free on Saturday afternoon? Meagan will be gone by then and it's my day off."

"That would be great," CC answered brightly. "Thank you."

"You're welcome." Jamie smiled once again. "Uhm CC . . ." The doctor paused, trying to gather her thoughts. "Are you seeing anyone?"

"Me?" CC laughed at the thought. "No. I haven't been dating anyone for a long time. It's been about ten months or so. Jamie, what is all of this about?"

"You're going laugh," Jamie stated with some degree of amusement.

"Why do I doubt that?" CC questioned her companion.

"Okay, so maybe you won't," Jamie conceded. "After the last time you and I were intimate, I went over to your place to see you. " CC raised her eyebrow in suspicion as she listened carefully while trying to keep her eye on the road. "Your car was there and Stevie's wasn't so I went around to the back door. The door was open and I heard noises."

131

"Noises?" CC questioned, still not getting the gist of the conversation.

"I heard someone . . . you know," Jamie stammered.

"No, I don't know," CC responded honestly.

"Having sex," Jamie finally blurted out.

"Oh?" CC laughed, and then her face dropped when she realized whom Jamie had heard. "Icky." She groaned in disgust. "That must have been Stevie and her little playmate, the contractor."

"No wonder it's taking so long to get that room done," Jamie said thoughtfully.

"Tell me about it," CC grumbled.

They drove in silence while CC processed the information. She knew that she should be focusing on the case. "So that's why you were avoiding me?" CC finally asked.

"Yes," Jamie confessed. "Look, I know I don't have any right to say anything about who you date. But it hurt when I thought that you had bedded someone else so quickly."

"Jamie," CC began slowly as she reached out and took Jamie's smaller hand in her own, "you are the first and only person I've been with in almost a year. I honestly want to see if . . ." CC stopped speaking abruptly as they pulled into the hospital-parking garage. "Sorry. Can we talk about this later? I really need to focus on Sandra right now."

"I understand." Jamie nodded in agreement. "I'm not looking forward to calling her parents."

"Are you all right?" CC inquired tenderly.

"Not really," Jamie admitted. "It's just such a shock. She was so young."

CC could see the pain in Jamie's eyes as she pulled the car into an available spot. She unhooked her seatbelt as Jamie did the same. As Jamie went to open the car door, CC halted her by reaching out and placing her hand on Jamie's shoulder. She watched as the blonde's eyes fluttered shut. Without question CC wrapped Jamie up in a warm and comforting embrace. "Why would anyone do this?" Jamie choked out. "She was just a kid."

"I know," CC said soothingly as she rubbed Jamie's back.

Jamie shifted once again, trying to make herself comfortable on the sofa. It was her own fault; she'd known Meagan was coming for a visit and she still hadn't gotten the spare room ready in time. Now she found herself fighting nightly to get comfortable on the sofa. Jamie sighed heavily as she began to flip through the channels on the television. "Four hundred channels and there's still nothing on." She grunted as she continued to search for something to watch.

It didn't help that she was accustomed to working at night. Now it was well after three in the morning, and she was wide-awake. She knew that a part of her insomnia was because of Sandra. The call to the energetic girl's parents had been difficult. They were flying in from Colorado in the morning. Jamie couldn't imagine what it must be like to lose someone so suddenly. It had been hard enough watching her mother's life slip slowly away. Sudden loss was something she dealt with constantly at work, and she still didn't know how to handle it.

The only bright spot in her day was CC. She felt good about having some of the confusion between them cleared away. The constant misunderstanding reinforced what she had already known. She and CC really didn't know one another anymore. "Maybe now we'll get the chance," Jamie said thoughtfully. "Wouldn't it be funny if we get through all this only to discover that we have nothing in common?" She chuckled. "Well, almost nothing," she murmured in a breathy tone as her mind flashed to CC kissing her way down Jamie's body.

Jamie felt the blush creeping across her body. "She is certainly good in bed." Jamie blew out a frustrated sigh. Jamie looked around the room, shyly wondering if her sister was sleeping. The blonde licked her lips in anticipation as she cupped her breasts. A soft knock at the front door disrupted her exploration. "This just isn't my day," the doctor growled as she clicked off the television and tossed the blanket aside.

She raced over to the door, thinking that the only person who would come calling at this hour was the woman she had just

133

been fantasizing about. She scowled when she looked through the peephole. "You've got to be kidding me," she growled as she swung open the door. "What are you doing here?" she snapped at Simon.

"I just wanted to see how you were," Simon stammered. "I heard about Sandra."

Jamie blinked in disbelief as the young Dr. Fisher rambled on. "How did you get my address?" she barked coldly as she folded her arms over her chest.

"I . . . err . . . Uhm . . ." the young man stuttered as he blushed.

"This stops now," Jamie fumed as she stepped outside and neared the tall lanky boy. Despite the fact that Simon was much bigger than she, the feisty blonde was making him cower in fear. She knew she could appear menacing when she needed to be. "I am your supervisor and that is all. We are not friends, and you are not permitted to invade my privacy. Is that understood?" she growled fiercely.

"Jamie, I just thought . . ." he began shyly.

"You thought wrong," Jamie barked as she watched Stevie's mini-van enter the parking lot. "And didn't your Momma tell you that it is impolite to address someone by their first name unless they invite you do so?"

"I just think . . ." he continued as Jamie watched CC exit the vehicle. The tall policewoman cast a curious glance over at her. "I just want to talk to you," he pleaded.

"No," Jamie responded firmly as she watched CC approach. *'Oh goodie, the cavalry has arrived. She's going to blow a gasket. I can feel it from here,'* Jamie thought fearfully.

"I have feelings for you, but I could accept just being friends," Simon continued pitifully as CC drew closer.

"Dr. Fisher, we are not friends," Jamie corrected the young man, trying to get rid of him before CC could intervene. "I'm only going to say this once more. I am your supervisor. Coming to my home was inappropriate. Now I suggest you leave."

"I just want to talk," he whimpered as he reached out to her. His movement was halted by CC's grip on his forearm. "Ouch!" he yelled as he turned angrily towards his attacker. "Let me go," he growled.

Jamie stepped back, noticing the young man's demeanor had changed dramatically. "I think the lady asked you to leave," CC said firmly, her hand still gripping his arm.

"This is none of your business," Simon spat out.

Jamie could see the intense look in CC eyes. "Caitlin," she said softly in an effort to diffuse the situation. There was a twinkle in CC's eyes as she turned towards the doctor. "Dr. Fisher was just leaving. You can let go of him now." CC's lips curled into a snarl.

"Back off," Simon snapped as he moved to push CC who then grabbed the young man by his throat.

"This is just great," Jamie grumbled. "Let him go. The kid's turning blue," Jamie pleaded.

"Is he going to behave?" CC asked, holding the struggling man up straight. Simon was choking.

"Simon, if CC let's you go, will you play nice?" Jamie inquired forcefully as CC lifted the man higher off the ground. Simon nodded. "Put him down," Jamie instructed CC firmly.

"All right," CC sighed as she dropped the man to the ground. "Hi, honey. I'm home." CC teased as Simon gasped for air and struggled to get to his feet. Jamie shook her head as she stepped closer to CC.

"You . . ." Simon growled as he reached out for CC. Jamie quickly stepped between the two. Simon instantly backed down. "Who in the hell is this creature?" he growled.

"I told you that I'm involved," Jamie stated flatly. Simon looked stunned as CC snorted triumphantly from behind her. "Now go home. I'll be back from my vacation in a couple of days. You and I are going to have a long talk," Jamie addressed him coldly. The young doctor nodded mutely as he rubbed his throat. He cast a cold stare at CC before stumbling off.

"You enjoyed doing that," Jamie moaned as she turned to find CC smiling.

"Just a little." The policewoman beamed in delight. "Who was that?"

"Long story," Jamie groaned. "Come in for some coffee, and I'll tell you." She ushered CC through the door. Jamie was anxious to get inside so they could stop giving a show to the entire complex.

"You're sleeping on the sofa?" CC inquired as Jamie closed the front door behind them.

"Meagan has my room while she's staying here," Jamie said softly, hoping that her sister wasn't awake.

"That can't be comfortable," CC noted thoughtfully.

"It sucks," Jamie agreed as she stretched her shoulders to alleviate some of the tension from her body. "But Meagan is leaving soon so it's not too bad."

Jamie stared at the tall brunette whom seemed lost in thought. "Jamie, I don't want you to take this the wrong way, but you're more than welcome to bunk with me," CC offered in a sincere tone. Jamie could only stare at CC in disbelief. Certainly she hadn't just said what she thought she said. "I'm not trying to hit on you," CC explained quickly. "I just thought you'd be more comfortable in a bed. We've slept in my bed before without anything happening. And this way you could get some real sleep."

"It would be nice not to be squished up on the sofa," Jamie reasoned as she wondered if she could trust herself sleeping so close to CC.

"It's settled then," CC responded casually.

"I'll just leave Meagan a note," Jamie said absently as she padded off to get a pen and paper.

"Tell her to come over in the morning, and the four of us can have breakfast together," CC added with a warm smile.

"Okay," Jamie answered her blankly, wondering if this was such a good idea. Jamie wrote the note quickly and left it on the coffee table. She grabbed her keys, wondering if she should bring anything else. Realizing she had everything she needed, she followed CC out the door and locked up behind them.

As they entered CC's home, Jamie still felt a little awkward. "I'm going to take a shower, and then you can tell me about Doctor Feel Good," CC said casually as she headed out of the room. "Jamie, thanks for accepting the invite. I'll be honest. I didn't like the looks of that guy, and I'll feel better if you stayed here," CC confessed in a shy tone.

"Thanks," Jamie said with smile, feeling better about the situation. She understood CC's overprotective nature, and it made her feel good knowing that her invitation was born from concern and not lust. "Go take your shower, and I'll make us some tea."

CC smiled in response and left the living room. Jamie went into the kitchen, filled the kettle, and put it on the stove. She couldn't shake the feeling of how natural the simple act seemed. She was going to brew tea, relax and talk with CC after each had experienced a long day. Something felt so right about the moment.

A short while later they were sitting on the sofa sipping their tea while CC played with Emma. "She is never going to sleep through the night if you keep waking her up when you come in," Jamie noted as she watched the two of them giggling.

"You sound like Stevie." CC smirked as she continued to play with the infant. "Doesn't she?" CC questioned her cooing niece. "So tell me about the guy on your front steps," CC inquired.

"He's one of the med students," Jamie explained nonchalantly. "Simon Fisher. He's had this crush on me," Jamie continued in a dismissive tone. "I ignored it at first, but lately he's been stepping over the line. I tried being nice, and then I tried being firm. I told him I wasn't interested, and I'm also his advisor so it would be inappropriate to interact socially. I even told him that I'm seeing someone." She groaned in disgust.

"He seems to be a bit slow on the uptake," CC said thoughtfully. "He didn't know that you're gay?"

"No," Jamie sighed as she rolled her eyes. "I know that some of the nurses told him that he was barking up the wrong tree. I don't understand him. I've been very up front about my lack of interest. I can't believe he showed up at my house."

"None of this sounds very good," CC said in a serious tone. "I don't want to alarm you but something about him makes me nervous."

"Don't worry," Jamie responded as she rubbed CC's shoulder gently.

"Hmm." CC grimaced.

"You probably scared him off." Jamie chuckled. "No," she said quickly as Emma reached for CC's teacup. "I'll take these into the kitchen," the blonde offered as she collected their cups.

"Thanks," CC responded.

Jamie rinsed their cups and then took a moment to brush her bangs out of her eyes and straighten her T-shirt and sweatpants. She rolled her eyes at her actions. She was enjoying their comfortable conversation. Still, sitting so close to CC who was clad in a pair of boxer shorts and a tank top, was wreaking havoc with her libido. "How am I going to share a bed with this woman?" she whimpered before reentering the living room.

Stevie had appeared and was cradling Emma as she chastised her sister for waking her daughter. "Told you so," Jamie taunted CC.

"Hey James," Stevie greeted her with a smile. "I hear you're going to be crashing here."

"Yeah, if you don't mind," Jamie said, feeling a slight degree of tension from Stevie.

"No problem," Stevie responded sincerely as she cast a cautioning look at the doctor.

"I'm beat." CC yawned as she stood. "I'm heading to bed."

Jamie was about to follow her when she caught Stevie giving her a slight nod. "I'll be there in moment," Jamie said softly.

"I meant it, Jamie," Stevie addressed her after CC had left the room. "It's not a problem. It's just that you two seem to have a real issue when it comes to taking things slowly."

"I know," Jamie conceded. "I'm not going to hurt your sister. I promise."

"Jamie, I really like you," Stevie continued. "I know I've been giving you a hard time, but my sister means the world to me. Honestly I would love to see the two of you work things out."

"Really?" Jamie said in surprise.

"Really." Stevie chuckled. "I just think maybe you need to get to know one another in the vertical position first."

"I'm trying," Jamie said with relief. "Goodnight, Stevie," she said as she touched the brunette's arm gently.

"Goodnight, James," Stevie said brightly.

Jamie entered CC's bedroom to find the brunette still awake. She closed the door behind her and climbed into bed. "My sister giving you a hard time again?" CC inquired with concern.

"You can't really blame her." Jamie yawned as she tried to distance herself from CC's warm and inviting body. "It's not like you and I haven't said the same things."

"I know," CC grumbled as she clicked off the lamp on the nightstand. "It's just so annoying coming from my kid sister."

Jamie chuckled lightly as she clung to the edge of the bed. "You know I invited you to stay here so you'd be more comfortable," CC said dryly. "I'm not going to ravish you if you move a little closer."

"How do you know I won't ravish you?" Jamie taunted CC as she rolled over on her side so she could look at her. Even in the darkness she could see CC's crystal blue eyes staring back at her.

"Goodnight, James," CC said softly, ignoring Jamie's comment.

"Goodnight, Caitlin," Jamie said softly in response as she unconsciously leaned in closer and placed a soft kiss on CC's lips. Jamie hadn't realized what she was doing until she felt CC's lips pressed against her own.

Jamie pulled back slightly, startled at how natural her actions had felt. CC cupped her face with her hands and brought Jamie's face down to her. Jamie felt CC's breath teasing her skin as she leaned into her touch. CC reclaimed her lips gently. Slowly mouths parted and tongues began to explore the warmth of the other's mouth. Jamie felt the spark of desire ignite within as her body pressed against CC's.

Jamie smiled down at CC as the kiss ended blissfully. She lowered her body so she could rest her head against CC's chest and smiled as CC wrapped her arms around her to hold her close. She still felt aroused by the contact, but she felt something else as well - she felt loved. She drifted off to sleep as she listened to the steady beating of CC's heart.

CHAPTER FOUR

CC stirred slightly in her sleep as she felt another person's warmth covering her body. The tall brunette moaned as she became aware of the sensual feeling of her nipple being teased while a firm thigh pressed against her aching center. CC kept her eyes shut firmly, not wanting the dream to end. It felt so real. A gentle breath caressed her breast making her body tremble in pleasure; her eyes flew open. The sensations grew stronger as she felt her left nipple being teased.

Looking down she saw Jamie lying across her body. CC's top had been pushed up and a sleeping Jamie was rolling and pinching her nipple. The blonde's firm thigh pressed against CC's heated center. "I'm in hell," CC grumbled as she tried to move away from the blonde's pleasurable touch.

Jamie whimpered as she pressed herself more tightly against CC's body. CC's breathing was becoming ragged as Jamie squirmed around on top of her. CC's mind and body engaged in an active battle of wills. It felt so very good to hold Jamie, and the blonde's gentle touch was driving her insane with desire. Yet making love again before they had a chance to work things out between them would be the wrong thing to do.

CC prayed for the persistent aching to cease. She lifted her body slightly in hopes of making her escape. Unfortunately the movement allowed the slumbering doctor to capture CC's breast in her mouth. Jamie began to suckle eagerly. CC found herself reeling from the sensation as her fingers laced around the back of Jamie's head.

CC's body took control as she pressed Jamie closer to her and arched her back, giving more of herself to her former lover. She pulled Jamie's body closer as she fell back down onto the mattress. The movement awakened the doctor; green eyes fluttered open in surprise. Jamie's face turned red as she lifted herself away from CC's chest. Her movement caused her thigh to press harder against the policewoman's center. "Sorry," Jamie blurted out as CC groaned.

Jamie was still straddling CC as the brunette gasped for air. CC's body was a quivering mass of arousal as Jamie moved slightly against her. "CC, I'm sorry," Jamie said softly as CC lowered her top to cover her breast. CC couldn't speak; she could only lie there trembling. Jamie started laughing. CC, who was still trying to breath normally, just looked up in despair. Jamie quickly clamped her hand over her mouth.

CC growled as she watched Jamie's body shaking from the stifled laughter. "This isn't funny," she managed to utter in a shaky tone. She watched in discomfort as Jamie bit down on her lip, trying to conceal her merriment. Jamie shifted slightly and once again her leg brushed CC's throbbing clit. CC's head rolled to the side as her body burned from the touch.

"Oh God," Jamie moaned from above her. CC's eyes fluttered shut, knowing that Jamie could now feel her wetness.

"Caitlin," Jamie said sweetly as she reached down and ran her fingers along CC's jaw line.

CC's lips quivered in anticipation as she found herself lost in the pool of jade staring down at her. "I know that look," CC said in a breathy tone. "Jamie, we can't."

"Why?" Jamie whimpered in dismay as her chest heaved and her eyes twinkled. "We can," Jamie asserted as her fingers continued their torturous trail along CC's chiseled features.

"I know we can," CC responded weakly as she leaned into Jamie's touch. "We shouldn't."

"I know that look you're giving me, Caitlin," Jamie continued in a husky tone. "You have the same look in your eyes that you had years ago when you were fighting against what our bodies wanted. You don't have to do the honorable thing. You need this. I can feel how much you want this." Jamie swayed her hips against CC's body, effectively conveying her message.

CC's will power was crumbling as her body arched against Jamie's. "What is it about you that drives me to the point of insanity?" Jamie uttered softly. "From the first moment I saw you I lost control."

"I gave you a speeding ticket," CC responded as she relaxed into Jamie's touch. Jamie laughed lightly. Both women were lost in the memory of that fateful afternoon.

"And then later that night you still asked me to dance after I made a complete fool out of myself," Jamie said lightly, her hands drifting from CC's face and down her body.

"Barely managed to ask you to dance," CC confessed as her body tingled from Jamie's touch.

"I couldn't believe how nervous you were," Jamie said with smile as her fingers continued to lightly caress CC's neck and then drifted to her broad shoulders. "That still amazes me."

"What's that?" CC sighed as her eyes fluttered shut her body tingling from Jamie's delicate touch.

"That underneath your tough cop image, you're shy," Jamie explained softly.

"Am not," CC grunted as she blushed slightly.

"You're sensitive and kind and gentle," Jamie cooed softly as her fingers drifted down CC's body and began to draw light circles across CC's firm abdomen. "Even when you were gone, and I thought that I hated you, I still missed your touch."

"Did you miss me?" CC inquired with uncertainty, and she captured Jamie's hands as they were about to find their way under her shirt. CC opened her eyes to find herself lost in the look of love Jamie was giving her.

"Yes," Jamie responded with sweet sincerity. "I missed your smile. I missed your laugh. I missed the way you get all shy when someone gives you a compliment. I missed the way you act like an overgrown kid. I missed the way you try to hide your tears when you watch a sad movie. I miss that look of sheer exasperation you get when I ramble on like an idiot. I miss the way you run your fingers through your hair just before you say something."

"I do all that?" CC uttered in surprise.

"And more," Jamie said tenderly. "For twelve years I just could not understand how someone so sweet and wonderful would just walk away from what we had without a word." Jamie paused as she collected her thoughts. CC tightened her hold on Jamie's hands, feeling the pain she had put the young doctor through. "And now I want to know why you waited all this time to tell me the truth," Jamie said in a sad voice.

CC brought Jamie's hands to her mouth. She turned them over and kissed the palms. "I thought about it so many times over the years," CC began slowly. "I just couldn't seem to get you out of my mind. It would be easy enough to track you down to find an address and send you a letter. I did run a check several times, and I could have written to you."

"Why didn't you?" Jamie questioned her as CC began to kiss each one of her digits slowly.

"Every time I would work up the nerve to do it, I kept seeing you kiss that girl," CC finally choked out.

"She didn't mean anything to me." Jamie sighed as her fingers trembled against CC's mouth.

"That doesn't make me feel better," CC responded honestly. "I loved you. You were everything to me. I fought to keep my career and then to get my body back in shape. Then I found myself fighting to get custody of Stevie. I was an emotional wreck having to face my mother in court. Knowing that she didn't care enough to come to me when I was in the hospital." CC could see the tears beginning to pool up in Jamie's eyes. "Then I went to you and had to face the reality that I had lost you. And I was angry that you could move on and forget about me so easily. I felt betrayed."

"Moving on with my life was anything but easy," Jamie choked out a bit harshly, "but I had to do it."

CC kissed Jamie's hands once again, enjoying the warmth she found there. "I know," CC said softly. "It hurt just the same." CC reluctantly released Jamie's hands. She reached up and brushed away the tear running down Jamie's cheek with her thumb. "And now by some miracle we've found one another again. And I am terrified that I'll find someway to screw this up."

"You are not alone on that one," Jamie said as she smiled. "Still . . ." the blonde added playfully as she swayed her hips once again.

CC gasped as their bodies pressed together. CC felt as if she was falling when Jamie's eyes darkened with desire. "Are you suggesting that while we get to know one another again, that we refrain from getting to know one another?" Jamie teased as her hands found their way up under CC's top.

"You're not making this easy," CC panted as Jamie's fingers teased her skin.

"Neither are you," Jamie said softly. "I know we shouldn't," Jamie concurred as her hands drifted further up CC's body. "I just can't help myself. Even in my sleep I want to touch you. I dreamt about you last night."

CC could only whimper in response. She knew that she was helpless to stop what was happening. Her body was on fire, and there was only one person who could extinguish the flames of desire. Jamie was the only one she wanted, and she was straddling her body. CC groaned as Jamie cupped her breasts. She felt Jamie lower her body. Jamie was now lying on top of her as her hands felt the swell of her breasts.

"Would it be so wrong to give in just this once?" Jamie whispered hotly in her ear just before she dipped her tongue inside.

CC groaned loudly as she clung tightly to Jamie's body. Since the night of the fire, the policewoman had been strung out. She needed Jamie's touch, and now she was trying to convince herself that Jamie was right. *'Would it be wrong to just give in to her desire?'* her mind debated.

From outside the doorway she heard laughter. Jamie's body stiffened at the sound. Both women scowled in disgust. "This is not fair," Jamie growled as she lifted her body slightly. CC smiled in agreement as her mind and body took notice that Jamie's hands were still pressed against her breasts; her eyes were still clouded over in a smoky haze. CC smiled as she moved quickly and flipped the small blonde over onto her back. Jamie squealed in surprise.

"This is why we never spent time at my apartment when we were dating," CC teased her as she balanced herself over Jamie.

"I always wondered about that." Jamie giggled lightly.

"It was too tempting being alone with you," CC confessed as she leaned down to steal a quick kiss. "We need to get up and have breakfast with our sisters."

"I hate being an adult," Jamie grumbled.

"Sucks, don't it?" CC laughed lightly as she climbed off Jamie.

Jamie bounced up off the bed. "You are certainly in a good mood this morning," CC noted as she pulled her hair up in a ponytail.

"I am," Jamie said as she tried fixing her rumpled blonde locks. "I haven't slept that well in ages. Thanks for letting me crash here."

"Anytime." CC yawned once again.

"Sorry about feeling you up in my sleep," Jamie apologized with a slight shudder.

"It's okay," CC conceded. "I just need to remember that you're a big pervert."

CC inhaled quickly as the doctor's hand swatted her hard against her stomach. "Ouch!" CC complained.

"Suck it up, you big baby," Jamie teased as CC yawned once again. "Someone needs her coffee."

CC nodded slightly before flashing a big pout. She fought back the laughter as Jamie rolled her emerald eyes in disgust. "Come on, hot stuff. Let's get you caffeinated."

"I'll be out in a second. I just need to change," CC explained quickly.

CC watched the confused look on Jamie's face change into a full-fledged blush. "Sorry." The blonde chuckled.

"No, you're not." CC scowled as the doctor dashed out of her bedroom. "Jamie, what am I going to do about you?" CC muttered as she dug out a clean pair of sweats. The policewoman changed quickly and joined the others in the living room.

"Good Morning, Sis," Stevie greeted her.

"Coffee," CC stated flatly.

"Glad you could join us," Stevie continued.

"Coffee," CC repeated, not understanding why her younger sibling failed to comprehend the urgency of the matter.

"Did you sleep well?" Stevie continued to taunt her.

"Coffee," CC growled.

"I'm sorry. Did you want me to make you some coffee?" Stevie inquired with a tone of mock confusion.

'Finally!' CC's mind screamed triumphantly. "Yes," CC grunted indignantly. Stevie folded her arms across her chest and stared at CC. *'Oops.'* CC cringed. "Please," she managed to squeak out meekly.

"I've already put it on," Jamie announced from behind her.

CC turned to find Jamie and Meagan sitting on the floor playing with Emma. "Baby." She grinned eagerly.

146

"No," Stevie grumbled. "My daughter will never learn to walk if you keep carrying her around."

"But..." CC began to protest.

"Jamie and Meagan are playing with Emma," Stevie scolded her.

"She's seems to be very focused first thing in the morning," Meagan commented.

"Yup. Coffee, baby, toss in a shiny thing, and my sister's morning is complete," Stevie grumbled.

"Actually I was talking about Emma," Meagan responded lightly as CC sneered at her.

CC was far from pleased at the way Jamie snorted with laughter. The blonde stood and walked over to her. "I'll get your coffee if you promise to behave," Jamie said softly as she placed a comforting hand on CC's stomach.

"Okay," CC conceded as Jamie began to rub her stomach in an all-too-pleasing manner.

"Funny. You seemed pretty wide awake back in the bedroom," Jamie whispered in her ear before removing her hand and making her way into the kitchen.

CC sighed contentedly, watching the sway of Jamie's hips as she left the room. *I really like starting my day this way,'* she thought blissfully. "Are you enjoying your visit, Meagan?" CC inquired as she watched Jamie's sister play with her exuberant niece.

"I'm having a great time," Meagan responded brightly. "Well, except for what happened yesterday."

"What happened yesterday?" Stevie inquired.

"One of Jamie's residents was murdered," Meagan explained in a hushed tone.

"Oh my God!" Stevie gasped.

CC chewed on her bottom lip as her mind began to review the case. Jamie handed her a mug of coffee. "Thank you," she said softly. "Speaking of which, I really need to talk to you about Sandra," CC said before enjoying her first sip of coffee.

"I figured as much." Jamie sighed heavily.

"What can you tell me about Dr. Fisher?" CC began slowly, not really liking that she had to disrupt the morning by bringing up business.

"Isn't that the guy who has a crush on you?" Meagan asked.

"Yeah," Jamie responded. CC could hear the discomfort in her voice. "What does he have to do with any of this?"

"Nothing I hope." CC shrugged. "I just need to go over some stuff with you since you were her supervisor," CC lied, not wanting to alarm Jamie with her suspicions. "Why don't we talk about this later? "

CC was happy when the subject changed. The four women relaxed and enjoyed a leisurely breakfast. Of course, Jamie occasionally brought up the subject. CC normally admired her overwhelming curiosity, this time it was working her last nerve.

Later after Jamie and Meagan had departed, CC and Stevie cleaned up. CC was feeling anxious since Meagan was leaving for home that afternoon. She didn't like the idea of Jamie being alone. After Emma had been changed, Stevie set her down on the carpet and allowed her to explore. "So what is it about Dr. Fisher you don't want Jamie to know?" Stevie inquired as they both kept a watchful eye on Emma.

CC grimaced at the question. "He has a crush on Jamie," she stated bluntly.

"And?" Stevie prodded.

"He isn't taking 'no' for an answer," CC continued thoughtfully. "He showed up on her doorstep late last night."

"That's a little creepy," Stevie commented.

"There's something about him that makes me uncomfortable," CC added. "We gave him the impression that we were a couple just to get rid of him, since 'take a hike' wasn't working."

"Uh huh." Stevie chuckled. "I bet you just hated acting like Jamie's girlfriend."

"He didn't react very well," CC said with concern.

"I don't like where this is going," Stevie said as she inhaled quickly.

"I think I scared him," CC said, not really believing what she said.

"You didn't hit him, did you?" Stevie groaned.

"No." CC shushed her. "I choked him." Stevie's brown eyes widened as they filled with shock. "Just a little," CC said, defending her actions. "He tried to attack me."

"You're afraid that you might have pushed this guy a little closer to the edge, aren't you?" Stevie stated fearfully.

"Yeah," CC admitted. "Would you mind keeping an eye on things while I'm at work tonight? I'm going to suggest that Jamie crash here again."

"Not a problem." Stevie instantly volunteered. "How did sharing a bed go?"

"Not bad." CC shrugged, recalling how wonderful it felt to awaken with Jamie in her arms. "We didn't have sex if that's what you're wondering."

"Who me?" Stevie scoffed. "So what does Jamie's stalker boy have to do with the murder?"

"Nothing, I hope." CC cringed as she spoke. Her fears were unsettling enough without having to say them out loud. "It's just that the victim looked a lot like Jamie."

"Jesus Christ!" Stevie's voice trembled as she spoke. "Well, that settles it. After Meagan leaves, Jamie is staying here until this case is over."

"James will never agree to that," CC argued.

"You'll think of something," Stevie reassured her.

CC did think of something. Oddly enough it was the truth; not the complete truth but enough for Jamie to agree to spend a few more nights at CC's place. CC was never one to play games. She had lost more women in her life because she refused to fall into that trap. As CC found herself taking yet another cold shower, she prayed that her willpower could withstand being so close to Jamie night after night.

Once she was dressed and ready to head out to work, she found her sister waiting for her. "Caitlin, I'm going out to dinner with Jamie," Stevie explained.

"Oh, is that why the peanut is all bundled up?" CC cooed as she tickled her niece.

"Jamie said you should take her car," Stevie continued, ignoring her sister's silly facial expressions. "The keys are on the counter."

"She offered me her car for the night?" CC questioned.

"James said that she knew that you were worried about leaving me without a car just in case anything happened with Emma," Stevie said with a smile.

"That was very nice of her to do." CC smiled at the thought.

"How did you get her to agree to crash here?" Stevie inquired.

"I told her that I would feel better if she stayed here at night," CC explained slowly.

"You didn't tell her what you suspect, did you?" Stevie asked her.

"No." CC scowled. "I don't want to worry her. What if I'm wrong? I'd just feel a little better knowing that she isn't alone at night."

"Regardless of what happens with this case, this guy sounds creepy," Stevie noted thoughtfully.

"I shouldn't be late. Have fun tonight," CC offered before kissing Emma and Stevie goodbye.

CC arrived at the station earlier than usual. She made a few telephone calls and then she placed the case files out in front of her and pondered them carefully. *'Talk to me,'* she urged silently, hoping to find some small detail that she had previously overlooked.

"Anything?" Max said as he sat down in his squeaky chair.

"Not yet." CC grimaced. "How did it go with her parents this morning?"

"They're devastated," he said sadly. "I can't imagine what that must be like."

"I made some calls to the hospital and set things up for tonight," CC explained as she silently agreed with her partner. "Her car is still in one of the garages. CSU is already over there.
"

"They just found her car now?" Max fumed.

"They have three different parking garages," CC explained slowly. "People coming and going twenty-four hours a day. It wasn't hard to overlook since no one knew that she was missing until yesterday. Why don't we head out to see what CSU has dug up, and then we can take a look at the video tapes from the monitors?"

"What do you want to bet that her tire iron is missing?" Max snorted.

"If it is then whoever took it would be on the video tape," CC said confidently. "After that, why don't we talk to some of the other employees?"

"The coworker and friends interviews - I hate those," Max snarled as they headed out towards the parking lot.

"There's one that you'll need to conduct without me," CC explained. "There's this guy who worked with her. He has a thing for Dr. Jameson."

"Do tell." Max chuckled as they climbed into his car.

"He showed up on her doorstep last night," CC continued. "I had a bit of a run in with him."

"Great," Max sighed as he drove them towards the hospital. "How bad?"

"Nothing too serious," CC hedged. "Max, this guy is definitely quirky."

"So this guy just showed up at her place?" Max inquired thoughtfully.

"Yes, and from what I gather he wants to get to know Jamie better," CC continued. "When I showed up, she was telling him to get lost."

"He didn't want to go I take it?" Max responded.

"No," CC confirmed. "He was polite enough with her. But when I stepped in, he snapped."

"Not good," Max grunted. "So we have a victim who looks a lot like Dr. Jameson. Captain Creepy is harassing her, and all three of them knew one another. Tell me, Detective Calloway, do you believe in coincidences?"

"No, I don't," CC growled as her fear grew. "What did you get from her parents about her social life?"

"According to them, she didn't have one," Max responded flatly. "You know how it is. They lived there, and she lived here."

"The landlady said she was quiet and a bit of a homebody," CC added. "With the schedule that these kids keep, it isn't hard to believe that she didn't have a social life. She never saw her going out with any guys."

"Which garage is it?" Max inquired as they pulled up.

"The southwest one. It should be the one around behind the hospital," CC instructed him. As they pulled up to the gate, CC noticed that there was no ticket dispenser, only a keycard slot. "Why would she park all the way back here if it's so far from the hospital?" she questioned absently. Max shrugged as he honked his horn, flashing his badge at the attendant so they could gain entrance.

As they approached the little blue Toyota, CC noted the flat tire on the back. "What do you have for me, Niezwicki?" CC asked the lead CSU investigator.

"Not much," the older man explained, scanning his clipboard. "No signs of a struggle. There are a lot of fingerprints. No blood that we can see. Looks like she ate her meals in the car; there's a ton of old coffee cups and fast food wrappers. Also the rear passenger tire is flat." He grunted. "And yes, we'll check it out when we get the car back to our garage."

"Was there a tire iron?" CC inquired.

The older man scratched his chin as he scanned his notes. "Yes," he confirmed finally. "The attendant over there was on duty the night your victim disappeared. His name is Terrell."

"Thanks. Let us know what you find once you get her back to the station," CC instructed. The man simply rolled his eyes. She knew that he knew what he was doing, but there was always that sense of urgency that made her feel as if she should remind the techs.

CC and Max introduced themselves to Terrell. The skinny older African American man simply nodded. CC could see the sadness in his eyes. "Did you know Dr. Bernstein?" CC inquired carefully.

"She was nice lady," Terrell responded softly. "Not like some of the other youngsters that come and go. She'd always stop and say hello. She'd ask about my family; she even baked me cookies at Christmas time. It's a damn shame, a nice woman like that dying so young."

"Yes, it is," Max agreed.

"Terrell, did you see her arrive the day of her last shift?" CC inquired in a soft tone.

"Yes, I did." Terrell nodded. "She was working an overnight. I try to keep track of when the young women are coming and going. It's so dark back here."

"Why would she park way back here instead of one of the garages in front?" CC asked; the question had been nagging her.

"Staff parking," Terrell responded flatly.

"Staff parking?" CC said in confusion. "I don't understand."

"The staff isn't allowed to park in the main garages," Terrell explained. "They're suppose to park back here so the patients and visitors can use the front garages to get in and out of the hospital easier. They even jack up the rates so the staff won't sneak in there. You need to get your ticket validated if you're a patient or a visitor. The desk even checks it on the computer to make sure that you aren't lying."

"I have a friend that works here, and she parks in the front lot," CC explained, knowing that she had seen Jamie park in the front.

"She must work the late shift," Terrell said with a smile. "There's no one here then who will validate a ticket. The rates drop at night. It's kind of understood that since visiting hours are over, and no one is coming in for an appointment, the staff can sneak into one of the main garages. It's against policy but everyone ignores it."

"And Sandra was working overnight and couldn't get away with leaving her car in the main garage," CC concluded. "Is that why there isn't a ticket dispenser?"

"Yes," Terrell confirmed. "They pay for a month's worth of parking in advance and get a key card which can only be used in the staff parking lot."

"Did you see her the night she disappeared?" Max inquired.

"No, sir," Terrell responded flatly. "It's strange but I don't remember anything about that night. Of course things are pretty dull back here. One night is just the same as any other."

"Did you see anyone who looked out of place?" Max continued.

"No, sir." Terrell sighed heavily. "Like I said it is pretty dull back here at night."

"This garage, is it just for doctors?" CC asked.

"No, it's for staff," Terrell explained.

CC grimaced; the scope of their investigation had just widened enormously. "If she had car trouble, would she contact you?" CC continued as her mind processed everything.

"Oh yes," Terrell responded sadly. "I stay in the office right over there." He pointed to the little room with the glass window that looked out over the garage. "We have mechanics on call if someone breaks down."

"So if they needed a jump start or had a flat tire, they could just tell you and you would call for assistance?" CC concluded. "I see you have video monitors in there. Can you see the entire garage?"

"Yes, Miss." Terrell nodded. "They skip around from floor to floor. I must have stepped out for coffee or something. I don't recall seeing her or anything unusual so I must have."

CC's heart broke at the forlorn expression on the older man's face. "Terrell, this isn't your fault," she reassured him. "We're going to find out who did this."

They questioned the man for a short while longer, and then Terrell gave them instructions on how to find the security office. They wandered the halls of the large hospital until they located it. "This place is huge." Max was huffing; the walk had strained the overweight man. "How does anyone find his or her way around?"

CC smiled at the panting man. "You know, what I find interesting is that no one stopped us as we were wandering around," she commented wryly. When they entered the security office a young man greeted them ands showed them to the director's office. The director was a large man. CC shook her head, instantly knowing the type. He was a big fish in a little pond. She could tell by the way he adjusted his belt that he was also a cop wannabe. He sneered when he saw CC. She stepped back and allowed Max to take the lead.

They showed their badges and introduced themselves. The way he addressed Max confirmed her suspicions. "I reviewed the tapes you requested," Dietrich began as he sucked on a toothpick. 'Oh goodie, this should be good,' CC's mind sneered.

"I didn't see anything that would help you," Dietrich continued as he sucked harder on his toothpick. *'There's a problem,'* CC noted in anger.

"We'll take them anyway," Max said firmly with a slight scowl.

"It's just that . . ." The man hesitated.

"Is there a problem?" Max taunted him.

"Well, there must have been a glitch," the large man mumbled.

"What sort of glitch?" Max pressed in an irritated tone.

"The tapes periodically rewind. We don't save all of them," Dietrich explained.

"That's not uncommon with surveillance equipment," Max noted. "Since her car was there for awhile, there still can be something that will help us. How long of a blackout are we talking about?"

"Ninety-seven minutes," Dietrich grumbled.

"What?" CC blurted out before she could stop herself.

"Now listen hear, Sweetie," Dietrich barked at her.

That did it, CC snapped. "Listen, Sparky. Just tell us something . . ." Max chuckled as she towered over the man. " . . . Just how long does the rewind normally take?"

"I don't have to put up with this," Dietrich bellowed in response. "I think you should leave."

"Guess again," Max interrupted. "This is a homicide investigation. Now give us the tapes and answer my partner's questions or we'll go over your head."

"Are you threatening me?" Dietrich fumed.

"Yes," CC and Max responded in unison.

"I run a tight ship here," Dietrich defended himself.

CC groaned, thinking how absurd it was that this man was trying to defend his job. "Really? Then why is it, in this day and age, that my partner and I wandered about without proper id and were never questioned?"

"It's the night shift. You can't get into the hospital without going through reception," Dietrich said, defending himself.

"Let me guess. You're not here at night." Max snorted in disgust.

"No," Dietrich conceded.

"How long does the blackout usually last?" Max repeated.

"Ten minutes," Dietrich finally confessed.

"Eight-seven minutes unaccounted for," Max grumbled. "Just enough time to flatten her tire and snatch her. Do you know why this happened? Were any of the other monitors affected?"

"No," the burly man grunted.

"How often do your men sweep that garage?" Max continued.

"Every half hour," Dietrich asserted firmly.

"Is that how often they're supposed to or how often they actually do?" Max pressed.

"My men follow my orders," Dietrich spat out.

"But you're not here at night," Max noted merrily.

"We'll take the tapes," CC said as her head throbbed. "And a list of your *men* who were on duty the night of the twenty-seventh. Also, we need a printout of who punched in and out of the garage during the time Sandra's car was there."

"Do you have any idea how long a list that will be?" Dietrich groused.

"Does the fact that a young woman is dead escape you?" CC fumed. "She was probably murdered in that garage. Now you can help us find out what happened or you can see your sorry excuse for a career swirling around the bowl."

Dietrich didn't say a word. He simply handed over the tapes and copies of the work log. He did agree to fax over the key card information. CC and Max took the material and left the man muttering bitterly behind them.

"You're beautiful when you're angry," Max teased her.

"I wanted to strangle that arrogant jerk," CC growled.

"Do you think she was killed in the garage?" Max questioned.

"No." CC sighed as they made their way to the Emergency Room. "I think she was grabbed there by someone who was smart enough to know that the monitors were down."

"Terrell?" Max questioned in disbelief.

"Doesn't fit," CC surmised. "I guess we'll know more when we view the tapes. Now let's go talk to her co-workers."

Throughout their interviews CC and Max discovered that Sandra Bernstein was the girl that Jamie and her parents had described. She seemed to be liked by everyone who knew her. Although Max and CC were used to that sentiment being expressed after someone had recently died, this time they seemed to be sincere.

CC and Max stopped by a vending machine and started filling it with an obscene amount of money just to get two cans of soda. "Oh goodie, there's the guy I was telling you about," CC said as she saw Dr. Fisher enter the hospital.

Jamie found herself laughing at Emma's antics in the restaurant. The infant was trying to get her hands on everything while Stevie and Jamie were fighting to clear everything out of her reach. This seemed to infuriate the child who screamed until her mother gave her one of her cookies to suck on. The waitress simply doted on the little girl.

"She's so beautiful." Jamie chuckled lightly as she peered over her menu at the adorable child.

"Gay men really do make beautiful children," Stevie agreed with a proud smile.

"I'll keep that in mind," Jamie responded quietly.

"Oh, thinking of getting one of these for yourself?" Stevie taunted her.

"I don't know." Jamie sighed. "I guess being around this little cutie got me thinking. Meagan is trying. Maybe I could just be the doting Auntie?"

"I don't know. You have that look in your eyes," Stevie said suspiciously.

"I guess I'm starting to think about things like having a family and a long term relationship again," Jamie said thoughtfully. "I haven't done that in a long time."

"The breakup left the two of you hurting. You both changed so much afterwards," Stevie noted with concern. "I know Caitlin never really tried to find someone else. Of course, for the first few years she was too busy raising me."

"She did a great job," Jamie asserted with a smile.

"Yes, she did," Stevie responded. "If she hadn't taken me out of there, God only knows what would have happened. The moment my father found out that Caitlin was in a coma he came after me. That's how I discovered she was in the hospital. Fortunately she had taught me a few moves so I could protect myself until I ran away."

"How did she manage to get custody?" Jamie inquired as she wiped some drool off Emma's face.

"I guess the FBI figured that they owed her and did some digging into my Dad's past," Stevie explained in strained tone. "Turns out he has a record for indecent assault on a minor. The courtroom was filled with cops from here and Rhode Island and a slew of FBI agents. What judge wouldn't pay heed to that? CC thinks that the judge was biased. I don't care. It got me out of there. What really hurts is that my mother still refuses to believe any of it."

"Do you hear from them?" Jamie inquired carefully.

"They both tried to get me away from CC's evil influence." Stevie laughed bitterly. "Especially after Emma was born. Now I have a restraining order, and the cops back home keep a careful eye on my father. He's in prison right now for trying to snatch a kid from a playground."

Jamie shivered as her stomach turned in disgust. "Let's talk about something else," Stevie suggested. "So roomie, did you pack your jammies?" Stevie teased as Jamie groaned.

"Do you mind my staying over?" Jamie asked.

"No," Stevie responded firmly.

"I was really unnerved when Dr. Fisher showed up at my house," Jamie finally admitted. "You know, last night was the best sleep I've had in ages."

"Snuggling up to a certain cop wouldn't have anything to do with that, now would it?" Stevie teased as Jamie blushed.

"Despite feeling safer over at your place, I have to confess it's a little hard sharing a bed with your sister," Jamie explained as she tried to hide her blush. "I know we need to take things slow, and in the end we may only end up being friends, but she is so damn attractive."

"I swear the two of you are just going to spontaneously combust someday," Stevie teased. "But you do need to get to know one another again."

"I know," Jamie groaned. "My head keeps telling me that, and so does my heart. Now if I could just get my body to listen, everything would be just fine. Speaking of spontaneous combustion, how's Emma's room coming along?"

"Emma's room is finished and so is the contractor," Stevie growled. "I can't believe she told you about that."

"Well, in her defense she had to," Jamie explained quickly. "I went over there one morning and kind of got the wrong impression. CC's car was there and yours wasn't and I jumped to the wrong conclusion."

"Oops," Stevie choked out.

"Either way, it really isn't any of my business," Jamie explained quickly. "It just . . ." Jamie hesitated as she tried to understand her emotions. She placed her menu down and began to rub her eyes. Stevie placed her hand over Jamie's.

"You're falling for her again," Stevie said bluntly.

"A part of me doesn't want to," Jamie responded in a fearful tone. "And another part of me wonders if I ever stopped loving her."

"Let's eat," Stevie said boldly as she gave Jamie's hand a light squeeze.

"Excellent idea," Jamie said with relief as she waved the waitress over and Emma cooed happily in agreement.

They placed their orders quickly and settled into a light chatter about the weather and their jobs. Just as their food arrived, Jamie's cell phone chirped. She rolled her eyes at the interruption. "Dr. Jameson," she snapped into the telephone.

"Jamie," the voice said in a strangled tone. A chill ran through her body as she realized whom the caller was. "I need to talk to you," he continued.

"How did you get this number?" Jamie demanded, fighting against the sudden fear that was welling up inside of her.

"Why are you doing this?" Dr. Fisher demanded.

"Is this call in regards to a professional matter?" Jamie addressed him sternly.

Jamie watched as Stevie's normally dark features paled. She could hear Fisher breathing heavily on the other end. "Is she there?" he spat out like a jealous lover. "That woman from the other night. Who does she think she is?" he demanded.

159

"That is none of your business," Jamie said curtly. "Nothing about my personal life is any of your concern. Do you understand that?"

"Jamie, why?" he pleaded.

"This conversation is over," she said firmly before disconnecting the call. Her hands were shaking as she set the phone down on the table.

"Jamie?" Stevie squeaked out nervously.

"It was him," she responded in an absent tone.

The weasel flinched slightly when he saw CC watching him and then he ducked into the doctor's lounge.

"Okay, Max. Let's go have some fun," she said with a feral grin.

"He doesn't like you." Max snorted as they made their way towards the doctor's lounge.

"I'm just going to rattle his cage a little bit and then turn things over to you," CC explained dryly before she slammed the door open. The young doctor squeaked as he quickly pulled up the scrubs he was changing into.

"Get out of here," Dr. Fisher demanded, his face burning bright red in anger.

"Relax. Trust me, you've got nothing I want to look at." CC snorted indignantly as Max rolled his eyes.

"If you don't stop harassing me, I'm going to call the police and have you thrown out," Fisher snarled in an arrogant tone.

CC and Max smiled as they pulled out their badges. "Too late." She said with a cocky smirk as they flashed their badges at him. She noticed that the bright red color vanished as his face turned ashen.

"You're a cop?" He trembled.

CC looked at her badge before placing it in her pocket and glaring at the nervous young man. "Yup," she snapped as she moved closer to him. She cast an icy glare at him, taking note of the beads of sweat trickling down his forehead. "You have a problem with that?" she pushed as he took a step back, banging into his locker. "Why so nervous, Doc? Been bothering my girlfriend again?" she taunted him. She watched as his eyes glazed over and his face again turned a brilliant shade of red.

"Calloway!" Max scolded her. "Back off," he said gruffly.

CC cast one last menacing glance at Dr. Fisher before taking a step back. "Women," Max sneered in Fisher's direction. "Must be PMS," he added with a shrug as Fisher glared at her. "Now, Dr. Fisher, we're just here talking to some of Sandra Bernstein's co-workers. I don't know what's wrong with her. Why don't you wait outside, Calloway, so I can do my job?" Max said firmly. CC stood her ground. "Get out before I have to put you on report," Max said harshly.

CC donned a sheepish pout before shuffling out of the room. Once she had closed the door, she smiled brightly. "Oh, that was good, Max." She chuckled softly before seeking out more of Sandra's friends. After she interviewed everyone she could find, she waited for Max. Her partner seemed to be taking forever. She'd glanced at her watch once again before she saw Max exit the lounge. He had a stony expression on his face as he nodded towards the doorway.

CC left the hospital and waited for her partner. Max looked back at the hospital as he came out, ensuring that no one was around. Since there were still people milling about, the two didn't speak until they reached the car. "So are you going to put me on report?" CC teased, trying to lighten the mood.

"You liked that, did you?" Max smiled slightly. CC noticed that his mood remained somber despite his smile.

"I was right?" she asked gravely as she leaned against the car.

"There is something wrong with that boy," Max responded in a heavy tone. "It wasn't so much what he said. There was just something about him that made the hair on the back of my neck stand on end."

"Tell me everything," CC said firmly.

"Well, he doesn't like you and can't understand why you're harassing him and his girlfriend," Max explained. CC's jaw dropped as her chest tightened. "Now everyone we've spoken to says that Sandra was the nicest friendliest person they had ever met, but this guy claims that he didn't really know who she was."

"Hard to believe." CC grunted as she began to grind her teeth. "They were in the same class and both under Jamie's supervision; he must have known her. On top of that, Jamie said that he used Sandra's death as an excuse to visit her. That was an awfully long interview to have with someone who didn't know the victim."

"Uh huh," Max grunted. "He had a lot of theories about the crime."

"That's interesting since he didn't know the victim," CC added with a slight sense of panic.

"Oh yeah." Max sighed. "And he asked a lot of questions about the case. He tried to seem casual about it but he was definitely fishing for information. Plus he loved talking about Dr. Jameson. Apparently they've been an item for some time; they just need to keep it quiet since they work together."

"He's our boy." CC groaned as her head began to pound. "Did he have an alibi for the night of the murder?"

"He claims that he was on duty all night," Max informed her. "We need to check him out. In the meantime, perhaps Dr. Jameson should stay away from home," he suggested carefully.

"She's staying with me," CC said flatly, trying to sound casual about the situation.

"Really?" Max said with amusement.

"Max," she growled at him.

"I didn't say anything." He laughed as he unlocked the car. "Calloway, if it is him, you need to back off."

"Max, I can't," she protested as she climbed into the car.

"If this weasel beat that poor girl to death, I don't want him getting off," Max said, chastising her.

CC grimaced, knowing he was correct. She reached into her pocket and switched her cell phone back on. They'd both turned their phones off in the hospital since it was unsafe to leave them on. CC's phone instantly began to vibrate. She checked her messages quickly. Her face turned pale as she listened to Stevie's frantic message. "Take me home," she snapped at her partner as she dialed Jamie's cell phone number.

"What is it?" Max inquired, not accustomed to his normally stoic partner looking so rattled.

"Just take me home," she choked out. "Come on, Jamie. Pick up," she pleaded as she listened to the ringing at the other end. "He called her," CC explained. "Fisher called Jamie earlier tonight."

"What did he say?" Max pried as he maneuvered his way through traffic.

"I have no idea but I'm going to find out," CC snarled as her heart raced. "Now just drive."

CC rushed into her home to find Jamie sitting on the sofa, calming reading a book. She paused for a moment, wondering when Jamie had started to wear glasses. The blonde peered up at her and gave her a curious look. CC fought back the urge to wrap the smaller woman up in her arms. Jamie looked so sweet and innocent, but CC could see the worry brewing in her eyes. "Stevie called you?" Jamie sighed heavily as she placed the book down and removed her glasses. "I asked her not to." She shifted uneasily.

"Why?" CC spat out as her younger sibling descended the staircase.

"Sorry, Jamie," Stevie murmured before nodding to Max who was panting heavily from chasing after his partner.

"It's okay," Jamie addressed her grimly. "Caitlin, I was going to tell you when you got home tonight," Jamie explained. "He didn't threaten me. He just wanted to talk."

"How did he get your phone number?" CC pressed, unable to keep the frantic tone from her voice.

"I don't know," Jamie said with a tremble. "I'm going to speak to my supervisor and have him reassigned." Jamie tried to sound calm but CC wasn't swayed.

"That's it," CC snarled.

"Yes," Jamie fumed as she jumped off the sofa.

CC started moving to confront her when she felt Max's hand on her arm. "Calloway, let me conduct the interview," he said in a soft tone.

"This isn't a police matter," Jamie argued.

"Perhaps not," Max said in a calm voice. "Why don't you tell me everything that's been happening while *Caitlin* finds something to keep herself busy." He smirked at CC.

The tall brunette grumbled under her breath as Stevie approached her. "Come on, tough stuff. Let's go upstairs so you can wake up your niece." CC curled her lip in displeasure as she allowed her sister to lead her away. Once upstairs, CC relaxed as she held Emma tightly to her chest.

After what seemed like an eternity, CC was allowed to return downstairs. If it hadn't been for the comfort of holding her niece, the policewoman would have thrown a major fit. Something about holding the cooing infant instantly relaxed her. After carefully placing Emma back in her crib, CC tried to roll the last vestiges of tension from her shoulders. She said goodnight to her sister and made her way back downstairs to her living room. Max looked unconcerned but CC recognized the calm demeanor that they would try to project so they wouldn't worry someone. She knew instinctively by the way he wouldn't meet her gaze that he was worried.

Jamie sat on the sofa absently running her fingers through her short blonde hair. The young doctor looked exhausted but seemed unaffected by the evening's events. Of course Jamie was unaware of the suspicions that both she and Max were hiding from her. CC swallowed hard, knowing that she would need to tell Jamie soon, and that the blonde was going to explode.

Jamie flashed a captivating smile up at CC that made her heart skip a beat. *'How do you do that?'* The brunette pondered as she approached the small blonde. *'You really are the one, aren't you? How am I going to focus on this case and deal with what's happening between us?'* CC smiled as Jamie stood. "Wait for me in the car, Max," CC instructed her partner. He simply nodded in response before leaving the two women alone.

Jamie took CC's hand and began to gently caress the back of it with her thumb. CC knew that Jamie was unaware of what she was doing. At times, touching like this just happened naturally between the two of them. "I might be late tonight," CC explained softly as she stepped slightly closer to Jamie.

"I'll be here," Jamie responded softly as she wrapped her arms around CC's waist and nuzzled her head against CC's chest.

CC sighed as she wrapped her arms around the smaller woman, allowing her body to absorb the heat from Jamie's body.

As CC inhaled the delicate scent of Jamie's shampoo, she pulled her even closer. Her heart was beating in a steady comfortable rhythm. The moment wasn't about sex or desire; it simply felt so right to hold the smaller woman. "Try to get some sleep," CC suggested before placing a kiss on the top of Jamie's head.

"I'll try," Jamie said softly.

"And lock up everything after I leave," CC continued as she reluctantly released her hold on the smaller woman. Jamie rolled her eyes at the comment. "And call me if anything, and I mean anything, happens." Jamie groaned with displeasure. "Humor me," CC persisted.

"Okay," Jamie agreed with a slight smile.

Then, as if the past twelve years had simply vanished, CC did something that felt completely natural. She leaned down and kissed Jamie goodnight. It was a short tender brushing of their lips and it took both women by complete surprise. They stood there for a brief moment, simply looking into one another's eyes as they both smiled brightly.

"That seemed so right," Jamie said in quiet wonderment.

"It did," CC responded in the same soft tone.

"Maybe we should do that more often?" Jamie suggested with a hint of playfulness.

"Oh yeah," CC answered enthusiastically. "I need to get going before Max thinks you kidnapped me or something."

"That could be arranged," Jamie said in a teasing tone as she ran her hands along CC's hips in a suggestive manner. "Tell me, Officer, where do you keep your handcuffs?" Jamie's hands started to run along the sides of CC's body in a mock attempt to find the handcuffs.

CC's eyes darkened with desire as she released a low tempting growl. "Wouldn't you like to know?" she taunted the blonde. "If you're good, maybe I'll show you sometime."

"I'm always good," Jamie responded in a husky tone.

"Oh boy," CC choked out. "Is it getting hot in here? I really need to go," she asserted as she maneuvered herself away from Jamie.

"Coward," Jamie teased her as she was leaving.

"Brat," CC shot back before exiting the townhouse.

She knew that she was sporting a silly grin when she climbed into the car. Max simply laughed at her. "Knock it off," she said, still unable to wipe the smirk off of her face. "Tell me what she said," she stated firmly while thanking the darkness that surrounded them. The last thing she needed was for Max to see the blush that she was certain covered her features.

Max continued to laugh at her expense before reviewing just what Jamie had told him. CC's anxiety grew as Max related the story on the way back to the station house. "So how did he get her phone number and address?" Max pondered aloud.

"Can't be that difficult in a place like that," CC reasoned. "She's a doctor. Her contact information must be lying around somewhere in case they need to call her in, like they did the night of the big fire. Fisher could have seen it in a Rolodex or on the computer. Hell, he could have probably just looked it up."

"If he isn't the guy that killed that girl, I still don't trust him as far as Dr. Jameson is concerned," Max explained with concern. "That boy is definitely living in his own world."

"That's one way to put it," CC grumbled. "Personally I'm going on record right now and saying that he's a big old nut job."

"Don't worry, partner," Max offered comfortingly. "Nothing is going to happen to Dr. Jameson. We just need to be careful. You're a little too close to this one."

"No kidding." CC grunted, feeling the earlier tension return full force.

Later, Max and CC were watching the garage videotape with bleary eyes. "That's not Terrell," Max noted as they watched. "He must not have been on duty at that time."

"We need to find out who that is," CC commented as she wrote down the time, "since it's close to the time our victim got off duty." They continued to watch. "We need to run the plates of the car that was parked next to Sandra's. It was there the entire time."

"It'll have to wait until RMV is open." Max grunted. "There is another glitch with the computer. This is so dull. How do those guys spend eight hours a day locked in those little booths?"

Just as Max made his inquiry, something on the screen caught their interest. "My, isn't she pretty," CC said with amusement. "If you like that 'hi, I'm a big slut' look. She seems to know our friend in the booth really well. Yes, she's going into the office with him. Oh gee, why do you think she got down on her knees? You think she dropped something?" Max snorted in amusement at her commentary. She continued merrily until something else caught her eye. "Wait, play that back," se said hurriedly.

"I didn't think you were into that kind of thing," Max taunted her as he complied with her request. "How far?"

"Right as she's stepping into the booth," CC explained quickly. "There! Pause it!" she shouted. "There in the opposite corner," she explained as she pointed to the screen. "Do you see who I see?"

"Dr. Fisher." Max grunted in agreement. "Not a clear picture, but I'm willing to bet that it's him. Let's run it and see when Sandra enters the garage," he explained as he hit the play button. The screen played for a few more moments, showing different images of the garage. Once again they could only see rows and rows of empty cars. The only other activity was the guy in the booth making out with his lady friend. Suddenly the screen went blank before resuming with the same images. Only this time the worker in the booth was quite alone. "There's our gap."

"Now we know why." CC groaned in disgust. "Our friend in the office had a date and didn't want it on film. If he's done this before, maybe some of the regulars know about it. Pause," she said suddenly as the camera showed Sandra's unattended car. "The car next to hers is gone."

"Just enough time to grab her," Max commented in disgust as he once again pushed the play button.

They both knew there wouldn't be anything to see but they had to double check. "According to the printout, Dr. Fisher punched in around the same time Sandra did the day before. And he punched out during the blackout."

"And who else?" Max pushed.

CC was about to protest when she caught the cautioning look in his eyes. "Okay, we'll give these to the computer boys and have them print out anyone who was parked there during the same time. Then we'll run all of their plates through the RMV," CC conceded.

"Good girl." He humored her. "It'll have to wait until tomorrow. Let's call it a night."

"It is tomorrow," she said.

"Too early though," Max grumbled.

"You know what sucks?" CC muttered.

"The coffee in the vending machine," Max teased.

"That too." CC smirked. "No, it's just that even if we match all of this up with Fisher it's still not enough for a search warrant. I'd love to see this guy's tire iron and have the lab boys spray some luminol in his car," CC remarked. The chemical could be illuminated with a black light and reveal any traces of blood, even if someone tried to clean it up.

"It's enough for a second interview," Max added hopefully.

"Which I can't be present for," CC snarled.

"We'll figure something out." Max patted her shoulder gently. "Let's get out of here before my wife forgets what I look like."

CC was exhausted when she got home. Between the tension and the lateness of the hour, every muscle in her body ached. She padded her way into the bedroom, trying to be as quiet as she could. She wasn't accustomed to having someone waiting for her in her bed. She smiled down at Jamie; she was curled up, clutching her pillow tightly. The heartfelt smile instantly bloomed into a full grin.

"I'm awake," a muffled voice said.

"Did I wake you?" CC asked in concern.

"No." Jamie yawned. "Come to bed," Jamie offered in a soft tone.

CC felt the tension quickly slip from her body as she replayed the sweet words in her mind. "I just need to take a shower," she explained as she bent down and placed a kiss on Jamie's forehead. The blonde mumbled something in response as she turned over. CC stifled the laugh that built inside of her when she heard the tired squeak in Jamie's voice.

CC quickly secured her sidearm and shed her clothing. After a long relaxing shower, she dried her long hair and dressed in a long T-shirt before returning to the bedroom. She closed the door quietly when she noticed that Jamie hadn't moved in her absence. Gently she pulled back the covers and slid into bed. She kissed Jamie's cheek before wrestling the pillow out of the blonde's grasp.

After fluffing her pillow to the desired firmness, she snuggled her body down and released a cleansing breath. *'This feels so right,'* she thought happily as she settled herself slightly closer to Jamie's warm body. Jamie's arms wrapped themselves around CC's waist. Once again CC found herself grinning like an idiot as Jamie nuzzled her neck.

Warm inviting kisses brushed the skin of her oversensitive neck. She moaned before she could stop herself as Jamie's mouth continued to suckle her neck. CC whimpered slightly as her body began to tingle with desire. "Are you awake?" CC choked out as she clutched the bedding tightly.

"Hmm," Jamie purred before running her tongue along CC's jaw line.

Jamie's hands slipped up under CC's T-shirt as her mouth began a slow tantalizing trail back to her neck and then over to her ear. CC whimpered once again as Jamie began to nibble on her earlobe. "I missed you," Jamie whispered hotly in her ear.

"Oh baby," CC groaned as her hands moved to Jamie's back.

Jamie shifted her body so that she was lying on top of CC. The brunette looked up to find Jamie's emerald eyes twinkling with delight as she ran her fingers along CC's full lips. The temptation was too great. CC's tongue peeked out of her mouth and began to caress Jamie's fingertips. She could feel Jamie's breath growing ragged as she captured one of the digits in her mouth. "You're driving me crazy," Jamie panted.

"Good." CC smirked as she recaptured Jamie's hand. She began to feast delightfully on each one of Jamie's digits as the blonde straddled her body. She could feel Jamie pressing her center against her firm abdomen. CC slipped her free hand down Jamie's body and under the waistband of her sweatpants. Jamie's hips ground faster as CC cupped her backside. As CC tortured Jamie's fingers with her tongue, her hand massaged the firm naked flesh of her cheek.

Jamie's hands slid up past CC's rib cage until she was cupping the brunette's full breasts. "Caitlin," Jamie pleaded as she began to roll CC's nipples between her fingers. CC's body arched as the pleasure of Jamie's touch set her body on fire. She released Jamie's digits from her mouth and cupped Jamie's other cheek, pulling her lover closer as the blonde rocked against her.

Somewhere in the back of her mind, CC knew that she should stop what was happening between them. Her heart and body took control and banished the thoughts. *I need this.* Her body screamed its need as Jamie pulled her T-shirt up. CC raised her arms, allowing the blonde to remove the garment. Jamie tossed CC's shirt across the room before lowering her mouth.

CC released a strangled cry as Jamie kissed the valley between her breasts. She kissed and tasted her way across CC's chest as she nudged the brunette's legs apart with her knees. CC lay there completely naked as her passion flowed freely. Jamie captured one of CC's aching nipples in her mouth and suckled it greedily while she pulled the other nipple with her fingers.

Jamie teased CC's erect nipple with her teeth and her tongue as CC wrapped her long legs around Jamie's body. CC began tugging at Jamie's clothing as their hips swayed in unison. CC released a hiss as Jamie continued to nibble and suckle her nipple. Jamie's T-shirt ripped as CC clawed at the material. Jamie raised her head; even in the darkness CC could see her flushed features.

Jamie lifted her body further up and, as her hips maintained a steady rhythm, she pulled her shirt from CC's tightly held grasp and yanked it off her body. CC's hands immediately reached out to capture Jamie's full breasts as they swayed above her in a tantalizing manner.

The doctor brushed away her advances and lowered her mouth to CC's other breast. She lavished the nipple with the same delightful attention she had given its twin. CC was squirming as she pulled on Jamie's sweatpants. She needed to feel her lover pressed against her, to have their overflowing desire merge until they collapsed. She used her long arms and legs to pull the pants down Jamie's body as the blonde feasted upon her breast.

Jamie pulled away from her. CC reached for her lover only to have Jamie gently lower her back onto the mattress. Jamie pulled the blankets down and then removed the last of her clothing. CC raised herself so she could watch her lover as she settled her body between CC's quivering thighs.

Jamie cupped her backside and raised CC's body to her mouth. The brunette draped her legs over the blonde's shoulders. Jamie began to slowly lick the inside of CC's thighs. "So wet," Jamie murmured against her skin as CC ran her fingers through Jamie's short blonde hair.

A warm breath blew through her damp curls and she trembled in response. Jamie's tongue slid slowly along her slick folds as she looked up at CC. Jamie's tongue circled her now throbbing clit, slowly teasing the brunette with each flicker. Jamie parted CC's swollen lips with two fingers as she sucked her clit into the warmth of her mouth.

CC's heart raced as her lover moaned in pleasure. CC raised her body higher, offering herself to the small blonde. Jamie drank in her wetness greedily as she held CC's thrusting body steady. CC cried out when her lover pressed her fingers against her opening. "Yes," she begged. "Please, Jamie."

Jamie entered her slowly as she continued to suckle her clit. CC's head fell back and her eyes fluttered shut as Jamie's fingers wiggled inside of her. She fought to control her breathing as she listened to Jamie murmuring in pleasure. Her body was on fire as she gave herself over to Jamie's touch. She wanted this moment to never end but her body trembled uncontrollably; she wouldn't be able to hold on much longer.

With one hand CC clutched the headboard; the other was firmly locked on the back of Jamie's head. A sheen of sweat covered her body as the bed banged against the wall. Jamie's hand and mouth worked in unison, driving CC closer to the edge as she called out the blonde's name over and over again. Jamie's teeth grazed her clit and she screamed out. Her body arched, lifting Jamie along with her as her mind went blank and the climax rushed through her.

Jamie held onto her as her nimble fingers continued to fill her. CC screamed again, unaware of disturbing noises outside. Her body rocked as Jamie encouraged the waves of ecstasy to continue. "Please," CC panted as she tried to pull her body away from her eager lover.

Jamie's mouth finally left her wetness and the blonde rested her head on CC's trembling stomach. The last vestiges of passion filtered through CC's body while Jamie's fingers remained inside of her. "You feel so good," Jamie murmured before kissing her stomach. CC whimpered as she felt Jamie's touch withdraw from the warmth of her center.

"You're trying to kill me." CC grunted as Jamie climbed up her body.

Jamie laughed lightly at the comment as she draped her naked body over CC's still quivering form. Jamie claimed her lips in a tender kiss as her thigh slipped between CC's legs. The brunette swooned, tasting her own desire on her lover's lips. As the kiss deepened, their bodies began to rock in a sensual rhythm. Jamie seemed to melt into CC as they wrapped themselves around each other.

CC clung to her lover as she felt Jamie's wet desire paint her thigh. She knew her lover could feel her wetness covering her thigh as well as their bodies fused together. Their hips began to grind wildly as Jamie moaned hotly into CC's ear. They continued to thrust against each other until their bodies arched against each other and screams of pleasure filled the room. They collapsed together and wrapped themselves up in the other's embrace. Laying in the darkness, CC simply enjoyed the feel of Jamie's body draped across her own.

The sound of breaking glass and a car speeding off disrupted their bliss. Both women sat up quickly, startled by the noise. "Stay here," CC instructed Jamie firmly as she climbed out of bed. She scrambled quickly to grab a pair of sweats and a shirt out of her bureau. Jamie started to dress as well. "Jamie," CC cautioned the blonde as she grabbed the lockbox her gun was in and began to spin the dial, fighting with the darkness to enter the correct combination. As she retrieved and checked her sidearm, two cell phones began to ring persistently.

Both women scrambled to find their cell phones. "It's me," they said in unison. CC listened intently to the dispatcher at the other end as she caught snippets of Jamie's conversation. "Did they see anyone?" CC asked in an urgent tone. "Damn," she grumbled. "I'll meet them out front." She disconnected the call and dialed Max's home number quickly. As she waited for Max to pick up, she heard Jamie say 'fudge nut brownies'. CC looked at the blonde with interest.

"The alarm company,. Jamie explained as she disconnected the call. "That's my code."

"Still have a sweet tooth," CC said with a smirk. "Max, there's been a break-in at Jamie's place. I'm going in with the unit."

"I'm on my way," her partner offered in a hurried tone.

"No." CC cut him off. "I'll fill you in tomorrow."

CC argued with Max for a short while longer as she wandered out into the living room. She found her sister standing there, clutching her daughter tightly. As she ended the call, she noticed Jamie trailing very closely behind her. "Something's happened at Jamie's place," CC explained. "Fortunately I've had a unit keeping an eye on things. Jamie, you stay here with Stevie," CC stated firmly.

"No way," Jamie argued.

"This is not open for debate," CC said in a calm voice. "Call the alarm company and let them know that the police are already here. Stay away from the window. I don't want anyone to know that you're staying here."

"But . . ."Jamie started to protest.

"No buts," CC said emphatically as she looked for her shoulder holster, her badge, and a jacket.

"Be careful," Jamie said softly.

"Always," CC reassured her.

The brunette was met by two squad cars; the four officers were already in full swing. She held up her badge. "Nice neighborhood you got here, Calloway," Roger Spenser said teasingly. CC looked at Jamie's townhouse to see the picture window had been smashed. CC's chest tightened as she looked at the broken mess.

"I'll get the keys from the owner," she muttered, trying to keep her emotions at bay.

"We've already talked to a few of the neighbors," Spenser continued. "They heard loud banging and someone shouting and then breaking glass. When the neighbors' lights started to go on, it must have scared him off. No one saw the car. We made a pass through here about fifteen minutes before it happened."

"Check the bushes and the trees over there," CC instructed the uniformed police officer. "Our guy might be lurking to see if the owner returns. She's at my place; we can slip in through the back."

"The owner is a friend of yours, right?" Spenser inquired.

"Yes," CC confirmed quietly. "We can go and talk to her after you guys do a sweep."

CC waited patiently as the officers checked every corner of the surrounding area. Then she escorted Spenser into her home. She found Jamie and Stevie sitting on the sofa, both looking very nervous. "Jamie, this is Officer Spenser. Spenser, this is Dr. Jameson and my sister Stevie."

"And I know who this is." Spenser beamed as he knelt down to tickle Emma. "This is little Emma," he cooed. "You know, your auntie drives us all crazy with your pictures."

"Do not," CC growled as Spenser chuckled. "Jamie, your front window was smashed. The neighbors heard someone banging on the door just before it happened. No one saw who did it."

"I can't believe this is happening," Jamie responded in a dejected tone.

"None of you heard anything?" Spenser inquired in a curious tone.

"I was upstairs when I heard the banging. The first thing I did was check on my daughter," Stevie explained.

"What about the two of you?" Spenser continued in confusion.

"I was busy," CC said quickly as she blushed deeply.

"Asleep," Jamie uttered as she blushed as well.

"Jamie, we'll need your keys," CC said in a rushed tone before Spenser could make any further inquiries. "We're going in through the back."

"They're in the bedroom," Jamie explained.

"Busy?" Stevie whispered in CC's ear.

"Shut up," CC growled.

"I'm going with you," Jamie said as she headed towards the bedroom.

"No." CC and Spenser responded quickly. "Jamie, no arguments. Why don't you and Stevie put on a pot of coffee? I'm sure the boys could use a fresh cup before they leave," CC said.

Emerald eyes glared at her before Jamie spun on her heel and headed into the bedroom. CC sighed and followed the irate woman. She grabbed her shoes as Jamie looked for her keys. "This one," Jamie explained as she handed the large set of keys over. Jamie cupped CC's face gently. The brunette leaned into the touch. "Be careful," Jamie repeated before placing a tender kiss on CC's lips.

CC nodded in response before putting her shoes on. "Why does this always happen?" Jamie said with a heavy sigh.

"What's that?" CC asked as she tied her shoes.

"Every time we make love, some sort of catastrophe happens," Jamie explained in a wry tone. CC chuckled lightly. "I guess we'll just need to keep trying," Jamie said with a smirk.

"Oh yeah," CC responded in a throaty tone.

Jamie snuggled closer to the warm body that was lying beneath her. She slowly opened her emerald eyes and smiled at the sight of CC's slumbering form. Her fingers began to gently trace the policewoman's chiseled features. She released a happy sigh. Despite the turmoil of the past few days, waking up in CC's arms seemed to make everything all right. "We really do belong together," she uttered softly so as not to awaken her companion. Of course, she still had to replace her living room window and then go back to work to face Dr. Fisher. "Doesn't matter." She shrugged happily as she continued to gently caress CC's face.

"What doesn't matter?" CC grumbled from beneath Jamie as a pair of crystal-blue eyes fluttered open. Jamie smiled as CC wrapped her arms tightly around her waist. "What's going on in that pretty blonde head of yours?" CC whispered softly in her ear, sending tantalizing shivers down her spine.

"Nothing. I'm just happy," Jamie murmured against CC's skin. Feeling her lover tremble beneath her, she couldn't resist placing a soft tender kiss on her neck. One kiss led to another as she felt her lover's pulse beat rapidly against her lips. CC moaned as Jamie began to suckle her neck.

The soft pleading whimpers CC was releasing fueled Jamie's desire and she pressed her body down onto the brunette's welcoming form. Jamie's lips began a slow torturous descent down CC's body while her hands ran up under the brunette's T-shirt. "James," CC moaned deeply as the blonde cupped the swell of the brunette's firm full breasts. "We don't have time for this," CC protested in a halfhearted tone.

Jamie snickered, not believing for a moment her lover wanted her to stop. She ran her hands back down CC's rib cage and grasped the hem of her T-shirt. Jamie slipped down CC's long form, leaving a trail of kisses in her wake as her hands raised the brunette's shirt. As she dipped her tongue into CC's navel she could hear a telephone ringing in the distance.

Jamie raised her head with a grimace and took in CC's amused gaze. "What do you think the chances are that the phone is for Stevie?" she inquired meekly as she sat up, removing her hands from CC's tantalizing body. CC laughed as she pulled down her shirt. "Good morning," Jamie said softly before brushing her lips across CC's.

"Good morning," CC responded with a soft kiss of her own.

The warmth of CC's lips tempted Jamie to resume her exploration of the brunette's body. The knocking on the bedroom door forced a scowl to bloom on her normally cherubic features. "It's us, isn't it?" Jamie groaned as she slipped off CC's body.

"Caitlin?" Stevie called from the other side of the door.

"Yeah, Stevie?" CC said with a slight chuckle.

"Phone call," CC's younger sibling offered apologetically.

"I'll be right there," CC responded. "Sorry, James." She sighed.

"I'll just go home and take a shower," Jamie said with a smile, knowing that CC was just as frustrated as she was. "We need to go car shopping and I need to call someone about my window. Who do you call about a thing like that?"

"God, it's Saturday already." CC groaned as she stretched out her back. "Where did this week go?"

"It hasn't been dull; I'll give you that." Jamie laughed. "Speaking of which, how bad does my place look?"

"It's just the window," CC explained as they made their way into the living room. "CSU cleaned away all the glass. We don't know what he broke the window with," she added thoughtfully before picking up the telephone. "Calloway."

Jamie wanted to pursue the conversation but, since CC was on the telephone, she turned her attention towards little Emma. She bounced the infant on her lap, watching the pensive _expression on CC's face as she spoke on the telephone.

"So what are your plans today?" Stevie asked as she brought a cup of coffee over to Jamie.

"Thanks," Jamie responded as she placed the cup down, away from Emma's inquisitive grasp. "I'm taking CC car shopping."

"Thank you," Stevie said enthusiastically.

"Are you still friendly with that contractor?" Jamie asked as Emma tugged on her hair, ear, nose, and any other body part she could reach.

"Why?" Stevie inquired suspiciously.

"I need to replace my bay window, and I honestly don't know who to call," Jamie explained quickly.

"I'll give her a call," Stevie offered with a slight smirk.

"Thanks," Jamie replied as she tickled Emma. "I have to go to work early tonight." She crinkled her nose at the thought of having to meet with her supervisor. "I need to talk to the Director of Emergency Medicine about my not-so-secret admirer."

"That guy is creepy," Stevie added in an ominous tone.

"Hmm," Jamie responded in a distracted tone as she watched CC out of the corner of her eye. The policewoman's one-word answers and fidgety mannerisms were putting Jamie on edge. "Who is she talking to?" she asked, trying to sound casual.

"Not sure," Stevie responded with a shrug. Jamie knew instantly that Stevie was lying.

Jamie handed Emma over to Stevie as CC was hanging up the telephone. "I'll bring this back," Jamie explained as she picked up her coffee mug. "Everything all right?" she asked CC as she sipped her coffee.

"Uhm . . . yeah," CC replied as she chewed on her lip nervously. "I forgot I had dinner plans with a friend tonight."

"Friend?" Jamie inquired cautiously.

"Co-worker," CC added. "I was hoping to spend time with you tonight."

"No problem. I have to work. Now I need to get cleaned up so I can take you out to look at some cars," Jamie reassured her, fighting the uneasy feeling building up in her stomach. "I'll be back in a few," she offered before placing a gentle kiss on CC's lips. The brilliant smile the brunette flashed her instantly calmed her fears.

After Jamie had showered she thought that maybe she should give her old friend Charlie a call. The large man was a good friend of hers during her undergraduate days. He was also the one who suggested she try Tai Kwan Do when she was looking for self-defense courses. Being very involved with the study he had suggested that she join him for a class or two. Later when they both ended up at George Washington it was Charlie who encouraged her to keep training. He returned to Boylston after his second year of med school deciding that being a doctor was not the path for him. They kept in touch and now he ran his own martial arts studio. With everything that had happened over the past few days a little sparring with Charlie might help keep Jamie calm and focused.

Later that day as they strolled around the dealership, CC looked like a kid in a candy store - a really big kid in a really expensive candy store. "What do you think?" CC asked eagerly as she rocked on the heels of her feet.

"Well . . ." Jamie replied, trying not to smirk at CC's enthusiasm, " . . . it's in your price range and you liked the test drive. You would feel comfortable driving with Emma in it . . . I say you should buy it, CC."

"Yeah?" CC practically gushed.

"Caitlin, just talk to the salesman." Jamie pushed her towards the impatient-looking gentleman who had been assisting them.

"Let's wrap this up, Sparky," CC called out to the man. He led them into the showroom and CC began to fill out the necessary paperwork. "Damn they ask a lot of questions."

"You're buying a car. There are things they need to know," Jamie said reassuringly.

"Miss Calloway, let me just run your Social Security Number for the credit check." The salesman, Gary, smiled brightly.

"Detective," Jamie corrected him.

"You're a policewoman?" He perked up even more.

"Homicide," CC mumbled as she poured over the endless forms.

"Oh?" he choked out. Jamie sensed that CC was about to get a very reasonable deal on her new vehicle.

They discussed the price and Jamie jumped in, haggling for the very confused CC. She knew that her friend had never bought a brand new car; in fact, this was probably the first major purchase CC had ever made. They finally agreed and Gary ran CC's credit check. "Oh no." He sighed heavily.

"What?" CC snarled. "I have good credit."

"What there is of it," Gary said. "Other than a couple of credit cards, there really isn't much here."

"I live within my means." CC shrugged.

"But you've never financed anything before?" he asked.

"So?" CC responded with an icy glare.

"Caitlin, a lack of credit history can be worse than a bad credit history," Jamie explained. "What if she had a co-signer?" she asked Gary.

"That would work," Gary responded eagerly.

"Wait a second," CC protested as Jamie held out her hand for the forms that Gary was sliding across to her.

"Caitlin, you like the Forester, and you need a reliable car," Jamie said quickly as she filled in the appropriate information. "Here," she said triumphantly as she handed the paperwork back to Gary.

"Okay, let's take a look at this, Miss . . . sorry, I mean Doctor, Jameson." The man was practically drooling when he read the information. "Any problems with student loans?"

"None, I've paid them off," Jamie explained. "I had a lot of scholarships so I didn't need that many."

Gary quickly punched the information into the computer. The way the man's eyes were lighting up Jamie knew that CC wasn't going to have any problems. "I don't like this," CC grumbled beside her as Gary gathered up the paperwork.

"I'm just going over to the finance guy," Gary explained. "I'll to see if he'll okay it without you're . . ." he said, hesitating for a moment. Jamie was familiar with the blank stare. " . . . friend," Gary tossed in quickly.

"James . . ." CC began hesitantly after Gary left.

"Caitlin, let me do this," Jamie cut her off. "I don't want to be worrying if you're going to be safe at night."

"You worry about me?" CC asked in a playful tone.

"Yes, you big Goober," Jamie groaned as she rolled her eyes. "The other night it was really strange; I could feel your vest under your clothes and it made me feel good."

"They're mandatory now," CC explained flatly.

"I wish they had been twelve years ago," Jamie grumbled bitterly. "Tell me about this friend you're going out with tonight."

"Huh?" CC stammered as her azure eyes widened in surprise.

"I see," Jamie sneered slightly as she began to grind her teeth.

"What?" CC said in a defensive tone.

"Old flame?" Jamie asked directly.

"No. . . Uhm . . . no . . . well, not really," CC babbled on.

"Uh huh," Jamie grunted as she continued to grind her teeth.

CHAPTER FIVE

CC played with her food, not really listening to Marissa. She just wanted to get out of the restaurant and call the station to find out if the RMV computers were finally working. She needed to know who's car was in the hospital garage that night. She wanted to kick the acting Governor's behind for the recent cutbacks that were stalling her accessing the information instantly. She had wanted to cancel the dinner with Marissa for many reasons. One, Marissa did not seem deterred by CC's lack of interest. Two, she was with Jamie and wanted to go check on her to see how she was. The list went on and on.

"You're not even listening to me, are you?" the perturbed medical examiner growled in frustration.

"Sorry, Marissa," CC apologized. "It's just this case," she explained, giving half the truth.

"Want to talk about it?" Marissa offered in a sincere tone.

"I think I know who the guy is," CC grumbled in a defeated tone.

"That's great." Marissa beamed. "Personally, I'll sleep easier once he's off the streets."

"So will I," CC confessed earnestly. "Too bad you can't get a search warrant just because someone gives you the creeps."

"Amen to that." Marissa lifted her glass of wine and toasted the idea. "It would certainly make my job a little easier. Then again, there's that whole infringing on human rights thing." Marissa groaned.

"I know, the rules are there for a very good reason," CC concurred. "Sometimes it's just so damn frustrating. "

"You'll put the case together," Marissa reassured her. "You're very good at what you do."

"Except I have to back off on this one," CC explained in a distant tone.

"Why?" Marissa asked in confusion.

"The guy works with someone that I'm close to," CC explained, not ready to go into the entire drama.

"Stevie? Doesn't she still run her own business out of the house?" Marissa persisted.

"It's not Stevie," CC hedged. "It's someone else."

"If it's just a friend then there shouldn't be a problem," Marissa continued, pushing the issue.

"Well . . ." CC winced as she tried to think of just how she was going to explain this one.

"Calloway, just a few days ago I asked you if you were seeing someone," Marissa said firmly. "You said no. Were you lying to me?"

CC took a sip of her drink and brushed her dark bangs back. "Not really," CC said slowly. "There is someone . . ."

"Why didn't you just say so?" Marissa laughed lightly. "If you're out with me tonight, it can't be all that serious."

CC was miffed by Marissa's words. "This is just dinner," CC pointed out. The cool confident smile Marissa flashed in response made CC even more agitated. "Marissa, I'm serious." In her heart CC knew that she was referring to more than their dinner engagement.

"I believe you," Marissa responded in a slightly condescending tone. "I also know that you've never been a U-Haul girl."

"Once," CC corrected her as her mind drifted to a certain blonde doctor. "I was once. Funny thing is, it's the same girl." CC had hoped that by being honest, Marissa would finally get the hint.

"So you're dating an old flame?" Marissa answered nonchalantly, seemingly unfazed by what CC had just told her. "After dinner do you want to catch the drag show over at Vapor?"

"No," CC declined, fighting to maintain a polite tone.

An hour later Marissa was pulling her Jeep into the parking lot for CC's house. Somehow CC had managed to finish her meal and maintain a polite level of conversation. Marissa was nice enough but she just didn't seem to understand that CC wasn't interested in renewing anything. The policewoman did end up agreeing to going for a cup of coffee after dinner. Somehow she managed to divert Marissa's flirtations and now she was home.

She just wanted to get out of the car, down a bottle of aspirin, and go to sleep. "Thanks for dinner," CC said as she reached for the door handle, hoping to make a quick escape. She never expected Marissa to do what she did next. *'What the hell?'* CC's mind screamed as she pried herself away from the intense lip lock Marissa held her in. "Marissa!" CC snapped as she pulled away.

Marissa's brown eyes stared at her in confusion. CC was just about to read the medical examiner the riot act when she felt the hair on the back of her neck rise. She knew Jamie was watching them before she turned to find a pair of angry emerald eyes glaring at her. "No," she gasped as she once again reached for the door handle.

"Jamie, wait!" CC called out as she scrambled out of the Jeep and ran after the furious blonde. "It's not what you think," CC explained as Jamie fumbled with the keys to her car. She reached the fuming doctor as she struggled to open her car door. "Jamie, let me explain," CC pleaded to Jamie's back. She could see the blonde's small hands shaking as she continued to fumble with her keys.

"I can't talk to you right now," Jamie choked out, keeping her back to CC.

"Jamie?" CC pleaded as she touched the trembling woman before her.

Jamie shrugged away from her touch; the bitterness in her action ripped a hole in CC's already fragile heart. Jamie turned to her, tears streaming down her beautiful face. "I have to go to work," Jamie choked out as she turned away once again.

"Please," CC begged fearfully. "It's always been you," CC said urgently as Jamie opened the door to her car. "I never stopped loving . . ."

"Don't!" Jamie snapped as she climbed into her car. "I can't do this right now."

CC's heart broke as she watched her lover wipe her tear-stained cheeks. CC opened her mouth to speak. She needed to explain everything before their lives once again spun out of control. "Not now," Jamie said stiffly, cutting off her attempt to speak. CC was frozen in horror as Jamie closed the door to her car. She watched helplessly as the love of her life started the car and drove off.

"What the hell was that all about?" Marissa demanded angrily from behind her. CC spun around and glared at the woman.

"That was the woman I love," CC spat out.

"What?" Marissa trembled in response. "I . . . I . . . didn't know."

"Maybe if you had listened to me just once tonight, you wouldn't have done something so asinine," CC fumed, the veins in her neck bulging as she spoke.

"Do you want me to explain things to her?" Marissa offered remorsefully.

"No," CC flared. "Stay away from her. Just go."

Marissa looked like a frightened rabbit before she made a mad dash to her car. CC stormed into her home and found Stevie standing there with a bewildered look on her face. "What the hell happened this time?" Stevie demanded.

"I swear I just thanked her for dinner, and the next thing I know, Marissa was trying to floss my teeth with her tongue," CC explained in exasperation.

"I hope you told her where to get off," Stevie snarled.

"I was about to when I saw Jamie standing there watching us," CC added as she flopped down onto the sofa.

"Oh no," Stevie groaned in sympathy.

"What am I going to do?" CC choked out, fighting against the tears threatening to spill.

Stevie just sat there in a stunned silence. "Why didn't Jamie let me explain?" CC suddenly asked, anger now overriding her sadness. "If she'd just waited and listened to me . . ."

"Hold on, Caitlin," Stevie said, cutting her off. "Give James a break on this one. She just caught you playing tonsil hockey with another woman."

"But I wasn't!" CC protested.

"I know that and you know that, but James only knows what she saw," Stevie explained in a soft comforting voice. "Come on, you're a cop. If you saw Jamie in the same situation, what would you think was going on?"

CC grumbled, knowing that her sister was right. She had to fix this and she had to fix it now. "What did Jamie say?" Stevie inquired carefully.

"Not much," CC said, the image of Jamie's face playing over in her mind. "She said she couldn't talk to me right now."

"That's good," Stevie said brightly.

"How is that good?" CC snapped.

"She didn't tell you to go to hell or shove whatever you want to say to her where the sun doesn't shine," Stevie offered as she placed a comforting hand on her older sibling's shoulder. "She's hurt but she still left the door open. She just can't handle talking to you right now."

"I need to talk to her," CC reasoned.

"She's at work; wait until she gets home," Stevie said in an effort to placate her sister.

"If she comes home," CC mumbled, realizing that in the past Jamie often sought comfort in the arms of another woman. CC felt the anger rise once again, only this time she wasn't certain whom she should be angry with. There was Marissa for acting like a total jackass. There was Jamie for not listening to her and jumping to conclusions. And there was, of course, herself for going out with Marissa in the first place.

"I need to see her," she said firmly as old demons fueled her fears. *'If Jamie hops into bed with another woman I don't think I can forgive or forget this time,'* her heart and her mind screamed. "Not this time," she hissed as her jaw locked firmly.

"What?" Stevie questioned.

"I have to see her," CC said in a strained voice. "I know her. I finally understand her and I can't let her think that I betrayed her. Because if she does, then she'll do something stupid."

"Such as?" Stevie asked in a fearful tone.

"Sleeping with someone who doesn't mean anything to her," CC explained dryly. "I won't go through that again."

"Good for you," Stevie responded with bravado. "But I don't think that's going to happen this time. Jamie is a bright woman and I think with everything that's happened in the past she'll listen to you once she calms down. But if she doesn't then you need to walk away."

"I know," CC admitted in a defeated tone. "No matter how much I love the girl, I can't start a relationship with someone who's going to run every time we have a little problem."

"You kissed someone else!" Stevie blurted out. "Look I understand it wasn't intentional but that is more than a little problem. Unwanted facial hair is a little problem. Seeing you making out with another woman is a catastrophe." CC glared at her sister who held up her hands in defense. "That's what she saw," Stevie explained quickly. "If it was me, I'd be pretty ticked off."

"So what am I supposed to do?" CC tried to think of just how she was going to get Jamie to listen to her.

"If you are so intent on seeing her before she gets home then do yourself a favor. Give it a couple of hours so both of you can calm down," Stevie explained softly. "Then go see her. She's at work. It's not like she'll be trolling the Emergency Room looking for a date."

"Fine," CC sighed in agreement. "Lend me your car. I'm not picking up my new one until Monday."

"Okay," Stevie said with relief. "Oh, and get her some flowers or something."

"Flowers?" CC said in bewilderment. "Where am I suppose to get flowers at this hour of the night?"

"Bring her something as a peace offering," Stevie said firmly.

"Somehow I don't think that Hallmark makes a card for this one." CC smiled slightly. " 'Sorry you saw me sucking face with another woman, but it isn't what you think.' "

"I don't know; they might," Stevie responded with a light chuckle.

CC glanced at her watch while her mind tried to make sense of the last half hour of her life. Stevie was right. She needed to find something to break the ice with Jamie. She only hoped that whatever she came up with wouldn't be tossed back in her face. CC decided that she should select something that at least wouldn't leave a scar if Jamie was angry enough to actually throw her peace offering at her.

Jamie was in a foul mood by the time she reached the hospital. She went straight to her locker and changed for her shift. Then she went to the ladies' room and checked her appearance. Just as she'd suspected, she looked like hell. Her eyes were puffy and red. "No wonder everyone stopped me to ask if I was all right," she grumbled as she washed her face. Once she looked slightly more human, she made her way to her director's office. She had asked him to stay late so she could talk to him. As she approached his office, she tried to get her mind to focus on her duties and not the sight of CC wrapped up in another woman's arms.

She just didn't understand it. Why would CC do something like that? "She wouldn't," she muttered to herself. Still the image was burned into her brain. "But she did," Jamie said heavily before knocking on Dr. Templeton's door. She took a calming breath as she heard his voice telling her to enter. "Jack," she greeted him, forcing her voice to take on a friendly tone.

"Are you all right?" the older man asked in concern as she took a seat in front of his desk.

"Fine," she lied. "Long day."

"Okay," he said as he sat behind his desk. Jamie knew by the older man's kindly tone that he didn't believe her. "So what's wrong?"

"Huh?" she stammered, not expecting the question.

"Something must be wrong for you to set up this meeting," he explained in a friendly tone. "Unless it's just my charming personality or boyish good looks."

Jamie laughed at the older man who was almost bald except for the white hair cropped closely to his ears. "Could be," she teased. "Actually I'm having a problem with one of my kids."

"Not doing their work load?" he inquired.

"No, it's more personal," Jamie began slowly, hoping that she was doing the right thing. "Simon Fisher has . . . well, at first I thought it was just a crush . . . but now it's become a problem."

Her boss shifted uncomfortably in his chair and furrowed his brow. "Tell me everything, "he said in a commanding tone as he took out a pad of paper and a pen. Jamie was suddenly uncomfortable and her chest tightened. "Jamie?" Jack offered in a comforting tone.

"It started a few weeks ago," Jamie said slowly. "He asked me to join him for a drink. I declined, explaining that it was unprofessional. He persisted but there was nothing about his persistence that bothered me at the time. I explained that I'm seeing someone when I realized that his interest went beyond friendship. As time went on, he continued to invite me out for social meetings. I declined each time. I tried handling the situation in a friendly manner; I tried handling it in a direct manner; nothing seemed to work. I thought I could handle it myself; it didn't seem very serious. That is, until he showed up at my home late one evening."

"He what?" Jack blurted out. "Sorry," he said, quickly regaining his composure. "Did you give him the address or invite him over?"

"No," Jamie stated, trying to maintain her calm professional manner. She knew that Jack had to ask but the question infuriated her just the same. "I told him to go away and he wasn't to invade my privacy ever again. The other night he called me on my cell phone and, no, I never gave him the number. It was the last thing I would have expected of him. My companion arrived when he was at my door and they got into an argument."

"That must have surprised him." Jack chuckled.

"Unfortunately, she's a cop," Jamie explained carefully as Jack winced.

"Let me guess. The police are looking into this now." Jack sighed heavily.

"I'm sorry, Jack." Jamie apologized, knowing that the police looking into the activities of one of their residents was not going to look good.

"Don't apologize, Jamie," Jack said in a fatherly tone. "You've explained that you are not interested in a social relationship, and he's met your partner. That alone should have given him a clue that he isn't your type."

"There's more," Jamie added shyly. "Last night someone broke my living room window while I was out. The police don't know who it was, but given Simon's past actions it doesn't look good."

Jack rubbed his brow in a weary motion. "I should suspend the bugger, but I'm afraid it will set him off," Jack said in a tired voice. "As of this moment he's reassigned to Warner and I'll have him moved to the dayshift. It's not fair to those who have earned that spot but I don't want him near you. Is he on the schedule for tonight?"

"Yes," Jamie responded.

"The moment he walks in the door send him to me. I'll wait and have a chat with him," Jack explained. "I'm afraid you'll be a little shorthanded tonight."

"Maybe he'll finally get the message," Jamie muttered with some sense of relief. "Thank you, Jack," she said as she stood.

Later she saw the pesky Dr. Fisher storm out of Jack's office. By the way he blew past her in a huff, she knew he wasn't happy about his reassignment. "Most people would be thrilled with being moved to days," she muttered nervously. Jamie went about her duties and tried to ignore the uneasy feeling she had regarding Dr. Fisher. She was also trying to block out the nagging questions that were haunting her about what she had seen in the parking lot at home.

"Okay, Mrs. Henderson, let me see if I can explain this one more time," Jamie began wearily as she tried to get across to the seemingly intelligent patient that suppositories weren't suppose to be taken orally. The woman was very upset when the prescribed medication failed to work. Jamie almost fell over when she realized that the woman was placing them in the wrong orifice.

"Dr. Jameson?" Stella said cautiously as she stuck her head in the exam room. "You have a visitor."

Jamie's stomach clenched slightly at Stella's news. She feared that it was Dr. Fisher coming back to bother her. "I'll be right out," Jamie responded in a tense voice. Then a sudden thought brightened her dreary mind. "Would you mind helping Mrs. Henderson?" she asked as she blinked brightly at the nurse who was now giving her a murderous gaze. *'Please,'* she mouthed in desperation.

"I'd be happy to," Stella responded sarcastically.

Jamie raced quickly towards Stella, shoving Mrs. Henderson's chart into her hands. She was tempted to do a happy dance as she fled the room, leaving Stella alone to deal with the confused woman. "Sweet freedom." She sighed happily. Then she braced herself for whoever her mysterious visitor might be. Slowly she walked towards the nurse's station.

Her heart skipped a beat when she spotted the familiar leggy brunette chatting with the staff. She smiled before she remembered that she was very angry with this woman. Jamie's green eyes narrowed as she approached CC. "Caitlin," she greeted her coldly.

"Can we go somewhere and talk?" CC inquired nervously.

Jamie curled her lips and pondered her options for a moment. "Fine," she finally agreed, knowing there must be some reasonable explanation for her actions if CC traveled all the way down there in the middle of the night. She was praying that she wasn't simply fooling herself.

She motioned for CC to follow her as she stepped outside into the cool night air. She turned back to find CC shuffling nervously in place, a small white paper bag held tightly against her chest. Jamie eyed her suspiciously. Suddenly the sight of the tall policewoman standing there, afraid to speak, struck her as humorous.

"Here," CC finally blurted out as she shoved the paper bag into Jamie's hands.

Jamie accepted the ice-cold package in confusion. Carefully she peeked inside. She smiled as she extracted a cold pint of ice cream. "Ben and Jerry's Vanilla Carmel Fudge," she said excitedly. "Is this a bribe?" she added quickly as she found a pair of brilliant blue eyes pleading with her.

"Yes," CC stammered. "Well, not a bribe really. More like a peace offering in hopes that you'll listen to what I have to tell you."

"This better be good," Jamie warned her. "Because catching you in a lip lock with another woman is going to take a lot more than my favorite flavor of ice cream for me to forgive you."

"True," CC conceded. "But before you go ballistic, let me explain. First off, I wasn't kissing her."

"Excuse me?" Jamie responded in a deep threatening tone.

"She was kissing me," CC explained quickly. "I was just about to tell her off when I saw you."

Jamie searched CC's eyes for any hint of deceit. She relaxed when she found nothing but sincerity staring back at her. "Go on," Jamie encouraged her.

"Marissa is an old flame," CC continued in a more confident tone. "But that was a long time ago and it was very brief. I've been completely honest with her about not wanting to continue things. I told her tonight at dinner that I'm seeing someone. Unfortunately, Marissa seems to be living in her own little world."

"Okay," Jamie responded slowly.

"Okay?" CC blinked in surprise.

"Okay," Jamie repeated with a shy smile.

"That's it?" CC grumbled.

"What were you expecting? The Spanish Inquisition?" Jamie chuckled as she enjoyed CC's discomfort.

"No but . . ." CC protested.

"Look, you can't help it if you're a hottie," Jamie said, cutting her off.

"I am not," CC groaned in amusement.

"I swear you never look in the mirror," Jamie said softly as she leaned over and brushed her lips against the taller woman's.

"There's something else I need to tell you," CC said softly as she wrapped her arms around Jamie's body. The blonde instantly leaned into her lover's touch. "What I started to say before you drove off was that I never stopped . . ." CC's words were cut off as Jamie's beeper blared loudly.

"Damn," Jamie spat out as she ripped the offending object off her waistband. She checked it quickly, her lips curling into a snarl. "I have to go."

"That's all right. This really isn't the setting I wanted to tell you what I have to say," CC said with a coy smile.

"I'll see you tonight," Jamie promised. She kissed CC quickly before rushing back into the hospital. Jamie's heart couldn't stop pounding as she contemplated if CC was about to tell her what she was hoping to hear?

CC heard the tentative knocking and sprang to her feet. She'd fallen asleep on the sofa after returning from the hospital. Her blue eyes tried to focus on her surroundings. She turned around to see a smirking Jamie standing out on the deck. CC stretched out her long frame and listened to the sounds of her back popping into place. "Damn, I hate falling asleep on the couch," she grumbled as she stumbled towards the back door.

CC unlocked the glass door and slid it open. "Good morning, Dr. Jameson." She yawned, quickly covering her mouth so she wouldn't overpower Jamie with her morning breath.

"What happened to you?" Jamie asked in amusement as she stepped into the townhouse.

"Fell asleep on the coach," CC responded with a scowl. "Now I feel like a mutant pretzel."

"Poor baby," Jamie cooed as she placed her bag on the floor and rubbed CC's stomach.

"Hmm," CC murmured as she relaxed into Jamie's touch. "It's my own fault. I was trying to wait up for you."

"Goober," Jamie grunted as she swatted CC's stomach playfully.

"Ouch!" CC exclaimed as she pouted.

"Big baby," Jamie teased her.

"Why are you coming in the back?" CC questioned her suddenly, thinking that it was a good idea.

"I had to get something from my place," Jamie explained shyly.

CC gave the smaller woman a curious glance. "Okay." CC shrugged as Jamie blushed slightly. "You're so cute when you blush," CC taunted the doctor who was once again rubbing CC's stomach. "Could you keep doing that?" CC inquired thoughtfully.

"Forever," Jamie responded softly as her hand drifted below CC's tank top.

CC smiled at the comment and captured Jamie's hand in her own. She raised the smaller hand to her mouth and brushed her lips against Jamie's quivering palm. "That too," she murmured against Jamie's skin. "Actually, I was talking about coming in the back door." Her jaw dropped as Jamie began to wiggle her fair eyebrows suggestively. CC squeaked in response and Jamie broke out in laughter. "My, you are in a feisty mood tonight," CC said as a brilliant smile emerged on her lips.

"I can't help it," Jamie said with a mock frown. "You see, I had this terrible fight with my girlfriend."

"Sounds awful," CC responded in a rich tone as she tilted her head down and began to nibble on Jamie's neck. Jamie moaned in response as CC lost herself in the taste of the young doctor's skin. "Tell me about it," CC said hotly in the blonde's ear before she suckled her earlobe in her mouth. Jamie whimpered with desire; the sound of her need sent shivers up and down CC's spine.

CC's hands took on a life of their own as one cupped Jamie's firm backside and the other slipped up to the gentle swell of her breasts. Her thighs began to tremble as Jamie's body melted into her own. A sudden hardness pressed into her hip, startling her. At first she thought it was Jamie's beeper but there was something else. "What the . .?" she asked in confusion.

Jamie pressed her fingers against CC's lips, stilling any further questions. "Are you?" Jamie inquired in a nervous tone. Her emerald eyes had grown dark and serious. CC blinked in confusion. "Are you my girlfriend?" Jamie's voice trembled slightly as she spoke. Gently CC removed Jamie's fingers from her quivering lips and tenderly kissed each digit.

She watched as Jamie's eyes grew darker, only this time they were filled with desire. "I never stopped . . ." CC began slowly as Jamie pulled her hand away and reached into her pocket. CC swallowed hard, knowing that she needed to say the one constant thought that had lain in her heart since the day she had first lost Jamie.

"Jamie . . ." she continued as the blonde removed something from her pocket. "I never stopped loving you," CC finally confessed as Jamie took her by the hand. She felt the coolness of metal being placed in the palm of her hand. CC looked down at her hand in confusion. Her heart raced as she saw the tarnished brass ring resting there. CC opened her mouth to speak but was unable to form the words.

"I've always kept it close to me," Jamie confessed in a determined tone. "At times I hated myself for being such a sap. Now I know that I was meant to find you again. I love you, Caitlin." CC fought the tears that were threatening to spill down her cheeks. She placed the brass ring back in Jamie's hand and closed the doctor's fingers over it. Then she raised Jamie's hand and placed it against the doctor's chest. She smiled as she felt the rapid beating of Jamie's heart.

"Well, I see you two have made up," Stevie snorted as she entered the room. CC growled in disgust.

"She brought me ice cream," Jamie piped in cheerfully as she tucked the ring back into the front pocket of her slacks.

"Ice cream?" Stevie groaned in disbelief.

"Hey, it was Ben and Jerry's," Jamie explained enthusiastically.

"Oh well, there you have it," Stevie grumbled as she rolled her dark brown eyes.

CC and Jamie yawned simultaneously and then grinned at one another. "I need to get cleaned up," Jamie said wearily. "As much as I would love to continue what we started, I think that tonight has been too much for both of us."

"Sorry," CC apologized sheepishly as she yawned once again.

"No worries, stud muffin," Jamie teased her. "Go to bed. I just need to take a shower and I'll be right there." Jamie reached up and brushed her lips against CC's cheek. "All I need tonight is for you to hold me and to wake up in your arms," Jamie whispered in her ear.

CC ran her fingers through Jamie's short blonde hair and nodded in agreement. Jamie shuffled off to the bathroom as CC watched the gentle sway of her hips. The spirit was definitely willing but the emotional roller coaster she had endured that evening had taken its toll. The policewoman diverted her attention to find her younger sister grinning at her. "What?" She scowled.

"Nothing." Stevie chuckled as she held up her hands defensively. "So you worked things out?"

"We're in love," CC gushed like a schoolgirl.

"No!" Stevie exclaimed sarcastically.

"Brat," CC growled.

"Jerk," Stevie shot back before she smiled up at CC boldly. "I'm happy for you," she added sincerely. "Now go to bed . . . stud muffin." CC sneered as Stevie rolled her eyes once again.

"Thanks," CC said softly before wrapping her sister up in a warm hug.

Feeling as if the weight of the world had been lifted off her shoulders, CC pranced into her bedroom. She climbed under the covers and smiled contentedly. Somehow knowing that she was waiting for Jamie to join her made the night seem calmer, the bed seem warmer, the mattress more comfortable . . . "Man, I've got it bad." She laughed at herself as she snuggled deeper into the mattress. Her smile faded as the pestering thoughts of reality invaded her senses. "I'm going to have to tell Jamie," she muttered as her mind focused on the very real danger Jamie might be in.

"You're going have to tell Jamie what?" Jamie's voice startled CC. The blonde chuckled as she crawled into the bed and snuggled up against CC's warm body.

"Jeez!" CC exclaimed as Jamie's cool hands slid up under her T-shirt and came to rest on her stomach. "Did you stop off at the freezer on your way in here?"

"Some big tough cop you are." Jamie snorted in amusement. "Tell me what you're hiding from me or my feet are going to join the party," Jamie threatened her as she ran the cold appendages up and down CC's long legs.

CC yelped as she tried to squirm out of the blonde's grasp. "Okay, I give up," CC squealed as Jamie held her down while placing her cold body parts in some very strategic locations.

"Sissy." Jamie laughed as she pinned CC to the mattress. "Now talk," Jamie demanded as her nipples brushed against CC's.

The brunette inhaled sharply from the contact. "Are you sure you want to talk?" CC offered in a breathy tone as her hips swayed slightly against Jamie's body.

She watched as the blonde's eyes fluttered shut and she began to bite down on her bottom lip. Jamie shook her head furiously. "Yes," she said firmly as her eyes snapped open. "No more secrets."

"Let go of me," CC responded as she nodded in agreement.

"No way," Jamie responded wickedly. "First tell me what you're hiding."

"I'm worried about your safety," CC explained in a solemn tone. Jamie stared down at her in confusion. "Simon Fisher. I think he was the one who broke your window, and I suspect that . . ." She hesitated, knowing she couldn't reveal any details of the investigation. " . . . I'm just worried that this might not be the last of it."

"I agree," Jamie replied quietly. "I've had him reassigned. He will be on the day shift for the rest of his rotation. My supervisor knows everything, including the police report."

"How did he take it?" CC asked fearfully.

"Not well," Jamie responded with a heavy sigh. "Jack, that's my boss, has contacted security to keep on an eye on him. I never wanted things to get this far. I mean, what if I'm wrong? But frankly Simon is beginning to frighten me."

CC simply nodded her head in response, not trusting her voice at the moment. She was more than a little frightened when it came to Dr. Fisher.

"Now is that it?" Jamie demanded playfully as she clasped CC's wrists a little more firmly. CC trembled as she watched her lover's eyes darken with desire.

"Yes?" the policewoman squeaked out.

"Good," Jamie purred as she pressed her body into CC's. The brunette could feel her lover's desire painting her thigh. "Now where do you keep your handcuffs?"

"Huh?" was the only response CC was capable of at that moment as her clit pulsated in a steady rhythm.

"Handcuffs, Officer," Jamie demanded as she began to trace CC's jaw line with her tongue and then the blonde licked her way up to CC's ear. "Do you want to play?" Jamie offered hotly in her ear.

"Top drawer of the nightstand," CC consented as she wrapped her long legs around Jamie's waist.

"Don't move," Jamie instructed her. She shifted her hold so that she now had CC's wrists pinned above her head with one hand while she frantically searched the nightstand with the other.

"Don't forget the key," CC cautioned her, recalling how embarrassing that could be. Of course, she wasn't going to get into that now. Jamie's body squirmed against her own as she extracted the small leather case from the drawer.

The doctor opened the case and removed the pair of silver handcuffs and held them up triumphantly as a positively evil grin crossed her lips. A deep growl rumbled in CC's chest as Jamie opened the cuffs. The clicking sound caused CC's breathing to become ragged as Jamie released her and placed one cuff on her wrist. CC stared at Jamie intently as she gently looped the free cuff through a rail on the headboard. "Okay?" Jamie inquired softly as she clicked the second around CC's other wrist.

"Oh yeah," CC reassured her, knowing that she could easily slip her thin wrists out of the loose restraints.

CC's pulse was racing as Jamie nudged her long legs apart and settled her smaller body between her thighs. Jamie traced her lips slowly as CC watched her every movement. The blonde reached down to the hem of her oversized T-shirt and quickly yanked the garment up off her firm body. "Ugh!" CC cried out as she tried to reach out to capture Jamie's breasts.

The blonde leaned forward, pressing her breasts into CC's face and reached behind CC's head to tighten the handcuffs. The silver rings weren't tight enough to inflict pain, but CC could no longer slip her wrists free. Unable to touch her lover with her hands, CC nuzzled her face deeper into her lover's cleavage and began to trace the valley with her tongue. "No you don't," Jamie chastised her as she pulled away.

The doctor captured CC's face between her hands and placed a searing kiss on her lips. CC moaned deeply as Jamie's tongue entered her mouth. The policewoman struggled against her restraints as Jamie explored her mouth thoroughly. Suddenly Jamie pulled away, placed a firm hand on CC's broad shoulder, and gently lowered her back onto the bed.

CC's eyes widened as she stared up at Jamie; her half-naked lover was clad only in a pair of dark emerald panties. CC whimpered as she watched Jamie cup her own breasts and began to roll her rose-colored nipples between her fingers. Her legs parted even further as she felt her wetness growing. Jamie continued to tease her nipples until they were fully erect.

Jamie's eyes burned into CC's as one of her hands began to slowly drift down her firm abdomen. CC yanked once again against her restraints as Jamie's hand dipped below the waistband of her panties. Jamie shifted her body so that she as now straddling CC's waist. The brunette could feel Jamie's desire pressing against her stomach as her lover began to stroke herself. "I want to see," CC pleaded as Jamie's hand increased its motion. Jamie shook her head as CC tried to press her thigh against Jamie's center.

Jamie laughed wickedly as she lifted her body just out of CC's reach. She leaned over CC's body while she continued to pleasure herself. CC released a frustrated growl as she tried in vain to reach her lover. "Please?" CC pleaded as Jamie's breasts swayed dangerously close to her lips. Jamie panted as her hand increased its sensual rhythm. Once again Jamie leaned back so that she was straddling CC's waist.

She removed her hand from the warmth of her center and brought her fingers up to CC's lips. The policewoman could smell Jamie's arousal and she lifted her head so that she could capture Jamie's fingers in her mouth. She growled once again as Jamie pulled her fingers away just as CC was about to taste her wetness. Jamie smirked once again as she began to paint one of her nipples with her own wetness. "Do you want to taste me?" Jamie inquired innocently.

"Yes," CC hissed in a tone that reflected how silly she thought the question was; Jamie simply quirked an eyebrow at CC. "Please?" CC added in a pleading voice as she felt her own desire threaten to overwhelm her. Jamie smiled in response as she lowered her body.

The blonde cupped her own breast and offered it up to CC's eager lips. The brunette moaned once again as her tongue flickered across Jamie's erect nipple. The taste of Jamie's wetness filled CC's senses as she suckled her nipple into her mouth. She struggled against the restraints as she continued to devour Jamie's nipple. She felt her lover's center rocking against her stomach as she began to pinch one of CC's nipples.

CC's head fell back as Jamie moaned and thrust wildly against CC's body. "Come for me," CC begged her lover.

"Not yet," Jamie panted in her ear. The feel of Jamie's hot breath fueled CC's desire. Jamie's hips stilled as CC tried to raise her body in response. CC was whimpering once again as Jamie's tongue dipped into her ear. Her stomach clenched as Jamie raised her shirt and began to kiss her way down her body.

CC's body arched as Jamie's mouth suckled one of her breasts and her hand slowly tortured its twin. CC could feel her entire being pulsate as Jamie teased her nipple with her teeth and her tongue. She lifted her body as far as she could in an effort to press her breast deeper into her lover's mouth. CC was on the brink of losing all control as Jamie turned her attention to her other breast.

CC's body thrashed against the mattress as Jamie continued to move from one breast to the other and then back again. "Please!" CC screamed urgently as her need for release reached the brink.

"Please what?" Jamie taunted her as she began to kiss her way down CC's body. "Tell me," Jamie demanded against her sweat-soaked body as she licked and tasted her way down to the waistband of her boxer shorts.

CC was ready to pass out as she looked down at her lover who was slowly pulling her boxer shorts over to her hips. "Tell me," Jamie repeated playfully before dipping her tongue into CC's navel.

"Please, Jamie." CC groaned desperately as she felt her shorts being lowered further down her body.

"Tell me," Jamie taunted her as she pulled the boxers off CC's quivering body.

"Fuck me," CC begged in a shaky tone as Jamie tossed her shorts across the darkened bedroom.

"Is that what you want?" Jamie asked in a torturous tone as she began to lick her way up CC's endless legs.

"Yes!" CC hissed as Jamie kissed the back of her knees. She was about to expand upon her demand when Jamie's lips caressed the inside of her thighs.

"Say it again," Jamie insisted as she licked CC's overflowing desire from her trembling thighs.

"Fuck me," CC whimpered as she felt her lover's breath caress the damp curls of her dark triangle.

She felt her swollen nether lips being parted as Jamie's tongue dipped into her wetness. "I love you," CC choked out as she fought the climax that was threatening to rip through her body. She could hear Jamie's murmurs of pleasure as she pulled her throbbing clit into the warmth of her mouth. CC's body arched sharply. She could feel Jamie steadying her body with one hand while she entered her center with the fingers on her free hand.

CC gripped at the chain of the handcuffs as Jamie filled her. Her body thrust wildly and Jamie held onto her while she plunged in and out of her wetness. She felt Jamie fill her deeper and harder as her ears began to buzz and the room began to spin. CC knew she was screaming as the orgasm tore through her, yet she was unaware of what she was saying.

CC's mind went blank as Jamie continued to pleasure her. She was dimly aware of Jamie's teeth grazing her clit as her fingers maintained their wild rhythm. Once again Jamie tried to hold her body while it convulsed in ecstasy. CC's vision was blurred as her lover continued pleasuring her. "Stop," she choked out. She felt Jamie's mouth and hand still as her body collapsed against the mattress.

Jamie rested her head on CC's trembling stomach as her fingers remained deep inside her center. CC rode out the last tremors of passion while Jamie kissed her stomach. "Jesus, Mary and Joseph," CC panted.

"What did you just say?" The blonde laughed as she raised her head and carefully slipped her fingers out of CC's wetness.

"I have no idea," CC confessed as her lover climbed her body. "Undo these," CC requested as she tugged on the handcuffs.

"If I must," Jamie said with a reluctant sigh as she leaned across CC's still quivering form to find the key. CC smiled as she heard the distinctive click of the cuffs being opened. She sat up slightly and rubbed her wrists as Jamie deposited the handcuffs onto the nightstand.

"It didn't hurt, did it?" Jamie inquired with concern. CC shook her head, letting her lover know that she was fine. She pulled her sweat soaked T-shirt off her body.

"So you want to play doctor now?" CC suggested eagerly as she pulled Jamie up onto her lap. Before the blonde could respond, CC flipped her over onto the bed and began to suckle the blonde's neck. The desperate whimpers her lover released encouraged the policewoman who was already lowering Jamie's passion-soaked panties.

CC found herself moaning urgently as she dipped her fingers into her lover's wetness. The abundance of her lover's passion coated her hand and CC knew that Jamie needed her now. She leaned back and quickly removed Jamie's underwear. The blonde opened herself up to CC's touch. The brunette happily accepted the invitation as she pressed her fingers against her lover's center.

CC captured Jamie's nipple in her mouth; she could still taste her musky desire as she entered her lover. She felt the walls of Jamie's warm, wet center grip her fingers, telling her that Jamie was already on the edge. She suckled Jamie's nipple furiously as she plunged in and out of Jamie's wetness while her thumb teased the blonde's clit.

Jamie's body rocked wildly beneath her as CC made love to her with wild abandonment. Soon Jamie was wrapping her legs around CC's body as she cried out in ecstasy. CC leaned over her lover's trembling body as she continued to wiggle her fingers inside of her. Jamie captured her wrist firmly and stilled her movements. "Baby I can't. I already did when I was pleasing you," Jamie confessed with a deep blush.

CC released a throaty chuckle as she removed her fingers from the warmth of Jamie's passion. She lay down beside Jamie and wrapped her in her arms. "I thought you were tired?" CC teased her still quivering lover.

"Second wind," Jamie choked out as CC tightened her hold on the smaller woman.

CC smiled contentedly as she relaxed into the feel of Jamie's body in her arms. Their heats beat in unison as they drifted off to sleep.

CC awoke in a blissful mood, the weight of Jamie's naked body lying on top of her own. She smiled as she ran her hands down Jamie's exposed back. She loved the feel of the blonde's skin caressing her fingers. She felt alive just by touching the young doctor. She nestled her nose in the blonde hair resting on her chest. CC drank in the scent; the scent that was distinctly Jamie refueled her desires. CC had always possessed a healthy libido but there was something about Jamie that drove her completely insane.

CC sighed deeply, thinking that since it was Sunday morning the couple was finally awarded the opportunity to simply relax. As the delightful thought occurred to her, the sound of a ringing telephone disrupted her bliss. "Kill it," Jamie murmured against her skin.

"You don't know that it's for me," CC reasoned, knowing full well that the ringing could only mean that their bliss was about to come to an end.

"Right," Jamie growled as her head snapped up.

CC swallowed as she found herself trapped in a fiery emerald gaze. "We had sex. Now all hell is going to break loose," Jamie grumbled. "Come on. You have a gun. Go shoot the telephone then climb back into bed with me," Jamie pleaded with a heart-wrenching pout. CC laughed as she watched the blonde push her bottom lip out even further and begin to blink her eyes that were now filled with a forlorn expression.

A soft tapping on the bedroom door invoked a deep scowl from both women. "Yeah, Stevie; I'm coming," CC muttered bitterly.

"No, but you would be if you'd simply shot the telephone," Jamie griped as she rolled off CC's body and buried her face in the pillow.

"Maybe it's nothing important," CC offered as she climbed out of bed. In her heart she knew that Jamie was right.

"Hah!" Jamie spat out as she burrowed her body deeper under the bedcovers.

CC simply pulled on a pair of sweatpants and tossed on a filthy T-shirt before making her way out of the bedroom. She could hear Jamie grumbling into the pillow as she clicked the bedroom door shut. She went into the kitchen for the telephone and found Stevie leaning against the kitchen counter, yawning loudly. "Did Emma keep you awake, Sis?" CC inquired innocently as she picked up the telephone receiver. She was unprepared for the pair of angry brown eyes that shot up and glared at her. Suddenly CC was fully aware that it wasn't her niece that had kept her sister awake all night. "Sorry," she offered sheepishly as she quickly snuck out of the kitchen. "Calloway," she barked into the telephone, keeping her back to her sister.

She could feel her sister's eyes boring a hole into her back as she spoke with Max. She got both good news and bad. All of the lab, RMV, and forensic reports were finally ready; whatever bureaucratic snafus had been holding them up were out of the way. The bad news was that it was Sunday and both detectives wanted to spend their day off with their respective families. "That's great! Keep us off the computers all week and get everything done on the weekend. Yeah, that'll help the budget," she growled. "I can't wait until this woman is out of office."

"Hey, I didn't vote for her," Max noted.

"No one did," CC said in exasperation. She hadn't liked the acting governor before she was moved up the food chain. Then, after being in office for less then an hour, the woman announced that she would never sign a bill that would allow same-sex unions. CC despised the woman.

"We could wait until tomorrow," Max suggested sympathetically.

"No," CC said with a scowl. "I want to wrap this up as soon as possible. I won't be able to sleep until I know that Jamie's safe." She heard her sister snort indignantly behind her. CC ignored Stevie's commentary and returned to the conversation with her partner. "If everything adds up to what we think it will, I need to talk to the Captain as soon as possible. I'm going to have to explain why I can't go anywhere near the prime suspect."

"Rousseau won't be a happy camper," Max grunted.

"Can't be helped," CC explained as she felt the weight of the situation bearing down upon her. "If Fisher is the guy, and we don't go to Rousseau now, then Fisher could possibly weasel out of this. I'll go down to the station today, and I'll meet with you first thing in the morning."

"You and Jamie are picking up your new car in the morning," Stevie quickly reminded her.

"Right. Sorry, Max. I can't get in until after noon," CC explained quickly. "I'm picking my new car up at the dealership."

"No kidding?" Max asked. "Well, it's about time you got rid of that piece of sh . . .."

"Hey!" CC cut him off indignantly as Max laughed heartily.

"See you tomorrow, Calloway, unless you come across something urgent today," Max concluded as they ended the conversation.

Once she had hung up the telephone, CC tried to sneak away before she caught any flack from Stevie. "What in the hell were the two of you doing last night?" Steve demanded loudly. CC froze in her tracks. The absurdity of the situation suddenly struck the policewoman as funny, and she decided to give as good as she got.

CC swallowed hard before regaining her composure. She turned to her younger sibling and curled her lips into a cocky smirk as she raised a single eyebrow triumphantly. "Do you really want to know?" she asked in a rich tone. Stevie seemed suddenly flustered as she grimaced at the question.

"God no," Stevie spat out emphatically as she shuddered in disgust. "I for one will be happy when you wrap up this investigation and the two of you can start having sex at Jamie's place."

"Oh, we've already done that," CC quipped proudly.

"Eww." Stevie blanched as she covered her ears. "TMI!"

"Just what are you teasing your poor sister about now?" Jamie inquired in a sleepy voice as she shuffled into the room wrapped in nothing but the blanket from the bed.

"Stevie heard us making love last night," CC explained flatly.

"Oh," Jamie responded with a loud yawn as she snuggled up against CC's body.

"CC?" Stevie sputtered.

"Oh pshaw," Jamie scoffed as she burrowed her head deeper into CC's body. "I had to listen to you and the lady contractor acting like a couple of sailors on shore leave."

"Yuck!" CC and Stevie groaned in unison.

"Now that we've all shared . . ." Jamie yawned as she wrapped her arms around CC's body and snuggled even closer. "Can we go back to bed?"

"I think you're just trying to suck all the heat out of my body," CC teased the burrowing blonde.

"Can I help it if you're like a portable Bunsen burner?" Jamie yawned as CC wrapped her long arms around the blonde's slender body. "Bed, please," Jamie pleaded in a weary tone.

"Sorry, Honey - duty calls," CC apologized as she pulled Jamie closer to her and placed a gentle kiss on the top of her head.

Emma's wails could be heard over the baby monitor. "Speaking of duty calling." Stevie sighed as she headed upstairs to her daughter.

"Why don't you crawl back into bed?" CC suggested as Jamie's emerald eyes fluttered shut and she nestled her head against CC's chest.

"Don't want to move," Jamie protested sleepily. "Want to stay like this forever."

CC chuckled lightly as she allowed herself to relax in the feel of Jamie's body resting against her own. "Hmm," she sighed contentedly as she ran her fingers through Jamie's short blonde hair. When she felt Jamie's breathing even out, she knew that her lover was about to fall asleep in her arms. "Come on, Sweet Pea," she whispered softly in Jamie's ear. "You need to get back into bed, and I need to take a shower."

Jamie mumbled something incoherent before stepping away slightly. "I'll make you coffee." The blonde yawned as she blinked her eyes rapidly in an effort to wake herself up.

"That's okay." CC smiled in return as she cupped Jamie's cheek with the palm of her hand. Jamie smiled as she leaned into CC's touch. Jamie rested her smaller hand on top of CC's.

"Go hop into the shower, and I'll make the coffee," Jamie encouraged her. "You haven't had any sleep either. I don't want you falling asleep behind the wheel." CC opened her mouth to protest, but Jamie spun her around and started to push her towards the downstairs bathroom. "No arguments. Since you'll be driving my car, I rather you were alert. Now get into that shower, Officer. Because the sooner you get there, the sooner you can get your cute ass back here," Jamie asserted more firmly as she swatted CC squarely on her backside.

CC yelped as her lover's hand made contact with her back end. "My, aren't we a pushy little thing this morning," CC responded playfully as Jamie shoved her into the bathroom. "Fine . . . I'm going." CC laughed as she turned to her lover. "Now get into that kitchen, woman, and fix me some coffee," she quipped before quickly ducking into the bathroom and locking the door behind her. She heard the knob turning as Jamie laughed on the other side.

"Just you wait." Jamie taunted her.

CC took her time in the shower, allowing the warm spray to slowly awaken her tired body. Making love with Jamie made her feel alive. It was strange to feel complete satisfaction and a constant yearning for more. She smiled, thinking that she was truly blessed for finding Jamie again. She finished her shower and dried herself before wrapping herself in a large towel and making a mad dash to her bedroom. As she pranced across the living room, she knew Jamie was watching her every move.

CC dressed casually in jeans and a light sweater and then she slid her gun into its holster. As she turned to leave the room, she felt as if she was forgetting something. When she spied her handcuffs resting on the nightstand, she blushed as she realized what was missing from her wardrobe. She bit back her laughter as she snatched up the leather case and the cuffs before walking into the outer room.

She found her sister and Jamie sipping coffee in the kitchen surrounded by a delightful aroma. Both women were now more suitably dressed in lounge pants and T-shirts; they ignored her as they watched Emma trying to stick her foot into her mouth. "I made you some eggs," Jamie said as she looked up with a smile.

"Thanks," CC said with surprise. "That was quick."

"I learned to make meals quickly when I was an resident," Jamie explained as she slid a plate of scrambled eggs and toast over to CC. She then moved quickly to pour a fresh cup of coffee for CC. "Here you go," Jamie offered as she began to sip her own coffee.

"Thank you," CC said warmly as she absently started folding up her handcuffs so she could put them in their case.

Jamie's eyes widened and she began to choke on her coffee. "Jamie?" CC said with concern as Jamie rushed over to the sink and spit her coffee out.

"I'm fine," Jamie got out as she cleared her throat and returned to the conversation.

"Are you sure?" CC continued as she finished putting her handcuffs in their case. She didn't stop to think about what she was doing since the action was so routine.

"Why do you have your cuffs out?" Stevie asked.

CC's movements halted as she suddenly realized what had caused Jamie's strange reaction. "No reason," CC lied as she quickly snapped the holder onto her belt. Stevie stared at her with an odd expression. Her eyes then moved to Jamie and then back again.

"Oh gross," Stevie choked out as her face screwed up in a most unnatural expression.

"What?" CC shot back innocently. Jamie once again spit her coffee into the sink as she began to laugh hysterically.

CC rubbed her temples as Wayne explained his findings in great length. "In English please, Wayne," she pleaded wearily, tired of his long dissertation on how he had compiled everything and the computer jargon. Of course, he felt a need to explain all the terms to her in great detail. "I just want to know who was parked where, and when they left the garage," she implored him.

"I made you a chart," he said sheepishly as he peered over his thick black plastic-framed glasses.

She rolled her eyes in exasperation as he handed her a very detailed chart showing who was parked where and when they punched in and out of the garage. She bit back the urge to spew a litany of harsh comments at the little man who definitely needed to spend more time outside of his tiny lab. "Thank you," she said sweetly as a blush spread from his neck up to what was left of his hairline.

She peered at the chart and was instantly surprised that the car parked next to Sandra's was not Dr. Fisher's. But his BMW had been parked a few cars down. The vehicle in question belonged to an Ellen Murdock who, according to Wayne's chart, exited the garage exactly one minute prior to Dr. Fisher. "Now that is interesting," she mumbled. "Wayne, I need a print out from the RMV for Ellen Murdock."

"Way ahead of you." Wayne beamed proudly as he shuffled through his stacks of paperwork and handed her the requested item.

CC smiled as he proudly handed her a sheet of paper that contained Ellen's address, date of birth, height, and anything thing else she would require. Her smile vanished and her heart lurched when she looked at Ellen's picture. The woman bore a stronger resemblance to Jamie than Sandra did. "I don't like this." She gulped. She placed the sheet down and steadied her nerves. "Okay, what about the background checks?" Her voice shook slightly as she addressed Wayne.

"Nothing outstanding," Wayne explained quickly. "The usual misdemeanors, domestic violence, parking tickets and so on. But I did do a nationwide scan since Boylston is a teaching hospital and people come from all over the country. I stumbled across something that I think you might be interested in," he explained as he handed a stack of printouts to her. "This one," he explained as he handed over a single report that he had carefully separated from the rest. "It kind of stuck out."

CC scanned the computer printout and felt her heart stutter in fear. To the naked eye it appeared to be nothing, the charges had been dropped. But it was who it was for that peeked CC's interest. "What time is it in San Diego?" she inquired absently.

"Just after nine a.m. They're three hours behind us," Wayne answered. "Here's the number."

"Good call, Wayne," CC praised the smaller man. "Assault charges. Interesting, Dr. Fisher."

CC quickly began to dial the telephone. After jumping through hoops to get authorization to make the long distance call, she was patched through. She said a silent prayer that someone involved with the case was available on Sunday morning so she wouldn't need to call back. After a series of transfers she was greeted by a gruff voice that sounded as if it had been exposed to unfiltered cigarettes for far too many years.

"Detective Brooks?" CC began cheerfully. "This is Detective Calloway from Boylston Mass. If you have a few moments, I'd like to ask you a few questions regarding an old case of yours."

"Anything to help out, despite what the Sox just did to our boys," he teased with a heavy cough.

"Oh, you can't blame us for the shape the Padres are in," CC countered. The man coughed while he laughed once again. *'Jesus, Dude! You really need to quit smoking before you cough up a lung,'* CC noted in disgust. "It's an assault case from six years ago . . ." she began carefully.

"Jesus H. Christ," he barked in anger. CC wasn't surprised by the reaction. "How the hell am I supposed to remember that?"

"Let's give it a shot," CC encouraged him dryly. "The victim was a Marylyn Steiner. . ."

"I remember," he cut her off in a grave tone.

"Why?" CC asked as her voice trembled.

"She's dead," he explained in a pained voice. "There was another girl as well. I know who did it; I just couldn't prove anything. The little bastard weaseled out of it. I never had a thing on him. Now he's going to be a doctor and two girls that I know of are dead. The initial assault wasn't really anything. The guy wanted to date Marylyn, and he grabbed her roughly by the arm. She dropped the charges. It was just that she looked so much like the first victim; I couldn't get past it. A couple of weeks later Marylyn turned up dead."

"How?" CC asked as her mouth went dry and her heart started pounding urgently in her chest.

"A combination of blunt force trauma to the head and manual strangulation," he explained quickly as if he had just witnessed the crime scene.

"Sexual assault?" CC continued, praying that she was wrong.

"No," he responded in a painful tone. "But he tried. No penetration or semen. Tell me, Detective Calloway, why the sudden interest in an old case so far away?" he asked wearily.

"I have a victim that matches the same M.O.," CC responded as she fought the bile rising in her throat.

"Blonde, short, with blue or green eyes?" he pressed in a disgusted voice.

"Yes," CC answered flatly.

"Was Simon Fisher in the area?" he asked in an excited tone.

"Yes," she responded gravely. "Tell me something. With either Marylyn or Natalie, did he give the impression that he had a relationship with either woman?"

"Marylyn," he confirmed. "When she first came to us, he copped an attitude that it was just a lover's spat. He was very convincing, but I just had a feeling. When Marylyn explained that she had never had so much as a cup of coffee with the guy, I knew that there was something wrong that boy."

The way his words eerily echoed Max's made her shiver. "Thank you," she said quietly. "Can you send me . . .?"

"I'll FedEx copies of everything out to you right now," he cut her off. "Calloway, could you keep me updated? I'll fly out there if you need me. I've got a ton of vacation time, and I would love to see this guy get what he deserves. "

"I'll let you know everything," CC promised.

"One more thing you should know," he cautioned her. "His parents have more money than God, and they've bounced him from one private school to another. They made it very difficult for us to investigate him."

"Are they on the West Coast?" CC inquired.

"One of the first families here in San Diego," he explained; she could almost hear the smile in his voice.

"Good." She gave him the address he could send the information before promising to send copies of her case files as well.

CC worked with Wayne a little while longer, knowing that she had to investigate every possibility before completely focusing on Fisher. Then she made her way down to the Forensics lab downtown. Dr. Corey McDowell wanted to speak to her. CC was more than a little curious as to why he needed to see her in person.

"Corey," she called out as she wandered through the cool room. The older man looked up from the microscope and simply stared at her with indifference. "Calloway," he greeted her dryly.

"Okay, Sparky. Tell me what's so important that I have to haul my butt down here on a Sunday," she pressed, feeling a need to go home and be close to Jamie. She didn't like what she had heard today, and the last thing she wanted was for the blonde to be out of her sight for even a moment.

"Good afternoon to you as well," he continued in the same dry fashion.

"Corey, your report didn't show any prints or blood in the victims car or at the garage," CC continued, ignoring his banter.

"Did you bring me anything?" he taunted her.

"No," she lied with a wry smile as she hid the bag of brownies from Rosie's Bakery behind her back. Corey had an incurable sweet tooth. He also had a wife that was very concerned about his health. CC learned early on that Corey would move mountains for any cop that would smuggle him some goodies.

"Hmm," he responded thoughtfully as he turned his attention back to his microscope.

"Well . . ." CC hedged playfully. "I might have a little something."

A smile formed on the older man's face as he returned his attention to the tall policewoman. "No donuts," he cautioned her. "For this I want something good." She smiled as she pulled the white paper bag out from behind her back. "Rosie's," he responded as he nodded his approval. CC handed him the bag. He peered in carefully and nodded his acceptance of her offering.

"Now what do I get?" she pressed. "Besides a warning not to tell your wife that I helped feed your sugar Jones."

"Your neighbor's window," he began in his slow fashion. Corey was a brilliant scientist; he loved to savor his work and he took his time revealing his discoveries. CC had learned a long time ago to simply allow the man to proceed at his own pace.

"Yes?" she said with interest as the man took a bite of one of the rich chocolate brownies. She watched with some degree of amusement as the man's eyes fluttered shut. She allowed him to savor his treat a little while longer.

"At first I was curious as to why I was doing work on a vandalism case," he continued thoughtfully. "Then I found traces of blood on the glass."

"What?" she blurted out.

"I spoke with one of the officers who was on the scene, and he assured me that no one had been cut," he continued slowly, ignoring her outburst.

"No, nobody was hurt at the scene," she confirmed.

"I've been hearing through the grapevine that your neighbor worked with the victim who was dumped in the park," he continued, his eyes growing slightly dim as he spoke. "And she bears a certain resemblance to Sandra Bernstein."

"Yes," CC choked out.

"I had Roget do some tests," he continued thoughtfully. CC could hear a hint of discomfort in his voice and it made her skin crawl.

"And just what did our blood expert find?" CC pushed as the gnawing feeling in the pit of her stomach grew.

"On a hunch, I had him run some DNA tests," Corey explained. "The blood was Sandra Bernstein's."

CC's body swayed slightly and she grasped the end of the metal table to steady herself. "You didn't by any chance find the object used to break the window?" he inquired hopefully.

"No," CC choked out, fighting the urge to throw up.

"I'm almost certain that whatever was used to break that window was also used to crush your victim's skull," he concluded gravely. "Here's the report."

CC thanked him as she accepted the report. She ran out of the building, ducking quickly through the maze of corridors until she found herself outside. She barely made it around the corner of the building before emptying the contents of her stomach. As she wiped her mouth, she was thankful that it was Sunday afternoon and no one was around to see her lose her composure. She flipped open her cell phone and dialed the number she knew from memory quickly. "Max, we need to talk," CC said.

Jamie looked around Harvard Square anxiously. She loved the weather; unfortunately so did everyone else and the popular spot was overloaded with tourists. She also noted a number of students wandering about aimlessly with a blank expression. "Oh yes, it's time for finals." She chuckled as she recalled the days when she survived on nothing but caffeine and determination. "I don't miss those days," she commented wryly.

"And what days are those, Blondie?" a friendly voice from her past mocked.

"Becky," she squealed like a schoolgirl as she spun around to greet her old friend.

The two women hugged one another tightly before Becky stepped back and took a good look at Jamie. "First, shame on you for taking so long getting together with me," she scolded Jamie who simply shrugged in response. "I was plotting to injure Frank just so I could see you at work."

"You'd wound your poor husband just to see me?" Jamie inquired with a smirk. "I'm touched."

"Come on. Let's get some food, and more importantly, margaritas," Becky offered quickly as she linked her arm in Jamie's and ushered her down Church Street.

Once they were settled at a table in the noisy Mexican restaurant, they dipped their chips in the rich salsa while sipping their margaritas. "So tell me everything you've been up to, including that glow you're sporting," Becky demanded as Jamie blushed. "Uh huh, so you're still a wanton woman these days? I never thought I'd see my little virgin turn into such a player."

"Well . . ." Jamie began shyly, knowing that once she told Becky the truth the woman was going to freak out. "I'm seeing someone."

"As in a steady relationship?" Becky choked on her cocktail before clapping her hands together. "It's about time. Of course, after what that bitch put you through I can certainly understand being gun shy."

"Well . . . Uhm," Jamie stammered.

"Tell me everything about her," Becky demanded.

"She's a cop," Jamie offered carefully.

"I never thought you'd go out with another cop after what CC put you through," Becky responded in surprise. "She must be very special."

"She is," Jamie responded proudly.

Becky gave her an expectant look, obviously waiting for more details. Jamie licked her lips and took another sip of her drink. "Come on, Jamie," Becky pleaded. "Tell me everything. Well, not everything but you know . . . everything!"

"You need to spend more time with adults," Jamie teased the schoolteacher.

"And you're stalling," Becky pressed. "What's wrong with her?"

"Not a thing." Jamie almost purred as she spoke. "Okay. Well, she's tall, almost six feet tall, and she has long dark hair and the most amazing blue eyes that I've ever seen in my entire life." Jamie felt a tingle of excitement as she described her lover.

Becky stared at her blankly as she processed the information. "Uhm . . . Jamie, she sounds a lot like CC," she said hesitantly. "Are you sure that wasn't the attraction? Not meaning to rain on your parade, but . . ."

"It's okay," Jamie cut her off, fully understanding her concerns. "You see, the reason she sounds so much like CC is because . . . she is CC."

"Are you insane!" Becky shouted loud enough to be heard over the din of the busy restaurant.

Jamie slid down in her wooden chair as everyone stared at them. "Hear me out," she pleaded quietly as the waiter delivered their lunch. "I think we need another round," she suggested and the waiter nodded. "Make hers a double," she said, taunting her old friend.

"She walked out on you," Becky flared after the waiter scurried off. "And getting me drunk won't change that."

"No amount of alcohol will change what happened," Jamie confirmed as she began to rub her temples. Her head was pounding violently. "You remember back then when I didn't hear from her?" Becky nodded in agreement. "You defended her. You told me that there was no mistaking the way she looked at me."

"Yeah," Becky responded suspiciously. "I was shocked that she turned out to be a jerk. And I could have kicked myself for defending her."

"You were right," Jamie blurted out. "She had a real good reason for not calling me back."

"What? Alien abduction?" Becky snorted indignantly. Jamie laughed at the comment as she recalled her own reaction when CC finally told her the truth. The waiter delivered another round of cocktails as Jamie stifled her laughter.

"Okay, brace yourself; this is going to take some time," Jamie cautioned her friend who looked as if she wanted to beat CC within an inch of her life. "It all started the morning she left my dorm room . . ."

A couple of hours later the two women were sitting in Dunkin' Donuts, working on their second cup of coffee in an effort to combat the tequila. "Wow," Becky muttered for the hundredth time. "So her sister confirmed all of this?" she inquired in amazement.

"Yes." Jamie nodded her confirmation. "It's all true. Not that I believed her at first."

"How could you?" Becky supported her. "Frank hears a lot of things down at the paper about all the tip offs and FBI corruption involving Whitey. It doesn't surprise me that a snitch would panic by being pulled over. You must have freaked when you saw her again."

"At first I thought it was some cruel twist of fate that we ran into one another again," Jamie explained as she recalled how badly she had treated CC. "And when I found out I was living next door to her, I was convinced that I'd been very bad in a past life. Now I just think it was meant to be."

"Wow." Becky glanced at her watch and grimaced. "It's late. Frank is probably pulling out what's left of his hair by now. I bet the kids are driving him up the wall."

"Your little ones are angels," Jamie protested.

"They're not so little anymore." Becky sighed. "But since you're coming over for dinner very soon," she threatened, "you can find out for yourself."

"I promise," Jamie vowed. "Walk me to the T station."

"No car?" Becky asked curiously.

"CC has it for the day," Jamie explained. "She's working a difficult case and had to go into work today. You know that girl they found in the park near Allston?"

"Oh, that poor thing," Becky sympathized as they stepped out into the warm sunlight. "Frank's sister walks by that park every day. "

"The girl was one of my residents," Jamie explained sadly. "She was really sweet and full of life. The whole thing is unbelievable. CC has been really overprotective since it happened."

"Good," Becky said firmly.

"Between the murder and a would-be Romeo following me around at work, she's been on edge," Jamie confessed sadly.

They walked to the train station and exchanged their goodbyes. "Be careful," Becky cautioned her before she descended the staircase for the red line train. As Jamie rode the train, she was unaware that her lover was frantically trying to reach her on her cell phone. Since the doctor was underground the urgent call wasn't being received.

After several transfers she got off at the green line station near her home. The beeping of her phone startled her as she stepped off the train. She noted that the sun was setting, and she briefly wondered if she should hail a cab instead of walking the three blocks to her house. Between fumbling for her telephone and searching for a taxi, she never noticed the black BMW sitting at the corner.

CHAPTER SIX

After Max had managed to calm her fears somewhat and get CC back into a professional mode, she felt more focused. Still it didn't quiet her heart that was still pounding furiously. CC called the station and tracked Wayne down just as the poor bugger was trying to leave for the day. She turned on the charm, knowing that it would take relatively little to convince Wayne to do what she wanted. Quickly the quiet little man was agreeing to contact the hospital to find out what Ellen Murdock did there and when she was scheduled to work again.

Once she'd completed the call, CC poured herself into Jamie's car. She griped the entire time about the lack of room in the little Honda, and for the first time that day she smiled, knowing that this time tomorrow she would be in her new SUV. She flipped open the small notepad she always carried with her and looked up Ellen Murdock's address. The one reassurance she had to keep her from going completely ballistic was that she knew Jamie was with Stevie. She was nestled safely away from any danger since there was absolutely no way that the unstable Dr. Fisher could know that she was there.

CC parked the Honda in front of the nondescript apartment building. The four-story brick structure looked like so many complexes that littered the city, built solely to house the state's growing population. She checked the buzzers for Ellen's apartment number. She found the woman's name and shook her head, knowing how dangerous it was for a woman to list her full name; it informed any passerby that she was a woman living alone.

CC tried the glass entrance door, knowing that quite often it would be unlocked because of a broken lock or simple negligence. This time the front door was locked. She pressed the buzzer for Ellen's apartment, which was located on the top floor. Then she waited. After what seemed like an eternity, she rang the buzzer once again. She rolled her neck and shoulders in a futile attempt to alleviate the tension that was growing with each passing second.

CC glanced at her watch and scowled. She pressed the small rectangular black button once again, this time leaving her finger firmly pressed against the button. She allowed the buzzer to ring until the tip of her finger ached in protest. Still no one responded. "Okay, she's not home," she griped as her cell phone chirped.

CC snatched the small blue phone from its holder on her belt. "Calloway," she barked into the tiny device. She heard a small gasp emanate from the caller.

"Uhm . . . Detective," Wayne stammered as CC's shoulder blades pinched tensely.

"Yes, Wayne," she droned in response as she began to grind her teeth.

"I found that information you wanted." Wayne's voice was trembling nervously as he spoke.

"Okay," she said slowly, not wanting to frighten the little man any further.

"Ellen Murdock is a pediatric nurse," he said, his voice still trembling as he spoke. "She's been on vacation since she got off work the night Sandra Bernstein disappeared. She was due back today only . . .."

"Only what," she snapped as her chest began to constrict.

"She failed to show up for her shift," Wayne blurted out quickly.

"Shit," she blurted out. "Wayne, I need you to send a CSU crew to Ellen Murdock's address. Call me when they're on their way in case I don't need them," she commanded him firmly, knowing in her heart that she would need the Crime Scene Unit. He agreed and she ended the call. She dialed Max immediately and gave him the address, telling him to get his fat butt there as soon as possible. She offered no explanation before she hung up on him.

She pressed the buzzer for the manager's apartment, praying that he would be home on Sunday. "What?" came the hostile response through the tiny speaker.

"Police," she answered firmly.

"Right," the voice scoffed before disconnecting.

CC emitted a feral growl before pressing the buzzer once again. "Knock it off!" the voice barked before disconnecting. CC pressed the buzzer, holding it firmly in place, knowing that she was disturbing the obnoxious individual on the other end.

"Look, its Sunday . . .!" the voice shouted angrily.

"And it's still the police!" she shouted in response. "I need to get into one of your tenants' apartments now!" She had considered threatening to shoot her way in but thought better of it at the last moment.

"Really?" the voice squeaked.

"Yes, really!" she fumed. "Now get up here and let me in."

The box disconnected and she was about to press the buzzer once again when a scraggly man approached the front door. She rolled her eyes at the man's appearance as she noted that he hadn't bothered to zip up his fly. "Why do they do that?" she muttered as she held up her badge. He gave her a wary look and examined the badge carefully before opening the door. "Its about time," she grumbled. "4H," she instructed him as Max pulled up to the curb.

"That's Miss Murdock's apartment," he responded in bewilderment as Max hustled to join her. Unfortunately, with Max's large build, it took him awhile to reach her.

"I know," she said as Max stopped beside her huffing and puffing. "This is my partner," she added with a nod to the winded man next her. The apartment manager simply nodded as he headed towards the staircase.

"Elevator?" Max gasped. The scraggly man simply shook his head in response.

"Fourth floor," she informed her wheezing partner. Max simply groaned as they began to ascend the staircase.

"I can't imagine that Miss Murdock would be in any trouble," the manager babbled as they climbed the stairs.

"Let's hope not," CC muttered softly.

"She's been away," the manager continued. "I was going to check on the place tomorrow. She must have forgotten to take her trash out before she left; the neighbors have been complaining about the smell."

Max and CC froze for a moment and stared at each other. "I already have CSU on the way," she explained softly as they continued to climb the stairs.

"Let's hope we're wrong," Max said, trying to reassure her. CC nodded in agreement although the constant gnawing in her stomach reminded her that she was right.

As they approached the door to Ellen Murdock's apartment, an all-too-familiar stench assaulted their senses. CC and Max knew what they would find inside. "Open it," she informed the manager who seemed unaware of what was happening. He complied with her request. "Stay here," she instructed him solemnly as he blinked in confusion.

Max pulled some rubber gloves from his pocket and handed her a pair. She gave him a questioning glance as she put them on. "I had a feeling," he explained grimly as he snapped on his own pair of gloves.

CC turned the doorknob slowly as the apartment manager cleared his throat. "Are you sure you can do this?" he questioned them.

"Yes." She sighed, knowing that the occupant was no longer in a position to complain. She opened the door and the foul stench engulfed them.

"What is that?" the manager groaned in disgust.

"Stay here," CC repeated as she and Max carefully stepped into the apartment.

"Why don't you open a window?" the man suggested as CC spun around and glared at him.

"I said stay in the hallway," she chastised him.

His mouth opened to protest when his face went suddenly pale. He clasped a hand over his mouth as his body started to convulse. CC and Max followed the direction of his eyes and found what they'd feared that they would. "Max, could you secure the scene while I take Mr. . . . " She blinked, realizing she didn't know the man's name. "Him," she finally grunted, "outside to wait for CSU to show up."

Max grimaced as she grabbed the man by the elbow and escorted him out of the apartment. She knew it gave Max the creeps being left alone at the crime scene. But she had no choice. She wanted to ensure that she was never alone at the scene just in case her suspicions were correct. She ushered the manager downstairs and watched as the man emptied the contents of his stomach into an azalea bush. Once he was calm she took his statement.

She discovered that his name was Ronnie Dunhill and he hadn't seen Ellen Murdock since a few days before her vacation was due to start. Her car was parked in the back and had been there since the night before she was scheduled to leave on vacation. She asked if he thought that was odd. He didn't since he was certain that she was planning on taking the train wherever she was going. The crime scene unit arrived and CC accompanied them up to the late Ellen Murdock's apartment.

Her first glance at Ellen Murdock's body was eerily familiar. "Just toss her in the park and she could be our last victim," Max noted dryly.

"Yeah," CC confirmed as she fought a wave of nausea. She wished they could open a window but she knew it would attract flies that would disturb the corpse. "Check everything," CC informed the technicians. "Her car is out back. I want that checked as well.

"Nothing on the answering machine," Max noted.

"Everyone expected her to be out of town," CC explained as she carefully examined the room. The sweat was pouring off her brow. "I'll be right back," she offered as she dashed out into the hallway.

"I never saw her react like that," one of the techs commented.

CC quickly grabbed her cell phone and dialed her home. "Stevie, let me talk to Jamie," she barked at her sister.

"Uhm . . . she's not here," Stevie responded timidly.

"What do you mean she's not there?" CC demanded in a blind panic.

"She's out with a friend," Stevie explained quickly.

"I told you to keep an eye on her," CC fumed.

"I know. I just took Emma to the park while she was asleep," Stevie defended herself. "By the time I got back she was gone. She left a note saying that she was meeting a friend for lunch. What the hell is going on, Caitlin?"

"I'm not . . ." CC's voice trembled. "Look, when she gets back, make her stay put. Do you understand?"

"Yes," Stevie confirmed adamantly.

"Sorry to yell," she mumbled quickly before disconnecting the call. She instantly called Jamie's cell phone and was bumped to her voicemail. "Jamie, call me right away," she blurted out frantically before quickly dialing the number once again. "Come on. Where are you?" she muttered when the voicemail greeted her once again.

"What is it?" Max asked from behind her.

"I don't know where she is," she whimpered, as her face grew pale.

Jamie moved across the street as she continued to fumble for her cell phone. She stood in the doorway of a shop; since it was early Sunday evening everything in the tiny village square was locked up tight. She punched her code into her cell phone so she could retrieve her voicemail. Her jaw hung open as she listened to the terror in CC's voice. "What the hell?" she said under her breath as she quickly dialed CC's cell phone.

She heard a car engine rev to life and out of the corner of her eye she spotted a black BMW pulling away from the corner. She shrugged as it drove off towards her street. Seeing a BMW in the neighborhood wasn't the least bit unusual. She was far too preoccupied waiting for CC to answer to think about it any further.

"Jamie!" CC snapped before the doctor could say *'hello'*. "Where are you?" she demanded loudly, causing Jamie to yank the cell phone away from her ear.

"Please tell me that you're premenstrual," Jamie shouted into her phone indignantly.

"Where are you?" CC repeated in a slow careful tone.

"Caitlin, you're scaring me," Jamie stammered as she looked around for a taxi. Finding none, she turned her attention back to her lover's voice.

"Jamie, will you please tell me where you are?" CC pleaded.

"I'm at the Boylston Village T stop," Jamie informed her in a desperate effort to calm her down. She could hear CC repeating her location to someone else.

"Jamie, I need you to do something for me. I need you to go into one of the shops and wait for me," CC instructed her carefully. "And don't ask me why."

"Why?" Jamie inquired before she could stop herself. Once again she found herself yanking the telephone away from her ear as CC released a frustrated growl. "Sorry. Reflex," Jamie explained sheepishly in her defense.

"Jamie, just go into one of the shops," CC barked at her.

"Caitlin, it's Sunday night. Nothing's open," Jamie explained. "Look, I'm just going to walk home and you can explain everything when you get there." She was ready to end the telephone call; frustrated by the thought that she could have been halfway home by now. It was getting dark and the tone of CC's voice frightened her.

"No! Take a taxi," CC ordered her.

Jamie sighed in exasperation, wishing she had started walking already. "There aren't any cabs," Jamie explained while she tried to calm her nerves. Normally she would have just told CC off for speaking to her like she was an errant child but she could hear the fear echoing in her lover's voice.

"Are there any people or cars around?" CC continued in a strained voice.

"Caitlin! You're scaring me," Jamie sobbed into the telephone. She was unable to hold her emotions back any longer.

"I'm sorry, baby," CC explained in a crestfallen voice. "I'll be there soon. Just hang on and wait for me or the squad car that's en route." Jamie released another sob. "If it's any consolation, I'm probably overreacting," CC offered lightly.

Jamie saw through the act instantly. Granted, CC was known to overreact at times, particularly where the blonde doctor was concerned. And Jamie knew she was guilty of doing the same thing when it came to the tall dark policewoman. Somehow the level of pure panic in CC's voice mixed with the sound of a siren blaring in the background didn't lead Jamie to believe that CC was simply overreacting. "I don't believe you," Jamie confronted her. "There's no one around. There was a BMW here earlier but it just left," she said as she tried to slow her rapidly beating pulse.

"A BMW?" CC echoed. "What color?"

"Black," Jamie responded slowly as the color drained from her face.

"Are you sure it is gone?" CC pushed.

"Yes." Jamie sighed in relief as she looked around to reassure herself.

"I'm almost there; just keep talking to me, baby," CC encouraged her.

"What would you like to talk about?" Jamie grunted in annoyance; she had a sudden urge to throttle her lover for scaring her half to death.

"What did you do today?" CC inquired in a casual tone that Jamie didn't buy for one second. Jamie scanned the dark square as the hair on the back of her neck stood on end. "Jamie?" CC prompted her.

"I had lunch with Becky," she finally responded. "You remember her; she lived on the same floor in my dorm."

"Oh yeah, she was a doll," CC responded. "What's she up to these days?"

"Married with three kids," Jamie explained. "I told her about us."

"How did that go over?" CC laughed.

"She asked me if I'd lost my mind." Jamie snorted as the urgency of the situation slipped away for a brief moment.

"And have you?" CC teased her further, lulling the young doctor into a false sense of security.

"Absolutely." Jamie laughed as she saw the flashing blue lights approaching her.

"Is that you?" she inquired, her smile fading as she saw a police cruiser approaching her. It came to a stop at the corner where she was standing. Two uniformed police officers quickly emerged from the car. One was a large man of color who would have towered over CC. The other was smaller, also dark-skinned, with a bushy moustache. The drastic differences in their heights struck Jamie as amusing.

"Dr. Jameson?" the taller man inquired.

"Yes," she responded with a smile.

A few seconds later she saw her small Honda approaching with a flashing blue light of its own. The car skidded to a stop behind the squad car, and CC struggled out of the front seat. Once again Jamie was amused as she saw the tall woman unfolding herself from the small car. "The SUV was definitely the right choice for her," Jamie noted under her breath. CC rushed over to her with a look of relief written across her chiseled features. Max looked weary as he trailed behind his tall partner.

"Hey Calloway," the smaller man greeted her. "The doctor seems fine. Anything else we can do you?" he offered sarcastically.

"Actually there is," CC said firmly as she scribbled on a small notepad. She tore off the top page and handed it to him. "Go to that address. No lights, no sirens. Drive by, check around, and keep doing it. Also keep an eye out for a black BMW."

"In this neighborhood?" the taller policeman grunted. "Could you be more specific?"

"The license plate is on the paper," CC snapped indignantly. "Call my cell if you find anything, and I mean anything."

The two officers nodded in understanding before climbing back into their car. Jamie looked at CC thoughtfully. "Are you all right?" CC inquired anxiously.

"Why is there a light attached to the roof of my car?" Jamie inquired thoughtfully.

"Don't ask," CC responded as she rolled her crystal blue eyes.

"Can I keep it?" Jamie asked hopefully as she turned off her cell phone and stuffed it back into her pocket.

"No," CC groaned.

"It has a siren too?" Jamie added with enthusiasm.

"No," CC lied.

"I heard it when you were talking to me," Jamie stated as CC went to get in the driver's side. "I don't think so," she said quickly as she nudged her lover out of the way. She climbed into the car and adjusted the seat. Jamie was amused as she watched Max and CC maneuver their larger bodies into her compact car.

Jamie reached over to the strange black box dangling from her cigarette lighter. "Don't - it's not a toy," CC chastised her as she swatted her hand away.

"Why can't I keep it?" Jamie pouted.

"It belongs to Max," CC grumbled. "Speaking of which, we need to get him back to his car and then go on to the station."

"I want to go home," Jamie protested.

"Not yet," CC groused.

"Oh come on; Stevie will be there," Jamie whined.

"No. I called her and sent her and Emma over to Brad's for the night," CC quickly explained. "Now we need to go to . . ."

"I'm not going anywhere until you tell me what's going on," Jamie stated as CC shrank back in her seat. "Out with it, Caitlin," she demanded.

CC was covered in nervous sweat and her hands were trembling. Jamie was still glaring at her awaiting some sort of answer. And she did deserve one. Just what could CC tell her without compromising the investigation or frightening Jamie even more than she already was? "I'm waiting," the blonde barked indignantly.

"Do you know Ellen Murdock?" CC began slowly.

"No," Jamie snipped.

"She works at the hospital, or rather she did," CC continued, reaching deep inside herself to gather the professional demeanor that usually came to her naturally. "She's dead." She watched in horror as her lover's lip began to quiver. "Jamie, I can't tell you everything. And I'm praying that my suspicions are wrong, but right now I feel that you're in danger. Please - you need to trust me. I can't lose you."

"Okay," Jamie responded with a slight tremble. "I trust you." The heartfelt sincerity in her words almost broke CC's heart.

She was at a loss as to what she could say in an effort to offer her lover some comfort in the frightening situation. Her cell phone chirped to life and she snatched it up quickly. "Calloway," she barked into the receiver. She listened fearfully to the caller. "Come get Max where you met us," she responded coldly. "Get out, Max."

CC and Max stepped out of the car and walked over to the corner to ensure that Jamie couldn't hear what they were saying. "They found his car around the corner from our complex. They're coming back for you. I'm taking Jamie somewhere safe. Call my cell and let me know what's going on."

"Where will you be?" Max inquired casually as he began to organize himself.

"I'm not telling anyone," CC responded flatly as Max looked up at her in surprise. "From what the detective in San Diego said, his family has some very deep pockets. I can't risk anyone knowing. I won't lose her."

"You won't," Max confirmed adamantly. "This guy is going to pay even if we have to . . ."

"Don't," CC snapped fearfully. Her stomach clenched as she wondered if she was capable of doing what she feared Max was suggesting.

"Get her out of here," Max reassured her. "We'll get him and send that bastard away. I'll call you when I get back to the station. Go," Max added firmly. CC could only nod in response before walking back to the car and climbing in. Jamie was staring blankly out the window. "Are you okay to drive?" CC asked her lover gently.

"No," Jamie answered flatly. Neither woman spoke as they got out of the small vehicle and switched positions.

As they entered the lobby of the posh hotel CC accepted the ticket from the valet. They hadn't spoken a word during the drive into the city. CC guided her lover to the front desk. Jamie seemed to be in a daze as she followed behind the tall brunette.

"Well, I'll be damned," a friendly voice greeted CC.

"Probably," CC taunted her old friend.

"Oh, you still say the sweetest things," Kendra teased her. "So what brings you here? Miss me, did you?"

"I need a favor," CC responded with a sorrowful look.

"Of course." Kendra snorted. "What happened? Did Stevie kick you out on your sorry . . ." The dark woman's words trailed off as Jamie stepped out from behind CC.

"Kendra?" Jamie spoke brightly and CC relaxed at finally hearing the sound of her lover's voice.

Kendra was about to hop over the desk when CC pushed her back. "Show some self control for once," she scolded her old friend. "I need a room."

"Of course. " Kendra nodded with a toothy grin. "Flowers, champagne, anything for the two of you."

"None of that," CC groaned as Jamie chuckled. "What I need is discretion and no names."

"Oh?" Kendra's face dropped as a scowl formed. "This is business."

"Not entirely," CC teased her friend as she took Jamie's hand.

"Now you're just messing with me," Kendra spat out with an evil growl.

"I'll explain everything," CC promised. "But for now I need a Bette Davis."

"Which means you need to get out of sight as soon as possible," Kendra replied thoughtfully as she nudged the desk clerk away from the computer. "Done," she said triumphantly as she snatch up a card key. "Follow me," she said confidently as she made her way around the long desk and waved off the bellhop.

"Bette Davis?" Jamie asked in confusion.

"I'll explain," CC once again promised as the three of them made their way to the stairwell.

"Second floor," Kendra explained.

"Sometimes when I've had problems getting a woman in need into a shelter, Kendra has helped out," CC explained as they climbed the stairs.

"I run the place and the hotel can write it off as a charitable expense," Kendra offered with a shrug. "I use names like Bette Davis or Rosalind Russell and the staff knows that it's a code for complete privacy. No one will bother you or mention your stay."

"That's very kind of you, Kendra," Jamie said with respect.

"I do what I can," Kendra said graciously as they exited the stairwell and she led them down the hallway. "The room isn't all that great," Kendra explained as she ushered them into a quaint room with a queen size bed, dresser, and television."

"This is very nice," Jamie said honestly.

"Not compared to our other rooms," Kendra pointed out. "It's very basic. No hot tub, wet bar, or anything but a bed and a television. But it's close to the ground floor and the windows face a brick wall so no one can see in."

"Perfect if you're in hiding," CC explained.

"All we really need is a bed," Jamie teased the tall brunette as she wrapped her arms around her waist.

"That's it," Kendra fumed as she grabbed Jamie and pulled her in for hug. "God, it's good to see you, Blondie." Once she released the giggling blonde, she glared at both of them. CC couldn't help but smile at her friend's antics. "Now fess up and tell me what's going on. Besides the fact that you're in some kind of trouble which you can't tell me about."

"Oh, you mean her?" CC taunted the tall ebony beauty as Jamie firmly swatted her on her backside. "Ouch. Again with the hitting?"

"You're such a baby," Jamie scoffed.

"Isn't she?" Kendra agreed. "So what happened? Did you finally swallow your pride and decide to listen to your old friend? I've been telling her for years that gorgeous women don't fall into your lap every day."

"You have?" Jamie gushed; CC blushed at the memory of Jamie literally falling into her lap the second time they'd met.

CC smiled at the blush Jamie was also sporting. "It's true," CC confirmed softly. "Almost every time we got together, Kendra would find someway to let me know just how big of an idiot I was to let you go," CC explained truthfully.

"She was right," Jamie responded in a husky tone. "But I was an even bigger fool."

CC was overwhelmed by Jamie's words and the misty gleam in her brilliant green eyes. She leaned over and brushed her lips against Jamie's soft trembling ones. As she felt her lover's tongue brush against her lips, she parted her own and allowed Jamie to explore the warmth of her mouth.

"Oh," Kendra gushed as the innocent kiss flamed into fiery desire. "Okay, enough," Kendra scolded them. "You're turning me on." CC's body was quivering slightly as she stepped away from her lover. "So tell me how the two of you got back together," Kendra persisted as CC maintained her distance from Jamie, knowing that she wouldn't be able to control herself if she was near her.

"Well, it was at the hospital," Jamie started.

"Right, the dead guy," CC added.

"I told you off," Jamie filled in.

"No, first you acted like you didn't know me," CC clarified.

"Right, then I told you off," Jamie agreed as Kendra stared at both of them with a baffled look.

"Then there was the other dead guy," CC continued.

"He wasn't dead," Jamie corrected her.

"Are you sure?" CC questioned her.

"Yes, and you were banging your head at the nurses' station. I still don't understand that one," Jamie expanded. "I told you off again."

"Then you checked out my ass," CC teased her with a smirk.

"I didn't," Jamie protested.

"You did," CC bragged. "Then we got drunk."

"And slept together." They added in unison.

"That's when you got back together," Kendra supplied gleefully.

"No," they moaned in unison.

"Jamie completely freaked out," CC continued with a grimace.

"Twice," Jamie added. "First for sleeping with you and then when I realized I lived next door to you."

"Oh right," CC agreed with an understanding nod. "Then Stevie told the both of us off."

"We played miniature golf," Jamie proceeded thoughtfully.

"Slept together," CC added with a blush. "Then there was the fire."

"Right," Jamie filled in. "Then I thought you were sleeping with the contractor and you thought I was sleeping with my sister."

"Eww!" Kendra blanched.

"Then the murder. And your stalker," CC supplied.

"Ringing telephones, doorbells, pagers, broken windows, you kissing the pathologist, ice cream, handcuffs, and somewhere along the line we realized that we're still in love with one another," Jamie concluded with a flurry. "Did I leave anything out?" she asked the giggling detective.

"No, honey; that's just about everything," CC agreed.

"Sounds very romantic," Kendra responded sarcastically. "Now I need to get back to work and try to figure out what you just told me. Are you sure you don't want any champagne?"

"Sorry, I'm still on duty," CC apologized. "And I have an early day tomorrow. Thank you for everything."

"My pleasure," Kendra responded with a smile. "I'll just leave the two of you alone," she said as she handed CC the card key. "I'd tell you to behave but apparently you don't understand the meaning of the word. Handcuffs and ice cream? I don't even want to know about that." She laughed as she departed.

"Should we call room service and order some ice cream just to mess with her?" Jamie suggested playfully. CC didn't respond to her lover's joke. Instead she wrapped Jamie up in her arms and clung tightly to the small blonde. "I need to be close to you," she said with a whimper. "I can't lose you," CC sobbed as the fear finally took complete control.

Jamie stepped back from CC's embrace, her emerald eyes burning into the brunette's soul. "You're not going to lose me," the small doctor vowed.

"I can't!" CC trembled.

"You won't," Jamie promised her once again as she reached up and claimed the taller woman's lips.

CC knew that she was trembling; she couldn't stop her body from shaking. For the first time in a very long time she was afraid. Her mind started to shut down as the fear gripped her rapidly beating heart. She was unaware that the kiss had ended or that Jamie was removing her clothing, until she felt herself being lowered onto the bed. She looked up in confusion at her lover who was leaning over her.

Jamie's eyes bore into her soul. The look of reassurance and love cast down upon her was the only answer Caitlin Calloway needed. She lay naked on the bed as Jamie slowly removed her clothing, only breaking her gaze or contact with CC's body when she needed to discard an article of clothing. CC felt her fears melt away as her lover's naked body lay down beside her own.

Jamie cupped her face with both of her hands; CC sighed as she melted into her lover's touch. This wasn't about their overactive libidos. This moment was about the love they shared for each other. "I belong to you," Jamie promised before she tenderly brushed CC's lips. "And you belong to me," she added before reclaiming the brunette's lips. "No one is going to take us away from each other. There isn't a force strong enough to break us apart again," Jamie promised as CC wrapped her arms around the smaller woman's slender waist.

CC gasped sharply as their breasts lightly brushed. "I love your body," Jamie confessed in a breathy tone as her small hands began to caress CC's broad shoulders. Jamie guided the tall policewoman onto her back and CC allowed her lover to take control, needing Jamie's touch to remind her of their deep unbreakable connection.

Jamie's body rested halfway on hers and halfway on the mattress as her nimble fingers began to trace every curve of CC's long smooth body. CC could feel her fears ebbing as Jamie watched her fingers elicit a trail of goose bumps along her body. As Jamie's fingers ran along the swell of her breasts, the blonde leaned in and placed a tender promising kiss on the brunette's lips.

Missing from Jamie's kiss was the urgent probing that would drive CC to the brink of insanity. In its place was the love they shared. This was what CC needed, not the overwhelming need to be sated. Tonight she needed to feel and be shown the love that Jamie felt for her. "Still with me?" Jamie inquired softly.

"Yes," CC responded firmly as her hand came to rest on the curve of Jamie's hip. Her fingers danced along Jamie's quivering flesh. Jamie flashed her an endearing smile as her fingers continued their gentle exploration.

Jamie's fingers trailed along her breast, circling and caressing but never quite touching her nipple. CC's fingers began caressing Jamie's flesh, drifting from the curve of her hip to the blonde's firm backside. CC allowed the tips of her fingers to simply glide along Jamie's flesh. Absent was the panting and groping until they both collapsed in exhaustion. Jamie sighed contentedly, mirroring CC's own inner feelings as she gently brushed her fingers across CC's nipple.

CC lifted her other arm and began to run her fingers through Jamie's short blonde locks. She gently massaged the blonde's scalp as Jamie's tongue peeked out and began to circle her nipple. She could feel Jamie relax into her touch, purring like a kitten as the blonde's tongue began to flicker slowly across her nipple.

Both of CC's nipples became erect and still she felt no desire to rush the moment they were sharing. Jamie's slow tender suckling reflected her own desire to take things slowly. Jamie's curls brushed against her thigh as she pressed it slightly into Jamie's center. CC moaned as Jamie's teeth grazed her now aching nipple. Jamie's body shifted slightly, nestling herself firmly against CC's thigh while pressing her own firm thigh against CC's center.

Their hips began to sway in a gentle sensual rhythm as CC continued to caress Jamie's back while still running her fingers through her hair. The soft scent of the blonde's shampoo filled her senses as she felt her lover's desire painting her thigh. "I love you." The honest words escaped from CC's lips as Jamie lifted her head and stared deeply into her eyes.

They continued to stare deeply into one another's eyes as their hips continued to dance slowly against each other. Their clits met, beating steadily with a soft loving desire as they melted into one another's touch. "I love you, Caitlin," Jamie whispered sincerely as they continued to thrust slowly against one another. Jamie supported herself on her arms, leaning above CC's body as her breasts swayed against the brunette's skin. CC clasped her lover's hips, gently guiding her to meet her growing desire.

CC lost herself in the feel of their wetness painting each other's bodies. The look of love in Jamie's eyes melted her heart and inflamed her passion as they began to thrust wildly. CC could feel the need for release growing between them. "I love you," CC choked out as she felt the climax steadily building. She fought against the tears that threatened to escape as they lost themselves in the beauty of the moment.

They climaxed together as soft cries escaped tight throats. Jamie curled up in CC's arms as their hearts beat in unison. CC clung to her lover, knowing that this was where she belonged. Holding Jamie in her arms was the only thing in the world that really mattered at that moment in time.

CC's azure eyes blinked opened as she heard the chirping sound of her cell phone. She untangled her body from Jamie's that was resting comfortably on top of her. The doctor grumbled sleepily in protest. CC kissed her lover's brow and tucked Jamie back under the covers. CC already missed feeling her lover next to her. The policewoman's body was slightly sore from the evening's activities.

After the sweet gentle affirmation of their lovemaking, the couple had climbed under the covers to cuddle. A simple touch and tender kiss and soon their bodies had complete control. "That girl is going to be the death of me." She yawned as she searched the darkened room for her cell phone.

"Are you complaining?" came the muffled query from her lover who still snuggled deeply into her pillow.

"Never," CC responded boldly as she tripped over her pants. Looking down she could see the glint of her cell phone. She picked it up and punched in her code to retrieve the message from the call she'd just missed. Not surprisingly it was from Max.

Her partner had called to fill her in on what was happening with the investigation. They had found the car, and before they could have it impounded for being parked illegally, the doctor had shown up. Max remained in the cruiser just out of the doctor's sight, listening to his explanation. He would have believed that the young doctor was just going to surprise his girlfriend if he didn't already known the truth. Max further explained that when he emerged from the cruiser, Dr. Fisher had paled. Max added that he had spoken with her neighbors and someone matching Dr. Fisher's description had been seen lurking around Jamie's townhouse. Max concluded that he put a rush on the forensics from the Murdock crime scene and he felt that they had enough to bring the good doctor in for another interview.

CC quickly dialed Max's cell phone. "Hey, buddy," she greeted him, hoping that the roughness of her voice wouldn't reveal her earlier activities. Max's chuckle quickly dashed that hope. "Did you make it home yet?"

"Yeah, I'm home and the wife is steamed," Max grunted.

"So you think we can bring him in for another round?" she pressed, eager to climb back into bed and hold her lover in her arms.

"He was in the area," Max explained. "Maybe your neighbors can ID him. He's still lying about his relationship with Jamie," he pointed out. "And she's already filed a complaint with us."

"And her supervisor at the hospital," CC informed him.

"Good," Max responded eagerly. "It's not enough for a restraining order but it's getting us closer to where we need to be."

"He's on the day shift now," CC continued. "Why don't we have him come in right after his shift? I know I can't be present but I really want to watch. Besides, if he's at the station I know Jamie will be safe at work. We need to do a follow-up with Terrell and the Romeo who was on duty the night Sandra disappeared."

"Sounds like a plan," Max confirmed. "Get in as soon as you can; we need to speak to the boss about all of this."

"I will," she promised before ending her conversation with Max.

Wearily she climbed back into bed with her lover. Jamie instantly nestled her body against CC's. "Now will you tell me what's going on?" Jamie inquired softly as she rested her head on CC's chest.

"Yes," CC agreed, feeling that her control had returned and her fears had been properly reigned in. "Ellen Murdock was a pediatric nurse and her car was parked next to Sandra Bernstein's the night she disappeared. She was on vacation so no one knew that she was dead in her own apartment. She was murdered in the same fashion that Sandra was as well as two other girls in San Diego. The only difference is that Ellen's body wasn't dumped. Two killings in one night - the killer probably didn't have the time to dump the body." CC looked down at Jamie who was still nestled against her chest and twirling a strand of CC's hair between her fingers.

CC didn't miss the pensive look on the doctor's face. She began to rub reassuring circles down her lover's back as she waited for some sign from Jamie that it was all right to continue with her story. "What does this have to do with me?" Jamie inquired in a disturbingly flat voice.

"All of these women had two things in common," CC continued slowly. "They were all blondes with green eyes, similar builds and features, and they all had some kind of contact with Simon Fisher. His car was parked near Ellen Murdock's and he left the garage immediately after she did."

"Wait, that still doesn't mean that I'm in some kind of danger," Jamie reasoned.

"Sandra Bernstein's blood was found on the glass shards from your front window," CC concluded as her hands stilled their soothing motion. A sharp gasp was the only response the blonde offered and CC understood that the discussion was over. She wrapped her arms tightly around Jamie's body and held her close to her. Their hearts beat in unison as sleep evaded them.

The following day was a flurry of activity. They returned home to find workmen awaiting Jamie's arrival so they could replace her front window. Jamie handled the situation while CC showered although Jamie didn't want to let her lover out of her sight. Once the workmen had finished and Stevie returned home, CC rushed to the bank to pick up the cashier's check she needed to deliver to the car dealership. When she returned home nothing looked amiss. Jamie and Stevie were playing with Emma, but a shadow hovered over them.

As they drove to the dealership CC she and Jamie were snapping at one another. She knew it was her fault but she couldn't stop herself from harping on what Jamie should do each time she entered her own home. She kept reminding her to check the alarm system and exit through the back door and enter CC's home in the same way. "I get it," Jamie finally screamed at her.

Jamie pulled her car off to the side of the highway; they sat there in silence as Jamie's knuckles turned white from gripping the steering wheel far too tightly. "I'm sorry, James," CC grumbled as she rubbed her aching brow.

"I can't live like this," Jamie uttered in a soft determined tone. "I love you, Caitlin, but you need to stop treating me like I'm a child."

"I know," CC groaned. "I know," she repeated in the same heavy tone, knowing that she was incapable of promising Jamie that she wouldn't fall into the same trap again. The stakes were far too high. "Jamie . . ."

"Caitlin, promise me that you'll at least try," Jamie cut her off in a softer tone as she finally released her grip on the steering wheel.

"Sometimes I feel like you can read my mind," CC commented wryly as she took Jamie's small delicate hands in her own.

"That's because I can and you should be ashamed of yourself," Jamie teased her.

For the first time that day CC actually smiled. The off color remark crept through the tension and got to her. "Let's go and pick up my new car," CC said. Jamie winked at her playfully while she put her car in drive and carefully reentered the insane flow of traffic along Rte. 128.

After they finished all the paperwork at the dealership CC found herself driving her new SUV while muttering to herself. She had asked Jamie to stick around and follow her to the station. The blonde doctor had adamantly refused, claiming that spending her time off hanging around the police station just wasn't her idea of a good time. CC insisted and Jamie told her to *bite her.* That's when CC realized that there was no way she was going to get her lover to comply with her wishes. She understood that Jamie was feeling like she was suddenly imprisoned and removed from living her life. It was a common reaction. And Jamie was right; CC couldn't be with her twenty-four hours a day. Of course that didn't stop her from calling in a favor to have a couple of plainclothes men follow the blonde around in her absence.

"Okay, Max; make me a happy woman," CC demanded as she planted herself on the corner of her partner's desk.

"Marry me?" her partner quipped. "No? In that case I'll just need to fill you in on the lab results."

"That was quick," CC said in relief. "Do I want to know how you managed to pull off this small miracle?"

"You can kiss your season tickets to the Sox's goodbye," Max responded flatly.

CC was about to explode when the thought of Jamie's safety overrode her anger. "Not a problem," CC confirmed confidently.

"You must be in love," Max pried.

"I am," CC answered the older man honestly. "How badly is that going to screw up this investigation?"

"So far it hasn't," Max reassured her. "Okay, first we have Sandra Bernstein's blood in Ellen Murdock's apartment, mostly in the bedroom but small traces in the living room and down the back stairwell. Nothing from her car. But the lock on the building's back door was jimmied as was the back door to her apartment."

"So he followed them and broke in and . . . How did he know which apartment?" CC threw out as an officer handed her a large FedEx package and a manila folder. She nodded her thanks as Max contemplated her question.

"The mailbox," Max concluded. "All he had to do was go in the back way."

"Thanks to the law in the Commonwealth that you must have front and rear exits to all dwellings, all he had to do was count," CC filled in as she tore open the package from San Diego.

"Her apartment number was marked on the trash barrels and recycling bin; she left them just outside her back door," Max supplied. "All he had to do was check the mailboxes and go in the back way. The locks on the front are really good but the ones in back look like someone was trying to save a couple of bucks."

CC set the case files aside for a moment and began to peruse the folder that the hospital had sent over. "No semen at the scene," Max continued.

"Our boy suffers from equipment failure," CC supplied.

"But vaginal secretions," Max continued.

"Ellen's?" CC inquired.

"And someone else," Max added. "The lab is working on that. Two wine glasses were found in the bedroom - one with Ellen's prints and one with Sandra's."

CC's head jerked up in surprise. "Damn, I'm an idiot," she snapped. "Remember how the landlady went on and on about Sandra not having a boyfriend or dating at all?"

"She just hung around with a few girlfriends from the hospital," Max finished as CC reached for the telephone on his desk. She quickly dialed her home number. "Stevie, let me talk to Jamie," she demanded before her sister could say anything.

'Yes?' Jamie greeted her gruffly.

"I'm not checking up on you," CC blurted out guiltily.

"It's okay if you are," Jamie responded softly.

"I'm not," CC reasserted adamantly. "I need to ask you a question."

"Okay." Her lover responded hesitantly.

"Was Sandra Bernstein gay?" the policewoman inquired carefully.

"Why?" Jamie inquired curiously. "Sorry," the doctor quickly apologized as CC groaned. "I never asked but I did get the baby dyke vibe from her."

"Thank you," CC said.

"What are you wearing?" Jamie taunted her in a sultry tone.

"Don't," CC blurted out as she felt her face flush. She said her goodbyes as Jamie cackled into the receiver.

"That's an interesting shade you're sporting, partner," Max teased her as she buried her face in the file she'd been studying. "So was Sandra playing for your team?"

"Jamie thinks so," CC confirmed as something on the page she'd been scanning caught her attention.

"How does that work - that whole gaydar thing?" Max threw out quizzically.

"Just a gut instinct," CC responded with a shrug. "Guess where Simon Fisher did his last rotation before the ER?"

"Pediatrics?" Max said hopefully. "We're getting so close."

"But we still don't have anything," CC grumbled. "Okay, we need to get the interviews set up for today and talk to the Captain."

"You have a theory; I can hear those wheels spinning," Max gloated.

"I need to talk to Carter," CC responded thoughtfully as she mentioned the department psychologist. "I'm just wondering about the two victims from California. All blondes with green eyes - what if they were gay too? I can't help but wonder if somewhere in Simon's life he lost a blonde girlfriend to another girl."

"Could be," Max agreed. "Then if the next woman he falls for or takes an interest in also turns out to be gay, it could be what set him off."

"Makes you wonder," CC said thoughtfully.

"What's that?" Max asked.

"Just how many bodies are we looking for?" CC concluded with dread.

CC and Max were sitting in the Captain's office; their supervisor's bushy white eyebrows were raised to his almost nonexistent hairline. "Could you repeat that?" the gruff older man sternly requested.

"We believe that Dr. Jameson is the killer's primary focus," CC repeated the information in a slow concise manner.

"Not that part," the Captain barked.

"She's my lover," CC reiterated boldly as she watched the vein in her supervisor's forehead begin to throb in an unnatural manner. *'Oh, that can't be good,'* she thought.

"And?" he urged her on as beads of sweat began to form on his brow.

"I had a physical altercation with the prime suspect," CC admitted.

"That's the part I needed to hear again." The robust man blew out a breath angrily. "So tell me something - was he the prime suspect before or after he hit on your girlfriend?"

"After," CC answered him, somehow managing to keep her cool façade intact.

"Captain, it's not like that," Max jumped in quickly to defend her.

"I know that," the Captain grunted. "I know that," he repeated confidently, diverting his gaze towards CC. "But I doubt that a jury will see it that way."

"You're right," CC agreed.

"Thank you," he responded with a heavy sigh.

"I don't agree," Max argued. "Calloway has never been alone with any evidence or at any of the crime scenes. We have documentation to support that," Max supplied eagerly.

"Yeah?" The Captain grunted with more enthusiasm.

"I went out of my way to ensure it and everyone and their brother has signed statements to that effect," CC explained. "We can show a clear line from the bodies to Dr. Fisher. And it has absolutely nothing to do with the fact that he's a creepy slime ball who's been sniffing after my girlfriend."

"No, you don't," the Captain corrected her. "From what I've heard, you haven't connected him to the bodies. Now when you bring me something that will make a judge sign a search warrant, then you'll have a clear line to the victims. In the meantime you don't have squat. But since you're no longer working this investigation, it doesn't matter."

"Captain?" CC began to protest. She'd known it might happen but she had to do anything she could to ensure that she was kept in the loop.

"No arguments," he cut her off.

"Captain, this is Calloway's case," Max defended his partner.

"No, it isn't," the Captain stated bluntly.

"Captain, hear me out," CC calmly interjected. "Fisher hasn't been charged. Max is following that angle and I'm simply pursuing the investigation to wherever it leads me. That includes any and all other possible suspects, including a list of known sex offenders who might fit the profile," CC explained in a cool confident tone.

"Bullshit," the Captain grumbled.

CC simply stared back at him with her stoic façade rooted firmly in place. She could tell by the way his bloodshot eyes were avoiding her gaze that he was beginning to waver. "No contact with Fisher," he warned her as he conceded to her wishes. Remaining on the investigation was more than she'd hoped for.

"There's more," CC continued, pleased by the turn of events.

"You're giving me a headache," the Captain groused bitterly.

"I know," CC responded with a cocky smirk. "I just wanted to give you a complete rundown on what we have."

"Tell me everything," he insisted in a warning tone. "Starting with the queer . . ." He halted his words as CC glared at him and then cleared his throat before continuing. ". . . I meant to say the gay angle."

"Of course you did," CC responded coldly. She understood it was more a generational thing with the captain yet it still didn't excuse the comment. She knew by the way his eyes avoided her own that her point had been made. "After speaking to Ellen Murdock's friends and family and doing a thorough search of her residence, we confirmed that Ms. Murdock was bisexual," CC explained, turning her focus towards the hard work she and Max had put in that day. "And she had on occasion socialized with Sandra Bernstein."

"They dated," the Captain added thoughtfully.

"Yes," Max confirmed. "DNA found at the scene confirms that the vaginal secretions belong to both victims."

"Blood and tissue samples collected at the scene lead to the obvious conclusion that both women were murdered in Ellen Murdock's apartment," CC picked up for him. "Ellen Murdock's blood is also present on the shards of glass from Dr. Jameson's front window."

"Do I want to know how the two of you managed to get all these lab results so quickly?" the Captain inquired with a curiously edgy tone of voice.

"No," the two detectives responded in unison.

The older man simply began to rub his throbbing temples once again. "Why dump one body and not the other?" he pondered aloud. CC and Max had been asking the same question since they discovered that both women were murdered at the same location.

"Not a clue," Max admitted. "We're hoping that Doc Carter might have some ideas."

"What else?" the Captain prodded them.

"Terrell, the attendant who's normally on duty in the back parking garage, has been eliminated as a suspect," CC continued. "He was logged on, but further investigation showed that he was at St. Elizabeth's Hospital at the time Sandra and Ellen departed the garage. His daughter and grandchildren had been involved in a minor car accident. He found out just after clocking in. His supervisor left him on the clock thinking he was helping the guy out by letting him collect a day's pay."

"Nothing that hasn't been done here." The Captain shrugged. "The supervisor confirmed this?"

"Yes, as did the staff at Saint E's," CC said. "Terrell didn't even know about it until we went over the dates and times with him. The sad part is that if Terrell hadn't been in Brighton looking after his family, those two women would probably still be alive. And that brings us to Saul Rumford."

"Romeo." Max snorted in amusement. "The kid who filled in for Terrell."

"Right, the one who shut the video down so he could have his knob waxed," CC supplied. "We have an interview set up with him in a half an hour. He isn't being very cooperative since the hospital canned him after finding out what he did."

"What about the girl?" the Captain pressed.

"We're going to try to get her name from him although it's possible she's a working girl," CC said. "Hard to say by the way she was dressed; she could have just been young. I don't know how useful she'll be since, based on her position in the booth, I doubt that she could see anything of interest."

"What about the two girls from San Diego?" the Captain inquired. CC handed him the file that she'd received. The Captain grimaced when he looked at the crime scene photos. "If I didn't know any better I'd swear I was looking at the Bernstein crime scene."

"I know," CC agreed. "Which brings us to another problem. This could be a serial killer." She'd been biding her time in bringing this up, knowing what the reaction would be.

"No Feds," the Captain shouted. CC gave him a wary look in response. "You want to bring them in? Why would you of all people want to do that?"

"Because they owe me," CC spat out. "And the stakes are too high for me to let this bastard get away."

Max and her Captain sat there in a stunned in silence. "They can get information that we can't," CC explained. "Like if the victims in California were gay. Right now we can't find anything to support that theory. Or if Simon has anything in his past that might show a prior history, and he isn't just some poor schmuck who has bad luck with women. And they can probably tie it up neatly so it looks like no one crossed any legal lines to get this information."

A chilly silence filled the room as her partner stared at her with a slack-jawed expression. CC had never thought she would be asking the same people who had covered up her shooting for help. But keeping Jamie safe outweighed everything else. "Anything else on the case?" the Captain stammered.

"No sir," CC responded casually.

"Well, keep me updated," he said in a faraway tone.

After they stepped out of the Captain's office Max was still staring at her in disbelief. "Don't fight me on this, Max," she cautioned him. "I won't lose her."

Jamie had a slight spring in her step when she entered the hospital. Despite the tension of the last twenty-four hours, she was elated by the time she'd spent with CC. And knowing that she wouldn't have to face Simon Fisher was an added bonus. "Good evening, ladies," she greeted the nurses who were busy pouring over their paperwork.

"You had sex," Evaline gasped.

"Jealous?" Jamie quipped with a bright smile.

"Yes," Evaline whined.

"Poor baby," Jamie offered with false comfort. "Well, time to get to work," she added brightly as she snatched a chocolate chip cookie from the tray sitting on the counter.

She entered the lounge area and went straight to her locker. She opened it, and with the cookie clenched between her teeth, began to change into her scrubs. As she pulled her lab coat out of the locker, a slip of paper fell to the floor. She stared at it curiously as she shrugged on the coat. With the cookie still firmly locked in her mouth, she bent over and picked up the piece of paper.

Jamie took the cookie in one hand and began to munch on it as she turned the paper over to see what it was. Her heart stopped when she saw the bold nondescript writing. The cookie fell to the floor as she stared blankly at the words - *'You're mine'*.

"What are you thinking?" Max inquired as CC stared through the two-way mirror. The sight of Simon Fisher sitting smugly at the shaky table made her stomach turn. "You're on to something. I can hear those squeaky wheels spinning in that noggin of yours," Max pressed.

"He's smart," CC explained dryly as Max blankly stared at her. "I mean he's really, really smart. He knows it and he likes to show it. Did you know that in San Diego the cops grilled him for hours and he never broke a sweat? They didn't have anything, and he knew it. Just like now; he knows we're focusing on him but we don't have any proof. That makes him happy. The good cop bad cop scenario is just going to amuse him."

"What would you like to do?" Max encouraged her.

"Go in there and tell him that you're sorry for wasting his time but you don't need to talk to him," CC continued thoughtfully.

"Excuse me?" Max sputtered.

"Go in and send him packing. Make sure he feels like he isn't important enough for you to waste your time on," CC concluded with a wry smile.

Max nodded in agreement and left her alone to watch Simon Fisher yawn in boredom. The door to the small observation room opened. CC didn't bother to look up; she knew whom it was. He sat in the chair next to her. She handed him the files that had been resting on her lap.

"So this is business and here I thought that you were missing me." The man grunted in amusement as he shifted in his chair.

"Take a look," CC instructed him firmly, never taking her eyes off Dr. Fisher. "Why would I be missing you, Mallory? The last time I saw you was over a decade ago. You were standing by my hospital bed reminding me how it would be in everyone's best interest if I pretended that the whole incident never happened."

"Calloway?" the man nervously began.

"Relax and take a look at those files," CC instructed him coolly as she watched Max finally enter the interview room.

"Doctor . . . Uhm . . . " CC smiled as Max seemed to fumble for the man's name. "Fisher," he concluded as he yawned and scratched his head. "Sorry to waste your time but I don't need you for anything."

"You're sitting here watching your partner dismiss a witness?" Mallory scoffed. CC ignored the man's arrogance; she watched in delight as Simon Fisher's face dropped in confusion. *'Just push him a little harder, Max,'* she mentally encouraged her partner. "Wait." Mallory's excited tone broke her concentration. "Two girls in Boston and San Diego? This is federal," Mallory stated eagerly.

"Stop marking your territory and listen," CC cut him off sharply.

"Then why am I here?" Fisher began to stammer.

"Sorry, must have been a mix up," Max said with a shrug. "I have no reason to talk to you. There's nothing you can help me with."

"Good boy," CC said with a smile.

"Well . . . Uhm . . . maybe I could be of some use," Fisher suggested timidly.

"Trust me, Doc; we don't need you," Max goaded him. "Sorry for the inconvenience."

"Mallory, you're not taking over this investigation," CC cautioned the irate man sitting next to her as she waited for Simon's next move. "You're going to work for us, and all of us are going to end up looking very good and a killer will be off the streets."

"It's a serial case. That makes it federal," Mallory asserted with a hiss.

"Shove it, Mallory," CC spat back. "Your office will work for us and reap much needed good press. I took two bullets because of your screw-up and your informant ended up dead. I'm trying to catch a killer. How about you? Is your ego really going to get in my way?"

"No," Mallory agreed with a grunt. "What do you need?"

"See this guy." CC pointed towards Simon. "Max told him that he doesn't need to speak to the police and he's free to go, but he's still there. I find that interesting. "

"Uh huh," Mallory conceded and CC knew that she finally had his interest.

"I want everything about him," CC stated flatly. "And I mean everything, right down to when he was potty trained."

"Anything else?" Mallory spat out sarcastically.

"Yes," CC answered in a flat even tone. "Don't even think about holding anything back or excluding me on this or your already soiled reputation will be looking a whole lot dirtier."

"Understood," Mallory gravely agreed. "Mind if I watch the show?"

CC nodded in agreement as her eyes remained focused on Dr. Fisher. Max had agreed to talk with the young doctor, claiming boredom and a chance to put his feet up. "So why did someone in your department ask me to come down here?" Simon inquired, trying far too hard to sound casual.

"That must have been my partner," Max grunted in disgust.

"That woman," Simon sneered.

"She doesn't like you." Max laughed. "I made the mistake of mentioning that you were in Dr. Jameson's neighborhood yesterday."

"What's so strange about me visiting Jamie?" Simon inquired with a shrug.

CC choked back the bile that began to rise in her throat. "Hey, you don't have to tell me." Max sighed. "But you know that kind," Max added in a disgusted tone.

"It's sad," Simon agreed. "Thinking that they don't want a man. Pathetic really."

"I know," Max agreed. "Makes me sick. But what can I do? Thanks to the bleeding hearts that run this state, I'm stuck with her."

"I just wish that she would leave Jamie and me alone," Simon explained, believing his own lies. "Frankly I'm tempted to file a complaint."

"Maybe you should," Max grunted. "Get the bitch out of my hair."

"Perhaps," Simon responded, sounding confused. "I wonder if she's somehow behind the vandalism at Jamie's home."

"Bingo," CC drew out with a confident smile.

"Vandalism?" Max responded, playing along with the charade.

"Someone broke her front window," Simon explained. CC noted the far away look in his brown eyes. "Smashed it with a tire iron."

CC and Max were drawn in by the young doctors' slip of the tongue. "Come on, Max; don't let him know that you know," CC whispered as she tightly clutched the armrests of her chair.

"That's terrible!" Max exclaimed. "And in such a nice neighborhood. I tell you the whole world is going to hell. You know, I can look into it for you. It could have been one of those freaks she encounters in the ER."

"I thought of that," Simon added. "That place is a cesspool. I'll be happy when my rotation is over." Max just stared at him blankly. "Right, you don't understand. We're rotated so we can learn from the different departments. Last time I was in pediatrics. All those screaming kids. But I did have a good thing going with one of the nurses."

"You're a real heartbreaker." Max chuckled. "I envy you."

"Well, you know." Simon blushed then his smile vanished. "But things with Ellen ended badly." The icy tone in his voice was making the hair on the back of CC's neck stand on end. Then suddenly his smile returned. "But it doesn't matter now that Jamie and I are together."

"That's what happens when you meet the right girl." Max smiled in agreement. "They clip your wings," he teased the young doctor. "Well, I should get back to work," Max grumbled as he stood.

"So how is the investigation into Sandra's murder going?" Simon threw out casually.

"Probably some lowlife freak that spotted her on the street," Max explained.

"Oh?" Simon mumbled in a dejected tone.

"Don't worry. It was probably just some loser," Max explained as he led Simon out of the room.

"Let me guess. This Jamie doesn't have a relationship with him?" Mallory inquired.

"Not in the real world," CC responded as Max entered the room. Her partner stiffened at the sight of the FBI agent sitting there.

"Max, this is Special Agent Mallory," CC made the introductions.

"We've met," Max grunted.

"He's going to tell us all about Dr. Fisher," CC taunted the federal agent. "Aren't you?" Mallory ignored her comment until she flashed him an icy glare. "In fact, you're going to get started right now."

"Of course," Mallory groaned as he stood and left.

Neither CC nor Max acknowledged the man's departure. "Did you get all that?" Max asked.

"I caught everything," CC responded grimly. "Jamie's broken window, the tire iron, and Ellen Murdock. It's still not enough."

"Did Jamie tell anyone about her front window?" Max inquired.

"Her supervisor," CC sighed.

"So it could have been common knowledge," Max processed.

"Still, I love the part about the tire iron." CC smiled. "Nothing like confirming our suspicions. At some point the good doctor is going to realize that he made that slip. Let's just hope we're in a better position by then."

The door opened and a uniformed officer poked his head inside. "Max, the head of security from Boylston General is on the phone for you," the young officer explained. Fear gripped

CC's heart. They rushed out of the room and to their desks. CC paced nervously while Max spoke on the telephone. "Well?" she demanded once he ended the call.

"Jamie is fine," he reassured her as she blew out a tense breath. "She found a note in her locker. Two words, *'You're mine'*." CC grabbed her car keys. "Sit," Max scolded her. "You can't go near the evidence. Stay here. I'll get the note, talk to Jamie, and take it to the lab," he explained carefully. CC opened her mouth, fully prepared to argue with him. "No," Max firmly asserted.

"I have to see her," CC protested.

"Call her," Max offered as he picked up his car keys.

CC had dialed the hospital before Max reached the door. "Dr. Jameson, please," she requested as she tried to still the erratic beating of her heart.

"Who's calling please?" a voice inquired and CC relaxed, knowing that extra measures were being taken to ensure Jamie's safety.

"Caitlin," she calmly offered.

"One moment please," the friendly voice said.

"Hey, baby," Jamie greeted her a few moments later.

"Are you all right?" CC asked in a soothing tone.

"A little shaken but hearing your voice really helps," Jamie responded softly.

"Max is on his way," CC explained.

"Oh?" Jamie responded and CC could hear the disappointment in the blonde's voice.

"I'm sorry, baby, but because of us I have to stay away this time," CC explained. Her own heart was breaking at not being able to be there for her lover. "I'm doing everything I can to put this behind us," she promised.

"I know," Jamie responded confidently. "I was just a little . . ."

"I know," CC responded as she caressed the telephone.

"Did I tell you that I dropped my cookie?" Jamie added brightly. CC laughed, knowing that her lover was trying to ease the tension. "You laugh?" Jamie scoffed. "It was chocolate chip."

"You'll have to explain that one to me when you get home." CC chuckled as she collected herself.

"Thanks," Jamie added softly. "I feel safer just by hearing your voice."

After CC ended the telephone call she looked at the clock again. *'Jamie might feel better, but I sure as hell don't,'* her inner voice grumbled. She was about to call Jamie back just to hear her voice one more time when the desk sergeant informed her that Saul, aka Romeo, had arrived. She had the sergeant show the little bugger to the interview room while she grabbed Larry Sorensen to join her.

"Why do you need a baby sitter?" Sorensen grumbled as he tried to finish his sandwich on the way to the interview room.

"Just do," CC responded curtly.

"So what did he do?" Sorensen asked as he took another bite.

"Got a blow job," CC casually quipped as she opened the door and Sorensen choked on his sandwich.

"So Saul, how are you?" CC inquired with a feral grin as she took a seat next to the brooding young man. "I'm going to tape this interview and Detective Sorensen is going to keep us company," she explained as she turned on the recorder and motioned to the detective who'd finally managed to spit out the remnants of his sandwich.

"Look, haven't you people done enough?" Saul spat out. "I lost my job; my father works in the cardiology department and heard why I was fired. I didn't see anything, and I don't have anything else to say," he sneered in challenge.

"This punk got a blow job?" Sorensen asked in amazement. "What did ya do - pay for it, kid?"

"That's it." Saul's voice cracked as he stood.

"Not so fast." CC stood to her full height so she could tower over the young man who still had acne and looked barely old enough to shave. "Saul, I'm really sorry you lost your job and embarrassed your daddy," she spat out sarcastically. "But not as sorry as I am that a woman died because the killer knew that he could get by you."

Saul swallowed hard as he slumped back down into his chair, his frightened eyes staring up at CC. "You've done this before, haven't you?" CC asked in an icy tone that scared even Sorensen.

"Yes," Saul squeaked.

"How often?" CC pressed.

"Whenever I work the late shift," Saul squeaked once again.

"You always shut the video off?" CC continued, still hovering over the man.

"Well yeah," Saul replied as if it was a silly question.

"Did you pay the girl?" CC continued.

"What?" Saul responded indignantly. "She's my girlfriend."

"We need her name and address," CC informed him.

"But . . ." he began to protest.

"No buts," CC cut him off. "A woman is dead. She'd be alive today if you'd only done your job," she pushed, not revealing that in fact two women were dead because Saul couldn't keep it in his pants. So far very few people at the hospital knew about Ellen and she wanted to keep it that way.

CC slapped a legal pad of paper and a pen down in front of the frightened youth. "Start writing and while you're writing you can tell us who entered the garage just before you shut the video down as well as everyone you can remember from the time the tape was off."

"There was that ferret-faced doctor who's always real snotty to me," Saul quavered as he scribbled furiously.

"Name?" CC pushed him.

"I don't know," Saul whined. "But I've seen him before; he always tries to watch when Shelia and I are together at work."

"Who else?" CC urged him on.

"Sandra Bernstein. I know her; she's real nice," Saul babbled on. "And Ellen something, she's a nurse in pediatrics, I think. I didn't see anyone else. But I was . . . err . . . busy."

"Thank you, Saul," she added in a patronizing tone.

By the time she'd finished with Saul, Max had returned and they compared notes. The note was at the lab and was nondescript. Jamie seemed fine and agreed not to go anywhere in or out of the hospital alone. Later CC made a quick stop before hurrying home. She smiled when she opened the door and found Jamie sitting on the couch waiting for her. She held up the white bag she'd stopped for and Jamie smiled.

"Pepperidge Farm soft baked chocolate chunk." Jamie sniffed. "You're too good to me."

"Yeah well . . ." CC grumbled.

Jamie smiled sweetly at her and took the bag of cookies as she kissed CC tenderly on the cheek. "Let's go to bed," Jamie whispered softly in the policewoman's ear as she took her by the hand. CC was sporting a goofy grin as her lover led her into the bedroom.

Jamie led her lover into the tiny bedroom, never wanting to release her hand. "I need to take a shower, darling," CC whispered softly in the darkness.

"Then I'll just have to join you," Jamie responded in a breathy tone as she turned and snuggled up against her tall lover. "Because I just can't seem to let go of you." She sighed deeply as she felt CC's hand caressing her back in a reassuring manner. "Sorry. With everything that's going on I'm feeling a little clingy tonight."

"Ssh," CC said in a voice just above a whisper as she placed a gentle kiss on the top of Jamie's head. "I'm feeling a little clingy myself. I just really need to shower before we go to bed," CC explained as she tightened her embrace.

"Let's go then," Jamie concluded with a sly smile. CC parted her lips to speak. Jamie quickly silenced her lover by pressing her fingers gently against CC's lips. "We'll just have to be quiet so we don't wake up Stevie or Emma. Quiet can be very nice sometimes," Jamie added seductively. She smiled as her lover's amazing blue eyes widened. Jamie couldn't see well enough in the dark but she was quite certain her lover was blushing.

Without a word Jamie led CC out of the bedroom and to the downstairs bathroom. CC leaned against the sink and watched the young doctor's every move. Jamie slid open the glass door and turned on the water. She allowed it to run so it could reach the appropriate temperature. Then she turned to her awaiting lover.

CC gave her a curious glance as Jamie slowly closed the distance between them. Jamie ran her hands along CC's broad shoulders and down her long arms. The brunette seemed to melt into her touch, giving herself over to Jamie's exploration. Jamie took her time as she ran her small hands back up CC's arms and then across her chest. She allowed her hands to soak up the feel of CC's soft cotton shirt as she cupped her firm full breasts.

Jamie allowed her fingers and the palms of her hands to continue caressing her lover's breasts as CC's breathing grew heavier and her nipples hardened from the blonde's touch. "I love the way your body responds to me," Jamie said softly as she placed tender kisses along CC's neck and her hands continued their exploration. CC moaned softly in response.

Jamie nuzzled her face in CC's long silky tresses. She loved the feel of her lover's hair caressing her skin and could lose herself in it for an eternity. The whimper CC released alerted her that her lover needed more attention. Jamie reluctantly pulled her face out of CC's hair and released her tender hold on her breasts. As the bathroom filled with steam, she slowly began to unbutton CC's blouse.

Jamie allowed her fingertips to graze CC's bronzed skin but never touched her where her need demanded. CC seemed completely willing to allow Jamie to set the pace. And tonight Jamie needed to take things slowly. The blonde could feel her own breathing become erratic as she removed CC's blouse, allowing it to fall onto the floor.

Jamie ran her fingertips along the bare skin of CC's shoulders while she lowered the straps of the woman's bra. Jamie's eyes were firmly fixed on watching the rise and fall of CC's chest; she trailed her fingers along the brunette's bra until she found the clasp in the back. With a swift motion Jamie released it and allowed the white lacy undergarment to hang loosely around her lover's body.

The heat was rising in the small bathroom as the steam created a mist around them. Jamie removed the taller woman's bra, allowing her fingers to once again caress her lover's skin. She tossed the garment onto the floor and then cupped her lover's breasts. She licked her lips as her hands wallowed in the feel of them. She explored the curve and weight of CC's breasts without touching her erect nipples.

Jamie fought off the temptation to suckle CC's nipples until her lover exploded in ecstasy. She watched her lover's breathing becoming more erratic; her own breathing mirrored her lover's. Her hands drifted down CC's ribs and felt the curve of her body. Jamie caressed the brunette's firm abdomen as CC released soft demanding moans.

As Jamie began to unzip CC's slacks, the taller woman kicked of her shoes. Jamie lowered the pants down CC's body, feeling every inch of exposed flesh in her path. She was kneeling before CC as she assisted in the removal of the brunette's slacks and socks. Jamie's hands slowly explored CC's endless legs, feeling the muscles twitching from her touch. She rested her head against her lover's quivering stomach as her fingers glided along CC's thighs.

Jamie tilted her head back and began to run her fingers along the elastic waistband of CC's panties. She smiled at the adorable underwear that had little blue smurfs on them. She almost laughed at the sight as she thought that it was adults like CC that kept novelty companies in business. Jamie kissed the taut muscles of CC's stomach as she began to lower the underwear. The scent of her lover's arousal filled her senses as Jamie pressed her body into CC's long legs.

Jamie rubbed her breasts against the brunette's firm thighs. She moaned as her nipples hardened through her nightshirt. Needing to feel more contact, Jamie quickly pulled off her top. She ran the hard buds across CC's thighs as she lowered her panties slowly down her legs. Once free from her lover's body, Jamie cast the underwear aside and once again ran her breasts up along CC's legs.

She could see the glistening signs of her lover's desire as she blew a warm breath through her dark curls. "Don't come," Jamie whispered before she parted her lover's swollen nether lips. CC growled in frustration as Jamie dipped her tongue in her lover's wetness. Jamie's tongue licked slowly along CC's lips, drinking in her desire. CC clutched the edge of the sink while Jamie's tongue flickered across her throbbing clit.

Jamie suckled CC's clit in the warmth of her mouth. She grazed her teeth across the aching nub while she caressed her backside. CC's thighs parted, inviting Jamie to explore her more deeply. Jamie suckled her harder as her hand massaged the firm flesh of her firm backside. As she felt CC's body trembling against her, the blonde retreated and stood beside her frustrated lover. Jamie kissed the brunette deeply, allowing her to taste her own wetness on Jamie's lips.

The blonde opened the shower door and tested the temperature of the water. After a quick adjustment she urged CC to enter the shower. Jamie stood just outside the glass door and watched CC immerse herself in the water. The sight of water dripping off CC's long beautiful body made her body quiver with desire. Once, years ago when they were dating the first time, Jamie had caught sight of a younger CC in the shower and almost exploded from the beauty she saw.

Now, over a decade later, Jamie felt the same stirrings of passion for CC. The brunette looked at her as she ran soapy hands over her body. Jamie watched as those strong hands lathered every inch of CC's body. She leaned back and watched each swirl of the bubbling lather that covered her lover. Jamie's hand slipped beneath the waistband of her sweatpants.

Jamie moaned as her own wetness painted her fingers. Her emerald eyes were firmly fixed on the soft movements of CC's hands while the blonde teased her own aching clit. She gasped as CC stepped under the spray of water and the lather ran down her body. Jamie's hips swayed urgently as she touched herself while CC began to wash her hair. By the time CC was rinsing the shampoo out of her long raven tresses, Jamie's hips were thrusting wildly.

She was panting as her hand slipped out of the warm wetness. She was close to the edge but wanted to climax with CC's body pressed against her own. She tugged off her sweatpants and threw them aside. Jamie stepped into the shower and closed the door behind her. She pressed her naked body against CC and ran her hands along her lover's wet naked flesh as the water beat down upon them.

CC turned and wrapped Jamie in her arms; their lips were soon locked in a fiery kiss as their bodies melted together. Not even a drop of water separated them as Jamie felt the cool tile wall pressing against her back. Each pressed a firm thigh against the other's aching mound. The kiss ended with both women gasping for air as they rode against the other's firm thigh. CC began to suckle Jamie's neck as the blonde clutched the taller woman's backside.

They thrust against one another urgently as their breasts pressed together. Jamie's body was on fire as they swayed together, each matching the other's frantic rhythm until they cried out. They clung to each other as their bodies trembled. Finally, each exhaled a heavy breath and they stepped back under the warm water and began to bathe one another, lingering on the more interesting body parts. Jamie once again found herself pressed against the shower wall and she wrapped her legs around CC's body. Her lover held her up with one arm while the other slipped between their bodies.

Jamie thrust against CC's body as her lover entered her. The blonde's hips rocked wildly as CC's fingers plunged in and out of her wetness. She muffled her cries as she climaxed against her lover's touch. They shared lingering kisses before returning to the task of actually getting clean. Drying each other off almost led to them returning to the shower, but since the water had already turned cold the couple climbed into bed. Jamie released a happy sigh as she snuggled her naked body against CC's. "I love you," she whispered as sleep claimed her.

CC was humming softly as she looked over the case files and forensic reports that were laid out on her desk. "You're in an awfully good mood," Max commented wryly as he looked over his own collection of reports. CC simply wiggled her dark eyebrows suggestively. "Oh, I see," Max surmised. "Still excited about the new car."

"Now that's why you're a detective," CC taunted him.

"Hmm," Max sighed as he nodded. "You might want to tell her not to leave so many marks next time."

"He he," CC chuckled with a broad smile.

Her telephone rang and she quickly answered it. "Calloway," she said into the receiver.

"Detective Calloway, this is Detective Brooks," the wheezing chain smoker greeted her.

"Detective Brooks, nice to hear from you," CC replied as Max perked up. "I was going to call you in a little while. I don't really have much but I want to keep you in the loop."

"I appreciate it." He coughed. "I might have something for you. The other day you asked if either of my victims were gay."

"Yes?" she responded eagerly as she twirled her pencil between her fingers.

"I don't know why I didn't recall it at the time. Marylyn wasn't but she did say something that might help you," he explained. "When Simon first started bugging her to go out with him, she told him that she was gay just to get rid of him."

"Interesting," CC noted. "What about Natalie, the other girl?"

"I did some checking, and she was a lesbian," Brooks confirmed. "Do you think this might be some kind of hate crime?"

"Not in the traditional sense," CC explained. "But it might be our boy's trigger."

"One more thing." Brooks coughed. "There've been some suits sniffing around the old files. You wouldn't know anything about that, would you?"

"Yeah," CC responded with a heavy sigh. "I know you probably don't want the feds around anymore than my boss does, but they promised to be good."

"I'd work with the devil himself if I could finally bring some peace to these girls' families," Brooks vowed.

"Feds, the devil - close enough," CC commented. "Thanks again, Detective. I'll keep you informed."

After she hung up the telephone, she filled Max in on what she had found. "Now Natalie complained about someone harassing, her but they could never prove that it was Fisher," Max thought out loud.

"Right," CC confirmed. "What about the lab report on the note from Jamie's locker?"

"Nothing," Max grumbled. "It could have been Fisher or Santa Claus for all we know. The paper is too common, the handwriting indistinct, and the only prints were Jamie's and hospital security."

"What? They couldn't find a pair of rubber gloves in the ER?" CC growled. "Yoyos. Don't these guys ever watch television?"

"Detective Calloway," a voice greeted her. CC looked up to find a very weary looking Agent Mallory staring down at her.

"Speak of the devil," she teased.

"I think that you, your partner, your Captain, and I should have a talk," he suggested in an exhausted tone.

Within a few moments the four of them were sitting in the Captain's office. Mallory handed the Captain a large file. "Everything you would ever want to know about Dr. Simon Fisher," Mallory explained; his demeanor and rumpled appearance told CC that he had given his all to find out everything he could.

"How many bodies? CC fearfully inquired.

"Nine we think," Mallory confirmed as CC's stomach turned. "Starting with his high school sweetheart - only there's no body for that one."

"Peachy," CC choked out. "Let's hear it."

"Simon Fisher of the San Diego Fishers has a sealed juvenal record for arson and torturing the neighborhood animals. A classic characteristic for serial killers," Mallory began in a slow careful tone. "His parents moved him from one private school to another whenever little Simon would get in trouble. Then about the time he turned seventeen, he met and started dating Janie Jensen. Simon seemed to clean up his act. His grades got better; he stopped setting things on fire and got accepted to a good college. The couple remained close until his sophomore year when Janie started college away from home. Everything seemed fine and then Janie disappeared. She was driving back to school at UC Santa Barbara after the winter break was over. Her car was discovered in a remote area off her route with a flat tire. Everyone assumed she broke down and some creep snatched her."

"You doubt that's what happened?" CC urged him.

"Normally I wouldn't but we did find out something very interesting," Mallory continued. "She and her roommate were involved. According to the roommate, a romance had begun and Janie was planning on breaking up with Simon. She'd never told anyone about it since her parents were so devastated by her disappearance."

"Was Janie a blonde?" CC asked, trying to keep her professional focus intact.

"Blonde hair, green eyes, and looked a lot like your victims," Mallory confirmed. "Here's her picture."

CC felt ill as she looked at the young girl who closely resembled her lover. "And the other victims?" CC pressed on, trying to remain focused and keep her breakfast from reappearing. The Captain slid the crime scene photos over.

"They could be our victims," the Captain noted.

"Same look, same MO, same lifestyle, same everything," Mallory pointed out. "And they either knew Simon Fisher, or he was in the area at the time. Several times he had a fictitious relationship with the victim. The only one that wasn't interested in women was Marylyn Steiner; we think she was his second victim."

"But she told him that she was gay just to ditch him," CC added.

"Yes, we found that out as well," Mallory confirmed, impressed with CC's knowledge.

"It really is him," CC said in slow steady voice as her heart pounded violently.

"Yes," Mallory confirmed. "And we can't prove a thing."
The four of them sat there in a stony silence until the ring of the Captain's telephone broke through the eerie silence. The Captain seemed tense as he concluded the call. "That was hospital security. Dr. Jameson received another note," he explained tensely.

"Ms. Durham, I'm Dr. Jameson," Jamie introduced herself as she stepped into the exam room. She was studying the chart the nurse had handed her and didn't look at her patient. When the woman failed to respond, Jamie looked up to see the woman staring at her coldly. It wasn't an unusual reaction since most people didn't come to see her because they were feeling good. Still, there was something familiar about the brunette who was giving her a murderous look. Jamie just couldn't put her finger on where she'd seen the woman before.

Jamie shrugged it off and went about examining the woman who proved to be quite uncooperative. "It looks like strep; I'm going to take a throat culture just be certain," Jamie explained as she scribbled some notes on Ms. Durham's chart. "Are you allergic to any antibiotics?" Jamie asked the scowling woman as the doctor's mind once again tried to recall why the woman was familiar. "Is that a no?" Jamie pressed when the woman failed to respond.

"Dr. Jameson, you have a call on line three," Evaline said as she stepped into the room.

"Thanks." Jamie nodded. "Could you take a throat culture for me while I take the call?" Evaline agreed and Jamie excused herself while her patient glared at her. Jamie shrugged as she picked up the telephone on the wall across from her unfriendly patient. "Dr. Jameson," Jamie greeted her caller.

"James, are you all right?" CC inquired frantically.

"Caitlin?" Jamie responded in confusion.

Suddenly a bedpan went flying past her head. Evaline screamed as Jamie spun around. Jamie was stunned to find her patient looking for something else to throw at her. Jamie dropped the telephone when her memory started working. "Oh shit. Liz," she muttered as she ducked a box of gauze. A security officer stepped into the room just as Liz's aim started to improve. "Dr. Jameson, are you all right?" the man inquired as he began to head towards Liz.

"Freeze!" Jamie shouted. "Now all of you calm down!" the blonde doctor asserted firmly. Thankfully everyone halted in his or her tracks. "Evaline, did you get the culture?" she asked quickly.

"No; she tried to bite me," Evaline responded bitterly.

"I'll get it," Jamie offered. "Why don't both of you wait outside. And you sit down," she growled at Liz.

"Dr. Jameson, I need to speak with you," the guard pleaded.

"I'll be outside in a moment," Jamie responded in a firm voice. He nodded, and then he and Evaline quickly left the room.

"Liz," Jamie began as she clenched her jaw.

"Now you know my name," the woman responded in a scratchy voice.

"Look, I know I'm a complete jerk," Jamie confessed in a harsh tone as she approached the woman with whom she'd shared a disastrous sexual encounter. "But if you don't behave, I'm going to call that large security guard back in here and have you restrained, and not in a fun way. Do you understand?" Liz simply glared at her. "I mean it," Jamie stressed. Liz still refused to answer her; Jamie watched the anger grow on the brunette's features. "Look, I may not have been the good time you were expecting in the backseat of your car, but I am a good doctor and that is why you're here."

"You used me to cheat on your girlfriend," Liz hissed.

"No," Jamie corrected her as she gathered the materials that she needed to get the throat culture. "Caitlin and I weren't back together by then."

"Don't hand me that 'we were separated' crap," Liz squawked.

"For twelve years," Jamie fumed, tired of the nasty predicament. Liz looked at her with a stunned expression. Jamie blew out a heavy sigh before finishing her explanation. "She was my girlfriend in college. We split up over a dozen years ago and recently got back together. That night I was with you I was still trying to sort out my feelings. Satisfied?" Liz nodded in agreement. "Good. Now open wide so I can get this over with. And if you try to bite me, I'll beat the snot out of you," Jamie added in a threatening tone. Liz nodded fearfully and opened her mouth as wide as she could.

Jamie was exhausted by the time she handed the culture to one of the technicians. Just as she did, the security guard approached her as CC, Max, and an older man she didn't recognize came bursting into the Emergency Room. "Now what?" Jamie grumbled as she rubbed her throbbing temples. Then she remembered that she'd been on the telephone with CC when Liz threw her hissy fit. "Just great," Jamie groaned as her lover made a determined path towards her.

"I'm fine," Jamie blurted out quickly as CC approached her. "It was just a difficult patient," she added, knowing that her lover was probably scared to death from what she'd heard on the telephone.

"What about the note?" CC inquired in a troubled tone.

"What note?" Jamie said in bewilderment.

"I haven't had a chance to tell her yet," the security guard interjected. "We found it on her car."

"Why don't Mallory and I find out about the note while you and Dr. Jameson get a cup of coffee or something?" Max offered.

"Sounds like a good idea," CC agreed as she led Jamie away from the inquisitive looks they were receiving. "You can tell me about your difficult patient," CC suggested as they stepped outside into the cool night air.

Jamie felt sick as they walked over to the tables in the deserted outdoor lunch area. She didn't want to talk about Liz with CC; the idea of what had just happened was making her stomach turn. "Why don't you tell me about this note instead?" Jamie suggested, hoping a change of subject would alleviate the sick feeling growing inside of her.

"I don't know anything yet," CC responded tensely as she sat down at one of the tables. "What's going on, James?" she asked.

"She was a mistake," Jamie began as she felt the tears welling up in her eyes. CC turned her gaze away and Jamie could feel a sudden coldness emanate from her lover. "Before we got back together, I didn't treat women with very much respect," Jamie confessed.

"If it was before we got back together, then I really don't need to know," CC responded honestly, the coldness seeming to ease.

"Then why won't you look at me?" Jamie pressed as her heart began to ache. CC didn't respond as she continued to look off in the distance. *'No more secrets. We promised each other that,'* Jamie reminded herself as she swallowed her fear. "I was with her, and I said your name," Jamie explained slowly. CC's head snapped around and she looked up at Jamie with a shocked expression. "I didn't even recognize her until I answered your call. She heard your name and flipped out."

"No small wonder." CC laughed. "I'm sorry; it's not funny. Come here," CC said with a smile as she held out her hand.

Jamie smiled shyly as she accepted CC's offer and climbed up into her lover's lap. "Look, we both have a past," CC explained as she wrapped her arms around Jamie's shivering body. "And it's going to show up. It might make things uncomfortable at times, but so long as these confessions are about the past it can't hurt us." Jamie's smile grew as she nestled closer to the warmth of her lover's body.

CC began to run her fingers through Jamie's hair and gently massaged her scalp. The young doctor felt her heart rate increase as she leaned into her lover's touch. Jamie's breathing was becoming erratic and she felt her nipples hardening as CC continued her gentle caresses. "Do you have any idea what you do to me?" Jamie asked in a breathy tone as she began to nibble on her lover's neck. CC moaned as Jamie's kisses grew more insistent. Jamie looked up to find herself captured by a lustful azure gaze. She reached up and pulled CC's face down to her own. Jamie's eyes drifted to her lover's soft lips.

Their lips brushed and Jamie's arousal grew. She ran her tongue along CC's lips while her lover's hands drifted down her back. Jamie parted CC's lips with her tongue and soon they were lost in a passionate kiss. The kiss deepened as Jamie cast off any worries of just where they were. CC suddenly broke away. "We need to get back inside," the brunette insisted suddenly in a cool tone as she lifted Jamie up off her lap. Jamie was stunned by the abruptness her lover displayed. Something about the tone of CC's voice frightened her.

Just as Jamie started to ask CC why she was rushing her back towards the hospital entrance, she had the uneasy feeling of being watched. "There's someone out there, isn't there?" she choked out as CC quickened their pace.

"Yes," CC hissed.

CHAPTER SEVEN

CC rushed Jamie back inside the hospital. Despite the safety the busy Emergency Room provided, CC still felt uneasy. She had been lost in Jamie's touch when she felt a chill run through her body. She hadn't wanted to frighten Jamie, but she knew that someone was watching. As much as she tried to write it off as just some passerby, she knew it wasn't true. It was as if she could feel the seething hatred boring a hole through her body.

"I'm sorry," CC apologized as she guided Jamie into the doctor's lounge. She felt as if she was failing to protect the one person who truly held her heart.

"I'm fine," Jamie reassured her as she ran her fingers along the policewoman's arm.

"I think we need to pull a Bette Davis again tonight," CC suggested wearily; she thought that another night hiding in the hotel would be the safest option for Jamie.

CC felt a chill wash over her as the door behind her opened; she watched as Jamie's emerald eyes widened fearfully. "What are you doing here?" Jamie hissed boldly as CC spun around, instinctively reaching for her sidearm. CC used her body to block Jamie from Simon's hostile glare.

"Get out," CC commanded as the young doctor glared at her and her lover.

"Why do you keep trying to interfere with us?" Simon questioned her in a distant tone.

"There is no . . ." Jamie began.

"Don't," CC cautioned her, noting the distant look in the young man's eyes. "He won't understand," she added knowing that Simon was lost in his own little world and would put his own interpretation on anything Jamie said.

"Maybe you'll understand this, Dr. Fisher," Jamie hissed. "You are not allowed on hospital property unless you're on duty. I believe that was explained to you. Now unless you want security to escort you out of here, I suggest that you leave."

CC was proud of her petite lover's bravado. Still, letting Simon Fisher out of her sight wasn't the best course of action. Out of the room would be a good idea. Yet CC couldn't touch the deranged young man without jeopardizing everything. For a brief moment she ran her fingers along the cold steel of her weapon, wondering if she should just end it there and then. She brought her hand down, knowing she couldn't cross that line.

The door opened once again and Max and Mallory stepped into the room. CC smiled slyly as she watched Simon's demeanor soften. "Dr. Fisher, I need a word with you," Max asserted firmly.

CC's heart pounded in her chest as Simon's eyes drifted to Jamie. "Janie, I don't understand why you're letting this creature be around you?" he offered in a casual tone. CC's eyes widened in horror as he called Jamie by the name of his high school sweetheart. She could see Max and Mallory stiffen as well. Simon simply sighed and calmly turned towards Max. "Detective, it's good to see you again."

"Always a pleasure, Dr. Fisher," Max appeased him. "In fact, I think I could use your help with something. Would you mind joining Special Agent Mallory and I down at the station?"

"Special Agent?" Fisher responded tersely.

Max approached Fisher casually and whispered in his ear. "Suits," he grunted loudly enough so CC and Mallory could hear him. "It's her fault. Don't worry; he's here to help us get rid of her."

"Good," Simon responded with confidence. "I'll just meet you down at the station," the young doctor added with an air of boldness.

"That would be a big help," Max appeased him as he followed the troubled young man out of the room.

CC's hands rested protectively on Jamie's shoulders as she looked at Mallory who lingered behind. "What is it?" she demanded as she continued to caress Jamie's shoulders.

"One of the garage attendants noticed someone lurking around Dr. Jameson's car," Mallory explained. "Sharp older guy thought it was strange and called security even though he wasn't stationed at that garage."

"Terrell," CC noted in appreciation.

"That's the guy," Mallory confirmed. "It was another note; only this time we got Dr. Fisher on tape. This could be the break we're looking for."

"What did the note say?" Jamie asked before CC had a chance to.

Mallory looked hesitant. "Special Agent, is it?" Jamie began irately. "I don't like it when people talk directly in front of me about things that concern me and then exclude me from the conversation."

"Well . . . Uhm," Mallory hedged.

"Tell her," CC spat out.

"*Stay away from her,*" Mallory responded. "That was it. Same bold non-distinct handwriting as the last note."

"He sure is subtle," Jamie grumbled.

"Maybe too subtle," CC noted thoughtfully. "We know it's a threat, but can we prove it? Still, with the complaints Jamie has filed here at the hospital and with us, it might be just enough to get us a search warrant. I really want to see this guy's tire iron. We're so close."

"Your guy Carter and our shrink are joining us down at the station. You want to come and watch the show?" Mallory offered. Normally CC would have been the first one out the door. She squeezed Jamie's shoulders, not wanting to leave her lover's side. "I've already called for an agent to follow Dr. Jameson."

"I think maybe I'll just . . . ," CC stammered.

"Caitlin, you should go," Jamie reassured her. "I'll be fine between hospital security, the FBI . . . that is who you are, isn't it?" Jamie asked Mallory who simply nodded. "And don't think I haven't noticed all the off-duty cops coming in with cases of the sniffles."

"I just . . ." CC began in an effort to explain her actions.

"Worry about me," Jamie finished for her. "I know, and you're right this time," Jamie agreed. "But if it wasn't for you, Simon probably wouldn't even be a suspect. I'd feel better if you were there to ensure everything goes right. Caitlin, the FBI are watching me," she repeated. "The worse thing that could happen is that another old flame drops in to tell me what I jerk I am."

"Okay," CC agreed. "I do want to talk to Dr. Carter and your profiler to see if they have any ideas about how to approach this guy. Plus I want to Marandize him." Mallory stared at her blankly. "I want anything he says to be put to use. He already thinks of me as the enemy. If I'm the one doing it, then he'll just blow me off for being a bitch. He'll probably forget I said it."

"Make sense," Mallory agreed.

"Hold him here for a moment," CC requested as she nodded to Jamie.

The moment Mallory left them Jamie was wrapped up in CC's arms. "Be careful," CC pleaded as she kissed the top of Jamie's head.

"You too," Jamie whispered softly. CC nodded in agreement and made her way back out into the hospital corridor, already regretting her decision to leave Jamie behind.

"Dr. Fisher." She scowled as curious hospital employees looked on. "You have the right to remain silent; anything you say can and will be used against you in a court of law."

"You can't be serious," Fisher scoffed.

"You have the right to an attorney. If you can't afford an attorney, one will be appointed to you," CC continued, completely unflustered by Simon's glare.

"Am I under arrest?" he taunted her.

"No," Max assured him. "She's just being her usual pain-in-the-ass self."

"Do you understand your rights as I've explained them to you?" CC pressed, wondering if the fact that he wasn't under arrest might present a problem down the road. Simon simply curled his lip in disgust. "Do you understand these rights as I've explained them to you, Dr. Fisher?" she repeated.

"Doc," Max encouraged him. "If you understand them, just tell her. It makes the whole thing legal and it will protect you down the road."

"Fine. I understand my rights, and no, I don't need an attorney," Simon spat out.

"Done this before have you?" CC taunted him.

"Come on, Doc; why don't you ride with us?" Max suggested. "No sense adding mileage to your car." Simon shrugged in agreement. "Oh, and that thing she said; I'm afraid it applies for the entire trip downtown and while you're at the station." Simon blinked in surprise; CC was suddenly worried that they might have overplayed their hand. "Don't you just hate all this legal crap?" Max added in disgust. Simon's face relaxed slightly. "You must be used to that with everyone trying to sue you doctors and rip you off."

"You have no idea," Simon agreed as he followed Max and Mallory out of the hospital.

CC breathed a sigh of relief and made her way out to her new SUV, thankful that they had taken separate cars. She spotted the agent Mallory had sent over instantly. "Why don't they just stamp FED on their forehead?" she pondered as she fished her cell phone out of her pocket. "Smithy, this is Calloway. I need a car towed," she explained with a sly smirk as she noticed Fisher's BMW parked illegally. "Might be a small problem. It's at Boylston General and it has MD plates," she said to the supervisor at the impound yard.

"No," Smithy flatly refused.

"It's illegally parked," CC argued.

"Those two letters on the plate means this bozo can park anywhere he wants to," Smithy carefully explained.

"There must be a way," CC pressed.

"Nope." Smithy sighed. "He can block Governor Swift's driveway and we can't touch him."

"Now there's an idea." CC chuckled. "Are you sure you can't touch it?" CC pleaded.

"Does the term illegal search and seizure mean anything?" Smithy chastised her. "Trust me; if we pick up a doctor's car from the hospital, anything you find won't mean spit. You could find Jimmy Hoffa in the trunk and it would be thrown out. Give me the tag on it and let me see if I can find anything out. You never know; they got the Son of Sam on parking tickets."

"You keep reminding me of that," CC grumbled before reading off Simon's plate number. "I ran it a few days ago and didn't come up with anything."

"With all the cutbacks and computer glitches we've had lately, you never know," Smithy said encouragingly.

"Thanks," she added before concluding the call

A slight sense of defeat embraced her as she was about to climb into her new car. Then she spotted a familiar figure passing by. "Terrell," she greeted the older man.

"Detective," he greeted her in return.

"Could you do me a favor?" she inquired as she handed him her business card. "See that black BMW over there?"

"Yup," Terrell responded with a scowl.

"Could you keep on eye on it for me?" she asked politely.

"My pleasure." Terrell said, nodding in agreement.

"Thank you," she added with sincerity.

"Dr. Jameson okay?" he inquired.

"Yes," CC reassured him. "Thank you for calling us."

"I'll keep an eye on her too," he promised.

She thanked him once again and climbed into her car. "Damn it; if only you had been on duty that night," she muttered as she pulled out into traffic. "Then again, with a whacko like Fisher it's just a matter of time," she reasoned as she raced towards the station.

When she arrived she met up with Max and Mallory. During her drive Smithy had got back to her with some interesting information. She brushed past the men and pulled out a street map. "Boys?" She beckoned them over. "Where's the good doctor?" she inquired quickly.

"Cooling his heels in Interrogation One," Max explained. "He didn't say anything useful on the drive down. Except what a pain in the ass you are. But I already knew that," Max teased. "I think he's onto us."

"Fine," CC conceded. "We knew it would happen. I tried to have his car towed."

"Not bright," Mallory chastised her.

"I know," CC admitted. "But Smithy ran his plates and he got a speeding ticket right here." She pointed to the map. "In the early morning hours on the night Sandra died."

"That's down the street from the park where she was dumped," Max fumed. "Why are we just finding this out now?"

"Somebody screwed up," CC grumbled. "But I think that and the fact that he was in the garage will get us our warrant. So what do you say, boys? Want to wake up a judge and then talk to the headshrinkers? After that the three of us can have a little chat with Simon while his car is being searched."

"I like it," Max agreed.

"Works for me," Mallory added with a smile.

"Mallory, you're smiling?" CC smiled in return. "I didn't think you knew how."

"My, things are getting exciting around here." The Captain smirked across the conference table at CC.

"Aren't they though?" CC confirmed as she looked around the room. There was Max; herself; the Captain; Mallory; Dr. Carter; Marissa; Dr. Richards, who was the profiler from the FBI; the local ADA; and, of course, a federal prosecutor. CC was certain that the last two would be pulling out the yardsticks if Fisher turned out to be their guy.

"Calloway, it's your show," the Captain instructed her with a slight gleam in his eyes.

"Let's start with you, Dr. Richards," CC began. "Dr. Richards is the profiler from Mallory's office. She's been given all the information regarding the victims only. She's been told nothing regarding the lead suspect. Let's see if we're on the right track. Dr. Richards, if you would?"

The middle-aged blonde brushed back a strand of long curly hair as she looked over her notes. "The victims suffered from strangulation, blunt force trauma, and attempted rape. Based on the attacks, the victims' lifestyles or alleged lifestyles, this is what I've concluded. Frontal strangulation shows his need for control. These women have probably rejected him. The attempt to rape them isn't, in his mind, rape. He honestly believes that they want him, but somewhere during the attack he knows that it isn't true. That explains the equipment failure. He knows what he's doing is wrong; that's why he crushes their skulls. He needs to cover up his mistake. And that's all he sees this as - a mistake. He doesn't consider his victims. He is far too self-centered to consider their needs. He's probably from a wealthy family that covered up any misdeeds he did to protect the family's image. He expects this. He is a white male, probably in his early to late twenties by now. The guy you are looking for has a sealed juvenile record. He probably started out with minor crimes at first then slowly escalated towards arson, animal mutilation, and violence towards others. Mommy and Daddy bailed him out. He thinks the world owes him a favor due to his station in life. He's a professional - a doctor, lawyer, or stockbroker - something fitting his station in life. He doesn't enjoy his work but he's expected to make something of his life and he resents it. He thinks that he should just be able to live off the family fortune and do whatever he wants. He's an overachiever although not because he wants to be. He's only a success because his family expects him to be one. Disappointing his parents is, in his mind, the worse thing he could do. They would probably cut him off, and he would have to actually go out and support himself, something that he feels is beneath him. He dumps his victims in the nude out in the open for several reasons. First and foremost is the shame; it's his final punishment to them for rejecting him. Secondly, he's smart, very smart, and knows that tossing them without clothing in an exposed area will disturb the forensic evidence. Next, the reason he didn't do this with Ellen Murdock is because he chose Sandra over Ellen. Killing them both was confusing to him. He sees them all as the same woman, the first one who rejected him. Which brings us to the first victim. Off the record, Janie is dead. There's not a doubt in my mind that he followed her. He probably just wanted to talk her into coming back to him. When she refused, he started to choke her for ruining his image. She would have been the perfect trophy wife.

Killing her was probably an accident; he panicked and hid her body. When he got away with it, his confidence grew. He's still seeking his trophy wife but he thinks it's the same girl. Okay, now who wants to hear the bottom line?" she teased as the others laughed. "I know it's a little dry but here it is. The killer is the same person in all the crimes. He's a rich spoiled brat with a borderline personality disorder. He has a violent nature. He's killing his first victim over and over again. In his mind they're all Janie. When he was confronted with two Janie's, he chose one to be her and simply forgot about the other one. He also blames Janie. Nothing is ever his fault. His position in life, his intelligence, and his youthful arrogance have convinced him that he's invincible. Questions?"

"Does he know what he's doing is wrong?" Rumford the federal prosecutor asked.

"Not when the attacks begin," she responded firmly as the rest of room released a collective groan. "Sorry folks; this one, in my opinion, is legally nuts. It's only during the attacks that he realizes what he's done. Afterward he may not even remember doing it. His subconscious knows and it kicks in just enough to aid in his ability to evade the authorities."

"How do we catch him?" Max inquired thoughtfully.

"Unless you catch him in the act or gather enough evidence, which will be difficult since most of the crime scenes are not pure, you'd have to set a trap," she said as CC's body tensed. "But with this guy it would take a lot of time. He has to meet the girl and be rejected by her and then his delusions need to grow until he's forced to act out."

Several eyes turned to CC. "Not going to happen, guys," she asserted harshly.

"We could use a policewoman," Mallory suggested.

"It won't work," Dr. Richards cut him off. "If he's found his new Janie then he knows everything about her, he won't be fooled by someone who looks like her. I agree with Detective Calloway. Putting a civilian in this guy's path is far too dangerous. I'm assuming that you suspect who the next intended victim will be."

"Yes, we do," CC confirmed. "That's if we're focusing on the right guy. Speaking of which, Dr. Carter, would you like to fill us in on your report?"

"My pleasure," Dr. Carter agreed. He was an older man with a rapidly retreating hairline and bifocal glasses. "Basically Simon Fisher fits Dr. Richards' profile perfectly. After reviewing the files and meeting with Dr. Fisher, I've come to the conclusion that I could write a textbook on this guy. He has a juvenile record for arson, animal mutilation, and assault. His high school sweetheart, Janie Jensen, disappeared after she dumped Simon for another girl. Everywhere he travels, girls who look a lot like Janie and either had or were believed to have had sexual interest in women, turn up dead. Now that's what I got from the files.

After speaking with the arrogant little jerk, this is what I've decided. He's rich, arrogant, and very smart. When in the company of women or men his own age, he behaves like the king of the universe. But he responds to Max and myself. He seems to want to prove himself to older men. We probably remind him of Daddy." Max snorted at the comment. "He hates gay women. He's convinced himself that they just need the right man. Sadly it's a view shared by far too many people, but with Simon it's very important for him to believe this. CC, you did a really smart thing when you had Max tell him to go home the other day because he had nothing important to offer him. His pride was hurt, and he's starting to view Max as a father figure. He stayed because he needed to prove himself to Max. Being dismissed by Daddy just can't happen. But I bet it has more than once. The interesting thing about this yahoo is that he functions really well with day-to-day life. When Max told him to file a report against CC, he should have jumped at the chance. He didn't because somewhere in his mind he knew that if he did he would have to face Jamie telling him that she wasn't interested in him and wanted him to go away. This guy's delusions run deep and so do his survival instincts. My suggestion is to have Max conduct the interview and have CC sit in. He trusts one and despises the other. It might be enough to get him a little off kilter. But I can't guarantee it will work. That's it."

"Thank you both," CC said as she mentally processed the information. "Marissa? What did the boys in the lab get?"

"We have blood, tissue, and fibers, most of which came from Ellen's apartment and the bodies," Marissa explained shyly, avoiding eye contact with CC. "We just need to match it to something. There are some carpet fibers that Stan found at the Murdock crime scene which he did trace to a carpet manufactured exclusively for BMW."

"That is good," Max said.

"Not really," CC grumbled. "She was a nurse. Chances are she knew one or two folks who drive Beamers." They all seemed to ponder the situation as CC wondered just how long Simon would sit quietly in the room they'd stuck him in.

"Now it's time for the lawyers," she began with a smirk. "Gentlemen, personally I don't care who gets jurisdiction. But I

274

feel that, based on the evidence, you'll never convict him on any crimes other than the ones that have happened here in the Commonwealth. All I want to know before our prime suspects walks out of here, because he's free to go and is probably ready to do just that by now, can you get us a warrant so we can get to his car before he does? Because if he's as smart as everyone keeps telling me he is, any evidence is going to go bye bye real soon if it hasn't already."

"It is on its way," ADA Griffin confirmed with a smile. "I woke up Judge Muller."

The police officers smiled. "I love Judge Muller. " The Captain smirked. "A policeman's best friend."

"Could it get thrown out later?" Rumford questioned fearfully.

"Let's hope not," CC grumbled, knowing that the dear old judge was very easy going when it came to handing out warrants. But a half way decent lawyer could maneuver around that. Her one glimmer of hope was Simon's arrogance. His ego would never allow his attorney to plead insanity if he went to trial.

"Fine. I'll have a team waiting to execute the warrant," the Captain barked. "Now you and Max go start your interview before Fisher walks out of here. Marissa, head down to the lab and wait. I'm assuming that the rest of you would like to watch?" The rest of the group nodded eagerly.

"Come on, Max. Let's go play good Dad cop and mean old lesbian cop." CC nudged her partner as they stood.

As they entered the interview room and found Simon idly twiddling his thumbs with a cocky smirk on his face, CC had to fight the urge to beat the man senseless. Simon smiled at Max and sneered at CC with a look of defiance. *'So you want to play? Fine!'* CC thought as she flashed the cocky little bugger a defiant sneer of her own. Max sat next to Simon while CC took a seat directly across from him. She flashed an amused look at him, silently telling him that she was going to win.

Simon stared at them blankly, not seeming to care that he was sitting in a police station with two cops staring at him. "So, Simon, what happened tonight?" Max proceeded in a fatherly tone. He almost sounded disappointed in Simon.

"Nothing," Simon protested with a whine.

"Something must have happened," Max scolded him. "Now just tell me; what did you do?"

"It wasn't me," Simon whined defensively. "She did this," he flared as he pointed towards CC.

CC smiled coldly at the flustered young man, thankful that the entire interview was being taped, videotaped, and witnessed by two prosecutors, her captain, and two of the top criminal psychologists in the area. She was also thankful that Simon was far too egotistical to request a lawyer.

"Simon?" Max continued in the same scolding manner. "You need to tell me the truth, son." *'Nice touch, partner,'* CC noted with pride.

"I didn't do anything," Simon insisted, his tone calming down. CC became nervous, as Simon seemed to be readily adjusting to the situation. "I just went to visit my girlfriend when this . . . *woman* . . ." he hissed, and CC was quite aware that wasn't the term he wanted to use, " . . . decided to stick her nose in our business."

"Simon, you need to tell me the truth or else I can't help you," Max continued. Simon seemed to relax even more. "Janie told me that she doesn't want to see you."

CC and Max flinched as Simon jumped out of his chair and threw it against the wall. "That's a lie," he shouted angrily. CC was certain that she could hear a collective gasp emanate from the observation room. She looked completely calm as she watched his face begin to twitch and his dark eyes dart from her to Max. "I . . . Uhm . . ." Simon floundered as she and Max shared a worried glance.

He was breathing heavily and clenching his fists tightly. "Simon, pick up your chair and sit down," Max instructed him firmly. Simon nodded his head and followed Max's instructions. CC's jaw clenched as she watched his breathing slow down. *'We lost him,'* she noted bitterly as she watched him calm down and lean back with a cocky smirk. He looked at both of them carefully. "Now, Simon, tell me what you were doing at the hospital," Max pushed.

"Why?" Simon responded smugly. "I don't want to talk to you anymore. If you have anymore questions for me, I want a lawyer."

'Game over.' CC sighed as she rubbed her temple. "That won't be necessary," she grunted. "We don't need this idiot, Max. You told me he could be helpful. I was right; he's worthless," CC offered in a dismissive manner as Simon's eyes darkened in anger. *'Come on, you arrogant little bastard - take the bait!'* her mind screamed as she glared at him.

"Fine." Simon smirked as he stood. "I'm leaving."

CC felt completely helpless as he walked out the door confidently. "We blew it," she groaned.

"No, you didn't," Dr. Carter reassured her as he and the others entered the room. "The cops in San Diego never got a rise out of him. He really sees Max as a father figure. But he's smart."

"Yeah, you keep saying that," CC spat out. "Now he's also pissed off and he's going after his Janie."

Jamie yawned as she stepped out of her car. She noted the ever-present car that had been following her since the hospital. She started to head towards CC's townhouse and stopped in her tracks. Remembering that she was supposed to enter through the back door, she turned towards her own house, noting the replaced front window. She smiled as she pondered whether or not Stevie had thanked the contractor.

It felt strange being in her own home after spending so much time with CC. She looked at the blinking answering machine then decided to check her messages and go through her mail before heading over to CC's place. "I can't wait for this to be over so we can start living our lives again." She sighed as she listened to messages from her sister, her father, and Becky. "Sorry, guys. Maybe when I stop looking over my shoulder, I'll be better at returning phone calls," she whispered, knowing that she was afraid of talking to anyone close to her, worried that she would cause more needless worry.

She shrugged off her leather jacket and headed up the stairs to gather clothing for the morning. She looked around and decided that once things were back to normal she was finally going to unpack and set up her new home. She felt slightly hopeful when she saw the police vans pull up and the officers start to ransack what she later would discover was Simon's car. "Please let this finally put an end to all of this," she prayed as she sorted through her clothing. She grimaced when she realized that her laundry was more than a little far behind.

She looked at her watch and out the window into the darkness. "There is no way in hell I'm staying here in the middle of the night just to do my laundry. I've seen enough bad movies to know that is just how those screaming, scantily dressed, high heel wearing bimbos buy it. I'll do it in the morning while the FBI is watching me," Jamie reasoned as she headed back downstairs.

The telephone rang just as she was heading towards the back door. She paused for a moment, listening to see if it was important. The silence after the beep made her edgy. "Janie," came the pleading whimper.

"Oh shit." A chill ran down Jamie's spine. "Time to go," she blurted out as she threw open the back door and raced out onto the deck. She reached into her pocket and fished the key to CC's home out of her pocket, slipping it between her knuckles so she could use it to defend herself if need be. An arm reached around her as a gloved hand covered her mouth. "You should have answered the phone," a voice hissed in her ear.

CC was back in the conference room listening to the reports. "They got the tire iron," the Captain exclaimed as he burst into the room. "Plus a coat from his apartment and samples from the carpet in his car. Everything is on its way to the lab."

Everyone seemed to relax and smile from the good news. The only one who didn't breath a sigh of relief was CC. "Where is he?" she demanded.

"He's being followed," the Captain reassured her. "It's too soon to make an arrest. We need the labs back first."

"Where is he?" CC repeated with a hiss. "Did he show up at his car or apartment?"

"No," Mallory said. "But he was on foot."

"He didn't take a cab?" CC choked out.

"No," Mallory responded in confusion. "He hopped on the green line."

"Not the red line which has a station right across the street," CC flared. "But the green line, four blocks over, which doesn't go anywhere near his home or the hospital. It also goes underground just enough times for whoever is following him to loose radio contact. The same train line that has a stop a few blocks from Dr. Jameson home? That green line, you stupid son of a . . ."

"Dr. Jameson is safe in her home," Mallory protested, as he turned paled. "My agent saw her enter and the lights go off. My agent is still watching."

"Did she get safely into my home?" CC screamed. "Mallory, did your agent see if she made it safely from her townhouse into mine?"

CHAPTER EIGHT

Jamie calmed her breathing as the man held her tightly and led her back into her home. She heard the glass door being closed. *'Just stay calm. Wait for your opening then run to Stevie or the FBI agent out front. Just go to the one you can reach first. No! I can't put Stevie or Emma in danger. I'll have to go out front,'* her mind reasoned as she fought against the fear building inside of her. She knew if she were going to survive she would need to keep a clear head. *'I promised her that I wouldn't leave her. I'm going to keep that promise,'* she silently vowed.

Simon's tight hold on her body prevented her from struggling. She calmed her breathing as he turned her around. There was a frightening blankness to his dark eyes. She kept her arms by her side as he tightened his grip around her throat. "Janie, you know that you belong to me," he rambled on in a distant voice, not really looking at her as his eyes glazed over.

Jamie felt lightheaded as his grip tightened and his free hand reached out for her shirt. She swayed slightly as if she was falling. In reality she was adjusting her stance. With a quick fluid movement she raised her left knee and struck him forcibly in the groin. His grip loosened as he stumbled back slightly while he winced in pain. She cocked her arm back, keeping her wrist straight and her elbow level. Then putting all of her energy in her shoulder, she hit in the face and dug the key she was still clutching into his left eye.

Simon howled in pain as he fell backward holding his injured eye. Jamie didn't waste any time as she made a mad dash for the front door. She fumbled with the locks on the door as the stunned Simon stumbled over and grabbed her by the hair. She shot her elbow back and delivered a sharp blow to his solar plexus. Simon gasped for air but still kept a firm grip on her hair. "Janie?" he panted in bewildered voice.

"My name is Jamie, you sick freak," she growled as she raised her left foot and slammed her heel into his foot. Simon screamed in agony as he released his hold on her and stumbled backward. Jamie spun quickly and adjusted her stance. Reaching out she grabbed his arm. Holding it tightly, she pulled him down slightly and then delivered a hard roundhouse kick to his kidney.

Simon howled as she released him with a slight shove. She watched as he crumpled to the floor. There was a frantic pounding on her front door. "What's the matter, Simon; didn't the other girls fight back?" she sneered at him as he looked up at her in pain and confusion. She turned and unlocked the front door, her hands shaking as she released the locks. She could hear CC's frantic voice on the other side.

Jamie threw the door open and a stream of police flooded her living room. The sight of her lover rushing into her home offered Jamie comfort and fear. The icy glare in CC's eyes as her hand reached for her sidearm sent a chill through Jamie. CC turned to her and the ice melted as her hand jerked away from her gun. Jamie breathed a sigh of relief as CC wrapped her arms around her and pulled her to her chest. Jamie released a sigh of relief and took a slight step back from CC's hold. "You're late," she teased her lover, hoping to wipe away the lines of fear that marred her chiseled features.

The lights clicked on as the police surrounded Simon's crumpled body. "Are you all right?" CC asked in a pleading tone.

"I'm a little shaken," Jamie confessed. "But I had a promise to keep and I did."

"Dr. Simon Fisher?" Max addressed the prone man. "You are under arrest for the murders of Ellen Murdock, Sandra Bernstein, and the assault on Jamie Jameson."

"Assault?" Simon protested. "I'm the one who's injured."

Everyone in the room looked down at Simon and then over at the tiny blonde CC was holding tightly in her arms. "You did that?" CC stammered.

"Yeah," Jamie responded with a calm shrug.

CC's jaw hung open as she stared down at Jamie. "Do you remember when I was in college and you told me that every woman should have some self defense training?" Jamie began to explain. "Well, for once I listened to you. Actually I ended up getting a brown belt. I enjoyed the discipline and structure of my training. You really should finish arresting him because he needs to go to the hospital. That eye doesn't look good and I'm worried that I may have damaged his kidney."

"Right," Max agreed, still staring at the tiny blonde in awe. Then he shook his head and refocused on the whimpering man on the floor. "Where was I?

"You're under arrest," Jamie supplied.

"Dr. Jameson?" Mallory interrupted as Max advised Simon of his rights and called for an ambulance. "We need to get your statement and take pictures of the bruises on your neck." Jamie tensed at the suggestion, wanting this to be over with. "Detective Calloway will be at your side the entire time," he added in a comforting tone.

"Okay," Jamie agreed as she took her lover's hand. CC gave her hand a reassuring squeeze as they left the townhouse and were greeted by a frantic Stevie who clutched a screaming Emma to her chest.

Later after they managed to calm both Stevie and Emma down, Jamie found herself at the police station. She had already endured having her neck photographed from every angle as well as the bruising on her arms from where Simon had restrained her. Despite the lack of serious injuries, Jamie felt violated. She was giving her statement to a room full of police officers as CC sat by her side.

"Then as he was choking me I kneed him in the groin," she said and every man in the room winced while every woman smirked. "As he fell back I jammed the key into one of his eyes. The left one, I think. I ran to the front door. It was locked and he grabbed me from behind while I was trying to unlock the door. He held me by the hair on the back of my head. I elbowed him in the solar plexus; he gasped and then I jammed my heel into his foot. As he was falling back, I delivered a roundhouse kick to his kidney. That's about it. I opened the front door after he collapsed on the floor and all of you rushed in."

"That's amazing," CC congratulated her.

"Thank you, Dr. Jameson." Max smiled over at her. "You really kept your cool and that saved your life."

"I was terrified," Jamie corrected him; CC's face dropped. "But I had someone very important waiting for me," she added as she smiled at CC who still looked despondent. "So what happens to Simon now?"

"Well, his injuries have been treated and he's under guard at the hospital," Max explained. "Some of your colleagues weren't very interested in treating him until we stepped in and reminded them it was in everyone's best interest to treat him like any other patient."

"I imagine that they were surprised at what happened. I know a lot of people thought I was overreacting when I filed a complaint," Jamie said. "He just seems so normal. Even I thought he was harmless until stuff started happening. And he never did anything around other people."

"Simon is very sick and very clever," CC added.

"He'll be arraigned and he has a team of lawyers and his parents flying in," Max continued grimly.

"What aren't you telling me?" Jamie pressed as she noticed everyone's gaze suddenly avoiding her.

"There's a problem," CC began carefully. "Our own experts have concluded that Simon is legally insane. Of course he'll still need to go through a more in-depth analysis. But it looks like he could plead insanity."

"Peachy," Jamie groaned as her body tensed. "So he goes to a mental hospital until he's deemed sane?" She felt her anger rise as she spoke. "He's done a psych rotation. He'll be out in no time."

"Let's hope his ego prevents him from copping a plea," CC added with a confidence that Jamie easily saw through as an effort to comfort her. Dr. Richards released a heavy sigh. Jamie didn't miss the warning look CC cast at the tall blonde.

"Sorry," the tall woman quickly apologized.

"You're not a cop?" Jamie noted thoughtfully.

"No." The woman smiled. "Well, I am, sort of. I'm Dr. Richards; I'm a profiler for the FBI."

"So, Doctor, what do you think will happen? And tell me the truth?" Jamie pressed.

"I don't want to frighten you," the tall woman responded.

"Too late," Jamie quipped.

"Okay," Dr. Richards conceded. "I think that unless Simon's parents are as arrogant as he is, and since they are the ones paying his lawyers, there'll be a plea bargain. They don't want this to get out and they'll want Simon sent away as quickly and quietly as possible."

They entered Jamie's townhouse; a sense of eeriness permeated it. The police had been through everything that might prove helpful. They'd taken Jamie's telephone since it had a digital answering machine in it. It was now evidence. CC watched her lover carefully as the blonde folded her arms across her chest and just stared at her living room.

It had broken CC's heart when, after hearing Dr. Richards's opinion on how things may work out, Jamie released a soft sob and squeezed her hand. "Take me home," Jamie requested in a small voice. CC nodded in agreement and led her lover out of the police station. The others could handle the police work from here on out. She had something far more important to do - she had to look after Jamie.

CC was edgy as she stood there and watched the dimness covering her lover's bright features. She felt helpless not knowing if she should just stand there saying nothing or if she should wrap Jamie up in her arms and hold her for an eternity. She took a shy step closer only to halt her movements when she saw Jamie flinch. "Maybe we should go to my place?" CC suggested in a soft voice.

"No," Jamie responded flatly without turning around to look at CC. "I'm not letting him drive me out of my home again," she spat out with conviction.

The tension loomed over them, as they remained standing in the same positions. "Who is Janie?" Jamie asked in a distant voice, keeping her back to CC.

"Janie Jensen was Simon's high school sweetheart," CC explained, fighting against the uneasiness that was welling up inside of her. Jamie spun around when she heard the name that was frighteningly similar to her own. "She disappeared several years ago after she broke up with Simon."

"Didn't anyone suspect him?" Jamie said incredulously.

"No," CC admitted. "No one, with the exception of her roommate, knew that she was planning on ending things with Simon. The roommate never told anyone because she didn't want to hurt Janie's parents with the reason why she was dumping Simon." Jamie stared at her as her emerald eyes silently asked CC to tell her everything. "They were lovers."

"What is it with him and blonde dykes?" Jamie wondered aloud.

"We think it always comes back to Janie," CC supplied. "The shrinks think he finds women who look and act like her and then he tries to woo them. When the romance fails he becomes lost in his delusions."

Jamie held up her hand to stop CC's explanation. "I get it," Jamie offered in a defeated tone. "You said she disappeared. They never found her?"

"No," CC responded grimly.

"Her poor parents," Jamie said as her eyes filled with tears. "Waking up every morning to face the day and then going to bed every night not knowing what happened to your child. I can't imagine the hell these people must be living in."

CC had to agree with her lover's observation. It troubled her that they would probably never learn the truth as to what happened to Janie Jensen. Simon wasn't going to tell them since CC felt quite certain that in his sick mind Janie was very much alive. Somewhere locked away in the disturbed young man's mind was the answer that would finally give Janie's parents the closure they deserved.

"How many?" Jamie's question broke CC's troubling thoughts. "How many girls did he kill?"

"We think that there were at least nine victims," CC informed her with regret as Jamie's tears finally escaped. CC didn't hesitate wrapping her lover up in her arms. "Ssh, it's all over now," CC reassured her.

"No, it isn't," Jamie protested weakly.

"Yes, it is," CC stated firmly as she guided Jamie slightly away from her body to look into her eyes. "It is over. Now will you do something for me?" Jamie nodded as she wiped the tears from her eyes. "Let me take you upstairs and hold you tonight." Jamie lifted CC's hand to her lips and kissed them gently.

"Call your sister first," Jamie choked out in a hoarse voice. "Stevie must be climbing the walls."

"Always the practical one," CC teased her with a wink.

"Yeah right." Jamie laughed.

CC called her sister and somehow managed to calm her fears. Jamie never left her side, needing to keep physical contact with CC. The policewoman knew the events of that evening were going to haunt her lover for a long time. After Stevie was reassured that they were safe, CC led Jamie upstairs and undressed her as well as herself. They climbed into bed and CC snuggled up behind her lover, spooning with the blonde. CC kept a tight hold as they drifted off to sleep.

Nightmares had plagued the young doctor; each time Simon's face had loomed over her in the darkness. She could still feel his grip on her throat as she awoke with a start. Comforting arms encircled her waist as CC whispered tender words in her ear. CC's words and touch eased Jamie back into slumber. The last bout of terror struck her just after eight in the morning. Once again CC soothed her and lulled the blonde back into sleep.

Jamie's emerald eyes blinked open once again, this time with more ease. She breathed a sigh of relief when she realized that she had finally slept peacefully for just over four hours. She caressed the large hands still pressed against her waist. She smiled as a gentle kiss brushed her hair. "Good morning," CC mumbled as her arms tightened around Jamie's body.

Jamie turned in CC's arms and smiled at the woman who had once again claimed her heart. "Good morning," Jamie responded before stealing a kiss.

"It's good to see you smile," CC commented thoughtfully.

"It feels good to smile," Jamie confessed as she laughed at her lover's appearance. CC's long hair was flying everywhere. "And why shouldn't I smile when I get to wake up next to you?"

"You're going to need to talk to someone," CC said hesitantly.

Jamie felt her anger rise at the comment. CC's arms wrapped her up in a warm embrace and the anger melted. "You're right," she conceded, not really wanting to relive what had happened. She knew her resistance to speak to a professional was normal. "I hate what he's done to us," Jamie spat out as CC's hands continued to make circles along her back. "I think you should speak to someone as well," Jamie suggested; she felt CC's body tense at the suggestion. "I saw where your hand was heading when you and the rest of the cavalry burst in last night."

"I wanted to kill him," CC stated bluntly. Jamie could feel the muscles in CC's body relaxing. "Then I looked into your eyes and the only thing that mattered was holding you."

"Do you want to go through the department or should I find someone at the hospital for both of us?" Jamie asked, not really looking forward at the prospect of seeking professional help.

"Hospital," CC agreed as she snuggled closer to Jamie's body. "There are no secrets at the station. I'd prefer no one knowing. Maybe we can get a group rate?" she added playfully.

Jamie allowed her fingers to begin exploring her lover's body. She loved the way CC's body reacted to her touch. "Now that's settled," Jamie began in an amused tone. "There's something else we need to talk about." Jamie smiled at the puzzled look her lover directed towards her. "You might have noticed that my little home is still a little unsettled. I haven't finished unpacking or decorating."

"I've noticed," CC responded wryly. "I was wondering if perhaps you weren't planning on staying."

"I'm staying," Jamie reassured her as she nestled her head against CC's chest. "And since I'm staying I think you should help me with the unpacking and decorating."

"Should I?" CC teased as Jamie's hand slipped to the curve of the brunette's hip.

"Yes," Jamie responded firmly. "Since I expect you to be spending a lot more time here."

"Okay," CC responded gleefully. "Hey, that wouldn't include shopping, would it?"

"Yes." Jamie laughed as she rolled CC onto her back and straddled her body. "Some big tough cop you are - afraid of a little trip to the mall," she teased her lover as she began to tickle her ribs.

"I'm not afraid," CC protested as she tried to swat Jamie's hands away. "And it's never just a little trip to the mall with you. It is more like an expedition to the moon."

"Sweet talker," Jamie teased as she poked her lover in the ribs.

CC yelped at Jamie's assault before capturing the doctor in her arms. Jamie relaxed into the feel of her lover's naked body pressing against her own. "We should try and get some more sleep," CC suggested. "We both have to go to work later." Jamie grumbled, not looking forward to facing the looks and questions from her co-workers.

"You can always take the night off," CC's offered.

It was tempting but Jamie wasn't going to stop living her life. Simon had disrupted it enough and she wasn't going to let him win. "I have to," Jamie asserted as she snuggled against CC. Soon both women drifted off into a blissful slumber.

CC was growing more and more agitated with each passing moment. The lawyers had arrived and now everyone was circling their respective wagons. The team of lawyers Simon's father had assembled was an impressive lot, each one dressed in a suit that was worth more than her yearly salary. There was one woman who troubled CC. She knew she recognized the woman who kept giving her icy glares, but for the life of her she couldn't figure out who she was.

The detective was becoming increasing aware that everyone on both sides was doing everything possible to drag the case out. She hated the effect it was having on her lover and decided to do something completely reckless. She gathered up her files and photos and went over to the hospital. CC marched down the hallway, noting the weary look on the police officer stationed outside of Simon's hospital room. On one side of the corridor stood the group of expensive suits crowded around a very distinguished-looking gentleman with a sorrowful look in his dark brown eyes. On the other side was her team. CC took one look at both packs of vultures and decided that she'd had enough.

CC held up her badge to the uniformed officer. "I'm going in to talk to him. Anyone care to join me?" she shouted and both camps seemed stunned. Suddenly both sides erupted in chaos as they argued over whether or not CC should be allowed to enter Simon's room. CC locked eyes with the only other person in the crowded hallway beside herself that wasn't speaking.

The man looked as if he was suffering from battle fatigue. His dark eyes were filled with a lost sorrowful expression. At times CC thought about the parents and families of those who kept her employed. It was unsettling because half of her experiences of coming face-to-face with the family of a killer ended with her understanding why they were the way they were. She knew that if someone out there had reached out and gotten them away from their loving families sooner, they might have been all right. The other half of the time she found herself looking into the same sadness she was looking at this moment. A confused parent who did everything humanly possible to raise their child right who was now wondering how the sweet child had become a monster.

"Annoying, aren't they?" CC addressed Mr. Fisher.

He blinked in surprise. She understood his confusion. He'd probably heard the whole story by now and was wondering why she didn't hate or blame him for his son's sickness.

"Yes," he finally responded in a weak pleading voice.

"Don't speak to her," the familiar large woman barked.

"Excuse me," CC snapped at the annoying woman. "She works for you, isn't that correct, sir?" she addressed the man. A faint flicker of a smile emerged on his lips.

"Yes, she does," he confirmed with a sad smile.

"Would you like to talk to me, Mr. Fisher?" CC asked him gently, fully prepared for his refusal.

"I just want to understand," he responded in a desperate voice.

"I think we all want that," CC concurred. She watched as Dr. Richards nodded to her, confirming that she was doing the right thing. "And you want to know about Janie."

"Yes," he choked out. "She was such a sweet girl. Her parents have been through hell. I can't believe that he would hurt her. But when I asked him, it was like the time I asked him if he'd dented his mother's car. His denial was very convincing, but he was holding the keys in his hand." His voice trailed off and CC could see the conflict waging in his eyes.

"Malcolm," one of the suits cautioned him.

"I have an idea," CC suggested as she ignored the arrogant lawyer. "When Janie disappeared, the police never suspected Simon."

"That's right," Mr. Fisher confirmed confidently.

CC could see the glimmer of hope rising in the man as he thought that perhaps this had all been some kind of horrible mistake. "That's because Simon decided to take an unexpected trip to the family cabin at Lake Tahoe and wasn't around when Janie disappeared," CC explained. "I just discovered this information in an old report this afternoon." CC continued as eager ears listened to her conversation with Simon's father. "With your permission, the FBI could search the cabin and the surrounding area."

The team of lawyers instantly shouted their objections, as Mr. Fisher mulled over the idea. CC simply stood there holding his gaze, allowing him to consider the idea while the others argued the point. A nurse finally stormed down the hallway and told everyone to be quiet. Something about the nurse's size and demeanor instantly quieted them. "Do it," Mr. Fisher finally agreed in a nervous tone.

"Mallory, get on it," CC instructed the agent firmly. Mallory stood there for a moment with a look of complete amazement as Simon's lawyers protested. "Mallory, do it," CC fumed as she shoved the address into his hand. He snapped to attention and ran off while the lawyers continued to grouse about illegal search and seizure.

"I'd like to speak to your son. Would you care to join me?" CC said to Mr. Fisher in the same comforting tone she'd used throughout their entire encounter. "Maybe we can finally get some answers."

"Absolutely not," the woman shouted in a shrill tone.

"Who are you?" CC finally snapped in disgust. There was something about this woman that made CC's flesh crawl. CC was searching her mind in an effort to remember who she was? The woman's beady eyes narrowed at CC's question. It was the way her eyes narrowed in disgust that brought back the memory. "Claudia," CC grumbled as she glared at the older wider version of her lover's college roommate.

"She can't work on this case," CC announced to the most elegantly dressed man in the group, assuming that he was the one in charge. The way he looked them both over confirmed her suspicions. "She was Dr. Jameson's roommate in college and I have first hand knowledge of her dislike for Dr. Jameson and her lifestyle." The other lawyers looked at Claudia with concern. "Come on, boys. She'll just try to make it look like the victims had it coming. You know that crap won't fly here."

"Excuse me?" Claudia snarled. "You're the depraved one. Who took advantage of her and then walked out on her."

CC smiled confidently as she heard Max growl behind her. "Actually I didn't," CC explained dryly. "I was wounded in the line of duty, and because of people like you, Jamie never knew because we had to keep our relationship a secret." Claudia and her co-workers seemed stunned.

"It's true," Max confirmed smugly.

CC and Mr. Fisher watched as the older attorney pulled Claudia aside. By the way she stormed off CC had a feeling that she wasn't very happy at the moment. "Good call," CC informed the lead attorney. "You were probably unaware that she's a homophobic religious zealot that could only hurt your case."

"You're still not going in there," the man chastised her with a smirk.

CC couldn't help smiling in response, as she liked this man; he'd seemed genuinely shocked by Claudia's views. "Why not?" CC reasoned, noticing that everyone's attention was focused on her. "Let's all be reasonable and put the yardsticks away for a moment." She watched as every man, with the exception of Mr. Fisher, become angry over her comment. Mr. Fisher seemed amused. "Your client was caught trying to attack Dr. Jameson. We found Ellen Murdock's and Sandra Bernstein's blood and glass from Dr. Jameson's front window on his tire iron and one of his jackets. His car was pulled over in the area where Sandra Bernstein's body was found. He was the only one seen in the parking garage at the time Sandra's tire was flattened."

She watched as Simon's lawyers grew paler as she revealed each detail. "And I think that we'll find Janie's body up at the cabin," she added in an apologetic tone to Mr. Fisher.

"But . . . ," the lead attorney began.

"He's nuts," CC cut him off. "Sorry, sir," she quickly apologized to Mr. Fisher. "It's true. Your son is not well. Do you honestly think he'll allow his lawyers to enter a plea of not guilty by reason of insanity? It doesn't matter what you think," she added before he could object. "You may be paying the bill, but at this moment he's their client." She saw the understanding dawn on his face. "Now boys, even if you get to enter that plea, which you probably won't, juries these days are pretty fed up with it. You know this. The jurors and everyone watching on Court TV will think you're a bunch of morons. Or do you want to wrap this whole thing up and provide some closure for the nine families of his victims? All I'm asking is a chance. It will just be you and your second chair." CC nodded to the lead attorney. "The federal prosecutor, our DA, Mr. Fisher, and myself. Come on. Wouldn't hammering out a deal now be in the best interest of your client?"

"You should run for office, Detective Calloway," the older man acknowledged with a smile.

"No, thank you." CC grimaced at the idea.

"Malcolm?" the man addressed Mr. Fisher.

"I agree with Detective Calloway," Mr. Fisher confirmed. "I just want some answers."

"I have to warn you that we may not get them," CC cautioned him. "Simon has a very slanted view of reality."

"I'm just finding that out," Mr. Fisher responded absently. "He told me that he and Dr. Jameson were a couple. It wasn't ever true?"

"No, sir," CC answered with a slight shiver. "Shall we?"

The six of them piled into the room as Simon sat up, his face still marred from Jamie's defense and his wrist handcuffed to the bed. "What do you want?" he snapped at CC.

After meeting his father CC couldn't understand how Simon ended up the way he did. She offered Simon a friendly smile as she took a seat next to his bed. He flinched away from her as his father stood next to him on the opposite side. "I have to remind you, Simon, that you are under no obligation to answer my questions," CC explained in a gentle tone. She no longer possessed the strength to hold onto her anger.

"That's right, Simon," the lead attorney reminded him. "But it might be in your best interest to cooperate."

"I didn't do anything," Simon flared, directing his tirade towards his father.

"Listen to Mr. Getz," Mr. Fisher instructed his son.

"Dad," Simon pleaded, "I just went to visit my girlfriend and the next thing I know this one barges in and arrests me. I think we should sue."

Mr. Fisher's mouth hung open in disbelief. CC calmed herself, recalling what the shrinks had said about Simon's subconscious defenses. "Simon, if you think that you should, then file a complaint," CC offered in a sincere voice. "Bring it all out into the open so Jamie can stand up in court and tell everyone that she loves me and not you."

"Lying bitch," Simon hissed as he strained against his shackled wrist to grab her.

Mr. Fisher simply stared in disbelief; CC didn't even flinch. "Oh, Calm down, Simon; your father is watching," she instructed him gently. She watched as Simon instantly calmed himself. "Simon, do you want to tell us what really happened to Janie?"

"Janie disappeared," Simon responded in confusion. "I keep hoping that somehow she'll be found."

"You may get your wish," CC explained, maintaining her composure. "Right now a team from the FBI is searching your family's cabin at Lake Tahoe." She noticed his face paled slightly.

"Why?" Simon inquired in bewilderment as his mind tried to sort out what was happening.

"Because that's where you hid her body," CC explained. "Where did you put her - the basement?" Seeing no reaction she pressed on. "The woods? The boathouse?" He flinched slightly and CC made a mental note to contact the team in California so they could check the boathouse thoroughly.

"No," Simon protested in a distant voice. "I just saw her."

"That must have been very confusing, seeing her in bed with another woman," CC continued, trying to focus on her case. "Even more confusing seeing two of her," she pressed as she watched the wheels in his sick mind spinning.

"It was," Simon mumbled.

CC glanced over at Getz who was rubbing his throbbing temple. *'Oh yeah, your client just shot himself in the foot and you know it,'* CC's mind reasoned. She reached over and pulled the tray table over. Slowly she placed a photo of one of his victim's bodies on the table. "How did it happen?" she asked casually as he studied the picture with a disinterested look. "Did you let just a little air out of her tire?" she continued as she placed another picture down. "You volunteered to follow her since you were heading up north," she offered as she slowly laid out the next set of pictures. "She pulled over and you offered to check the tire," she continued. His face remained blank as she placed the photos of eight of his victims before him. She refused to look up at his father, knowing that this was probably killing the poor man. "Thinking that having her stranded out in the middle of nowhere would be the perfect opportunity to talk some sense into her. You were changing the tire for her and she refused to listen to reason," she went on. She fought back the tears as she placed a photo of her lover before him. "You didn't mean to start choking her, did you?" she pushed. She watched his face begin to twitch slightly as his fingers caressed Jamie's photo.

"No," he muttered as Getz groaned in defeat.

CC placed the last photo of a young happy Janie Jensen before him and watched as the tears slipped from his dark eyes. "The tire iron was just there," CC supplied. "You just wanted her to understand that she belonged to you."

Simon's breathing was becoming erratic as his face turned red. Everyone watched as his fist clenched and the veins in his neck bulged out. Suddenly he shoved the table with the photos away, sending them flying across the bed. "Get out!" he screamed. Everyone except CC flinched. She simply began gathering up the photos and replacing them in her folder.

"She belonged to you, didn't she?" she pushed, fearful that she had gone to far.

"She'll always belong to me, you queer," he bellowed. "This is your fault. If you'd just left her alone, none of this would have happened. She's mine and I had to show her that!"

"Simon, shut up," Getz warned him.

"What?" Simon stammered. "Can't you see that this is her fault?" he said accusingly as Getz rolled his eyes in amazement.

"I need a moment with my client," Getz said with a heavy sigh.

"Of course," CC agreed as she gathered her things. She cast an understanding look at the weeping Mr. Fisher before she and the prosecutors left the room.

Jamie walked into the doctor's lounge and found her lover sitting at the table with a weary expression. "It's over," CC said in a soft voice. Jamie's heart clenched, uncertain what CC was talking about.

"What's over, Caitlin?" Jamie carefully inquired.

"Simon," CC explained as she blew out an exhausted sigh. "He'll be flown to California tomorrow. I had a hunch and we found Janie Jensen's body. It sent him over the edge and his lawyers are working out a deal with the feds. He'll be locked up in an institution for the criminally insane. It won't be some place he can just fake his way out of. We were able to close all the cases."

Jamie felt the pressure of the last couple of weeks slipping from her body as she stood behind her lover and began to rub her shoulders. "I'm almost done for the night," Jamie offered in a soothing tone as she continued to knead CC's broad shoulders. "Let's go home."

"How did it go for you tonight?" CC inquired in concern.

"It was hard at times," Jamie confessed wearily. "There were lots of questions and looks of pity. But I got through it."

The day had indeed been arduous for the blonde doctor. She could understand the discomfort her colleagues felt being around her. Just what do you say to someone after you discovered they were stalked and attacked by another co-worker? Yet if one more person approached her and asked how she was holding up, she might just set someone on fire. All she wanted to do at this moment was go home and wrap her lover up in her arms. Her emerald eyes drifted to the soft curve of CC's neck. Jamie licked her lips; her throat suddenly went dry as her mind decided that there might be one or two other things she wanted to do when they got back home.

Jamie could feel the heat rising in her body as her eyes drifted along her lover's body. Maybe she just needed to reconnect with her lover after everything they'd endured in the last twenty-four hours. Or maybe it was just the fact that her lover was the most beautiful passionate woman on the face of the planet. Either way Jamie was forming some very interesting plans for when the two of them were alone later.

"What are you thinking?" CC inquired in a sultry tone as she captured Jamie in a lustful stare.

"I'm thinking about . . ." Jamie blushed deeply as she felt her body react to CC's look. "Never you mind what I'm thinking. I need to get back to work."

Her name being paged confirmed her need to return to her duties. "Should I meet you at your place?" CC suggested in a hushed tone as someone entered the lounge.

"Yes," Jamie responded as she leaned over and kissed CC on the cheek. "And don't bother bringing your jammies," she added hotly in her lover's ear. Jamie's nipples became erect as her lover shivered from her words.

"Hi, Jamie," the Asian man greeted her with a shy smile.

"Hi, Shilin," She said as her hands continued to caress CC's shoulders. "Shilin, this is my partner, Caitlin."

"Nice to meet you," he said warmly as he offered his hand to CC who stood to greet him.

"A pleasure," CC responded as she accepted his hand.

Jamie hid her amused smirk; her lover towered over the smaller man who was drinking in all of her assets. CC turned to her with a shy smile. "I'll see you at home," CC offered shyly.

Jamie understood her lover's discomfort and uncertainty as how she should act around her co-workers.

"Just let yourself in," Jamie instructed her as she reached up and placed a promising kiss on CC's lips. She almost broke out in gales of laughter at the goofy grin CC sported. "I shouldn't be too long now that Shilin is here; maybe I can duck out a couple of minutes early."

"Thanks a lot, Jameson," Shilin grumbled. "I haven't even put my scrubs on yet."

Jamie waved goodbye to CC as she flashed a cocky smirk at Shilin. "Damn, Jameson; you have to tell me how to get one of those," the doctor said appreciatively as he poured himself a cup of coffee. He sniffed the brew and wrinkled his nose in disgust before tossing it out.

"It is simple," Jamie responded proudly. "When you see the brass ring, just reach out and grab it and don't ever let go."

"Oh, is that all?" He laughed as Jamie walked out of the lounge.

Later that evening Jamie's heart swelled when she entered her townhouse. The living room was lit by candlelight. On the coffee table were a dozen roses and a note taped to a bag of Pepperidge Farms Nantucket Chocolate Chip Cookies. "You do know the way to my heart, Detective," Jamie said with a wry smirk as she read the note that instructed her to follow the rose petals.

Jamie shrugged off her leather jacket, blew out the candles, and began to follow the trail of rose petals that led up the staircase. She continued to shed her clothing as she followed the delicate petals to her bedroom. The blonde doctor was completely naked as she stepped through the bedroom door. The sight that awaited her made her breath catch.

Her body trembled, the palm of her hand rested against her chest and she felt her heart pounding beneath her hand. The room was lit only by candlelight, revealing rose petals leading up to and covering the bed. Nestled comfortably on the large bed was her lover, holding another dozen roses and clad only in a long red silk robe. CC sat up and placed the roses on the nightstand before curling her finger and beckoning Jamie to join her.

Jamie stood there frozen, completely mesmerized by the sheer beauty in front of her. "Jamie," CC beckoned her in a husky tone.

"I'm sorry. You just took my breath away," Jamie confessed as she somehow willed her feet to move across the room. Slowly she crawled up on the bed and hovered over her lover. "I love you," she confessed before kissing her lover.

It was a slow lingering kiss that stoked the fire already burning inside the blonde as she lost herself in the feel of silk and rose petals. CC rolled her over onto her back and Jamie's body burned from the feeling of CC's silk-covered body on top of her while soft rose petals kissed her naked back. CC's hands began to roam as the kiss deepened. Jamie felt complete as CC poured her love into her kiss and touch.

When their lips separated Jamie was panting as her body pulsated with desire. She shivered as her lips continued to tingle. CC traced her ear with her tongue. "I want to make love to you," CC whispered in a hot breath before beginning to nibble on Jamie's earlobe.

"I'm yours," Jamie offered in a breathy voice as CC's mouth and tongue began to worship her neck.

Jamie wrapped her fingers in CC's long raven tresses while CC kissed and tasted her way down to the valley between Jamie's breasts. The doctor's body arched in response as her lover's tongue traced the swell of her breasts. "Caitlin," she moaned with needy desire as she felt CC's tongue circle her nipples without touching them. CC continued to tease her as the brunette's hands drifted down Jamie's body.

Jamie moaned deeply as CC's fingertips danced lightly along her skin. She fumbled as she tried to reach between their bodies to undo the tie on CC's robe. The feel of silk was intoxicating but she craved the touch of her lover's body. CC gently guided her hands away as she lifted herself up. She smiled down at Jamie and once again the blonde felt her heart skip a beat.

Crystal blue eyes held Jamie captive as she felt her wetness grow. CC gently clasped her wrists and guided them up over Jamie's head. "Please," Jamie begged as she lost herself in CC's gaze. The brunette smiled down at her; she held Jamie's wrists firmly with one hand while she undid the tie of her robe with the other. CC leaned down as she released the tie only to reveal a slight glimmer of the bronze flesh that was lying beneath. CC reclaimed her lips, keeping her body a hair's breath away from Jamie's quivering form.

The loosely hanging robe and CC's soft tresses caressed Jamie's body as her lover once again kissed and tasted her way down her body. Jamie squirmed beneath her in a desperate attempt to feel more of CC's body. "Caitlin!" she cried out as CC sucked her nipple into her mouth. Jamie slipped her knee between CC's firm thighs and pressed against her warm wet center. CC suckled the erect nipple harder while she rode against Jamie's thigh.

CC still held Jamie's hands above her head while her mouth feasted upon her breasts, moving from one to the other. Jamie's hips arched up as she felt her lover's desire paint her thigh. Jamie rocked against her lover's body urgently; CC's body moved in unison with her. As their bodies swayed in a wild rhythm, CC released her hold on Jamie's wrists. The blonde's tiny hands instantly slipped beneath CC's silk robe and began to caress the brunette's skin as CC's hands cupped her backside and guided Jamie's body to melt into her wetness.

CC's head flew up as Jamie began to tease her nipples with her fingers. Both women were gasping as they lost themselves in the sensual rhythm. Jamie cried out as her clit danced against CC's firm thigh. Jamie felt herself nearing the edge as their bodies began to thrust more insistently. She groaned as she felt CC slowing their frantic pace.

Jamie relaxed into the slower rhythm as she pulled CC's robe slightly off her shoulders while they engaged in another promising kiss. Her mind understood their need to slow down and savor the moment for as long as they could, yet her body was screaming for release. CC cupped her face in her hands as the kiss came to a slow reluctant end. Their breath mingled as they stared deeply into one another's eyes.

Jamie rolled both of them over so that they were lying side by side. "I can't believe how truly beautiful you are," CC said in wonderment as Jamie blushed at the compliment. Jamie slowly removed CC's robe as her lover's fingertips gently explored her skin. "I love you," CC offered on a soft breath as they continued to slowly touch each other. Their hands drifted lower and lower with each tender caress.

Jamie sighed as she dipped her fingers into CC's wetness while her lover mirrored her actions. Slowly they each explored each other's slick folds while their fingertips occasionally brushed the other's throbbing clit. They stole sweet tender kisses while they slowly entered one another. Each of them parted their thighs, welcoming the other's touch as they filled one another. Their nipples brushed as they slowly began to glide their fingers in and out of the other's center.

The kisses grew deeper as the rhythm of their fingers increased while they stroked each other's clits and their legs wrapped around each other's body. They both neared the edge as desire consumed them. Jamie felt as if she was ready to explode as she slipped her fingers from the warm wetness of CC's center. Once again CC mirrored Jamie's actions as the blonde shifted so that she was now kissing the inside of CC's thighs.

She felt her lover parting her as she nestled herself between CC's trembling thighs. Jamie moaned into CC's wetness, as her lover tasted her. The scent of CC's desire filled her as she began to drink in her passion. They feasted upon one another, beginning slowly as they dipped their tongues deep inside the other. Soon they began to suckle one another's clit as fingers replaced their tongues.

Jamie suckled CC harder as she thrust her hips against the brunette's touch. She could feel her body trembling as she drank in more of CC's passion. She heard CC's muffled cries of pleasure as her own climax overtook her. They screamed in ecstasy as they continued to pleasure one another. They collapsed against each other and began to lick away the last traces of passion from the other's body while the aftershocks trickled through them.

Jamie murmured in pleasure as she moved up her lover's body. CC wrapped her long legs around Jamie's slender body as the blonde kissed her lover deeply. Her mind reeled as she savored the taste of their wetness mingling on their lips. Once again Jamie entered her lover with two fingers as CC cupped and massaged her backside. Jamie plunged in and out of her lover, adding another digit as CC's body thrust against her own.

CC's head fell back as she cried out Jamie's name. CC pulled her down and began to suckle the pulse point on her neck while she guided Jamie's hips down. Jamie cried out as she clutched her lover's body and their clits once again danced against each other. Jamie's mind was spinning as CC entered her. They rolled around as CC plunged in and out of her. The energy slipped from Jamie's body as she exploded once again and collapsed into a quivering heap.

CC kissed her brow sweetly before helping the still trembling blonde under the covers. Jamie snuggled up in CC's loving embrace and smiled as she felt their hearts beating in unison. Sated and spent, the blonde doctor drifted off to sleep.

A few weeks later Jamie was walking hand in hand with CC at Cold Springs Park. "I can't believe she's walking and talking," CC commented in amazement. They watched the energetic Emma stumble along on her chubby legs before plopping down on her butt as her mother followed close behind.

"Well, something similar to it," Jamie noted in amusement.

"Do you think it's strange that she can't say Mama or Caitlin clearly but she can say cookie perfectly?" CC teased. "You haven't been coaching her, have you?"

"Look - the Carousel," Jamie cried out, avoiding the accusation.

"Merry-go-round," CC corrected her as they approached the ride.

"Carousel," Jamie argued.

"You are so stubborn." CC snorted in amusement. "So, Dr. Jameson, do you want to go for a ride?"

"Yes," Jamie responded with a smile as she squeezed CC's hand. CC gave her a gentle squeeze in response before releasing her grip and walking over to purchase their tickets.

As Jamie watched her lover she realized that she was more deeply in love with this woman than she thought possible. "Ready?" CC asked with a brilliant smile that made Jamie weak in knees. Jamie simply nodded in response, not trusting her own voice. They waited for the carousel to stop spinning and the other passengers to get off.

"I love you," Jamie vowed as they stepped up onto the wooden floorboards of the antique carousel.

"I love you too," CC responded as she helped Jamie up onto a white carved horse and rested her hand on the small of Jamie's back. The calliope music began as the ride began to move and CC rested her head on Jamie's shoulder. Jamie smiled as they began to go around. They had wasted far too many years before returning to the beginning. Jamie released a happy sigh, thankful that she was finally back where she belonged.

"CC, there's something I need to ask you," Jamie began hesitantly.

"Yes," CC answered before Jamie could ask her question.

"You don't know what I'm going to ask," Jamie cautioned her.

"Whatever it is, the answer is yes," CC readily agreed.

"Good, we can start moving your stuff in tonight," Jamie informed her.

"Most of my stuff is already at your place." CC laughed.

Jamie leaned over and kissed her as her horse glided up and down. "Actually there's something else I need to know. How much trouble can I get into for not paying a speeding ticket?" Jamie inquired playfully.

"A lot," CC commented as she gave Jamie a curious glance. "When did you get this ticket?"

"Twelve years ago," Jamie confessed with a slight cringe.

"You mean to tell me that you never paid that." CC inquired with a boisterous laugh.

"I just never got around to it," Jamie protested weakly.

"So, Jamie, are you going to try and catch the brass ring again?" CC asked as she caressed Jamie's shoulder.

"Caitlin, I already caught the brass ring. And this time there isn't a power in heaven or on earth that will ever cause me to let it go," Jamie vowed as she stared deep into her lover's eyes. The ride came to an end; they stepped off, hand in hand, to catch up with Emma and Stevie and start the next chapter of their lives together.

THE END

About the Author...

The real Bio:

Mavis Applewater was born in Massachusetts in 1962. As a child she was an avid reader and honed her creative side to major in Theatre at Salem State College. While supporting herself and waiting for her big break, she became a "resident" and well-known bartender at a nightclub in Cambridge, MA.
Mavis has done several commercials and lots of extra work but her creative juices were still flowing so she turned to another one of her hidden talents, writing. This jump-started her writing career and culminated into several manuscripts, one of them being "The Brass Ring".
Currently Mavis lives with her partner of 11 years; they reside in the North Shore area of Massachusetts.

Ok Sam I hope that is sufficient enough and what you were looking for, below is my more accurate version *eg*

Mavis Applewater, writer of most excellent stories, is still a blanket thief and hates to do laundry! However, I am willing to overlook these things because, after 11 years, she still takes my breath away.

A sneak peek …

Connecting Hearts

By Val Brown and M J Walker

[an excerpt]

The examination room, Denise observed, was of an average size and although it was typically clinical in appearance, it definitely had a much more comfortable feel to it. She realized it seemed you get what you pay for and she was suddenly very glad she hadn't stuck with the National Health System for this. Sara deserved the best as far as her niece was concerned.

Standing next to a large, grey, comfortable examination table, Doctor Macarthur took Sara's hands. He leaned forward slightly, the ends of his stethoscope hanging from around his neck. His white and blue stripy shirt was unbuttoned at the cuffs with his sleeves rolled up tight to his elbows. "Okay, Miss Jennings, Sara. I would just like you to squeeze my hands if you will."

Sara did as requested.

"As tight as you can."

Sara squeezed with all her might.

Nodding, but his expression blank, Doctor Macarthur released her hands and moved down to the bottom of the table. "Alright, Sara. Now I would like you to place your feet against my hands and push as hard as you can."

Again Sara did as bade, all under the watchful eye of her niece who sat beside the examination table observing the young blonde doctor carefully. *This guy doesn't look more than twenty-five years old,* she mused.

Sara pushed against Macarthur's hands as requested. She held a fixed expression of concentration as she pushed as hard as she was able.

"Okay." The Doctor released Sara and gently laid her feet back down on the examination table. "I do have a few more things I would like to do, Sara, but first I would just like to ask you a couple of questions."

"Ask away." Sara replied.

Macarthur leaned against the table. "You have said that you started feeling periods of cramping and twitching at first. You began to have trouble swallowing at times and you felt increasingly weak and tired. These are all classic symptoms of MND. Do you feel these symptoms have progressed?"

Denise looked down at her feet, knowing the answer to the Doctors question was obviously yes. Every now and then she would hope that maybe the hospital had made a mistake and had wrongly diagnosed Sara, but as the days wore on she realized it wasn't so.

The old woman nodded. "My right hand has started cramping a lot. Sometimes I am finding it hard to pick things up, or objects just fall out of it. This morning I had trouble dressing myself and found it incredibly tiring to climb the stairs."

Denise looked up surprised. "You never said anything."

"I didn't want to worry you, DJ. I do need to be able to do these things by myself."

The poet frowned. "Maybe so but whenever you do need help, no matter what, I will always be there for you. Always." She sighed. "I know it must be hard for you, but you must understand that I want to do whatever it takes to help you."

Sara nodded quietly. It was hard, and she was positive Denise understood this. They were both very much alike: independent and private people. The notion of having to rely on somebody else for assistance was almost unthinkable. At the same time Sara knew that she would much rather have her niece helping her than anybody else.

Doctor Macarthur nodded. "We have discussed the progressive symptoms of Amyotrophic Lateral Sclerosis and you are well aware that what you are experiencing will and is advancing." The Doctor moved over to a small desk and looked down at a small pile of different coloured folders on the surface.

Sitting rigidly in her chair, Denise watched Doctor Macarthur nervously as he picked up a large manila folder and opened it up, briefly scanning the documents inside. She then turned worried eyes to Sara who was smiling at her with a gentle understanding expression. The poet frowned wondering what her aunt was thinking.

"Okay, the purpose of this talk is because I think we need to discuss your making a living will." The Doctor turned his eyes towards Sara with a soft smile.

Sara nodded briefly.

"Living will?" Denise questioned. "Why does she need to make a living will?"

Macarthur looked at Denise, pulling small circular spectacles from his nose. "This is a standard procedure in your aunts situation. I hope you don't mind, DJ, but I need to be blunt with you here and explain MND in its advanced stages."

Sara looked away. It was terrifying to think about how this disease was going to affect her, yet she had accepted it. What else could she do? Go into denial, cry, scream to the world that it wasn't fair? Sara knew that the only way she was going to cope with her disease was to accept that there was nothing she could do to stop it and nothing she could have done to prevent it. It may not have provided much comfort but it did help her to face her future a little easier. This was going to happen.

"MND is a neuromuscular disease characterized by a progressive deterioration of motor nerve cells in the brain and spinal cord. Basically when the motor neurons can no longer send impulses to the muscles, the muscles begin to waste away." Macarthur looked intently into Denise's blue eyes. "This is progressing rapidly in your aunt's body and for patients in the later stages of MND there is usually a complete paralysis… even though their mind will remain unaffected. Do you understand what I am saying, DJ?"

Denise nodded, stunned. "You mean…" She looked towards her aunt. "Sara will eventually become paralyzed yet still be full conscious mentally."

Sara reached out and took Denise's hand.

"Which is why we need a living will." Macarthur added. "We need to know in advance exactly what Sara's wishes are. If there comes a point that she will no longer be able to breathe, will she want a ventilator to maintain that? If her heart were to stop beating, would she want CPR? Would she want a feeding tube for nourishment if she were no longer able to ingest food?"

An expression of confused disbelief crossed Denise's features. She swallowed hard as the Doctor's words took shape in her mind and she realized that her worst fear was to transpire. Sara was to experience much discomfort in the later stages of her illness and the worst of it would be that she would probably not be able to communicate her thoughts, feelings and needs.

Lowering her head, Denise closed her eyes and massaged her forehead as she tried desperately to will her emotions under control. She couldn't lose herself right there and right at that moment. She couldn't. Taking a very deep breath, the poet looked back at Sara with a pleading expression in her eyes.

Clearing her throat, Denise spoke. "Um… I… Sara?"

The old woman nodded sadly. "I am aware of this, DJ, and I want you to know that when that time comes I trust you to carry out and enforce my wishes."

"Wishes?"

Sara shook her head and blinked as tears clouded her eyes. "I don't want to rely on any artificial forms of life support, DJ. When that time does come," a tear escaped Sara's eye as she watched Denise desperately trying to keep control of her emotions, "I want to die peacefully. What point would there be in prolonging the inevitable?"

"Inevitable?" She could feel her control slipping. Salty tears stung her eyes as her breathing laboured. She rose swiftly. "Excuse me a moment please?" Denise said as she fled from the room as quickly as she could.

Out in the hospital corridor, Denise stormed down the hallway passing doctors and patients alike as she desperately searched for the exit. She noticed a green sign to her left and took the turn, finding a small door leading towards the outside world. The rain was still falling fast and furious as Denise pushed open the door and walked swiftly into the heavy downpour. Leaning against the wall her head fell back against soaked masonry as she closed her eyes against the onslaught of rapid raindrops and insistent tears.

She thought of all that Sara had gone through in her life, of all the things that had happened. She thought of the woman whom she had come to love as her own mother. She thought of this terrible disease and its increasing hold upon her. The effects it was to have and the inevitable outcome. And she cried.

Two hours later Denise sat in the quiet confines of her study. She and Sara had been home a short while and Sara had retired to her room for a rest, the events of the morning leaving her drained and emotional. Denise sat at her computer, staring at an empty screen. She had hoped to take her mind off things by trying to work, but it seemed she was less than able to concentrate.

Denise hadn't been able to give her response to Sara concerning her living will and had asked for a short while to think about her request. With anything else, Denise knew she would deny Sara nothing, but this was different. She just didn't know whether she could enforce her aunt's last request for an uncomplicated and dignified death. Denise wanted it to seem an unfair request to make, but inside she knew Sara asked her because she loved, respected and trusted her. It just hurt too much and if Denise was to admit it, to herself as much as anybody else - she needed help.

Unconsciously her hand moved to her top desk drawer and she pulled out a small slip of paper. Opening it slowly she read the address. As hard as it was, Denise had to accept that she needed to speak to this Nurse again and as she accessed her email account, she wondered what she was to say.

Nurse Martin,
Denise stopped and deleted the words. She started again:

Miranda,
She stopped again; didn't she say to call her Randa? Denise thought.

Randa,

I sincerely hope that you don't mind that I contact you but as you may recall you gave me your address not long ago on the Brightwood consultation room. I will admit that this is hard for me to do but I think I need your help, some advice.

Today I found out that my aunt intends to make a living will. I discovered just how debilitating and dreadful her disease is and for once I am wondering how I am going to cope with watching her declining health. I accept that there is nothing that can be done to prevent this from happening, but I don't know how I am going to be able to watch as this disease slowly takes her away from this world.

She is dying. I know that, I have to accept that. I am writing to ask for any help and advice you may be able to give concerning her comfort and progression during this time. I want to do whatever I can to help her and although I am finding it very hard to accept some of her decisions concerning the later stages of her disease I know that I want her to experience as little discomfort as possible. I want to help her however I can.

I hope that I haven't imposed on you at all, and any help you can give me will be very much appreciated.

Yours faithfully,
DJ

Reading over what she had just written, Denise's hand covered her mouse as she moved to the small 'send' icon in the corner of her screen. She paused, debated cautiously as to whether she was making the right decision in taking this step and as she realized that she could no longer deal with the events alone; she clicked the icon and sent her e-mail.

This book is available through **Limitless Corporation, Dare 2 Dream Publishing** at www.limitlessd2d.net

Order More Great Books Directly From Limitless, Dare 2 Dream Publishing		
The Amazon Queen by L M Townsend	20.00	
Define Destiny by J M Dragon	20.00	
Desert Hawk by Archangel	15.00	
Indiscretions By Cruise	18.00	
A Thousand Shades of Feeling by Carolyn McBride	18.00	
The Amazon Nation By Carla Osborne	20.00	
Spirit Harvest by Trish Shields	15.00	
Encounters, Book I By Anne Azel	22.00	
Encounters, Book II By Anne Azel	25.00	
Memories Kill By S. B. Zarben	20.00	
Deadly Rumors by Jeanne Foguth	20.00	
	Total	

South Carolina residents add 5% sales tax.
Shipping is $3.50 per book and will be via UPS.

Watch for these and more upcoming titles:
Visit our website at: http://limitlessd2d.net

Please mail your orders with a check or money order to:

**Limitless, Dare 2 Dream Publications
100 Pin Oak Ct.
Lexington, SC 29073**

Please make checks or money orders payable to: Limitless.